Political Theory, Science Fiction, and Utopian Literature

Political Theory, Science Fiction, and Utopian Literature

Ursula K. Le Guin and *The Dispossessed*

Tony Burns

LEXINGTON BOOKS
A division of
ROWMAN & LITTLEFIELD PUBLISHERS, INC.
Lanham • Boulder • New York • Toronto • Plymouth, UK

Published by Lexington Books
A division of Rowman & Littlefield Publishers, Inc.
A wholly owned subsidiary of The Rowman & Littlefield Publishing Group, Inc.
4501 Forbes Boulevard, Suite 200, Lanham, Maryland 20706
http://www.lexingtonbooks.com

Estover Road, Plymouth PL6 7PY, United Kingdom

British Library Cataloguing in Publication Information Available

Library of Congress Cataloging-in-Publication Data

Burns, Tony, 1953–
  Political theory, science fiction, and utopian literature: Ursula K. Le Guin and
the dispossessed / Tony Burns.
      p. cm.
  Includes bibliographical references and index.
1. Le Guin, Ursula K., 1929–, Dispossessed. 2. Le Guin, Ursula K., 1929– —
Criticism and interpretation. 3. Le Guin, Ursula K., 1929– —Political and social
views. 4. Science fiction, American—History and criticism. 5. Science fiction,
English—History and criticism. 6. Political fiction, American—History and
criticism. 7. Political fiction, English—History and criticism. 8. Utopias in
literature. 9. Politics in literature. I. Title.
 PS3562.E42Z59 2008
  813'.54—dc22   2008005845

  ISBN: 978-0-7391-2282-2 (cloth : alk. paper)
  ISBN: 978-0-7391-2283-9 (pbk. : alk. paper)
  ISBN: 978-0-7391-4487-9 (electronic)

This book is dedicated to my mother, Mary Burns (née O'Connell), who will be 82 years old this year, and to the memory of my father, Robert Burns (1922–1989).

Contents

Acknowledgments

Some material in chapter 7, section 3, 278–85, on Le Guin's approach to ethics, and in chapter 10, section 3, 414–25, on Le Guin's relationship to Marxism, is taken from Tony Burns, "Marxism and Science Fiction: A Celebration of the Work of Ursula K. Le Guin," *Capital and Class*, 84 (2004): 141–51. I am grateful to the editors of this journal for allowing me to reproduce this material here.

Material relating to various parts of the book was first presented in the form of papers delivered at various conferences. I would like to thank the audiences at those sessions for the valuable feedback they provided. The papers and conferences in question include the following: "Hegel, Anarchism and Utopia in the Writings of Zamyatin and Le Guin." Paper presented at the Thirty Second Annual Meeting of The Society for Utopian Studies Conference, 4–7 October 2007, Toronto, Canada; "The Place of H. G. Wells and Ursula K. Le Guin in the Parallel Histories of Science Fiction and Utopian Political Thought." Paper presented to a panel on the theme of "Political Theory and Science Fiction" at the Workshops in Political Theory—Fourth Annual Conference, Manchester Metropolitan University, UK, September 2007; "Hegel and Anarchism." Paper presented at the annual conference of the Political Studies Association of Great Britain, University of Bath, UK, April 2007; "Anarchism and Utopia in the Thought of Zamyatin and Le Guin." Paper presented to a panel on "Anarchist Political Thought" at the annual conference of the European Society for Utopian Studies, Zaragoza, Spain in 6–8 July 2006; "Aristotle and the Debate Between *Nomos* and *Physis* in Ancient Athens." Paper presented to a panel on Ancient Greek

Political Thought at the Annual Conference of the American Northeastern Political Science Association, Philadelphia, PA, United States, 17–19
November, 2005; "The *Iliad* and the 'Struggle for Recognition' in Hegel's
Phenomenology of Spirit." Paper presented to a panel entitled "Art, Aesthetics and Politics" at the Workshops in Political Theory—Second Annual Conference, at Manchester Metropolitan University, 7–9 September
2005; "Science and Politics in *The Dispossessed:* Le Guin and the 'Science
Wars.'" Paper presented at the annual conference of the European Society for Utopian Studies in Porto, Portugal, July 2004.

I would like to thank Larry Wilde (Nottingham Trent University, UK),
Ruth Kinna (Loughboro University, UK) and Jeffery Nichols (Mount An-
gel Seminary, U.S.) for taking the trouble to read and comment on the first
draft of this book.

Thanks also to Barbara and David Baggaley, and to Paula Wadding-
ham, for their valuable assistance in relation to child care. Without their
help at certain crucial points, the book would have taken even longer to
appear than it has.

Last but by no means least, my thanks go to Helen Baggaley for putting
up with me when writing this book, especially in the final stages, indeed
for putting up with me generally, and to Emily and Ursula just for being
there.

1

Introduction

This is a book about political theory and science fiction. It is a contribution to a project upon which I have been working for some time, the aim of which is to introduce students of political theory to the concepts and issues which are central to that discipline using works of literature and film, including works of utopian/dystopian literature and science fiction. The book's primary focus is on the work of Ursula K. Le Guin, especially *The Dispossessed*, which was first published in 1974 and received the accolade of being awarded both the Hugo and the Nebula prizes by the science fiction community for that year, which is a rare achievement. The book seeks to explore the philosophical underpinnings of that work, especially its understanding of the nature of scientific knowledge and scientific progress. It also attempts to draw out the ethical and political implications of that philosophy, as these are to be found in the novel. Its broad approach is interdisciplinary and it touches on issues which might also be discussed by students of philosophy (especially the philosophy of science and moral philosophy) and literature.

Le Guin is, of course, an anarchist, and it has often been said that *The Dispossessed* is an attempt on her part to embody the principles of anarchism in a novel, and hence that, so far as its political implications are concerned, *The Dispossessed* is best thought of as Le Guin's contribution to the cause of promoting anarchism, or of recommending what Le Guin considers to be the anarchist way of life to her readers. From this point of view, Le Guin's text is in effect a work of political theory, where this expression is used to designate a form of writing the purpose of which is to engage in speculation about normative issues relating especially to the moral or ethical question, oft discussed since it was first formulated by Plato, of how one ought or ought not to live. Advocates of this reading of *The Dispossessed* would be willing to concede, however, that if this text is indeed a contribution to political theory nevertheless it is a somewhat unusual one, given that at the same time it is *also* a novel, and hence a work of literature, a product of the creative imagination. Consequently those who read it must either pay as much attention to such things as characterization, plot, formal literary style, use of dialogue, and so on, as they do to any abstract ideas or theoretical speculation about questions of ethics and politics which it might contain. Or alternatively, as Krishan Kumar has suggested, they can and should be willing to simply set aside, as is often done in the case of Plato's dialogues, a consideration of such things precisely because they consider them to be irrelevant for the purposes of students of social or political theory as opposed to students of works of literature.[1]

Most, though as we shall see not all, commentators on Le Guin consider *The Dispossessed* to be a contribution to the utopian tradition in the history of political thought and in literature. According to these commentators *The Dispossessed* is a literary utopia. It is true, they argue, that it is in some respects significantly different from other works of utopian literature, or from more traditional literary utopias, not least because it is indeed a *novel*, and hence is even further removed from works such as Thomas More's *Utopia*, from the ideal-typical work of political theory, which is (allegedly) a purely theoretical treatise containing nothing but abstract ideas, formally presented (without employments of the various stylistic devices available to creative writers), which presents an argument the purpose of which is to answer some important normative question or other. However, despite these differences, it remains a literary utopia nonetheless, albeit of a new kind. Indeed, it is often suggested that *The Dispossessed* is a major contribution to the reinvention or revival of utopian writing which occurred in the second half of the twentieth century, and which was a reaction to a period in which such writing had become unfashionable, and in which those authors with an interest in utopian/dystopian political thought tended to produce literary dystopias rather than utopias, for example texts like Zamyatin's *We*, Huxley's *Brave New World*, and Orwell's *1984*, which are often considered to be dystopian in the sense of being anti-utopias. A number of expressions or descriptive labels have been used in an attempt to capture the significance of this development, but perhaps Tom Moylan's description of *The Dispossessed* as a new form of "critical utopia" is probably the best one. It is certainly the one most commonly cited in the secondary literature on Le Guin.

Those who think about *The Dispossessed* in this way tend to associate the utopian impulse with a desire to improve existing society morally or to make it better. It is the impulse to question and criticize society in the light of some moral or ethical ideal. It should be noted that this is a broad understanding of the idea of utopia, one which does not associate it with that of a perfect or ideal society. According to this understanding *all* normative theorizing and questioning of existing society must be considered to be utopian. Nor is this way of thinking about the notions of utopia and the utopian necessarily associated with that of impracticality, unless, of course, it is assumed at the outset (as arguably Nietzsche thought) that the very idea that anyone could act morally or virtuously or altruistically, out of concern for the well-being of others rather than one's own self-interest, is itself an impractical one.

One of the distinctive features of the present work is that it seeks to question the interpretation of *The Dispossessed* and its significance presented above by suggesting that, despite her personal commitment to the cause of anarchism, so far as questions of ethics and politics are concerned there is, nevertheless a decidedly *conservative* dimension to Le Guin's writing, and perhaps even her philosophical outlook more generally, which has been overlooked by most commentators on her work, though not all.

This book is not only about the work of Le Guin. It also spends some time, at various points, discussing the work of H. G. Wells, who laid the foundations for the development of science fiction as a genre in the twentieth century, and who was an important influence on most if not all of those contributors to the genre who followed him, including Le Guin. A number of issues with which we shall have to deal, and which are important for understanding certain aspects of Le Guin's work, were first dealt with by Wells.

Having spent some time researching and writing about the writings of Zamyatin and Le Guin independently of one another, I have come to the conclusion that for anyone wishing to understand Le Guin it is extremely fruitful to relate her work to that of Yevgeny Zamyatin. Consequently, in addition to Wells, the book also devotes quite a lot of time and attention to the views of Zamyatin, whose name comes up frequently. I argue that a fruitful way of introducing a discussion of Le Guin's views about a number of subjects, including issues in the philosophy of science on the one hand and ethics and politics on the other, is to consider them as a reaction to those of Zamyatin. Le Guin refers explicitly to Zamyatin on a number of occasions in her essays, and allusions to his work can also be found in her short stories and in her novels. Indeed, the core theme of Le Guin's *The Dispossessed* is that of the nature of science and scientific knowledge and the role of science and scientists in society, or the ethical and political implications of developments in science and technology. In particular *The Dispossessed* has to do with the ethical dilemmas confronted by those individual scientists (often considered to be "geniuses") who are the immediate architects of all scientific progress, the novelty of whose thinking brings them into conflict with the conventionally accepted wisdom of their own society. Zamyatin refers to such individuals as the "heretics" of science and I argue that this is a theme which Le Guin inherits from him. Like Galileo, the central character of *The Dispossessed*, the brilliant physicist Shevek, is a "heretic" in the specific sense in which Zamyatin employs the term.

Broadly speaking, then, although this book is about philosophy and politics in the writings of Le Guin, much of it is a consideration of themes which are to be found in the work of both Zamyatin and Le Guin—especially where there is evidence to suggest that Le Guin inherited the theme in question from the work of Zamyatin. I will seek to explore the *similarities* which exist between the works of these two authors where they exist. At the same time, however, I shall also say something about the important *differences* which exist between Le Guin and Zamyatin, either because Le Guin incorporates a theme which is absent in the work of Zamyatin, or because although it is present, nevertheless it is understood in a different way by Le Guin from the way in which it is understood by Zamyatin. The general line I shall take throughout is that although with respect to any particular theme there is good reason to think that Le Guin has been in some way inspired by the earlier work of Zamyatin, nevertheless she is also quite critical of the way in which Zamyatin deals with the theme in question, or the conclusions which he draws from his engagement with it. In these cases, Le Guin tends not to reject the views of Zamyatin outright. On the contrary, she considers them to be an important aspect of "the truth" so far as the theme in question is concerned. At the same time, however, she recognizes the limitations of Zamyatin's thought, and of his way of dealing with the theme in question. Hence, she seeks to incorporate what is of value in Zamyatin's ideas into her own account, which, therefore, goes beyond Zamyatin's whilst at the same time preserving those elements of Zamyatin's ideas which Le Guin considers to be valuable.

With one recent exception, namely Phillip Wegner's *Imaginary Communities: Utopia, the Nation and the Spatial Histories of Modernity*, which was published in 2002 and contains a chapter entitled "A Map of Utopia's 'Possible Worlds': Zamyatin's *We* and Le Guin's *The Dispossessed*,"[2] it appears not to have been generally recognized by commentators that Le Guin's science fiction is heavily indebted to the work of Yevgeny Zamyatin, and especially to Zamyatin's *We*. Wegner's book is, perhaps, the one significant exception to the generalization that commentators on Le Guin have largely ignored her relationship to Zamyatin. It will, however, become clear in this and in later chapters of the present work that my own reading of Zamyatin's *We*, of Le Guin's *The Dispossessed*, and of the relationship which exists between the two texts, is quite different from that of Wegner. If people were to think about it at all, the conventional understanding of the relationship between the two texts would probably be to say that Zamyatin's *We* is a *dystopian* text and that Le Guin's *The Dispossessed* is a *utopian* text, at least of some kind. In his book Wegner challenges this view, but only insofar as it touches on the work of Zamyatin. He does so by suggesting that Zamyatin's *We* is an example of a literary utopia and *not* a dystopia, as is often (in his opinion) erroneously thought. In Wegner's view, therefore, *both* of these texts are literary utopias. Indeed, Wegner refers to them as "these two great narrative utopias" of the twentieth century.[3] The interpretation presented below might *also* be thought of as challenging what probably would be the conventional view of the relationship between Zamyatin and Le Guin but in a different way from that of Wegner, by arguing that it is better to think of these two texts as being neither utopias nor dystopias, but as *novels* dealing with the themes of utopianism and/or dystopianism in politics. The significance of this will be explained later.

My reading of the relationship of Le Guin to Zamyatin might be thought of as a part of a wider project relating the work of Ursula K. Le Guin to both that of Zamyatin and Dostoevsky. Whenever a commentator chooses to discuss the work of three different thinkers this immediately, of course, creates a triangular framework of possible relationships, in this case the relationship between Dostoevsky and Zamyatin; that between Zamyatin and Le Guin;[4] and finally that between Le Guin and Dostoevsky. Quite a lot has been written about the first of these.[5] Relatively little has been said about the second or the third, despite the fact that in the case of the third it is evident that Le Guin owes quite a lot to Dostoevsky, if only negatively, because of what in his work she rejects.[6] Indeed, as more than one commentator has noted, Le Guin's *The Dispossessed* might be seen as a response to the implicit critique of anarchism which is to be discerned in Dostoevsky's own work *The Possessed*.[7] I shall say one or two things about Le Guin, Dostoevsky, and what Irving Howe has referred to as the "political novel" in chapter 6. However, where relevant, my main focus throughout will be the relationship between Le Guin and Zamyatin.

Both Zamyatin and Le Guin have very clear philosophical beliefs concerning the nature of knowledge in general and of scientific knowledge in particular. They also have definite ideas about morality or ethics. And in each case there is a close relationship between the two. It is Zamyatin's epistemological skepticism which leads to his nihilism, and hence to his commitment to a certain kind of anarchism associated above all with a certain interpretation of the philosophy of Nietzsche. Similarly, it is Le Guin's rejection of skepticism and her (arguably idiosyncratic) belief in the possibility of objective scientific knowledge, which inspires her rejection of nihilism, and her distinctive approach to the fundamental problems of ethics and politics. In this area Le Guin's thinking seems to me to be based on the assumption that there is such a thing as a natural moral law. It is this assumption, in turn, which provides the basis for Le Guin's commitment to her own form of (ethical) anarchism. If Zamyatin and Le Guin are both anarchists, then, they are nevertheless anarchists of a quite different type. Zamyatin is an anarchist in the tradition which begins with Max Stirner and runs through Nietzsche to that form of anarchism today which has been variously referred to as "postmodern anarchism," "poststructuralist anarchism," or simply "post-anarchism."[8] Despite recent efforts by a number of commentators to develop a constructive postmodern or poststructuralist ethics, which I discuss in chapter 7, in my opinion this recent form of anarchism is to be associated with skepticism in epistemology and nihilism in ethics and politics. Le Guin, on the other hand, is a social anarchist. She rejects the notions of skepticism, so far as questions of knowledge are concerned, and nihilism in ethics, and embraces the quite traditional idea that there is such a thing as human nature, and that by nature man [*sic*] is a social and political animal, or a moral being. In short, whether one is talking about questions in science and philosophy, on the one hand, or ethics and politics on the other, her outlook is not that of contemporary poststructuralism or postmodernism. If one must employ temporal categories to characterize this outlook, then it would be more accurate to say that it is "modern" rather than "postmodern." Indeed, it has a striking affinity with the classical anarchism of the nineteenth century, as this is to be found in the writings of such figures as Bakunin and Proudhon. Although, I hasten to add, I do not wish to imply that Le Guin would be willing to endorse all of the beliefs of these two classical anarchists, especially those of Bakunin.

I have said that both Zamyatin and Le Guin are anarchists, and there is a sense in which this is obviously correct—but, even so, it not entirely accurate. For it must not be forgotten that they are *also* creative writers, novelists—and this, as we have seen, complicates matters somewhat. In Le Guin's case the reason for this, as we shall see, has to do with her understanding of what the task of the novelist actually is. Central to my argument that there is a surprising conservative dimension to Le Guin's work is a distinction which, following a lead provided by Yevgeny Zamyatin and Georg Lukács, I make between what I shall refer to as two "Le Guins," or more accurately, two component elements of Le Guin's character, namely Le Guin insofar as she is considered to be a political *activist* and an anarchist, on the one hand, and Le Guin insofar as she is considered to be a *novelist* or a creative writer on the other. In an important essay devoted to the work of H. G. Wells, the significance of which for any interpretation of Le Guin I discuss in chapter 2, Yevgeny Zamyatin distinguishes between "two Wellses" and claims that it is important to make such a distinction if we wish to adequately understand Wells's work and assess its historical significance. Similarly, and perhaps more pertinently in the present context, when writing about Sir Walter Scott in his work on the historical novel, Lukács also distinguishes between two "Sir Walter Scotts," one of whom was actively engaged in the politics of his day and who possessed the ideological beliefs commonly associated with an English Tory in the first half of the nineteenth century, and the other of which was Scott the artist, or writer of historical novels, the ethical and political significance of whose work was more complex, and whose writings expressed certain beliefs which had implications for existing society which were much more critical than any of the beliefs held by the Scott who was a small-minded Tory gentleman. In what follows I make a similar distinction in the case of Le Guin. I shall, however, be presenting an inverted version of Lukács assessment of Sir Walter Scott. For in my view, unlike Scott as Lukács understands him, in the case of Le Guin it is Le Guin the creative writer and novelist whose outlook might be said to be in some sense politically conservative, whereas it is the other Le Guin, the political activist, whose beliefs might be said to be critical of existing society in Lukács's sense of the term.

This reading of Le Guin brings me into conflict with Carl Freedman who in an important recent work, *Critical Theory and Science Fiction*, presents Le Guin as a novelist whose work is "critical" in the sense in which Lukács considered the work of Sir Walter Scott to be. Indeed, Freedman argues that there is an affinity between Le Guin's basic outlook and that of the "critical theorists" of the Frankfurt School. Although I do not agree with everything that Freedman says, nevertheless I consider his work to be extremely important for anyone who wishes to understand Le Guin, and I refer to it on more than one occasion. This is partly because one of the core themes of the critical theory of the Frankfurt School, that of the ethical and political implications of developments in science and technology, is one which is also central to the work of Le Guin.[9] A second reason is that, as again in the case of critical theory, I think that a good "way in" to understanding many of the issues which are raised by Le Guin is to relate what she says about them to the philosophy of Hegel. I discuss Freedman's interpretation of Le Guin in some detail in chapters 2 and 10.

This distinction between Le Guin the political activist and Le Guin the novelist is one which is occasionally (but not by any means systematically) made by Le Guin herself.[10] For example in her introduction to *The Word for World is Forest*, Le Guin points out that in the 1960s she was associated with "the peace movement" and in consequence, because she "was in it," she then had "a channel of action and expression for my ethical and political opinions totally separate from my writing."[11] Similarly, in an interview with Jonathan Ward, Le Guin states explicitly that in general "my social activism is separate from my writing."[12] My reason for making this distinction in the present work is because I think that it is extremely useful for anyone seeking to understand Le Guin's attitude toward a number of important issues. One implication of making it is that it allows us to differentiate between the moral or *ethical* criteria which might be used to evaluate Le Guin and her conduct as a political activist, on the one hand, from the *aesthetic* criteria which might be used to evaluate Le Guin and her works as a creative writer. For example, I think it is fruitful to think that it is Le Guin the political *activist* who is an anarchist, whereas Le Guin the writer, or Le Guin the *novelist*, is not. For there are numerous occasions where Le Guin states explicitly that she thinks that being any kind of political ideologue, and hence also, of course, an anarchist, is a bad thing because it gets in the way of one's efforts to be a good writer. Remarks of this kind evidently contradict what Le Guin says elsewhere about anarchism.

I am not sure that this contradiction in Le Guin's character, her life, and her work could be resolved even if it was felt that it is desirable to do so. Moreover, as we shall see, there are good reasons for thinking that irresolvable contradictions of this kind are a fundamental part of Le Guin's general philosophical outlook. They are to be found in both the natural and the social worlds and, so far as the latter is concerned, are to be found at the heart of all human existence in society. They are central to what is usually referred to as "the human condition." Indeed, it is contradictions of this kind which generate the ethical dilemmas which, for Le Guin, provide the novelist with the raw materials for their work. It is not too surprising, therefore, that such a contradiction can be found in Le Guin's own life and character. To employ a concept which is important for understanding Le Guin's views regarding the aesthetic form of the novel, this seems to me to be what defines her as the individual "character" that she is.

For this reason I think that there is a striking similarity between Le Guin's general philosophical outlook and the views of Hegel.[13] I am in broad agreement with those recent commentators who have suggested that it is a familiarity with the philosophy of Hegel, as well as (or perhaps even instead of) a familiarity with Taoism, which best helps us to understand Le Guin's attitude toward the problems of philosophy, ethics, and politics. There are, of course, different readings of Hegel's philosophy. This is an issue which I discuss in Chapters 3 and 10. I suggest there that the reading of Hegel (which I refer to as the Centrist reading) which best helps us to understand Le Guin insofar as she is a novelist or a creative writer, as opposed to an anarchist or a political activist, is significantly different from the one which is traditionally associated with Left Hegelian-ism. It is a reading of Hegel which has conservative rather than radical political implications. Consequently, it is a reading which has little to of-fer a critical theory of society of the kind usually associated with the Frankfurt School, or with the Hegelian Marxism of aesthetic theorists such as Georg Lukács.

Le Guin's interest in fundamental ethical dilemmas is something which, like Hegel, she has in common with Greek tragic drama. And al-though Le Guin is, of course, usually thought of as a science fiction writer, nevertheless I think she shares the view that in some ways works of liter-ature (whether tragic dramas or novels) are better suited to deal with complex moral problems, as they impact on the lives of individual "char-acters," than formal treatises of moral philosophy, which generally as-sume that all moral problems are susceptible of a straightforward "ra-tional" solution, much like a problem of arithmetic or geometry. This is something which Le Guin has in common with Zamyatin. I hope that the reader will agree that one of the significant features of the present work is the fact that it attempts to connect a discussion of the moral and political thought of the ancient Greeks, especially as this is carried out in tragic drama, to the analysis of works of contemporary science fiction. If teach-ing the political theory of science fiction necessarily requires an orienta-tion toward the future nevertheless, at least in the case of the work of Le Guin, this task cannot be undertaken without some grasp of the way in which what are assumed to be fundamentally the same moral problems have been dealt with by creative writers in the distant past. Again one of the arguments of the book is that an important mediating link between "past" and "future" in this particular connection is the philosophy of Hegel, and his twentieth-century disciple Georg Lukács, whose writings again I consider to be fruitful for anyone seeking to understand Le Guin's views on the novel.

The structure of the book is as follows. In chapter 2, I begin by attempting to locate Le Guin's *The Dispossessed* against the background of the history of utopian/dystopian literature, a history which, in the twentieth century, be-came interwoven with that of science fiction. To be more specific I consider the work of two of Le Guin's most significant predecessors, H. G. Wells and Yevgeny Zamyatin. Focusing on an essay which Zamyatin wrote about Wells in the early twentieth century I argue that this suggests a "quasi-Hegelian" reading of the history of utopian/dystopian literature, within which there are just three main phases of development, that of the tradi-tional literary utopia (which is not a novel), that of the dystopian science fiction novel, and finally that of the utopian science fiction novel. I sug-gest that it is this reading which provides the source for the view that Le Guin's significance for that history is that she is the person responsible for writing the first utopian science fiction novel, *The Dispossessed*. I also suggest that there are reasons to question the value of this way of thinking about the history of utopian/dystopian literature and about Le Guin's place within it, reasons which I explore in more detail in chapters 5 and 6.

In chapter 3, I explore the philosophical underpinnings of Le Guin's work. Le Guin has often been characterized as someone who embraces the outlook of Taoism. This chapter explores what this might be taken to mean, especially given that commentators seem not to be able to agree with one another over the issue of what Taoism is, or what it is that Taoists actually believe. One point made in this chapter is that, as Le Guin understands it, the outlook of Taoist philosophy is strikingly similar to the dialectical way of thinking about the world which is more often associated with the philosophy of Hegel, or with Marx and Marxism. A number of commentators have suggested that Le Guin's dialectical approach to questions in the philosophy of science, on the one hand, and to problems of ethics and politics on the other, has been inspired more by her engagement with Marxism than it has by her reading of Taoist literature. And they have done this because Le Guin's (allegedly idiosyncratic) understanding of Taoism is very different from their own. In this chapter I bypass any discussion of Le Guin's relationship to Marx and Marxism and attempt to relate Le Guin's dialectical outlook directly to the philosophy of Hegel. I argue that Hegel's philosophy has been an important influence on a number of major thinkers in the history of anarchism, including especially Bakunin, Proudhon, and Zamyatin. It also provides a fruitful way of approaching Le Guin's writings, above all *The Dispossessed*, insofar as they touch on a number of important philosophical or metaphysical issues. This is especially true of the way in which Le Guin deals with the philosophical problems associated with the notion of change and which are centered around the notions of Being and Becoming, two ideas which are of fundamental importance for anyone seeking to understand either Hegel's philosophy, on the one hand, or the General Temporal Theory developed by the physicist Shevek, the central character of *The Dispossessed*, on the other.

In this chapter I also distinguish between three different possible readings of Hegel, which I characterize as "Right," "Left," and "Centrist." I associate Left Hegelianism with the radical or revolutionary politics espoused by anarchist figures such as Bakunin and Zamyatin and argue that the reading of Hegel with which Le Guin's views have the strongest affinity is the Centrist one, a reading which is reformist in terms of its political implications, and, therefore, politically conservative, in one sense of that term.

In chapter 4, I begin my examination of the relationship which exists between the views of Zamyatin and Le Guin. After noting some textual affinities between their writings, I turn to consider their views regarding the nature of science, scientific knowledge, and the idea of scientific progress. I argue that Zamyatin's views on these subjects provide a fruitful way of understanding those of Le Guin, both in one of her earlier short stories, "Schrödinger's Cat" and in *The Dispossessed*. Nor is Le Guin unaware of this fact, as she refers in one of her essays to Zamyatin as being someone who "knows about truth" in this area. I try to show that at least some of Le Guin's views are inspired by those of Zamyatin, although at the same time Le Guin is an original and creative thinker who does not simply take these ideas up and embrace them uncritically. On the contrary, she engages with them, probes them carefully, lays bare their faults, whilst at the same time incorporating what she considers to be of value within them into her own work. This is especially true of Zamyatin's views on change, which may be associated with the Sequency Theory of Time discussed in *The Dispossessed*.

I start chapter 5 by considering the question of whether *The Dispossessed* should be thought of as a work of science fiction, in the specific sense in which Le Guin understood this term in the 1970s, especially in her important essay "Science Fiction and Mrs. Brown." I suggest that in fact it is not. It is, rather, a novel in the tradition of European Realism, albeit with a scientific theme. I then turn to consider the question whether *The Dispossessed* should be thought of as being a literary utopia, a literary dystopia, or something else. Again I argue that in fact it is something else, namely a novel dealing with the theme of utopianism in politics. It is most fruitfully considered as a novel about utopianism in politics rather than a literary utopia. My argument is based partly on the particular reading of Zamyatin's essay on H. G. Wells discussed in chapter 2 and an application of that reading to Le Guin. However, it is also based on a reading of Le Guin's essays written in the 1970s around the time that *The Dispossessed* was first published. I attempt to show that on the basis of the views which Le Guin expresses in these essays regarding the issue of what a literary utopia is, or is supposed to be, it follows that *The Dispossessed* should not be considered to be a contribution to this particular genre. Indeed, I argue that in the 1970s Le Guin took seriously the view that the idea of a "utopian novel" is a contradiction in terms. Consequently, because *The Dispossessed* is undeniably a novel, at that time she had significant doubts regarding its possible status as a literary utopia. In my view, if Le Guin's reasons for thinking this are taken seriously then they bring into question the commonly accepted view that *The Dispossessed* is best thought of as an example of a new kind of literary utopia, a "critical utopia" in the sense in which Moylan uses this term. I also point out that Le Guin's views on this subject appear to have changed and are now quite different from what they were in the 1970s.

In chapter 6, I consider the implications which the question of the status of Le Guin's *The Dispossessed*, as being either a novel or a literary utopia, has for any assessment of the political significance of this work. Le Guin is usually (and rightly) considered to be an anarchist, and *The Dispossessed* is usually associated with the ideology of anarchism. It is thought to be an "anarchist novel" just as much as it is thought to be a "utopian novel." Here I suggest that for Le Guin the idea of an anarchist novel, also, is a contradiction in terms. Hence, for Le Guin, insofar as *The Dispossessed* is anarchist it could not be a novel; and insofar as it is a novel it could not be anarchist. I also maintain that, although she is hesitant about it, on the whole Le Guin prefers to think of it as a *novel* in the strict sense of the term rather than an anarchist pamphlet. As such in her view it could have no overt political message at all, of any kind, not even an anarchist one. In this respect, paradoxical though it may appear, given that she is conventionally thought of as the author of works of science fiction, Le Guin is best thought of as a writer working within the tradition of nineteenth century European realism.

Additionally, I claim that although Le Guin does not seem to be consciously aware of it, her understanding of what a novel is, and of what novelists do, is such that it could only ever have political implications which might be said to be in some sense conservative. In other words, the very form of the novel as a style of writing, as Le Guin herself understands it, is politically conservative. There is, therefore, a tension or contradiction in Le Guin's work, especially *The Dispossessed*, between her commitment to anarchism as a political activist, on the one hand, and her determination as a creative writer to write a novel about anarchism rather than a political pamphlet espousing the cause of anarchism on the other.

Chapter 7 considers Le Guin's approach to questions of ethics by relating it to what I claim is the traditional account of "the moral point of view." It considers the distinction which Le Guin makes between "ethics" and "morality," and it compares her views with the "virtue ethics" of Alasdair MacIntyre, the "situation ethics" of Jean-Paul Sartre and Simone de Beauvoir, and the "postmodern ethics" of Emmanuel Levinas. I argue that Le Guin's approach has more in common with the traditional account than it does with these other doctrines, at least as they are conventionally understood. One of the claims that I make here is that Le Guin adopts a "deontological" approach to ethics. She is, therefore, critical of ethical "consequentialism," especially "utilitarianism," and of those versions of anarchism which rely on these doctrines.

In chapter 8, I turn from discussing ethics to consider the closely related issue of anarchist politics. Here I relate Le Guin's ethical views to four different "ideal-typical" accounts of anarchism, which differ from one another over the issue of the relationship which ought to exist between "ends" and "means" in politics. I also continue my comparison of the views of Le Guin and Zamyatin by turning to consider their attitudes toward anarchist politics in respect of this issue. I attempt to show that there is a similarity between Le Guin's attitude toward the views of Zamyatin in this area and her attitude toward Zamyatin's views on science and scientific progress. I present Le Guin as being someone who is inspired by Zamyatin's ideas and seeks to incorporate them, suitably modified, into her own work; but who is at the same time not uncritical of them. In particular, as in the case of science and scientific knowledge, Le Guin distances herself from Zamyatin's enthusiasm for the philosophy of Nietzsche. She rejects Zamyatin's moral nihilism just as she rejects his skepticism. For Le Guin humanity is by its very nature an ethical animal, or more accurately a moral being. This view of human nature informs Le Guin's commitment to a social anarchism which is quite different from the anarchism of Zamyatin precisely because it is grounded on a positive affirmation of "the moral point of view." Here also, then, I shall argue that although Le Guin does owe a great deal to Zamyatin, that is not by any means to say that she simply endorses the views of Zamyatin without criticism, or that there are no significant differences between them, and I shall say something about these as well.

In chapter 9, I consider three further reasons for thinking that, despite the fact that Le Guin is an anarchist, there is nevertheless a conservative political dimension to her writing, focusing on Le Guin's Taoism, her commitment to the principles of scientific realism, and her views on human nature or "the self," all of which might be thought to be inconsistent both with her commitment to anarchism and with the suggestion that *The Dispossessed* is a literary utopia, in the sense of being a depiction of a society (Anarres) which its author considers to be a "utopian" society.

Chapter 10, the conclusion of the book, considers some of the criticisms which have been brought against Le Guin and her work especially by commentators with an interest in Marxist aesthetics. Just as Le Guin does not consider it to be her task as a novelist to either criticize or condemn existing society but simply, by focusing on the lives of a particular set of characters, to present a literary depiction of the ethical dilemmas confronted by those who attempt to change society for the better, so also I do not consider it to be my task as a commentator either to criticize or defend Le Guin so far as her activities as a novelist are concerned. I do suggest, however, that in the past some Marxist commentators have missed the point when criticizing Le Guin because they did not make the distinction between Le Guin the political activist and Le Guin the novelist. Confusing criteria of aesthetic evaluation with criteria of moral and political evaluation, they have condemned Le Guin the novelist because she was not also an activist seeking to promote either their, or indeed her own, ideological beliefs or political ideals in and through her creative writing. In other words they have criticized Le Guin for not being sufficiently "engaged" politically. They have condemned her for not doing as a *writer* something which, given her own views on art and writing, she could not possibly have done. Had Le Guin done what some of her Marxist critics have demanded of her, she would have compromised her own understanding of what a good writer or a good novelist is. She would have transformed *The Dispossessed* from what it is, that is to say a novel, into something else, namely an anarchist political pamphlet—a didactic text with a dubious claim to possessing that aesthetic value which Le Guin associates with a good work of literature.

In chapter 10, I also discuss Carl Freedman's interpretation of Le Guin. Freedman is one of the few Marxist critics who has actually praised rather than condemned Le Guin because of the political implications of her work, which he considers to be radical and critical of existing society. In an important recent text, *Critical Theory and Science Fiction*, Freedman seeks to associate Le Guin's dialectical philosophical outlook with the critical theory of the Frankfurt School and suggests that it might indeed, therefore, be said to be a "critical utopia" in Moylan's sense. Given that I do not myself consider Le Guin's text to be a literary utopia at all, the reader will not be surprised to find that I disagree with Freedman's reading of Le Guin. Although I agree with Freedman that Le Guin's basic philosophical outlook is indeed a dialectical one, and one which does indeed have an affinity with the philosophy of Hegel, nevertheless I argue against Freedman that the interpretation of Hegel's philosophy which Le Guin's outlook resembles most closely is the Centrist reading presented in chapter 3, a reading which because it acknowledges that there is a tragic dimension to all human existence in any society is necessarily, for reasons which will become clear, *un*-critical of any existing society, and which is again, therefore, basically conservative in terms of its political implications.

These criticisms of Freedman amount to the claim that his reading of Le Guin fails to capture at least some of the concerns which she has insofar as she is a novelist. I finish the book on a less critical and more upbeat note by drawing attention to the fact that, insofar as she is an anarchist, Freedman is absolutely correct to draw our attention to the similarity which exists between Le Guin's "humanist" approach to questions of ethics and politics and the critical theory of the Frankfurt School. However, this does not necessarily imply a direct intellectual debt on Le Guin's part either to the Frankfurt school or indeed to Marxism. This is so because such a strand of thought can be traced back, independently of Marxism, through the anarchist tradition, to a common source, namely German philosophy at the end of the eighteenth century and beginning of the nineteenth centuries, especially the philosophy of Hegel. In my view, far from this being a weakness in Le Guin's outlook, as some commentators would suggest, this is one of the great strengths in her work. It is this, more than anything else, which ensures the continued relevance of Le Guin's *The Dispossessed* today.

NOTES

1. Krishan Kumar, *Utopia and Anti-Utopia in Modern Times* (Oxford: Blackwell, 1987), 25.
2. Phillip E. Wegner, "A Map of Utopia's 'Possible Worlds': Zamyatin's *We* and Le Guin's *The Dispossessed*," in *Imaginary Communities: Utopia, the Nation and the Spatial Histories of Modernity* (Berkeley, Los Angeles, London: University of California Press, 2002), 147–82. Wegner rightly points out, 173, that the connection between Le Guin and Zamyatin "although rarely noted" in discussions of *The Dispossessed*, are "suggested by Le Guin herself." I came to the idea that it is fruitful to compare and contrast Le Guin's *The Dispossessed* with Zamyatin's *We* independently of Wegner, and became aware of Wegner's book only after completing the first draft of the present work.
3. Wegner, *Imaginary Communities*, 181.
4. The editions I have used are Yevgeny Zamyatin, *We*, trans. Bernard Gilbert Guerney, intro. Michael Glenny (Harmondsworth: Penguin, 1972 [1924]), references by D-503's diary "Entry" number and page, and Ursula K. Le Guin, *The Dispossessed: An Ambiguous Utopia* (London: Granada, 1983 [1974]), references by chapter number and page. For some earlier reflections of mine on the writings of Zamyatin and Le Guin, considered independently of one another, see Tony Burns, "Zamyatin's *We* and Postmodernism," *Utopian Studies*, 11, no. 1 (2000): 66–90 and Tony Burns, "Science and Politics in *The Dispossessed*: Le Guin and the 'Science Wars,'" in *The New Utopian Politics of Ursula K. Le Guin's* The Dispossessed, eds. Laurence Davis and Peter Stillman (Lanham, Md.: Lexington Books 2005), 195–215.
5. See Richard A. Gregg, "Two Adams and Eve in the Crystal Palace: Dostoevsky, the *Bible* and *We*," in *Major Soviet Writers: Essays in Criticism*, ed. Edward J. Brown (New York: Oxford University Press, 1973), 202–08; R. L. Jackson, *Dostoevsky's Underground Man in Russian Literature* (Mouton: The Hague, 1958); Gary Saul Morson, *The Boundaries of Genre: Dostoevsky's Diary of a Writer and the Traditions of Literary Utopia* (Evanston, Ill.: Northwestern University Press, 1981); G. Pomerants, "Euclidian and Non-Euclidian Reasoning in the Works of Dostoevsky," *Kontinent*, 3 (1978): 141–82; Patricia Warrick, "The Sources of Zamyatin's *We* in Dostoevsky's *Notes from the Underground*," *Extrapolation*, 17, no. 1 (1975): 63–77.

6. At one point Le Guin describes Dostoevsky as a "violent reactionary." See the prefatory remarks to Ursula K. Le Guin, "The Ones Who Walk Away from Omelas," in *The Wind's Twelve Quarters*, Vol 2 (London: Granada, 1980 [1973]), 112.

7. See James Bittner, "Chronosophy, Aesthetics and Ethics, in Le Guin's *The Dispossessed: An Ambiguous Utopia*," in *No Place Else: Explorations in Utopian and Dystopian Fiction*, eds. Eric Rabkin, Martin H. Greenberg and Joseph D. Olander (Carbondale: South Illinois University Press, 1983), 251; John P. Brennan and Michael C. Downs, "Anarchism and Utopian Tradition in *The Dispossessed*," in *Ursula K. Le Guin*, eds. Joseph Olander and Martin Harry Greenberg (New York: Taplinger, 1979), 117; Carl Freedman, *Critical Theory and Science Fiction* (Hanover and London: Wesleyan University Press, 2000), fn. 17, 118; Darko Suvin, "Parables of De-Alienation: Le Guin's Widdershin's Dance," in *Positions and Presuppositions in Science Fiction* (Kent: Kent State University Press, 1988), 138; and Victor Urbanowicz, "Personal and Political in *The Dispossessed*," 153.

8. See Todd May, *The Political Philosophy of Poststructuralist Anarchism* (Pennsylvania: Pennsylvania State University Press, 1994); Todd May, "Is Poststructuralist Political Theory Anarchist?" *Philosophy and Social Criticism*, 15, 2 (1989): 275–84; Saul Newman, *Power and Politics In Poststructuralist Thought: New Theories of the Political* (London: Routledge, 2005); Saul Newman, *From Bakunin to Lacan: Anti-Authoritarianism and the Dislocation of Power* (Lanham: Lexington Books, 2001). For a discussion of the work of Le Guin in connection with this issue see Lewis Call, "Postmodern Anarchism in the Novels of Ursula K. Le Guin," *SubStance* 36, no. 2 (2007): 87–105 and Lewis Call, *Postmodern Anarchism* (Lanham, Md.: Lexington Books, 2002).

9. For this see Herbert Marcuse, "From Negative to Positive Thinking: Technological Rationality and the Logic of Domination," in *One Dimensional Man: Studies in the Ideology of Advanced Industrial Society* (London: Routledge, 1991 [1964]), 144–69; Jurgen Habermas, "Technical Progress and the Social Life-World," in *Toward a Rational Society* (Boston: Beacon Press, 1970 [1968]), 50–61; Jurgen Habermas, "The Scientization of Politics and Public Opinion," in *Toward a Rational Society*, 62–80; Jurgen Habermas, "Technology and Science as 'Ideology,'" in *Toward a Rational Society*, 81–122. Andrew Feenberg, *Transforming Technology: A Critical Theory Revisited* (Oxford: Oxford University Press, 2002); Andrew Feenberg, *Critical Theory of Technology* (Oxford: Oxford University Press, 1991).

10. See for example Ursula K. Le Guin, "Introduction" to *Planet of Exile*, in *The Language of the Night*, 141, where Le Guin says that "my form of action is *writing*."

11. Ursula K. Le Guin, "Introduction" to *The Word for World is Forest*, in *The Language of the Night*, 151.

12. Jonathan Ward, "Interview With Ursula K. Le Guin," in Ursula K. Le Guin, *Dreams Must Explain Themselves* (New York: Algol Press, 1975), 34–35. It should be noted that, some would say significantly, Le Guin qualifies this judgment in the case of *The Dispossessed*. "Except," she goes on, "perhaps, for this last book, *The Dispossessed*, in which being *utopian*, I am trying to *state* something which I think desirable" (my emphasis). As we shall see, if all that *The Dispossessed* did were to state what Le Guin considers to be desirable, then by Le Guin's own aesthetic cri-

teria it would be a failure as a novel, as a work of *literature*, as opposed to a work of political theory, an anarchist political pamphlet, or a literary utopia.

13. For some remarks about the relationship between Le Guin and the philosophy of Hegel see Burns, "Science and Politics in *The Dispossessed:* Le Guin and the 'Science Wars,'" in *The New Utopian Politics of Ursula K. Le Guin's* The Dispossessed, eds. Davis and Stillman, 202–3 and fn 31, 211; Carl Freedman, *Critical Theory and Science Fiction*, 112; Bulent Somay, "From Ambiguity to Self-Reflexivity: Revolutionizing Fantasy Space," in *The New Utopian Politics of Ursula K. Le Guin's* The Dispossessed, eds. Davis and Stillman, 236; and Mark Tunick, "The Need for Walls: Privacy, Community and Freedom in *The Dispossessed*," in *The New Utopian Politics of Ursula K. Le Guin's* The Dispossessed, eds. Davis and Stillman, 129–48.

2

Science Fiction and the History of Utopian Literature: H. G. Wells, Zamyatin, and Le Guin

In this chapter I examine a quasi-Hegelian reading of the history of science fiction in relation to that of utopian/dystopian political thought. I also consider the place which both H. G. Wells and Ursula K. Le Guin have to play within that history. The account I offer is inspired by my reflections on an essay about Wells which was written by Yevgeny Zamyatin and published in 1922.[1] According to this speculative "history," Wells's science fiction is important for the history of utopian/dystopian political thought because, after nearly 500 years of utopianism, it marked a major transition from utopian to dystopian writing and, therefore, a radical or even revolutionary transformation of the genre, both in terms of its content and in terms of its stylistic form. So far as their content is concerned the works associated with the tradition became dystopian rather than utopian. So far as their stylistic form is concerned, they became novels, or at least novelistic tales. Moreover, the writings of Le Guin in the late 1960s and early 1970s are also thought to mark a significant point of transition. This is so because they are thought of as representing a return to the earlier tradition, in that they are utopias rather than dystopias. However, this is not a simple return, as certain features of the works produced in the history of the genre in its predominantly *dystopian* phase are preserved, in particular their aesthetic form. Thus, like Wells, Le Guin also is associated with an important nodal point of transition in the history of the genre, the birth of a new kind of literary utopia, which Tom Moylan has referred to as the "critical utopia."[2]

Focusing on *The Dispossessed* (which was published in 1974), I will challenge this account of the significance of Le Guin and her work. I will argue that, although Le Guin's views on this issue in the 1970s were never entirely clear, and although they have become much clearer since, there is at least *some* evidence to support the view that at the time at which she wrote it, Le Guin thought (in my view rightly) that *The Dispossessed* is best thought of as being not a literary utopia at all, of any kind, and, therefore, not a utopian novel, but rather a *novel* pure and simple—a novel dealing with the theme of utopianism in politics. I begin, however, with a discussion of the question of H. G. Wells and his place in the history of utopian literature, especially as this question is addressed by Zamyatin. For, as we shall see, Zamyatin's views on this subject might fruitfully be thought of as providing a possible source of inspiration for this widely accepted interpretation of Le Guin.

UTOPIA AND DYSTOPIA IN THE WRITINGS OF H. G. WELLS

Was H. G. Wells a utopian writer, a dystopian writer, or perhaps both? This is a complicated issue concerning which there is considerable disagreement. Commentators have answered this question in five different ways. First, there are those who locate Wells unequivocally within the utopian tradition throughout his life (or whose remarks about Wells leaves them open to such an interpretation), and who, therefore, overlook the dystopianism of Wells's early writings, especially the science fiction stories written in the 1890s, which are often thought to be "pessimistic." This category includes Marie Louise Berneri, J. O. Bailey, Basil Davenport, Carl Freedman, Elizabeth Hansot, George Kateb, A. L. Morton, Mark Rose, Judith Shklar and Phillip Wegner.[3] Second, there are those who overlook the utopian nature of Wells's more "optimistic" later writings, from *A Modern Utopia* onward, and who in consequence locate Wells, again unequivocally, within the dystopian tradition. For these commentators it is the dystopian writer of the 1890s who is the "real" or authentic H. G. Wells. As we shall see, this category includes Yevgeny Zamyatin. It also includes Alexandra Aldridge, who contrasts what she refers to as the "real" Wells, who endorsed the principle of "cosmic pessimism," and who was a major influence on later dystopian writers such as Zamyatin, Huxley, and Orwell, with "the mythic 'other side of Wells,'" that is, the "sanguine scientific rationalist" later Wells who was a "utopian" writer and an "optimist."[4] Anthony West (Wells's son) and Patrick Parrinder might also, perhaps, be placed in this category.[5]

Our remaining categories contain commentators who claim that Wells was *both* a utopian *and* a dystopian writer. However, this claim can be understood in at least three different ways. First, it has been maintained that Wells's thinking and writing went in phases, and that he *alternated* between dystopianism and utopianism throughout his life. Second, it has been argued that Wells's thinking and writing evolved over time from dystopianism to utopianism and remained there. Thus the dystopian and utopian phases of his development can be thought of as being related *sequentially*. Third, it has been asserted that throughout his life Wells's thinking and writing could be associated with both the principles of utopianism and dystopianism at the same time and even in the same works. In short Wells writings, like his life and his character, are riven by *contradictions*.

Bearing these distinctions in mind, we may now say that our third category of commentators includes those who think that throughout his life Wells *alternated* between writing dystopian (pessimistic) works and writing utopian (optimistic), depending upon his mood, or his personal circumstances, or his assessment of the state of the world generally. This is the view of Chad Walsh, who maintains that Wells was "a man far more complex than either his admirers or his detractors have usually recognized. There was a deep streak of pessimism in him, which found expression in such dystopian tales as *The Time Machine* and *A Story of the Days to Come*." However, Walsh goes on, Wells *also* "had his optimistic *periods*, times when it seemed that mankind was showing some hopeful signs of rationality and altruism and that the human venture could be guided in good directions" (my emphasis). It was, for example, Walsh maintains, "during one of those times of hope that he wrote *A Modern Utopia*."[6] Some of the statements made by Krishan Kumar (whose views on the subject are inconsistent) indicate that he also might be placed in this third category.[7]

Category four contains those who maintain that Wells underwent a process of sequential *development* from being a dystopian writer in his early writings, the great science fiction novels and tales of the 1890s, to being a utopian writer in his later years, beginning with *A Modern Utopia* (first published in 1905). These commentators suggest that generally speaking, in any particular phase of his intellectual development, Wells was a consistent rather than an inconsistent thinker. However, the later Wells was consistent in a different way from the earlier Wells. For example, the later Wells, starting with *A Modern Utopia*, held different views and had a different understanding of himself and his vocation as a writer than the earlier Wells of the 1890s, the Wells who was the author of the dystopian science fiction stories which made his name and gave him his reputation. This fourth category includes Robert C. Elliott, Elizabeth Hansot, Mark. R. Hillegas, John Huntington, Krishan Kumar, Frank E. Manuel and Fritzie P. Manuel, Frank McConnell, W. Warren Wagar, and Jack Williamson.[8] In this connection, Frank and Fritzie Manuel have cited Wells as a particular example of what they consider to be a general tendency in the history of utopian thought and literature. In that history there have been times, they claim, when technological developments have "appeared to exert force in two opposing directions," finding expression in "both utopias and dystopias," which have sometimes been "written by the same author at different points in his life."[9] Similarly, Krishan Kumar has claimed that the later Wells "*reverses* himself" (my emphasis). For out of "the *anti*-utopian portraits of his early science fiction, such as the Martians of *The War of the Worlds* and the Selenites of *The First Men in the Moon*, he constructs the not very dissimilar Utopian Samurai of *A Modern Utopia* and *Men Like Gods*." Thus, according to Kumar, "in his own person," Wells made "the passage from anti-utopia to utopia in the decades of the 1900s." Indeed, thereafter he became "the most imposing and influential utopian target for later anti-utopians."[10] Writing in a similar vein, Jack Williamson has argued that "the shift in Wells's thought around the turn of the century is so great that by 1905, the author of *A Modern Utopia* seems almost a different man."[11] From then on, Williamson maintains, Wells was "not only the principal target of anti-utopian attack but also, in his early science fiction, the most resourceful and most influential of all the attackers."[12]

Like those of Kumar, Frank McConnell's views on the subject of Wells's intellectual development are inconsistent, though in an interesting and revealing way. On a number of occasions McConnell states that Wells's *early* writings, the science fiction stories of the 1890s, are works of *utopian* rather than dystopian fiction. For example at one point he maintains that "whatever else it is—and it is many things—*The Time Machine* (1895) is certainly an exercise in that curious literary subtype called *utopian* fiction."[13] And elsewhere he claims that Wells's *The Island of Dr. Moreau* "is another post-Darwinian *utopia*" (my emphasis).[14] Considered in isolation these remarks suggest *prima facie* that McConnell should be placed in the first of the five categories referred to earlier. However, things are not as simple as this. For McConnell also states that the characters of *The Island of Dr. Moreau* (1896) "play out their grisly melodrama in a landscape, on an island, which is precisely nowhere (as is proper for a utopia, even an evil one;"[15] that Wells's *When the Sleeper Awakes* (1898–1899) "is a grim utopia indeed";[16] and indeed that the moon in *The First Men in the Moon* is in fact "a nightmarish *dystopia*" (my emphasis)[17] These assertions suggest that when McConnell describes Wells's early science fiction stories as literary *utopias* he is using the word "utopia" in a very specific sense. From this point of view all literary productions which depict an imagined alternative society and which could be used to criticize an existing one might be said to be utopias, irrespective of whether their authors consider the imagined society in question to be either better or worse than the society in which they live. In my view this use of the word "utopia" is far too vague, and is likely to confuse the reader, who might well think (rightly) that there is an important difference between believing that a work is a literary utopia, on the one hand, and believing that it is a literary dystopia on the other. Moreover, it is clear from what McConnell says elsewhere in his book that, despite his claim that Wells's early science fiction tales are utopias, his more considered view is that Wells *did* undergo a process of transition or development from a *dystopian* to a utopian writer around the beginning of the twentieth century.[18] It is for this reason that McConnell should be placed in category three or four above and not category one.

I note in passing that McConnell's very broad and misleading use of the term "utopia" is also employed by a number of other commentators. For example, Richard Gerber employs the term in this sense when he describes Huxley's *Brave New World* and Orwell's *1984* as *utopias*, something which Gary Saul Morson has severely criticized him for.[19] Carl Freedman, Lyman Tower Sargent, and Tom Moylan, have also suggested that the term "utopia" might legitimately be used in this broad sense.[20] In my view, however, not only is such a usage undesirable because of the possible confusion it might cause, it is also inconsistent with the view, which is also held by Sargent and Moylan, that when interpreting a text it is necessary to pay attention to the intentions of its author. I say more about this issue in chapter 5.

There is some evidence to support the view that as a commentator on his own work Wells himself should be placed in this fourth category, together with Hillegas, Kumar, the Manuels, and Wagar. A number of commentators have argued that some time early in the twentieth century Wells made a self-conscious decision to stop writing *novels* and to start writing texts of another kind; a decision which amounted, in effect, to a commitment to writing utopian rather than dystopian works in the future. Thus, for example, in his disagreement with Henry James, Wells wrote in 1915 that "there is, of course, a real and very fundamental difference in our innate and developed attitudes towards life and literature. To you literature like a painting is an end, to me literature like architecture is a means, it has a use." "I had," Wells continues, "rather be called a journalist than an artist."[21] Wells also makes remarks which support this reading in a radio broadcast on "Utopias" which he delivered in 1939. As Patrick Parrinder has noted,[22] this broadcast suggests that the later Wells thought of himself in the 1890s as being primarily a writer of "anticipatory tales" rather than of literary utopias. But it also suggests that Wells thought of himself as being a writer who, somewhat later, had occasionally indulged in utopian speculations, or had at least "tried a little excursion of that sort."[23] This broadcast indicates quite clearly, however, that those earlier works which in 1939 Wells considered to be literary utopias do *not* include any of his science fiction stories of the 1890s, or even *A Modern Utopia*, which Wells evidently thought was an essay *about* utopias and utopian literature, or "a summary of utopian ideas," rather than being an example of a utopian text in the strict sense of the term.[24] Rather, the stories which Wells refers to in this context are *In the Days of the Comet* (1906) and *Men Like Gods* (1922). It is clear, then, that in his 1939 broadcast Wells was of the opinion that *none* of his early writings of the 1890s, that is to say his works of science fiction, were literary utopias. They were all of them "anticipatory tales," or what we now refer to as works of dystopian literature.

Evidence supporting the claim that Wells's thinking and writing evolved over time, and that he should, therefore, be placed in category four above, can also be found in the preface to *Seven Famous Novels*, a reprinted collection of Wells's early stories of the 1890s, which was published in 1934. There Wells identifies what is now referred to as "science fiction" with the "anticipatory tales" referred to above and points out to his readers that he had given up writing such stories. For, he says, "the world in the presence of cataclysmal realities has no need for fresh cataclysmal fantasies."[25] Although Wells does not actually use the word "dystopian" in this context, his association of his anticipatory tales of the 1890s with the notion of "cataclysm" clearly indicates that he considered his early science fiction stories as falling within what is now referred to as the category of dystopian rather than utopian fiction. The views expressed by Wells in the 1930s, therefore, tend to support the judgment of Hillegas, Kumar, the Manuels, Wagar, and of other commentators in category four above, that at some point in the early 1900s Wells made a deliberate decision to stop writing dystopian science fiction and to become a utopian writer.

In the fifth category are those commentators who maintain that it is difficult to pigeonhole Wells by attempting to periodize his thinking and writing along the lines indicated earlier. According to them, it is true that Wells was *both* a utopian *and* a dystopian writer. However, this is true of him neither *alternately*, as commentators in category three maintain, nor *sequentially*, as commentators in category four suggest. Rather it was true of him at all times throughout his life. On this reading, then, Wells was always an inconsistent thinker whose writings are shot through with contradictions. Consequently at any one moment, for example even in his *A Modern Utopia*, which is commonly held to be a utopian work, he was *at once* both a utopian and a dystopian writer. He was always both excited and optimistic about the possibilities of scientific and technological development for social progress, whilst also at the same time being aware of and sensitive to its dangers.

How might these inconsistencies and contradictions in Wells's writings be explained? Some commentators have offered a psychological explanation for them. Arguments of this kind take three forms. First, it is suggested that Wells's vacillations were a reflection of the inconstancy of his temperament generally. This is the view of Chad Walsh.[26] Second, it is suggested that Well's inconsistencies are a reflection of his mood or of "the state of his personal and professional life" at the time of writing a particular work. This is the view of Krishan Kumar.[27] Third, it is suggested that Wells's inconsistencies are a reflection of his basic inability to engage in any sustained process of logical or systematic thinking. For after all he was, it might be claimed, a creative or imaginative writer and not a political theorist or a logician. This appears to be the view of W. Warren Wagar, who states that Wells "was never a subtle or systematic thinker, or even a thinker at all in the most solemn sense."[28] It is also the view of Jack Williamson, according to whom Wells was "never a systematic thinker." In Williamson's opinion, because he was "uncritical of his own ideas" Wells had a tendency to be "their captive more often than their master."[29]

A more charitable interpretation of Wells would be to suggest that, as in the case of Ursula K. Le Guin somewhat later, the contradictions in Wells's thinking are a reflection of the contradictory nature of the phenomena about which he chose to write and that, like Le Guin, Wells is a "dialectical" thinker, or rather was one in the 1890s and early 1900s when he wrote *A Modern Utopia*. John Huntington, for example, has argued that "the coexistence of opposites is a fundamental structural element in all of Wells's early fiction"[30] and that a "technique of thinking by means of oppositions and mediations informs the structure of all of Wells's work" at that time.[31] According to Huntington, in these stories Wells addresses a number of problems to which "though no 'answer' is finally produced," nevertheless the "act of mediation" associated with Wells's style of writing does at least make "the author and his audience alive to the complex dynamics" of the problems in question.[32] It is precisely this, in Huntington's view, which makes Wells's science fiction stories fascinating for the reader. The interest of Wells's early work, he says, "lies in his willingness to tolerate and explore contradiction with restlessly seeking to simplify and resolve its tension."[33] Huntington notes that this is the main difference between the writings of the early and the later Wells. For the later Wells, the *utopian* writer, has a "tendency to seek single answers and solutions" to complex moral and political problems—to "see contradiction, not as the expression of the complexity of human desire and the contradictory seekings and interests which have so far prevented any easy settlement of social problems, but simply as muddle, a confusion that some clear, directed thinking will resolve."[34] In the later works, then, "contradiction," which Huntington notes was for the early Wells "essential to the understanding," has come to be thought of as something that "must be resolved by attaining some kind of unity, usually by disproving or discarding *one* of the opposing elements of the contradiction."[35] Huntington makes no mention here of either Hegel or Le Guin. In my view, however, the characterization which he offers here of the dialectical outlook in the science fiction of the early H. G. Wells has obvious associations with Hegel's philosophy. Moreover, such an outlook is necessary for any adequate understanding, not just of the early H. G. Wells, but also of the writings of Le Guin, especially *The Dispossessed*. I note in passing that a logical implication of Huntington's remarks here is that Wells's early science fiction stories should be thought of as being neither exclusively *utopian* nor exclusively *dystopian* works. Rather, they should be thought of as being *novelistic* through and through.

Interestingly, Huntington suggests that this way of thinking also finds itself in Wells's *A Modern Utopia*, which in consequence "contains a strong *anti-utopia* element," (my emphasis) the existence of which has been completely overlooked by some commentators.[36] Gary Saul Morson also adopts, and ably defends, such a dialectical approach to the understanding of Wells's *A Modern Utopia*.[37] According to Morson, "a number of readers have, despite Wells's warning against simplistic and humorless interpretations," taken this work as "*unambiguously* utopian" (my emphasis).[38] In Morson's view, this "sunny reading" overlooks a number of deep shadows that Wells casts over his utopian passages."[39] Morson himself prefers to think of *A Modern Utopia* as a "meta utopia."[40] As such it is "an account of an imagination in dialogue with itself."[41] It is the story of "an inconclusive consideration of utopian and anti-utopian philosophies" in one and the same work,[42] or the story of one mind's (Wells's) "constant alternation between a vision of a "comprehensive scheme" for universal happiness and a contrary vision of the forces that make the first vision absurd."[43] It might, in consequence, in a telling phrase for those familiar with Le Guin's *The Dispossessed*, be said to be an "*ambiguous* utopia" (my emphasis).[44] As such it is a text which contains a "complex dialectic" of both "utopian *and* anti-utopian visions" (my emphasis).[45]

Morson points out, quite rightly, that most of those commentators who have interpreted *A Modern Utopia* as being straightforwardly a literary utopia tend to ignore the stylistic devices which Wells's employed when writing it.[46] In particular, they overlook the fact that Wells explicitly "distances" himself from the viewpoint, and the views, expressed by the apparent "author" of the book, or from the person whom Wells refers to as the "owner of the voice," who is presented to the reader as being the person who wrote the book.[47] It is this person who presents the ideas which are associated with utopianism in the book. But this utopian dimension of the work tells only one-half of the story in the text. Side by side with it there is, Morson notes, one of the most penetrating critiques of utopianism in politics ever written.

The philosophical underpinnings of this critique of utopianism in literature are to be found in Wells's essay "Skepticism of the Instrument," appended to the text. This, Wells tells us in his "A Note to the Reader," contains "the heretical metaphysical skepticism upon which all my thinking rests."[48] In this essay Wells follows Nietzsche and Dostoevsky and rejects the philosophical "rationalism" or the Platonism which, in his view, underpins all utopian speculation. Thus, for example, he has his "author" maintain that "rationalism" of this kind implies "almost everything that we are endeavoring to repudiate in this particular work."[49]

Moreover, in addition to this general attitude of philosophical skepticism, the critique of utopianism which Wells develops in *A Modern Utopia* rests upon two further principles. First Wells points out through the character of the "author" that those who write literary utopias tend to deal in abstract ideas rather than with the lives of real persons or concrete individuals.[50] Second, he has his "author" observe that the utopian writers have a tendency to think of the societies they are describing as being "perfect" and, therefore, "static," or not subject to change. They do not appreciate that, as the pre-Socratic philosopher Heraclitus rightly maintains, all things are changing in at least some respects all of the time. For Wells's "author," as for Heraclitus, Nietzsche and Zamyatin, change is the basic principle of all life.[51]

In "A Note to the Reader," which is placed at the very beginning of *A Modern Utopia,* and in words which prefigure the later thinking of Zamyatin in a striking way, Wells maintains that the rationalist in ethics and politics, and, therefore, presumably also the "utopian" thinker, is someone who sees things in "black and white." Such persons like "everything in hard, heavy lines, black and white, yes and no." Consequently, "they do not understand how much there is that cannot be presented at all in that way." They "cannot count beyond two" and deal "only in alternatives."[52] In short, although Wells does not actually use the word, what the utopian "rationalist" in politics lacks is indeed, as Morson suggests, a "dialectical" outlook on life. It is, perhaps, especially noticeable to readers familiar with Le Guin's *The Dispossessed* and its subtitle, *An Ambiguous Utopia,* that Wells should express this point by reference to the notion of "ambiguity." Utopian rationalists, he maintains, might be criticized for demanding a "scientific language," one "without *ambiguity,* as precise as mathematical formulae and with every term in relations of exact logical consistency with every other."[53] The similarity between the views which Wells expresses here and those of Zamyatin is obvious. The similarity between these views and those of Le Guin is much less so, especially to those who wrongly consider *The Dispossessed* to be, like Wells's *A Modern Utopia,* a work of *utopian* literature.

One manifestation of the dialectical complexity of human existence is the tension between that which is "universal" and that which is "particular." In the sphere of ethics and politics this manifests itself as a tension or even a "contradiction" between the abstract ideas or ideals associated with political utopianism, and which are the usual concern of the political theorist, on the one hand, and the "real lives" of concrete individual characters or "personalities" living in a particular society at a particular time, which are the usual concerns of the novelist or creative writer, on the other. In the final pages of *A Modern Utopia*, in his capacity as "chairman" or commentator on the ongoing dialogue between the works ostensible "author" and its other central character, the "botanist," Wells tells the reader that the point of adopting this stylistic device was so that he could deal with both of these two dimensions of human existence, the universal and the particular, at the same time or in the same work. His intention, he says, was to connect the abstract utopian theorizing with the lives of particular "personalities," or, in the case of the "author" or "owner of the voice," with just "one individual's aspiration" toward "utopia."[54] Wells notes here that traditionally utopian writing deals with the abstract ideas and ideals which are usually associated with some "comprehensive scheme" of things and not with the lives of "individuals." In his own case, Wells suggests that such a comprehensive utopian scheme of things must always be one in which individual personalities "float."[55] He explicitly acknowledges, however, that "the two visions are not seen consistently together, at least by me, and I do not surely know that they exist consistently together."[56] Thus, for example, in the case of the two central characters of *A Modern Utopia*, when "one focuses upon these two" and their individual lives then that "wide landscape" which is utopian society and utopian theory immediately "becomes indistinct and distant." On the other hand, however, as soon as "one regards *that*," (my emphasis) or focuses one's attention upon this wide landscape, then immediately "the real persons one knows grow vague and unreal."[57] "Nevertheless," Wells continues, although this is true, he finds himself unable to "separate these two aspects of human life, each commenting on the other."[58] For although this contradiction or "incompatibility" between that which is "great" or the "abstract," on the one hand, and that which is "individual" on the other, is one which he "could not resolve" (not surprisingly, since it is not resolvable), nevertheless in his opinion it is the very stuff of life.

It is for this reason, Wells says, that he felt compelled to construct *A Modern Utopia*, the work, in the particular way that he did. His intention, he states in his "A Note to the Reader," was to achieve a balance throughout between "philosophical discussion on the one hand and imaginative narrative" on the other.[59] It is clear from the final paragraphs of *A Modern Utopia*, that what Wells is really interested in, as a creative writer, is not abstract utopian theorizing for its own sake, but rather in the impact which the "desire and need for utopia" has had in the past, has now, and will have in the future, on individual human beings or, in the final words of the book, on "the daily lives of men."[60] In my view, once again it is readily apparent that the views on utopian politics and literature which underpin Le Guin's *The Dispossessed* are already here, *in nucleo*, in Wells's *A Modern Utopia*.[61]

These remarks suggest that although he is fascinated by the idea of utopia and by traditional literary utopias, nevertheless at the same time, both as a creative writer and someone with ethical and political ideals of his own, Wells is acutely aware of their limitations. It is true that in *A Modern Utopia* Wells occasionally flirts with the idea that, as Kenneth Roemer has suggested, what he is doing in this work is revising or reinventing the idea of utopia rather than abandoning it or rejecting it.[62] There are occasions when he would have the reader believe that this text is indeed itself an example of a certain (new) kind of literary utopia. At the same time, however, there is also evidence to support the view that what Wells is actually doing in this work is something else, namely commenting on the obvious limitations of utopianism in ethics and politics. For Wells's text evidently does contain a trenchant *critique* of utopianism in politics. Everything that we find, later on in the writings of Zamyatin, and which today is so often associated with *dystopian* political thought, is already to be found, not just in Wells's early works of science fiction, but also in his *A Modern Utopia*. Moreover, it would be foolish to ask which of these two sides of Well's thinking in this text reflects the views of the "real" Wells. For Wells insists upon the validity of both of these two contrasting and opposed points of view, each of which he evidently considers as capturing an important dimension of human existence.

Both Mark Hillegas and Christopher Collins have suggested that it is fruitful, in Hillegas's words, to consider Zamyatin's *We* as a "parody" of the kind of utopianism which is to be found in the writings of the later Wells, especially in *A Modern Utopia*,[63] which they consider to be straightforwardly a utopian work. According to Hillegas, "the rationalism and regimentation" to which Zamyatin is opposed in *We* was also "a strong element" in Wells's *A Modern Utopia*.[64] Hillegas maintains, therefore, that in *We* Zamyatin "wrote more of a critique of Wells than he probably ever realized," especially given his enthusiasm for Wells's earlier works of science fiction. According to Hillegas, Zamyatin appears to have been unaware of the existence and/or contents of *A Modern Utopia*, and hence also of the chronological development in Wells's thinking, specifically his transformation from being a dystopian writer in his earlier works of science fiction to being a utopian writer in *A Modern Utopia* and in later works. In fact, however, as his essay on Wells indicates,[65] it is not the case that Zamyatin was unfamiliar with Wells's *A Modern Utopia*. Indeed, a number of the core *anti*-utopian ideas in *We* are simply inherited by Zamyatin directly from Wells's text without significant alteration. This is true of Zamyatin's emphasis on the Heraclitean principle of change as a law of life. It is also true of Zamyatin's emphasis on the "irrational" character of the world generally, as is evidenced by the role of "irrationality" in the spheres of logic and mathematics. A reading of Wells's *A Modern*

Utopia, together with his essay "Skepticism of the Instrument," published as an appendix to it, indicates that these are beliefs which Zamyatin and Wells have in common, rather than beliefs which separate them. In my view, then, Zamyatin came to his judgment that Wells is not a utopian but an anti-utopian writer not in ignorance of, but in full knowledge of, the contents of Wells's *A Modern Utopia*. In effect, therefore, he explicitly denies that Wells moved from being a dystopian to being a utopian writer, as is suggested by commentators such as Hillegas, the Manuels and Wagar. For this reason I agree with Kumar's claim that Collins (and by implication also Hillegas) sees Zamyatin "too exclusively as a *reaction* to Wells, rather than, as Zamyatin himself saw things, a *continuation* of him" (my emphasis).[66] I also agree with Alexandra Aldridge's suggestion that, unlike Zamyatin, "Hillegas did not comprehend Wells's thought well enough" to see "the constant that runs through it."[67] Zamyatin would, I think, have wholeheartedly endorsed George Kateb's assertion that "Wells's modern utopia is not really a utopia, in the fullest sense, at all."[68]

It is arguable that Wells's *A Modern Utopia* is not itself a literary utopia. It is rather an essay about the history of utopian thought and literature. Patrick Parrinder has claimed that Wells "*never* produced a major utopian book" (my emphasis).[69] And there is at least some evidence in *A Modern Utopia* (which most commentators do consider to be a utopian text)[70] which supports this claim. Hence, also, there is at least some evidence to support Zamyatin's view that, so far as he was a creative writer, Wells was throughout his life *always* if not overtly anti-utopian then at least someone who, though tempted by the siren song of utopianism, nevertheless remained skeptical about utopianism in politics and wary of its obvious pitfalls. Zamyatin considers Wells's *Men Like Gods* to be the only exception to this generalization. He therefore agrees, on this occasion, with Wells's own assessment of *Men Like Gods* as a utopian work. In my opinion, though, even this work of Wells is not unequivocally an example of a literary utopia. For one of the points which Wells emphasizes within it is that a utopian society is not one in which real live (i.e., "imperfect") human beings could actually live. This is an unusual point for someone who is allegedly writing a literary utopia to make. I am inclined, therefore, not to take Wells's and Zamyatin's later assessment of this work too seriously.

ZAMYATIN'S ESSAY ON WELLS, SCIENCE FICTION, AND DYSTOPIAN LITERATURE

In an essay entitled "H. G. Wells" Zamyatin has some extremely interesting comments to make about science fiction as a genre of writing and its relation to utopian/dystopian literature.[71] So far as we are concerned, there are two questions here which are especially significant, to each of which Zamyatin has an answer. The first question is what was the trajectory of development of the utopian/dystopian tradition over the course of the nineteenth and twentieth centuries—the main turning points and the writers associated with them? The second question is how is the history of the utopian/dystopian tradition related to that of science fiction? At what point and with which writer did these two histories become fused?

The immediate context for Zamyatin's essay is his attempt to explain to his readers what contribution was made by H. G. Wells to the historical development of these two styles of writing. According to Zamyatin, there are actually "two Wellses." One of these is an "author of *realistic novels*," (my emphasis) whereas the other is the author of what Zamyatin refers to as works of "social fantasy," or "sociofantastic novels."[72] Zamyatin does not himself use the expression "science fiction" in his essay, but the works which he describes as being "sociofantastic" are in fact what today we would refer to as Wells's science fiction. It should be noted that when Zamyatin makes this distinction between the two "Wellses" he does so in a way which suggests that in his opinion works of science fiction are not and could not be realistic novels. At first sight it is not clear whether Zamyatin says this because he thinks that works of science fiction are not and could not be novels at all, in the strict sense of the term; or whether he says it because he thinks that although works of science fiction can indeed be novels, nevertheless they could not be realistic. Zamyatin's remarks support each of these two possible interpretations of his views.

It is clear from Zamyatin's essay that although Zamyatin does have a high opinion of Wells, nevertheless he does not think that, as a writer of "realistic novels," Wells could be included amongst authors of the first rank. Zamyatin makes a distinction between literary "geniuses" and those who are at best "talented," and he includes Wells firmly in the latter category, comparing him unfavorably with Dostoevsky in this regard.[73] In Zamyatin's opinion, it is the second of the two "Wellses" who is the most interesting, and this is so because he "has almost single handedly created a new genre" of writing,[74] or "a new, original variety of literary form,"[75] which again we would today characterize as science fiction. Zamyatin suggests that, given Wells's obvious limitations as a novelist, were it not for this second Wells, the first "would not have found a place among the brighter stars in the astronomical catalogue of literature."[76]

What are the characteristic features of science fiction, or this new genre of writing which Wells almost single-handedly created, and hence of Wells's own writings, as Zamyatin understands them? According to Zamyatin, there are two such features, having to do with the social content of these writings and with their artistic form respectively. The first of these

features, which relates to their content, is the fact that they are *not* literary utopias. This is so partly because their authors of literary utopias
"paint" what they consider to be pictures of "ideal societies." Thus,
"translating this into the language of mathematics," Zamyatin maintains, "we might say that utopias bear a + sign." They represent the optimistic, positive or affirmative attitude about the world which is
adopted by their authors, and which they recommend to their readers.
In Zamyatin's view, Wells's works of science fiction *lack* this quality. On
the contrary, Zamyatin claims that "most of his social fantasies bear
the – sign." They reflect the pessimistic or negative attitude of their author. Their purpose is not to look forward to consider the possibility of
a better or morally superior society in the future, but to focus on the
present. As Zamyatin puts it, they are "almost solely instruments for ex-
posing the defects of the existing social order," rather than for "building
a picture of a future paradise."[77] In short, one could say that as Zamyatin understands them, Wells's works of science fiction constitute not
"negative utopias" (arguably a contradiction in terms) but rather, as
Chad Walsh has suggested, "inverted utopias."[78] Zamyatin himself does
not actually use the word "dystopia" in his essay. Nevertheless, it is
tempting to suggest that he would have considered any work of this
kind (that is to say an inverted utopia) to be what today we refer to as a
literary dystopia, had he been familiar with the meaning of this term. As
we shall see, however, it is arguable that such a characterization of Zamyatin's understanding of Wells would be inaccurate. For it might be suggested that there is *more* to Wells's works of science fiction, as Zamyatin understands them, than the fact that they are literary dystopias, if
by that expression one means simply a text which represents an intellectual inversion of the traditional literary utopia.

The second feature which Zamyatin associates with the works of Wells,
and with science fiction generally, has to do with their aesthetic form, or
with the style of writing adopted by their author. And that is that these
works take the form of "the novel." They are novelistic. In this regard Zamyatin insists they are quite unlike traditional literary utopias. Zamyatin is
very clear about this. The traditional utopia, he says, "is always *static*; it is
always *descriptive*, and has no, or almost no, *plot dynamics*" (my emphasis).[79] In short, it is *not* properly speaking a novel.[80] Wells's works of science fiction, on the other hand, *do* possess these qualities, although not to
the eminent degree that they are found in a "great" writer. If in a traditional literary utopia, and by implication *also* in a modern inverted utopia,
we find that "static well-being" and "petrified paradaisiac social equilibrium are logically bound" with "a static plot and absence of a story line,"
then Wells's science fiction should not be thought of as being an *inverted*
utopia at all. This is so because an inverted utopia would be just as de-

scriptive and lacking in character and plot as the utopian form which preceded it and inspired it. According to Zamyatin, however, Wells is, on the contrary, a writer of "sociofantastic *novels*," within which "the plot is always *dynamic*, built on collisions, on conflict" and the story is always "complex and entertaining" (my emphasis).[81] In short, Zamyatin is of the opinion that H. G. Wells is not at all a writer of literary dystopias, if we use this expression to characterize what are simply inverted utopias. He is rather a *novelist* whose main theme is the impact of developments in science and technology on society and the "collisions" and "conflicts" which this generates in the lives of his characters.[82]

These views of Zamyatin disagree with those of both Tom Moylan and Krishan Kumar. In his *Demand the Impossible*, Moylan does not make a clear distinction between the traditional literary utopia and the "utopian novel." For example at one point he states that "central to utopian fiction" is the "alternative world imagined by the author." The society projected by the author, he says, "has long been seen as what the *utopian novel* is 'about.'"[83] And elsewhere he refers to "the *traditional utopian novel*" within which the "characters" are "secondary to the society itself" (my emphasis).[84] Thus Moylan identifies utopian fiction generally with the utopian novel. The remarks just cited indicate that he thinks that Thomas More's *Utopia* is a novel. Similarly, Kumar states, that "the utopia is closer to the *novel* than to any other literary genre; *is* in fact a novel, though not necessarily of the kind that we have come to identify too exclusively with its nineteenth-century form and focus."[85] Kumar concedes, however, that most traditional literary utopias are not "good" novels. For, he goes on to say that "very few utopias stand out as great works of literature—More's *Utopia* and William Morris's *News from Nowhere* are among the best—and in many cases utopian authors are perfunctory in the extreme in their selection and use of the form. The didactic purpose overwhelms any literary aspiration."[86] Zamyatin's view on the other hand, with which I agree, is that for this very reason it is better to think of traditional literary utopias as not being novels *at all* in the strict sense of the term, but as possessing a quite different literary form. This is so because within them issues such as characterization and plot (although they are undoubtedly addressed in some rudimentary form) are strictly subordinated to issues such as ideas and social context.

It is clear from what Kumar says in the passage quoted above, however, that his disagreement with Zamyatin is more one of terminology rather than substance. For Kumar acknowledges that the traditional literary utopia is indeed primarily a didactic rather than a "literary" work. In this connection Kumar makes some remarks in the preface to his *Utopia and Anti-Utopia in Modern Times*, which are especially significant. "Strictly speaking," he says, "the literary utopia—as opposed, say, to the political treatise—is the *only* utopia." All of the "utopias" dealt with in his book, in contrast, are really best thought of as being "*novels*, imaginative works of fiction," rather than "utopias" (my emphasis). And the reason for this is plain. For "on the whole, utopias are not very distinguished for their aesthetic qualities as works of literature." What is interesting about them is, rather, "the nature and quality of their ideas about individuals and societies." And, indeed, it is "chiefly as contributions to social thought" that Kumar considers them. According to Kumar, as a general rule it is the *anti-utopia*, at least in modern times, which "has been more effective than the *utopia* in evoking literary qualities of a vivid and compelling kind." This is borne out, Kumar maintains, specifically in the case of H. G. Wells, by "the well known contrast between the literary power of Wells's early anti-utopian fables and the more hackneyed quality of his later utopian writing."[87] In my view, however, the best way of making the point that Kumar wishes to make here, which does seem to me to be substantially valid, would be to distinguish, not between a "poor" utopian novel and a "good" one, as Kumar himself does, but rather between a traditional "literary utopia," on the one hand and a "novel" on the other.[88]

It is interesting to think about Zamyatin's *We* in this way. For if there is anything to be said for the above analysis then it follows that it is incorrect to think of *We* as being even one example, let alone *the* classic example, of a literary dystopia. Indeed if we apply this line of reasoning, which as we have seen is suggested by Zamyatin himself, to Zamyatin's own text then we would have to conclude that *We* also is best thought of as a *novel* rather than a literary dystopia in this particular sense of the term. That is to say, it is a *novel* dealing with the theme of utopianism in politics rather than an inverted utopia or a negative utopia.

Such a reading has been suggested, albeit somewhat halfheartedly, by Gary Saul Morson. I say "halfheartedly" because Morson's views on this subject are not entirely consistent. Morson interprets Zamyatin's *We* in two quite different and opposed ways at different times, either as a traditional literary dystopia or, alternatively, as a novel. For instance, Morson often refers, quite traditionally, to Zamyatin's *We* as an example, or even *the* classic example, of a literary dystopia, understood in this case as an "anti-utopia."[89] Texts of this kind, he maintains are "parodies" of the utopian literary form.[90] As such, like the utopian form itself, their aim is primarily (if not solely) a "didactic" one.[91] Literary dystopias are *not*, therefore, novels. For the novel is a genre of writing which must be clearly distinguished from that of the utopia, and hence also from the "parodic" inversion of that particular literary genre.[92] Although it is true, Morson concedes, that "like the novel" the classic "anti-utopian" text does also bring into question the "utopian" claim to possess absolute truth or certain knowledge regarding moral, social, or political questions.[93] Thus, in a manner similar to that of Zamyatin in his essay on H. G. Wells, Morson suggests at times that a literary dystopia is simply an inverted version of a classic literary utopia, possessing the same literary merits or rather demerits.

On the other hand, however, there are occasions when Morson also appreciates that if this were indeed the case then it would be difficult to defend the claim that Zamyatin's *We* should (or even could) be thought of as an example of a literary dystopia, precisely because of the fact that it is a work of art which suffers from none of the aesthetic inadequacies just mentioned. On these other occasions, therefore, Morson takes a different tack and refers to *We* as being a *novel* in the strict sense of the term. He suggests that, as such, it should be clearly distinguished from those works falling into the category of literary dystopia precisely because it focuses on such issues as "plot," "character," and the development of "personality."[94] At no time, however, does Morson suggest that Zamyatin's text might be thought of, as Frederic Jameson has claimed, as being a *utopia*—or as containing within itself (if only implicitly) a utopian vision of a better society.[95]

In connection with this issue of the literary status of Zamyatin's *We*, Robert C. Elliott has claimed that such works "are as far removed from the *novel* proper as are *News from Nowhere* and *Island*."[96] Elliott's reason for thinking this is that the novel "traditionally focuses on human character," whereas "negative utopias" like *We* "depict a society in which human character can hardly be said to exist at all." Presumably, in Elliott's view, this is because all of the individuals in *We* have been reduced to the status of a "number" and might in consequence be said to lack any individual character. It is worth noting at this point that in her essay "Science Fiction and Mrs. Brown" Le Guin endorses Elliott's view that a novel must focus on character. However, she disagrees with Elliott over the question of whether Zamyatin's *We* is a work within which "human character can hardly be said to exist at all." For in her view the individuality of Zamyatin's D-503, as a *particular* human being or as a "character," is evident throughout this work.[97] For this reason it might be suggested that Le Guin, too, thinks of Zamyatin's *We* as a novel about utopianism and its discontents rather than a literary dystopia, at least some of the time. I take it that this is what she has in mind when she says that *We* is a "dystopia which contains a hidden or implied utopia,"[98] that is to say, it is a work of literature which (like *The Dispossessed*) contains both "utopic" and "dystopic" elements. In my view, though, it would have been more accurate if Le Guin had said that it is this which makes Zamyatin's *We* a *novel* rather than either a literary utopia or a literary dystopia.[99] It should, however, be noted that, like those of Morson, Le Guin's views on this subject are not entirely consistent. For elsewhere she refers to *We* as being a "dystopia" or a "negative utopia" *as well* as being a "science fiction novel."[100]

It is especially noteworthy that when Zamyatin makes the distinction between static and dynamic utopias and dystopias in his essay on Wells he actually has *two* things in mind. Again one of these has to do with sociological content and the other with aesthetic form. In the first case, the issue is whether the *societies* being portrayed in the texts in question are ideal or perfect, and hence subject to change or not. In the second case, the issue is whether the *texts* in question are merely descriptive, lacking in characterization and plot, and so on. In other words, for Zamyatin, dynamic *texts*, as opposed to dynamic *societies*, are novels rather than either literary utopias or dystopias. What differentiates a dynamic text of Wells from a classical literary utopia, apart from the fact that it carries a "minus sign," and is, therefore, a dystopia and not a utopia, is the *additional* fact that it is a novel, or is novelistic, in the strict sense of the term. Those commentators who have discussed this issue have noted that for both Wells and Zamyatin the idea of a dynamic utopia or dystopia is connected to the view that the imaginary societies being depicted in each case are thought of as undergoing a process of historical change and development. It is rare, however, to find a commentator who has picked up on the idea that, for Zamyatin at least, the notion of a dynamic utopia or dystopia has as much to do with the issue of literary style as it does with that of sociological content. For example, Alexandra Aldridge has discussed Zamyatin's idea of a "dynamic utopia" in his essay on Wells, but overlooks the fact that for Zamyatin this idea has as much to do with the *aesthetic form* of the text as it does with the nature of the particular *society* being depicted within it, specifically whether that society is thought of as changing or not. Aldridge seems reluctant to accept Zamyatin's claim that Wells's "sociofantastic novels" are *not* literary utopias. However, it is not clear whether she objects to Zamyatin's claim that they cannot be utopias because they carry a minus rather than a plus sign, in other words because they are dystopias, on the one hand, or to his claim that they cannot be utopias because they are novels, on the other.[101]

One way of thinking about Wells relationship to the history of the utopian/dystopian tradition of literature would be to think about that history in the same way as Zamyatin thinks about the history of science, by reference to the notions of "inversion" and "displacement," about which I shall say more in chapter 4. As Tzvetan Todorov has suggested, speaking quite generally, "a new genre is always the transformation of one or several old genres: by *inversion*, by *displacement*, by combination" (my emphasis).[102] According to this line of reasoning, it is incorrect to think of a literary dystopia as being simply an "inverted utopia," or no more than what Zamyatin says is a literary utopia with a "minus sign." Rather, it is better to think of a literary dystopia as being a text which possesses similar characteristics to those which Zamyatin associates with

Wells's works of science fiction. To think about a literary dystopia in this way involves appealing not just to the notion of inversion, but also to that of displacement. From this standpoint, then, a literary dystopia properly speaking is not simply a descriptive text, lacking in dramatic narrative, characterization, and plot. Rather, it is a novel or a "dynamic" text as Zamyatin understands that term.

On this view, in the history of utopian/dystopian literature, it might be said that such a process of inversion *and* of displacement took place at one and the same time in the writings of H. G. Wells. Prior to Wells there were no literary dystopias of any kind. Consequently, there were no "inverted utopias," or texts which are merely descriptive, lacking the characteristics which Zamyatin associates with dynamic literary works. The very first literary dystopias were, therefore, not just inverted utopias but *also* novels properly so called. Hence, Zamyatin suggests, in the history of the utopian/dystopian literary tradition a "break" or a revolutionary transformation occurred at the end of the nineteenth and beginning of the twentieth centuries. Before this time there were only literary utopias, possessing the descriptive/didactic character noted earlier. Afterward, there were indeed literary dystopias. These, however, possessed the character of being not simply inverted utopias, but also that of being novels, in the strict sense of the term. As such, in addition to portraying societies in change, they were also what Zamyatin refers to as dynamic texts, or works with a strong emphasis on dramatic narrative, characterization, and plot. According to this schema, then, Zamyatin maintains that there are no literary dystopias at all which are not novelistic in character. The class of merely descriptive literary dystopias, or dystopias considered as being nothing more than inverted utopias is, as logicians say, a null class.

It is evident from Zamyatin's essay that he considers Wells to be the founding father of the literary tradition which today we refer to as science fiction. Moreover, rightly or wrongly, he also maintains that it is in the writings of H. G. Wells that the history of the utopian/dystopian literary tradition merges or fuses with that of science fiction. According to Zamyatin, however, the writings of Wells which fall into the category of science fiction are all dystopias rather than utopias. In short, Zamyatin is of the opinion that Wells not only wrote the first dystopian novels, or novelistic tales, he also wrote the very first works of science fiction.

Keith Booker has stated that Zamyatin's *We* "is often considered to be the first genuine modern dystopian text."[103] It is not clear exactly what Booker understands by the term "dystopian" in this context. But if, as seems likely, he thinks of Zamyatin's *We* as being a literary dystopia as well as, or perhaps even because of, the fact that it is a novel, then I think Zamyatin himself would have disagreed with this judgment. It is clear from his essay on Wells that Zamyatin considers himself to be, not the originator of a new literary tradition, what we now refer to as dystopian literature, but rather simply as a follower of H. G. Wells. Although Zamyatin does not use the word "dystopia," it follows from the analysis presented above that, in his opinion, H. G. Wells did not just create the new genre of science fiction, in effect he also created, at the very same time, the new genre of dystopian literature. Zamyatin's remarks imply that in his view science fiction and what we now call dystopian fiction, at least at their inception, were actually one and the same thing. Mark R. Hillegas's assertion that "the great anti-utopias of the twentieth century" are a part of a "single kind of fiction, for which there is no other name than science fiction," might in this regard be said to follow the lead provided by Zamyatin's essay on H. G. Wells.[104]

It should be noted that Zamyatin's and Hillegas's *identification* of the two genres of science fiction and dystopian literature has been subjected to criticism. According to Booker, for example, although it is true that dystopian fiction "resembles science fiction, a genre with which it is often associated," and although it is also true that there is "a great deal of overlap between dystopian fiction and science fiction" and that "many texts belong to both categories," nevertheless generally speaking "dystopian fiction *differs* from science fiction" because of its "attention to social and political critique," something which Booker does not think can be found in all science fiction.[105] Against this view, however, as we have seen, Zamyatin suggests that this was not the case when the genre of science fiction first came into existence, although of course this judgment is consistent with the view that the paths of the two genres have diverged thereafter.

From the standpoint of the categorial schema outlined by Zamyatin in his essay, Wells's *A Modern Utopia* might be said to be a transitional work. As Jack Williamson has suggested, it is "transitional in form as well as in thought, showing Wells midway between the literary artist and the propagandist."[106] It is neither a traditional literary utopia, on the one hand, nor a novel about utopianism in politics on the other. Considered from the point of view of its artistic form, it is something else. In Zamyatin's schema it could not be said to be the first example of a *utopian* novel. Zamyatin is very clear about this. He claims, in effect, that Wells's contribution to the historical development of the utopian/dystopian literary tradition was to write the first *dystopian* novel. According to Zamyatin, the *utopian* novel, if it existed, would constitute an inversion of the genre of the *dystopian* novel, a genre which, in its turn, constitutes both an inversion and a displacement of the traditional literary utopia. The accolade of being the first person to write a utopian novel, in the strict sense of the term, could, therefore, only be awarded to a novelist who in the *later* history of utopian/dystopian literature came after H. G. Wells. At this point it is appropriate to consider the work of Le Guin.

WELLS, LE GUIN, AND THE HISTORY OF UTOPIAN LITERATURE

It is interesting to consider the writings of Le Guin in the light of Zamyatin's essay on Wells, in the context of the two questions raised at the beginning of the preceding section. First, where does Le Guin stand in the history of the utopian/dystopian literary tradition? Or what has been her contribution to the historical development of that tradition? And second, where does Le Guin stand in the history of science fiction, specifically in connection with the issue of its fusion with that of utopian/dystopian literature? I shall address these questions more fully in chapters 5 and 6. However, it is convenient to make a few preliminary remarks about them here. As I suggested earlier, with respect to these questions there is a view which, although it is not stated explicitly, seems to me to be strongly implied in the writings of a number of commentators, and with which I disagree. This view is in effect a "quasi Hegelian" speculative account of the history of utopian/dystopian literature and its relationship to science fiction. According to this view, something similar to Zamyatin's suggestion that at the end of the nineteenth century H. G. Wells created almost single-handedly a new genre of writing, in effect that of the dystopian novel, might also (with a suitable inversion) be said of Le Guin in the 1970s. On this reading, like H. G. Wells, Le Guin can also be associated with the creation of a new subgenre of writing, namely that of the *utopian novel*, which also happens to be a work of science fiction. This is Le Guin's contribution to both the history of utopian/dystopian literature and to that of science fiction. And it is a *major* contribution, the significance of which justifies the claim that Le Guin is a writer of the stature and significance of Wells himself. For in the entire history of utopian/dystopian tradition, from Thomas More to the present, there have been only three significant turning points. The first was the creation of the tradition of the literary utopia in the writings of More. The second was the transformation of this traditional literary utopia into something qualitatively different, namely the dystopian novel (which is also a work of science fiction) in the writings of Wells. And the third was the further transformation of the dystopian novel of Wells into something which is again qualitatively different, namely the *utopian* novel (which is also a work of science fiction) of the 1970s; a transformation which is associated, above all, with Le Guin's *The Dispossessed*. According to this schema, the utopian science fiction novel of Le Guin might, therefore, be said to constitute a theoretical synthesis of the traditional literary utopia (More), which is neither a work of science fiction nor a novel, with the science fiction novel (Wells), which is not a literary utopia. This third subgenre might legitimately be said to represent a return to, or a revival of, the earlier tradition of utopian writing, *provided* that it is understood that those who write such works are, as it were, operating at a "higher level." It is in this sense only that one could talk about a work like *The Dispossessed* as having, as Tom Moylan has put it, employing a characteristically Hegelian expression, "negated the negation of utopia."[107]

As examples of commentators who seem to me to hold this view of Le Guin and her significance, or something very similar to it, at least implicitly, we can take Hoda Zaki and Carl Freedman. Zaki has claimed that "utopian literature" in the traditional sense "is conspicuous in its absence" in the twentieth century. In her view, however, this does not mean that "the death of utopian thought" in its entirety then occurred. For what Zaki refers to as the "utopian propensity" or the utopian "impulse" transferred itself and is now "alive and flourishing in another medium," namely that of "the science fiction novel."[108] It is true, of course, that not all works of science fiction in the twentieth century could be characterized as *utopian* in Zaki's sense. For a number of them are works of *dystopian* and not utopian literature. Nevertheless, Zaki's suggestion provides a clear indication of the significance which she attaches to the work of Le Guin, and especially *The Dispossessed*. For this is a text which, like a number of other commentators, Zaki considers as *the* classic representation of this new tendency. Of all of the Nebula Award winning texts surveyed by Zaki in her important study of twentieth century American science fiction, Le Guin's *The Dispossessed* is, she claims, "the most overtly utopian."[109] According to Zaki, both Le Guin's *The Dispossessed* and *The Left Hand of Darkness* may be placed in the category of "utopian" literature, or the utopian novel, because "they critique the present, depict imaginary societies, and anticipate the future." Moreover, both novels "endorse societies which are superior to the author's own."[110] They are, therefore, "utopian novels" as well as being works of science fiction.

The great strength of Zaki's analysis of the history of utopian/dystopian literature, and of Le Guin's place within it, is that she recognizes the need for us to distinguish between those works which are utopias and those which are dystopias. Its weakness, however, is the lack of any sense that Le Guin's writings constitute an important *new* development in the history of the utopian/dystopian literary tradition, rather than a simple (or as Hegelians would say "un-mediated") revival or return to an earlier form of utopian writing. The reason for this is that Zaki does not make a conceptual distinction between the aesthetic form of the traditional literary utopia and that of the novel. She thinks of Le Guin's writings as contributions to "political philosophy" or "political theory," rather than utopian/dystopian literature, and has no interest in questions of aesthetic form in contrast to intellectual or ideational content.[111]

Carl Freedman argues that the invention of science fiction as a new genre of writing in the late nineteenth and early twentieth centuries was eventually to lead to the "reinvention" and hence the "energization" or "revitalization" of the "older genre" of utopian literature.[112] He acknowledges, however, that this process did not constitute a "return" in the straightforward sense of a simple repetition. In his view, in comparison with the newly developed *"novelistic* genre of science fiction" the more traditional genre of utopian literature "necessarily lacks *novelistic* resources" (my emphasis).[113] The literary utopia prior to that time was in consequence essentially *"prenovelistic"* (my emphasis).[114] "The very characteristics of the literary utopia," he says, "are precisely those that distinguish the genre from the novel."[115] For example, the traditional literary utopia employs "a generally monologic authorial style that tends to foreclose any properly novelistic clash and heterogeneity of different voices."[116] "By contrast," he maintains, "the novel, and particularly the science fiction novel, involves a much higher level of dialectical complexity."[117] Freedman suggests, then, that utopian writing becomes novelistic precisely when it merged with "science fiction," which is itself a "novelistic genre."[118] He maintains that the *"synthesis* of science fiction with the older form," that is the traditional literary utopia, "amounts to the transformation of utopia into the *utopian novel"* (my emphasis).[119] Unlike Zaki, then, Freedman *does* appreciate the value of making a distinction between the form of a traditional literary utopia and a utopian novel, and this is the great strength of his analysis. However, its weakness is that Freedman does not appreciate the importance of making a conceptual distinction between utopian works on the one hand and dystopian ones on the other.

This weakness of Freedman's analysis is best exemplified by what he has to say about the respective parts which Wells and Le Guin have to play in the history of utopian/dystopian literature. As we have seen, Freedman has a very clear perception that the transition from traditional literary utopia to the *utopian novel*, and the fusion of the history of utopian/dystopian literature with that of science fiction took place at the same time. The crucial question, though, is *when* exactly did this occur, and which writer is the decisive figure to be associated with this transition? To be even more specific, does Freedman think that this transition took place at the end of the nineteenth century in the writings of H. G. Wells, or does he think that it took place in the 1970s in the writings of Le Guin? Freedman's views on this subject are inconsistent. Sometimes he maintains that the key figure was Wells, whilst at other times he maintains that it was Le Guin. The reason for this inconsistency is because Freedman neglects to make the distinction between the concept of a utopian novel and that of a dystopian novel when writing about this issue.

Thus, for example, there are passages when Freedman makes it clear that in his view the key figure here is Wells and not Le Guin. As Freedman himself puts it, "it remained for H. G. Wells," at the end of the nineteenth century, to "fuse the generic tendencies of utopia and science fiction and thereby produce a literary utopia that is critical (and so philosophically utopian) not only in its didactic content but also in its novelistic form."[120] It was H. G. Wells who was responsible for the "great vitalization" of the traditional literary utopia which was "made possible by the advent of science fiction." And it was Wells who initiated "the transformation of utopia into the *utopian novel*" (my emphasis).[121] It is, Freedman maintains, "owing to Wells more than to any other particular author that nearly all significant literary utopias," including Le Guin's *The Dispossessed*, are now works of "science fiction as well."[122] Freedman agrees with Zamyatin, then, that H. G. Wells was the decisive figure so far as the origination of the new literary genre of "the science fiction novel" is concerned. There is, however, an important difference between the views of Zamyatin and those of Freedman. For as we have seen, Zamyatin argues, in my view rightly, that Wells's science fiction stories of the 1890s are what today we would call works of dystopian and not utopian literature.

Freedman maintains that the transition from the genre of dystopian literature or the dystopian novel to that of the utopian novel (which is also a work of science fiction) amounts in effect to the emergence of what, following Tom Moylan, he refers to as the "critical utopia." One implication of this is that Freedman recognizes that at least one aspect of the transformation he is characterizing has to do with an innovation in literary form as well as in the ideational content of the works in question. Another implication is that Freedman maintains that the allegedly new type of utopia, the "critical utopia," came into existence not in the 1970s with Le Guin but in the early years of the twentieth century in the work of H. G. Wells. Unlike Zamyatin, therefore, again Freedman locates Wells within the *utopian* rather than the *dystopian* literary tradition. He associates the works of Wells with a "+" and not a "−" sign. And he thinks that Le Guin was responsible for a reinvigoration of the tradition of utopian writing in the sense that her work constitutes a revival of interest in the writing of utopian novels, an enterprise which was initiated by H. G. Wells at the end of the nineteenth century.[123]

It should be noted that one thing which Freedman does not do (and arguably *could* not do) is specify which work, in particular, he has in mind when he claims that it was H. G. Wells who wrote the very first *utopian* novel which was also a work of science fiction. One obvious candidate here is Wells's *Men Like Gods*, which was published in 1923. However there are problems with any such suggestion. One of these is that *Men Like Gods* is not a work of science fiction. Another is that there are good reasons for not considering it to be a work of utopian literature. Zamyatin's reading of this work is interesting in this regard, for he accepts that it is indeed a literary utopia. It is, he suggests, the one and only literary utopia which was ever written by H. G. Wells. It is clear from what Zamyatin says about this work, however, that he does not consider it to be a utopian *novel*. In Zamyatin's opinion (rightly or wrongly), *Men Like Gods* should be thought of as a continuation of the traditional literary utopia, mainly because of its very "thin" characterization.[124] Zamyatin does not deny that Wells wrote at least some literary utopias. What he does deny, however, is that Wells *ever* wrote a utopian *novel*—or at least a utopian novel which is also a work of science fiction. In his view those works of Wells which are literary utopias are not science fiction novels, and those works which are science fiction novels are not literary utopias.

Zamyatin is not alone in offering this assessment of Wells. Much more recently Jack Williamson, too, has suggested that most of Wells's "later work" is "topical journalism, propaganda for the world state, or popular education." The "science fiction," Williamson maintains, "was done before he gave up his art to champion great causes."[125] Similarly, Frank McConnell also offers some support for Zamyatin's interpretation of Wells, although McConnell's views on this subject are, as we have seen, not always consistent. For example he suggests at one point that Wells underwent a transformation from being a dystopian to being a utopian novelist at the beginning of the twentieth century.[126] Elsewhere, however, he states that "to invent a utopia as a *storyteller* and to mean it as a *social and political thinker* are perhaps always irreconcilable habits of mind" (my emphasis). The "great tragedy" of Wells's career, in McConnell's view, is that the "closer" Wells got to being a *utopian* thinker and writer, "the farther he got from the *art* of fiction" (my emphasis);[127] in other words, the farther he got from being a *novelist*. In short, here at least McConnell concedes that the later Wells, who was indeed a utopian writer, ceased to be a novelist, and, therefore, could not be properly described as a *utopian novelist*. This, I take it, is precisely the point which Zamyatin is making in his essay on Wells.

It is, I think, difficult to question Zamyatin's judgment here. Consequently, it is difficult to accept Freedman's view that the works of science fiction which Wells wrote in the 1890s might be classified as *utopian* novels. Freedman, however, is adamant that this is indeed the case. He insists, for example, that Wells's *The Time Machine* falls into this category. As Freedman himself puts it, "the first key text here is *The Time Machine*." For "not only does this novel inaugurate the science-fictional *utopia*," but, Freedman goes on, it is also "the first text in which the crucial temporal and historical dimension of science fiction becomes completely explicit."

For this reason *The Time Machine* is, in his opinion, "the most significant version of *utopian* literature in the first half of the twentieth century" (my emphasis).[128] The "synthesis of science fiction with literary utopia" which Wells initiated in this particular text produced what Freedman, again following Tom Moylan, refers to as a "critical utopia."[129]

I note in passing that Moylan himself associates the notion of a "critical utopia" with the new developments in utopian/dystopian writing (and in science fiction) which occurred in the 1970s, and which he associates especially with Le Guin. *Pace* Freedman then, Moylan would not consider *The Time Machine*, or indeed any of the works of Wells, to be a critical utopia in his sense of the term. Moreover, the reason for this is obvious. It is that Wells's *The Time Machine* is a *dystopian* and not a utopian work. According to Freedman, however, at the time it was written *The Time Machine* was arguably "the most critical utopia, in formal terms, to date." Indeed, when Wells wrote it he "established new utopian potentialities for science fiction itself."[130]

I outlined earlier a "quasi Hegelian" history of utopian/dystopian literature (and of science fiction) which I think is implicit in Freedman's account of the views of both Wells and Le Guin. Considered from the standpoint of that history, the remarks which Freedman makes explicitly about H. G. Wells, and the part which he has played within it, are open to a number of criticisms. One of these is that Freedman simply gets Wells wrong. For, as we have seen, he interprets Wells's works of science fiction as *utopian* rather than dystopian texts. A second criticism is that this leads Freedman to misrepresent the developmental trajectory of the history of utopian/dystopian literature. For he also wrongly claims that one of the key moments of transition in that history, the development of the *utopian novel* which is also a work of science fiction, actually took place at the very end of the nineteenth century rather than, as most commentators would maintain, in the 1970s. Moreover, in so doing, Freedman overlooks the true significance of Wells and his work, which is that Wells is to be associated with the rise of the *dystopian* rather than the utopian science fiction novel. Finally, Freedman's mistaken assessment of Wells and his significance for the history of utopian/dystopian thought leads to a parallel misunderstanding of the significance of the writings of Le Guin for that history. To be more specific, it is associated with a downplaying of the importance of Le Guin and her work. For by attributing the rise of the *utopian* (science fiction) novel to H. G. Wells at the end of the nineteenth century, it is evident that what Freedman does not do, and could not then do, is associate that new development with Le Guin in the 1970s. He is, therefore, compelled to be much more modest in the claims which he makes for Le Guin than he would have been had his assessment of Wells been correct.

All of the above comments about Freedman's understanding of H. G. Wells, Le Guin, and their respective contributions to the history of utopian/ dystopian literature are based on the remarks which Freedman makes explicitly in his book about Wells. But Freedman's explicit comments about Wells contain an implicit evaluation of the significance of Le Guin. Indeed, the relevance of Freedman's interpretation of Wells for our understanding of his assessment of Le Guin and her importance is readily apparent. Freedman acknowledges that Le Guin's contribution in the 1970s was of considerable significance. Up until that time, throughout most of the twentieth century, the vast majority of works written from the standpoint of the utopian/ dystopian literary tradition had been dystopian novels and *not* utopian ones. According to Freedman, Le Guin's writings, therefore, especially *The Dispossessed*, are important because they *do* represent a return to, a reinvention or a reinvigoration of the utopian tradition, in the specific sense that, just like the earlier works of H. G. Wells, it too is a *utopian* (science fiction) novel. It is arguable, however, that from the point of view of the "quasi-Hegelian" speculative history referred to earlier, this is to damn Le Guin with faint praise. For this assessment does not do justice to the real nature of Le Guin's contribution, which according to this line of reasoning was in fact to do for the utopian/dystopian tradition something similar to what Wells himself had done earlier, namely initiate a new nodal point of transition; a transition which amounted, not simply to a straightforward return to an older form of writing, originated by Wells at the end of the nineteenth century, namely the *dystopian* science fiction novel, but rather to a qualitatively *new* form of writing, the *utopian* science fiction novel. Le Guin's contribution, therefore, was a "revolutionary" one. It is a contribution which is no less significant for the history of utopian/dystopian literature, and of science fiction, than that of Wells himself.

Freedman's explicit remarks about Wells and Le Guin in respect to this issue are not entirely consistent. For example, in his discussion of Wells, despite his insistence that Wells was a writer of *utopian* science fiction novels, Freedman also claims at one point that although works like *The Time Machine* are indeed "utopias," they are not positive but "*negative* utopias" (my emphasis).[131] And it as such that they represent "the most significant version of utopian literature in the first half of the twentieth century."[132] Again, however, it is arguable for reasons given earlier that this usage is seriously misleading. Moreover, from the standpoint of the speculative history we are discussing this usage makes it extremely difficult to delineate with any degree of precision the exact trajectory of the important developments which have occurred in the history of utopian/dystopian literature from the late nineteenth century onward. In particular, it makes it much more difficult for us to assess the importance of both H. G. Wells and Le Guin respectively for that history.

A similar inconsistency can also be found in Freedman's explicit comments about Le Guin. For example, having seriously underestimated the importance of Le Guin's work for the history in question by misrepresenting, or at least exaggerating, that of Wells, nevertheless Freedman also makes remarks which indicate that he is well aware of Le Guin's true significance. For example at one point he states that "*The Dispossessed* is not only *the* central text in the post-war American revival of the positive utopia, but, arguably, the most vital and politically acute instance of the positive utopia yet produced, at least in the English speaking tradition."[133] From the standpoint of the speculative history which I think is implicit in Freedman's account this assessment of Le Guin and her significance is absolutely correct. It is evident, however, that, although it is correct, it is not consistent with Freedman's explicit claim that Le Guin's significance is that her writings represent a return, or a reinvigoration, or a reinvention of that particular tradition of utopian writing which was first initiated by H. G. Wells. For as Zamyatin argues, and as we have seen Freedman himself also occasionally acknowledges, Wells did not write what Freedman refers to here as "positive utopias," that is to say *utopian* science fiction novels. Nor did he write "*negative* utopias" (a contradiction in terms). What he actually wrote were *dystopian* science fiction novels, or novelistic tales. It is arguable, then, that Freedman is wrong to claim that Le Guin's *The Dispossessed* is a contribution to a literary genre which was originated by Wells. Rather, it constitutes a new and radical departure both in the history of utopian/dystopian literature and of science fiction.

I have suggested that the views of both Zaki and Freedman might both be associated with a "quasi Hegelian" history of utopian/dystopian literature in its relationship to science fiction. That history might be said to be a theoretical synthesis of their two accounts, each of which has both strengths and weaknesses. The strength of Zaki's account is that it does make the conceptual distinction between works of literature which might be categorized as utopias and those which are dystopias. Its weakness is that Zaki does not distinguish between the ideational or sociological content of a particular text and its aesthetic form. In particular, she does not differentiate between a literary utopia, on the one hand and a novel on the other. Freedman's account might be said to suffer from similar failing, but in reverse, as it were. For the strength of his account is that, unlike Zaki, he does make the important distinction between the form of the traditional literary utopia and that of the novel. Its main weakness, however, when it is considered from the standpoint of this account, is that Freedman does not explicitly distinguish between those novels which are utopian and those which are dystopian.

It is obvious that the views which Zaki and Freedman state explicitly could in principle be combined in such a way that a third position, that of the "quasi-Hegelian" speculative history referred to above, is generated. According to this third account, it is necessary that we make *both* of these two conceptual distinctions, and not just one of them. First we must distinguish between traditional literary utopias and novels and second we must distinguish between dystopian novels and utopian ones. From the standpoint of our speculative history it is only if we make both of these distinctions explicitly, which neither Zaki nor Freedman do, that we will be able to adequately understand the history of utopian/dystopian literature in relation to that of science fiction, and especially the parts which H. G. Wells and Le Guin have respectively to play within that history.

CONCLUSION

I have spent some time outlining the ideas which are associated with what I have referred to as the "quasi-Hegelian" speculative history of utopian/ dystopian literature which, in my view, can be found if only implicitly in the writings of a number of commentators, including Moylan, Zaki and Freedman. I am not aware of any commentator who has made an explicit attempt to develop systematically such an approach to the understanding of the history of utopian/dystopian literature in relation to science fiction. And I am not aware of any commentator who has sought explicitly to examine the writings of either H. G. Wells or Le Guin from the standpoint of such a history. Nor is this at all surprising, as the assumptions associated with such a history, once they have been made explicit, and once they have been compared with the actual history of utopian/dystopian literature, can be seen to be impossibly crude. Nevertheless, I do think it is fruitful to consider Le Guin and her work from this point of view. I should emphasize, however, that this is not because I agree with the particular reading of Le Guin and *The Dispossessed* which is associated with the speculative history referred to above, and which is in a sense generated by it. On the contrary, I think that this reading is seriously misleading. To be more specific, I do not think it is helpful to think of Le Guin's *The Dispossessed* as being a *utopian novel*. Nor therefore, *a fortiori*, do I think it is helpful to think of it as being the *first* literary production of that type. Hence I do not think that *The Dispossessed* represents a major turning point in the history of the utopian/dystopian tradition of the kind which is suggested by this speculative history because it is allegedly the first utopian novel which is also a work of science fiction.

In connection with this issue, if we rely on the remarks which Le Guin herself has made about over the last three decades then the evidence is conflicting. Nevertheless, in my view there is at least some evidence, *pace*

Zaki, Freedman, and the speculative history of utopian/dystopian literature which is implicit in their writings, that no matter how much her views have changed since she first wrote *The Dispossessed* in the 1970s, Le Guin did not then think that she had written a new type of literary utopia, a "utopian novel." In chapters 5 and 6, I shall argue that there is evidence in the essays which she wrote at this time that, like Zamyatin before her, Le Guin was of the opinion that the very idea of a literary utopia which is *also* a novel is a contradiction in terms. According to this reading of Le Guin, in her own estimation when she wrote *The Dispossessed*, Le Guin did not think that she had written a literary utopia at all. Rather, she thought that she had written something quite different, namely a *novel* dealing with the theme of utopianism in politics.

NOTES

1. Yevgeny Zamyatin, "H. G. Wells," in *A Soviet Heretic: Essays by Yevgeny Zamyatin*, ed. Mirra Ginsburg (Chicago: University of Chicago Press, 1991), 259–90.

2. Tom Moylan, "Beyond Negation: The Critical Utopias of Ursula K. Le Guin and Samuel R. Delany," *Extrapolation*, 21 (1980): 236–53; see also Tom Moylan, *Demand the Impossible: Science Fiction and the Utopian Imagination* (London: Methuen, 1986).

3. Marie Louise Berneri, *A Journey Through Utopia* (London: Freedom Press, 1982 [1950]), 293–310; J. O. Bailey, *Pilgrims Through Space and Time: Trends and Patterns in Scientific and Utopian Fiction* (Westport, Conn.: Greenwood Press, 1972 [1947]), 148; Basil Davenport, "Introduction" in *The Science Fiction Novel: Imagination and Social Criticism* (Chicago: Advent, 1969 [1959]), 12; Carl Freedman, *Critical Theory and Science Fiction*, (London: Wesleyan University Press, 2000), 81; Elizabeth Hansot, "H. G. Wells's *A Modern Utopia*," in *Perfection and Progress: Two Modes of Utopian Thought* (Cambridge, Mass.: MIT Press, 1974), 147–58; George Kateb, "Introduction," in *Utopia*, ed. George Kateb (New York: Atherton Press, 1971), 7–9; Mark Rose, *Alien Encounters: Anatomy of Science Fiction* (Cambridge, Mass.: Harvard University Press, 1981), 10; Judith Shklar, "The Political Theory of Utopia: From Melancholy to Nostalgia," in *Utopias and Utopian Thought*, ed. Frank Manuel (Boston: Beacon Press, 1966), 110; Wegner, *Imaginary Communities: Utopia, the Nation and the Spatial Histories of Modernity* (Berkeley, Los Angeles, London: University of California Press, 2002),109–19, 185; A. L. Morton, *The English Utopia* (London: Lawrence and Wishart, 1978 [1952]), 237–52, 262.

4. Alexandra Aldridge, "Ambiguities in the Scientific World View: The Wellsian Legacy," in *The Scientific World View in Dystopia* (Ann Arbor, Mich.: UMI Research Press, 1984 [1978]), 19.

5. Anthony West, "The Dark World of H. G. Wells," *Harper's*, 214 (1957), 68–73.

6. Chad Walsh, *From Utopia to Nightmare* (Westport, Conn.: Greenwood Press, 1975 [1962]), 52.

7. Kumar, *Utopia and Anti-Utopia in Modern Times* (Oxford: Blackwell, 1987), 177–79.

8. Robert C. Elliott, *The Shape of Utopia: Studies in a Literary Genre* (Chicago: University of Chicago Press, 1970), 85–86; Mark. R. Hillegas, *The Future as Nightmare: H. G. Wells and the Anti-Utopians* (New York: Oxford University Press, 1967), 4–5, 17–20, 30–31, 34, 36–37, 47–48, 57; Hansot, "H. G. Wells's *A Modern Utopia*," 146–47; John Huntington, "Utopian and Anti-Utopian Logic: H. G. Wells and his Successors," *Science Fiction Studies*, 21 (1982), 122–23; Krishan Kumar, *Utopia and Anti-Utopia in Modern Times*, 129. See also 66, 103–04, 110, 128–29, 168–69, 181–82, 185, 187–88, 190–91, 205–07, 225–25; Frank E. Manuel and Fritzie P. Manuel, *Utopian Thought in the Western World* (Oxford: Blackwell, 1975), 776; Frank McConnell, *The Science Fiction of H. G. Wells* (Oxford: Oxford University Press, 1981), 144–46, 153–54, 171–72, 184–85, 192; W. Warren Wagar, *H. G. Wells and the World State* (New Haven: Yale University Press, 1963), 33, 80–83, 86–87, 206–43, 252, 272.

9. Manuel and Manuel, *Utopian Thought in the Western World*, 776.

10. Kumar, *Utopia and Anti-Utopia in Modern Times*, 129.

11. Jack Williamson, *H. G. Wells: Critic of Progress* (Baltimore: Mirage Press, 1973), 5.

12. Williamson, *H. G. Wells: Critic of Progress*, 135.

13. McConnell, *The Science Fiction of H. G. Wells*, 71.

14. McConnell, *The Science Fiction of H. G. Wells*, 89. See also 162–63: [*The First Men in the Moon* (1901)] "is almost a voyage into the idea of *utopian* fiction . . . [Wells] . . . is, as it were, examining the elements of a positive *utopia*" (my emphasis).

15. McConnell, *The Science Fiction of H. G. Wells*, 106.

16. McConnell, *The Science Fiction of H. G. Wells*, 153.

17. McConnell, *The Science Fiction of H. G. Wells*, 158.

18. See McConnell, *The Science Fiction of H. G. Wells*, 144: "Wells did not really become a utopian novelist until some years after *The Time Machine*"; and 146: "What turns an apocalyptic novelist into a utopian? . . . [W]ith the turn of the century, Wells himself turned from the former to the latter voice."

19. Richard Gerber, *Utopian Fantasy: A Study of English Utopian Fiction Since the End of the Nineteenth Century* (London: Routledge, 1973 [1955]),123; also 99–100, 117, 120, 122–23, 127; Morson, *The Boundaries of Genre: Dostoevsky's Diary of a Writer and the Traditions of Literary Utopia* (Evanston, Ill.: Northwestern University Press, 1981) 72–73.

20. Freedman, *Critical Theory and Science Fiction*, 81–83; Lyman Tower Sargent, "Utopia: The Problem of Definition," *Extrapolation*, 16 (1975), 137; Moylan, *Scraps of the Untainted Sky: Science Fiction, Utopia, Dystopia* (Boulder, Co.: Westview Press, 2000), 74.

21. H. G. Wells, "Letter to Henry James, 8th July 1915," in *Henry James and H. G. Wells: A Record of Their Friendship, Their Debate on the Art of Fiction and Their Quarrel*, eds. Leon Edel and Gordon N. Ray (London: Rupert Hart Davis, 1958), 264.

22. Patrick Parrinder "Utopia and Meta-Utopia ," in *Shadows of the Future: H. G. Wells, Science Fiction and Prophecy* (New York: Syracuse University Press, 1995), 96.

23. H. G. Wells, "Utopias," *Science Fiction Studies*, 27 (1982), 119.

24. Wells, "Utopias," 120. As Williamson, says, *H. G. Wells: Critic of Progress*, 123, it is "more *essay* than novel" (my emphasis).

25. Bailey, *Pilgrims Through Space and Time*, 119.

26. Walsh, *From Utopia to Nightmare*, 53.

27. Kumar, *Utopia and* Anti-*Utopia in Modern Times*, 179.

28. Wagar, *H. G. Wells and the World State*, 60.

29. Jack Williamson, *H. G. Wells: Critic of Progress*, 1.

30. John Huntington, "Thinking by Opposition," in *The Logic of Fantasy: H. G. Wells and Science Fiction* (New York: Columbia University Press, 1982), 21.

31. Huntington, "The Logical Web," in *The Logic of Fantasy: H. G. Wells and Science Fiction*, 59.

32. Huntington, "The Logical Web," 59.

33. Huntington, "The Dreams of Reason," in *The Logic of Fantasy: H. G. Wells and Science Fiction*, 116.

34. Huntington, "The Dreams of Reason," 116.

35. Huntington, "The Dreams of Reason," 116.

36. Huntington, "Anti-Utopia in Wells's *A Modern Utopia*," in *The Logic of Fantasy: H. G. Wells and Science Fiction*, 167–68.

37. Gary Saul Morson, *The Boundaries of Genre: Dostoevsky's Diary of a Writer and the Traditions of Literary Utopia*, 146–55.

38. Morson, *The Boundaries of Genre*, 147.

39. Morson, *The Boundaries of Genre*, 148.

40. Morson, *The Boundaries of Genre*, 153.

41. Morson, *The Boundaries of Genre*, 153.

42. Morson, *The Boundaries of Genre*, 153.

43. Morson, *The Boundaries of Genre*, 154.

44. Morson, *The Boundaries of Genre*, 154.

45. Morson, *The Boundaries of Genre*, 154.

46. For this issue see also June Deery, "H. G. Wells's *A Modern Utopia* as a Work in Progress," in Donald M. Hassler and Clyde Wilcox eds., *Political Science Fiction* (Columbia: University of South Carolina Press, 1997), 26–42; David Y. Hughes, "The Mood of *A Modern Utopia*," *Extrapolation* 19 (1977), 59–67; and Kenneth M. Roemer, "H. G. Wells and the Momentary Voices of *A Modern Utopia*," *Extrapolation*, 23 (1982), 117–37.

47. H. G. Wells, *A Modern Utopia*, in H. G. Wells *A Modern Utopia and Tono Bungay* (London: Odhams Press, n.d. [1905]), 313.

48. Wells, *A Modern Utopia*, 309.

49. Wells, *A Modern Utopia*, 322.

50. Wells, *A Modern Utopia*, 317, 322, 325, 330.

51. Wells, *A Modern Utopia*, 315, 322.

52. Wells, *A Modern Utopia*, 310.

53. Wells, *A Modern Utopia*, 321.

54. Wells, *A Modern Utopia*, 492.

55. Wells, *A Modern Utopia*, 492.

56. Wells, *A Modern Utopia*, 492.

57. Wells, *A Modern Utopia*, 492.

58. Wells, *A Modern Utopia*, 493.

59. Wells, *A Modern Utopia*, 310.

60. Wells, *A Modern Utopia*, 493.

61. A possible intermediary between Wells and Le Guin in this regard is Robert Elliott's "The Aesthetics of Utopia," chapter 6 of *The Shape of Utopia*, especially 113–16. For example, Elliott states, 115, that Wells "felt that 'the conflicting form' he has devised" for *A Modern Utopia* "could not finally dissolve the incompatibility of the materials he was working with: the large generalities of the ideas, the insistent specificity of the characters"; and, 116, "if the writer of utopia could translate the ideas of his fiction into the experience of his characters, as the *novelist* does, then it would seem that he could escape from the thinness of which Wells complains. Clearly he can show human beings living in what he takes to be utopian conditions; but it appears to be almost impossible for him to create *characters* of any dimension who enact the constitutive ideas of utopia. He cannot make them *interesting*" (my emphasis).

62. Roemer, "H. G. Wells and the Momentary Voices of *A Modern Utopia*," 118. See also John Partington, "*The Time Machine* and *A Modern Utopia*: The Static and Kinetic Utopias of the Early H. G. Wells," *Utopian Studies*, 13, 1 (2002), 57–68; and John Partington, "The Death of the Static: H. G. Wells and the Kinetic Utopia," *Utopian Studies*, 11, 2 (2000), 96–111.

63. Hillegas, *The Future as Nightmare*, 185. Christopher Collins, "Zamyatin, Wells and the Utopian Literary Tradition," *Slavonic and East European Review*, XLIV (1966), 351–60.

64. Hillegas, *The Future as Nightmare*, 105.

65. Zamyatin, "H. G. Wells," 268.

66. Kumar, *Utopia and Anti-Utopia in Modern Times*, fn. 7, 462.

67. Aldridge, "Ambiguities in the Scientific World View: The Wellsian Legacy," 26.

68. George Kateb, *Utopia and Its Enemies* (New York: Schocken Books, 1972 [1963]), 220. It should, however, be noted that throughout most of this book Kateb consistently refers to Wells as a friend of "utopia" rather than one of its "enemies," cf. 10, 12, 70, 79, 95, 115, 156, 197–99, 202, 218, 220–21, 231, 235.

69. Patrick Parrinder, "Utopia and Meta-Utopia," 96.

70. This seems to be true even in those cases where a commentator has written specifically about the style of writing adopted by Wells in this text. For example, both June Deery and Kenneth Roemer maintain that *A Modern Utopia* is indeed a literary utopia, in at least some sense of that term. See Deery, "H. G. Wells's *A Modern Utopia* as a Work in Progress," 27; Roemer, "H. G. Wells and the Momentary Voices of *A Modern Utopia*," 118.

71. Yevgeny Zamyatin, "H. G. Wells," in *A Soviet Heretic*, 259–90. For a discussion of Zamyatin's relationship to Wells see Edward J. Brown, "The Legacy of H. G. Wells," in *Brave New World, 1984 and We: An Essay on Anti-Utopia* (Ann Arbor: Ardis, 1976), 46–53; Christopher Collins, "Zamyatin, Wells and the Utopian Literary Tradition"; and Patrick Parrinder, "The Future as Anti-Utopia: Wells, Zamyatin and Orwell," in *Shadows of the Future: H. G. Wells, Science Fiction and Prophecy*, 115–26.

72. Zamyatin, "H. G. Wells," 285. See also Elliott, *The Shape of Utopia: Studies in a Literary Genre*, 109–16. Like Zamyatin, Elliott nevertheless also makes a distinction between Wells the "author" (of novels) and Wells the utopian "writer" or commentator.

73. Zamyatin, "H. G. Wells ," 285, 288–89.

74. Zamyatin, "H. G. Wells ," 285.

75. Zamyatin, "H. G. Wells ," 287.

76. Zamyatin, "H. G. Wells ," 285.

77. Zamyatin, "H. G. Wells," 286–87.

78. Chad Walsh, *From Utopia to Nightmare*, 26–27.

79. Walsh, *From Utopia to Nightmare*, 26–27.

80. See Thomas M. Disch's remark, cited by Lyman Tower Sargent, "Eutopias and Dystopias in Science Fiction: 1950–75," in *America as Utopia*, ed. Kenneth M. Roemer (New York: Burtt Franklin, 1981), 348, that "'Paradise has a considerable flaw, however, from the narrative point of view. It is anti-dramatic. Perfection doesn't make a good yarn.'"

81. Zamyatin, "H. G. Wells," 288–89.

82. This is not the view of Lovat Dickson, however, who maintains, *H. G. Wells: His Turbulent Life and Times* (London: Macmillan, 1971), 107, that Wells's early science fiction stories are not "novelistic." Lovat Dickson maintains that these works are "*not* novels of character" (my emphasis). He also states, 106, that *Love and Mrs. Lewisham* was Wells's "*first* novel of character; his first attempt to get on terms with the art of the novel" (my emphasis). According to Dickson, Wells's earlier "scientific romances" had in fact "depended on incident and description" rather than individual character. The "human personality," Dickson maintains, has "no effect upon the flow of the incident."

83. Moylan, *Demand the Impossible*, 36.

84. Moylan, *Demand the Impossible*, 38.

85. Kumar, *Utopia and Anti-Utopia in Modern Times*, 25.

86. Kumar, *Utopia and Anti-Utopia in Modern Times*, 25.

87. Kumar, "Preface," in *Utopia and Anti-Utopia in Modern Times*.

88. Kumar, "Preface," in *Utopia and Anti-Utopia in Modern Times*. For Kumar's assessment of Wells's *A Modern Utopia*, see also Krishan Kumar, "A Book Remembered: *A Modern Utopia*," *New Universities Quarterly*, 36 (1982), 3–12.

89. Gary Saul Morson's *The Boundaries of a Genre*, 76, 115–16, 142.

90. Morson, *The Boundaries of a Genre*, 115.

91. Morson, *The Boundaries of a Genre*, 138.

92. Morson, *The Boundaries of a Genre*, 77.

93. Morson, *The Boundaries of a Genre*, 121.

94. Morson, *The Boundaries of a Genre*, 132–35.

95. See Frederic Jameson, "The Utopian Enclave," in *Archaeologies of the Future: The Desire Called Utopia and Other Science Fictions* (London: Verso, 2005), 21; Frederic Jameson, "Synthesis, Irony, Neutralization and the Moment of Truth," in *Archaeologies of the Future*, 176–77; Frederic Jameson, "Journey into Fear," in *Archaeologies of the Future*, 202.

96. Elliott, *The Shape of Utopia: Studies in a Literary Genre*, 120.

97. See especially Le Guin, "Science Fiction and Mrs. Brown," in *The Language of the Night: Essays on Fantasy and Science Fiction*, ed. Susan Wood (New York: Perigee Books, 1979), 104–05.

98. Le Guin, "Science Fiction and Mrs. Brown," 105. For commentators who maintain that Zamyatin's *We* is *both* utopian and dystopian (and for this reason an ambiguous work, like Le Guin's *The Dispossessed*) see Frederic Jameson, "The

Utopian Enclave," in *Archaeologies of the Future*, 21; Frederic Jameson, "Synthesis, Irony, Neutralization and the Moment of Truth," in *Archaeologies of the Future*, 176–77; Frederic Jameson, "Journey into Fear," in *Archaeologies of the Future*, 202; and Darko Suvin, *Metamorphoses of Science Fiction* (New Haven and London: Yale University Press, 1979), 259.

99. The suggestion that Zamyatin's *We* is not a literary dystopia has been made before. The commentators in question, however, almost invariably claim that *We* is best thought of as a *utopian* rather than a dystopian text. In other words they simply invert rather than displace the traditional reading of Zamyatin. For this "utopian" reading see Jameson, "Synthesis, Irony, Neutralization and the Moment of Truth," *Archaeologies of the Future*, 177; Mark Rose, *Alien Encounters: Anatomy of Science Fiction* (Cambridge Mass: Harvard University Press, 1981), 167–75; Peter Ruppert, *Reader in a Strange Land: The Activity of Reading Literary Utopias* (Athens: University of Georgia Press, 1986), 105–18; Suvin, *Metamorphoses of Science Fiction*, 255–59; Wegner, "A Map of Utopia's Possible Worlds: Zamyatin's *We* and Le Guin's *The Dispossessed*," *Imaginary Communities*, 147–82.

100. Le Guin, "Science Fiction and Mrs. Brown," 105, and "The Stalin in the Soul," in *The Language of the Night*, 211–12.

101. Alexandra Aldridge, *The Scientific World View in Dystopia*, 25.

102. Tzvetan Todorov, "The Origin of Genres," *New Literary History*, 8 (1976), 161, cited Rose, "Genre," *Alien Encounters*, fn. 5, 198.

103. Keith Booker, "Zamyatin's *We*: Anticipating Stalin," in *The Dystopian Impulse in Modern Literature: Fiction as Social Criticism* (Westport, Conn.: Greenwood Press, 1994), 25.

104. Hillegas, *The Future as Nightmare*, 5, 7.

105. Keith Booker, "Introduction" to *The Dystopian Impulse in Modern Literature: Fiction as Social Criticism*, 19.

106. Williamson, *H. G. Wells: Critic of Progress*, 123.

107. Moylan, *Demand the Impossible*, 10.

108. Hoda M. Zaki, "Utopian Thought and Political Theory," in *Phoenix Renewed: The Survival and Mutation of Utopian Thought in North American Science Fiction: 1965–1982* (San Bernadino, Calif.: Borgo Press, 1988), 13–14. See also 26, where Zaki states that "the fledgling field of science fiction seemed to emerge as a substitute, assuming the features of modern utopianism"; 39, where she refers to the "continuity of utopian thought in the genre of science fiction"; and 113, where she refers to science fiction novels "that self-consciously evoked the utopian tradition."

109. Zaki, "Ursula K. Le Guin," in *Phoenix Renewed*, 89. See also 114 where Zaki states, without demurring, that *The Dispossessed* has "been hailed by scholars of science fiction as signaling the rebirth of utopian literature."

110. Zaki, "Ursula K. Le Guin," in *Phoenix Renewed*, 80.

111. Zaki, "Ursula K. Le Guin," in *Phoenix Renewed*, 2.

112. Freedman, *Critical Theory and Science Fiction*, xvii–xviii, 78, 81.

113. Freedman, *Critical Theory and Science Fiction*, 80.

114. Freedman, *Critical Theory and Science Fiction*, 80.

115. Freedman, *Critical Theory and Science Fiction*, 80.

116. Freedman, *Critical Theory and Science Fiction*, 80.

117. Freedman, *Critical Theory and Science Fiction*, 80.

118. Freedman, *Critical Theory and Science Fiction*, 80.

119. Freedman, *Critical Theory and Science Fiction*, 81.

120. Freedman, *Critical Theory and Science Fiction*, 81.

121. Freedman, *Critical Theory and Science Fiction*, 81.

122. Freedman, *Critical Theory and Science Fiction*, 83.

123. Freedman, *Critical Theory and Science Fiction*, 81.

124. See Zamyatin, "H. G. Wells," 266: "And, finally, in 1922 . . . Wells in one of his latest novels, *Men Like Gods*, leads the reader off into the happy land of utopia"; 286: "Wells's sociofantastic novels are *not* utopias. His only utopia is his latest novel, *Men Like Gods* . . . Only *Men Like Gods*, one of his weakest sociofantastic novels, contains the sugary, pinkish colours of a utopia"; 288: "The elements of classic utopias are *absent* from Wells's works (with the sole exception of his novel, *Men Like Gods*)" (my emphasis).

125. Williamson, *H. G. Wells: Critic of Progress*, 16.

126. McConnell, *The Science Fiction of H. G. Wells*, 146.

127. McConnell, *The Science Fiction of H. G. Wells*, 153–54. See also 172: "By the end of his career, of course, Wells had come to a kind of defiant agreement with his critics . . . And since his adversaries had been telling him for years, that he had ceased being a *storyteller* and become a *preacher*, he naturally insisted that that was what he meant to do all along" (my emphasis); also 182: "Wells began more and more to abandon the possibilities of pure fantasy, free imagination, for the strictures and the grey disciplines of social and economic preaching: he began turning his stage into a pulpit—and botched the carpentry of the thing. I have mentioned this estimate of Wells's career and have suggested that it is deeply unfair to the later Wells at his best. But it is necessary, at this point, to admit that it is not entirely unfair to the later Wells in general."

128. Freedman, *Critical Theory and Science Fiction*, 82.

129. Freedman, *Critical Theory and Science Fiction*, 81.

130. Freedman, *Critical Theory and Science Fiction*, 81.

131. Freedman, *Critical Theory and Science Fiction*, 82.

132. Freedman, *Critical Theory and Science Fiction*, 82. As we have seen, Freedman is not the only commentator to use the term "utopian" in this way. See Richard Gerber, *Utopian Fantasy: A Study of English Utopian Fiction Since the End of the Nineteenth Century*, 99–100, 117, 120, 122–23, 127; Frank McConnell, *The Science Fiction of H. G. Wells* (Oxford: Oxford University Press, 1981), 71, 89, 162–63; Tom Moylan, *Scraps of the Untainted Sky*, 74; Lyman Tower Sargent, "Utopia: The Problem of Definition," 137.

133. Freedman, *Critical Theory and Science Fiction*, 114.

3

Le Guin's Dialectical Approach to Questions of Philosophy and Politics

LE GUIN, DIALECTICS, AND THE PHILOSOPHY OF TAOISM

More than one commentator has observed that Le Guin's philosophic outlook is a "dialectical" one. In my view it is a question of some interest to ask what the source of that outlook is. In this chapter I shall first consider Le Guin's relationship to Taoism and second the affinities which exist between Le Guin's ideas and the philosophy of Hegel. Le Guin's enthusiasm for Taoism is evident in *The Left Hand of Darkness, The Lathe of Heaven*, and *The Dispossessed*.

But what, exactly, is meant by "Taoism" here? There is a popular understanding of the philosophy of Taoism which identifies it exclusively with the principle of Being rather than Becoming, or with the notions of order, harmony, stability, and permanence as opposed to those of conflict, disorder, transience, and change. This is the understanding of both Darko Suvin and William Barber.[1] And it must be conceded that there are times when Le Guin herself also endorses such an understanding. For example, in her recent edition of the *Tao Te Ching* she suggests that for Lao Tzu "new is strange and strange is uncanny. New is bad. Lao Tzu is deeply and firmly against changing things, particularly in the name of progress."[2]

However, if this is an accurate account of the views associated with Taoism then it seems clear that, at certain time in her life (especially in the 1970s when she wrote *The Dispossessed*) there have been occasions when Le Guin could not and should not be thought of as being unequivocally a Taoist. It would, rather, be more accurate to say that Taoism constitutes just one aspect of her own philosophical outlook. For there is another, equally important aspect of Le Guin's thinking, which emphasizes the importance of the principle of change, and which has affinities not with the philosophical beliefs of Parmenides, Plato, or Lao Tzu, but rather with those of Heraclitus, H. G. Wells, and Zamyatin. Darko Suvin, for example, interprets Le Guin as being not a Taoist at all, but as a properly "dialectical" thinker, precisely because he understands Taoism to be a philosophy which is committed to the principles of harmony and balance, and hence also to the idea of a synthesis or compromise, between two different and independent, rather than interdependent, points of view. On the other hand, however, "the ambiguities never absent from" Le Guin's work, Suvin maintains, do "not primarily flow from a static balancing of two Yin-and-Yang type alternatives, two principles or opposites" between which a "middle Way of wisdom leads." Consequently, although Taoism "has undoubtedly had an influence" on Le Guin, in Suvin's view (writing in 1988) any attempts to "subsume" Le Guin under Taoism are not only "doomed to failure" now but also "retrospectively revealed as inadequate even for her earlier works." Rather, Suvin insists, the "Leguinian ambiguities are in principle *dynamic*." That is to say, in Le Guin's thinking, "to every opposition or contradiction there is, as Mao Tse Tung would say, a principal aspect which is dominant or ascendant and by means of which that contradiction renders asunder the old, transforming it into the new."[3]

It should, however, be noted that Le Guin's views on the subject of Taoism are not consistent. For example, she makes it clear in her "A Response to the Le Guin Issue," which was published in *Science Fiction Studies* in 1974, that although she is happy to identify herself with the outlook of Taoism, she nevertheless disagrees with her critics over the question of just what such identification involves. In particular, she resists the suggestion that the "static" vision expressed by Orr in *The Lathe of Heaven* does accurately represent the Taoist way of thinking about the world, precisely because she recognizes that Orr's views tell only one side of the story. Le Guin would, I think, at least at times, have some sympathy for Elizabeth Cogell Cummins's suggestion (which would no doubt come as a surprise to a number of commentators, including Jameson and Rabkin) that, far from being a "static" way of thinking, similar to the philosophies of Parmenides, Taoism should rather be associated with the notion of "constant change," and hence also with the philosophy of Heraclitus, which from the time of Plato onward has usually been considered to directly contradict that of Parmenides. According to Cogell Cummins, "the key to Taoism is that change is eternal" and "reality is process." Consequently if we wish to grasp what is involved in Le Guin's commitment to Taoism, which according to Cogell Cummins, Le Guin has correctly understood, it is necessary that we accept that Le Guin's outlook is "in principle," not at all static but rather, on the contrary, a "dynamic" one.[4] From this standpoint, Le Guin is of the opinion that is wrong to think of Taoism as being identical with either one or the other of the two modes of thinking, the "Yang" and the "Yin," identified earlier. For there is an important sense in which the Taoist way of looking at the world must embrace *both* of these, despite the fact that they contradict one another.

This way of thinking about Le Guin's relationship to Taoism has been hinted at by Donald Theall.[5] According to Theall, Le Guin offers a "reinterpretation" of Taoism, which must be considered to be in a sense a new departure. As Theall puts it, "while balance is obviously a central feature of her writing, she also takes the concept of ambivalence very seriously, stressing history as perpetually upsetting the balance and creating new tensions." In his opinion Le Guin "sees balance as a dynamic principle mediating between oppositions." Her views constitute, therefore, a "sharpened *reinterpretation* of the Taoist conception of balance" (my emphasis). Like Suvin and Barber, however, Theall insists that Le Guin's outlook is not authentically Taoist. In his view it is, rather, "in some ways similar" to that of the "socialist humanist" Leszek Kolakowski, who has "pointed out that an acceptance of contradiction did not automatically result in *a* simple balance based on the reconciliation of opposites."[6]

There are times, then, when Le Guin thinks (rightly or wrongly) that the Yin and the Yang of Taoism are not simply "opposites" which might exist independently of one another. It is not possible, she maintains, for us simply to "compromise" between them. Nor can we produce a peaceful harmony by reconciling the tension which exists between them. We cannot synthesize them in a manner which achieves a third way of thinking which actually resolves the contradiction which they embrace. Le Guin points out that it is "all too often" maintained that for Taoists "Yin and Yang are opposites between which lies the straight, but safe, Way." As an account of Taoism this is, Le Guin maintains, "all wrong."[7] Against this view, Le Guin presents an alternative understanding of Taoism which appears to have been inspired by her familiarity with the notion of "dialectics," as this is to be found in the writings of Hegel and Marxism. Indeed, she suggests at one point that those of her critics who misunderstand Taoism would do well to familiarize themselves with the principles of "Marxian dialectics." They should read, for example, the writings of the Sinologist Joseph Needham, who was, Le Guin points out, himself "a Marxist."[8]

According to Le Guin's understanding of Taoism, then, the two principles represented by the notions of Yin and Yang stand not simply in opposition but in contradiction to one another. Each on its own is an "abstraction" and neither can subsist independently, or even be thought of independently, of the other. Moreover, the tension which exists between them could never be resolved. It is, of course, possible for someone to seek to synthesize these two principles in some way, thereby producing a third form of thinking which embraces the insights of both. And it may even be appropriate to say that the final outcome of such an attempted process of synthesis could be associated with a certain kind of harmony or resolution. But this particular type of harmony or resolution is a most peculiar one, as it does not preclude the possibility of tension, contradiction, and, therefore, conflict, between the component principles which create and sustain it. As Le Guin has put the same point, more recently, "the reversals and paradoxes" on the *Tao Te Ching* are indeed "the oppositions of the Yin and the Yang—male/female, light/dark, glory/modesty," and so on. However, the "balancing act" between these "oppositions" which is undertaken by Taoism "results in neither stasis nor synthesis."[9]

In her response to her critics, this is the view which Le Guin associates with Taoism, properly understood. According to this understanding, the way of the Tao is the way of logical paradox and contradiction. Confronted by such a paradox, the good Taoist does not seek to resolve the contradiction or deal with the problem which it poses by identifying with either one of its two "sides" or the other. Rather, the good Taoist embraces the contradiction itself, despite the fact that it cannot in principle be resolved. This is the "way" of the Tao, just as it is the way of life itself. It is, presumably, for this reason that in *The Lathe of Heaven* one of Le Guin's chapter headings is the following paradoxical assertion taken from the saying of the Taoist philosopher Chuang Tse: "'To let understanding stop at what cannot be understood is a high attainment. Those who cannot do it will be destroyed on the lathe of heaven.'"[10] Philosophically speaking, this is an attitude which does not necessarily imply a critique of reason and science, though it might imply a critique of certain ways of thinking about them. Indeed, as in the work of Fritjof Capra, which Le Guin occasionally cites,[11] it might be said to represent a call for us to revise our understanding of science and the scientific attitude; a call to break down the barriers between science, on the one hand, and philosophy, mysticism, and religion, on the other.

If we read Le Guin's writings in the light of her commitment to Taoism, understood in this particular sense, then we get some interesting results. For example, if Le Guin were indeed to identify herself with the "one sided" views of George Orr in *The Lathe of Heaven*, then by her own account she would not be a good Taoist. In my view, *pace* Jameson and Rabkin, this is an indication that Le Guin does not make this identification at all. Similarly, in the case of *The Dispossessed*, if it is true that the central character in the novel, the physicist Shevek, represents Le Guin's own views; and if it is also true that when she wrote *The Dispossessed* Le Guin then endorsed the understanding of Taoism which has been attributed to her by some of her critics; it would follow that Shevek would have to be presented in this text as being committed to a certain form of utopianism, of the Yin variety, which identifies itself exclusively with the Simultaneity Theory of Time. It is clear enough, however, that Le Guin does not present the character Shevek in this way. The conclusion to be drawn from this is not that the outlook of Shevek/Le Guin is not Taoist, but rather that we should not have a partial or one-sided understanding of Taoism.

Charlotte Spivack has claimed that for Le Guin "the basic principles of Odonianism" in *The Dispossessed* "are congruent with those of Taoism."[12] There is, of course, some truth in this, but only if it is understood that for Le Guin Taoism, properly understood, is a thoroughgoing dialectical philosophy. One consequence of this is that if we take, for example, Le Guin's view of the relationship which exists between the two societies on Anarres and Urras (specifically A-Io) in this text, then Le Guin's understanding of Taoism leads her *not* to make a straightforward "either-or" choice between the principles associated with them, but rather to embrace the contradictory totality which is them both. This is an outlook which, as in the case of the notions of Yin and Yang, or the respective views of Haber and Orr in *The Lathe of Heaven*, sees that the one "side" of the story could not exist without the other. It sees the necessity of both and in consequence also accepts, or is resigned to, the existence of both. For those who think that if Le Guin could not be said to be straightforwardly a conservative thinker there is nevertheless at least a conservative dimension to her work, it is precisely *this* which constitutes the conservative element in her thinking. For such an attitude must involve some kind of accommodation on her part with the principles which underpin the social order on Urras (A-Io).

THE AMBIGUITY OF HEGEL'S PHILOSOPHY: RIGHT AND LEFT HEGELIANISM

As we have seen, a number of commentators have noted that Le Guin has a tendency to think dialectically about most issues, whether these relate to natural science or to ethics and politics, and it is an interesting question to ask what the source of inspiration for this outlook might be. In the preceding section I discussed one possible answer to this question, namely that Le Guin derives her inspiration from the philosophy of Taoism. Some commentators, in contrast, have sought to relate Le Guin to Marxism, assuming (not entirely implausibly) that if her mind-set is indeed a dialectical one then it is quite likely that her commitment to this way of thinking was derived through a critical engagement with the views of Marx and Marxists. Yet other commentators, however, have sought to bypass this line of reasoning and have drawn attention to the affinity which exists between Le Guin's philosophical beliefs and those of Hegel. In short, they have sought to relate Le Guin ideas to those of Hegel directly, independently of the possible or actual filter of Marxism. In this section I would like to pursue this last line of inquiry further. For despite Le Guin's commitment to anarchism there *are* striking similarities between some of the philosophical ideas which underpin her work and those of Hegel. Nor is this too surprising. The classical anarchist tradition before Le Guin, especially the work of Bakunin, also owes a great deal to Hegel, and Le Guin might be thought of as continuing in that tradition. The philosophy of Hegel, however, can be and has been interpreted in different ways, and the political significance of that philosophy is quite different, depending upon the interpretation which is offered.

Since the nineteenth century there have been two dominant, and quite different (indeed diametrically opposed), interpretations of Hegel's philosophy as a whole, which are usually associated with the notions of "Right Hegelianism" and "Left Hegelianism" respectively.[13] According to both interpretations Hegel's philosophy as Hegel himself understood it was nothing more than a conservative sanction of the social and political *status quo* in Germany in the 1830s and 1840s. The difference between the two is that the Right Hegelians of that time considered this to be a good thing, whereas the Left Hegelians deplored it. Additionally, the Left Hegelians also found the solution to this problem in Hegel's own philosophy, which in their view did contain at least one element which might be put to critical use, and which was indeed potentially both radical and revolutionary, namely Hegel's endorsement of the principle of dialectics. This, it should be noted, is something which anarchism had in common with Marxism at that time. For the members of both movements were for a while committed Left Hegelians.

A good way of approaching the issue of the ambiguity of Hegel's philosophy, and its relevance for an assessment of the work of Zamyatin and Le Guin, is to begin by focusing on the ancient dispute between the pre-Socratic philosophers Parmenides and Heraclitus regarding the nature of reality. As is well known, Parmenides understood reality by reference to the notion of a static Being and, therefore, like Plato (at least according to the conventional reading of Plato's views) denied the reality of change. In his view, the appearance of change in the world is merely an illusion. In its fundamental nature nothing in the world ever really changes. Against Parmenides, however, Heraclitus insisted that it is the appearance of permanence and stability which is illusory. And that change itself, or the principle of Becoming, is the only thing which is permanent and, therefore, truly real.[14]

Where did Hegel stand in this dispute? Not surprisingly, given the ambiguous nature of Hegel's philosophy, his attitude toward this issue has been interpreted in different and opposed ways.[15] Some commentators have interpreted Hegel as being in effect a follower of Parmenides, or a

Platonist who attaches no importance at all to the principle of change.[16] Sidney Hook, for example, has claimed that "Hegel's difficulties with time were notorious." According to Hook, Hegel "cannot grant its 'reality'," since this would "involve him in a logical contradiction—as, for Hegel, those things which are truly real [ideas or concepts, TB] are necessarily timeless." On the other hand, however, Hook maintains, Hegel "can hardly dismiss the phenomenon of time altogether." He is compelled, therefore, Hook concludes, to "acknowledge its 'existence'," if not its "reality," which "he does so grudgingly."[17] This Platonic reading of Hegel may be associated with Right Hegelianism. For it seems clear enough that if in general nothing ever *could* change in its essentials, then that is true of society also. Consequently, there is no point in even attempting to undertake a revolutionary or radical transformation of any society. Other commentators, however, have taken the contrary view and interpreted Hegel as being a follower of Heraclitus, and hence someone whose philosophy focuses *exclusively* on the principle of Becoming rather than that of Being. This is the reading associated with Left Hegelianism.[18]

In my view each of the two diametrically opposed interpretations of Hegel's philosophy outlined above is partial, one-sided, and, therefore oversimplified. Each interpretation captures just one important aspect of Hegel's thought and ignores another. Neither Right Hegelianism nor Left Hegelianism, therefore, succeeds in capturing the complex and contradictory nature of Hegel's philosophy as a whole. For correctly understood, Hegel's philosophy attaches importance to *both* the principle of Being and that of Becoming for any adequate intellectual comprehension of the world. Michael Inwood accurately captures Hegel's true position in respect to this issue when he says that although later Greek philosophers "shared, for the most part, Plato's preference for Being over Becoming," the German philosophers of the nineteenth century [i.e. Nietzsche, TB], on the other hand, "tended to prefer Becoming to the rigidity of Being." Against this "one sided" Heraclitean reading of Hegel, Inwood correctly points out that as a matter of fact Hegel did *not*, like Heraclitus, "abandon being altogether in favor of unremitting flux," or the principle of pure Becoming. Rather, Inwood rightly argues, Hegel's philosophy presents a dialectical synthesis in which both the principle of Being and that of Becoming have a necessary part to play.[19] I shall call this third reading, which I consider to be correct, the "Centrist" reading of Hegel.

MARXISM AND LEFT HEGELIANISM

In his well-known essay on Feuerbach, Engels illustrates the two diametrically opposed readings of Hegel's philosophy associated with Right and Left Hegelianism by making a distinction between Hegel's philosophical

system and his dialectic *method.*[20] According to Engels, what I have described as Right Hegelianism focuses exclusively on the conservative side
of Hegel's thought—his philosophical system—and ignores his dialectic
method. Engels argues that it is for this reason that in the end the political conclusions of Hegel's *Philosophy of Right* are from the standpoint of
this reading "extremely tame."[21] According to the Left Hegelianism of
both Marx and Engels, Hegel's "dialectic method," on the other hand,
sees everything as changing and developing all of the time. It could never,
therefore, permanently sanctify any existing political state of affairs. Consequently, it has radical political implications. As Engels puts it, this
method represents the "revolutionary character of the Hegelian philosophy" as a whole, once it has been extracted from the philosophical system
with which it is currently associated.[22] From the standpoint of Engels's
terminology then, we might say that Right Hegelianism with its exclusive
emphasis on the principle of Being focuses solely on Hegel's system and
ignores his method, whereas Left Hegelianism, with its exclusive emphasis on the principle of Becoming, does the opposite. Against each of these
two opposed interpretations of Hegel's philosophy, however, an advocate
of the Centrist reading of Hegel would argue, as Sidney Hook has done,
that Hegel's system and his method are in fact "indissoluble."[23]

Marx captures what he takes to be the revolutionary aspect of Hegel's
philosophy very well when he suggests (wrongly as it happens) that if we
look at the world from an Hegelian point of view the *only* truly permanent
thing is change itself. As Marx puts it (citing Lucretius' *De Rerum Natura*,
which he studied whilst a doctoral student between 1839 and 1841), from
the standpoint of the Hegelian philosophy "the *only* immutable thing is
the abstraction of movement" (my emphasis) itself—"*mors immortalis.*"[24]
In a well-known passage alluding to Hegel's philosophy Marx claims that
it only *seems* to "glorify the existing state of things." For although this philosophy certainly does include "in its comprehension an affirmative
recognition of the existing state of things" nevertheless at the same time,
Marx argues, it also includes "the recognition of the negation of that state"
and of "its inevitable breaking up," because it regards "every historically
developed social form as in fluid movement" and, therefore, "takes into
its account its transient nature not less than its momentary existence."
Consequently like Engels, Marx concludes that suitably interpreted
Hegel's philosophy is in fact "in its essence critical and revolutionary."[25]

We may note in passing that this assessment of Marx's understanding
of Hegel and Hegelianism is entirely consistent with the standpoint of
what is usually referred to as "orthodox Marxism." For, like classical anarchism, orthodox Marxism was also opposed to what its proponents considered to be political "utopianism," or to the construction of blueprints
for ideal societies, just as it rejected the notion of static perfectionism

which is often associated with utopian theorizing.[26] Moreover, for this very reason, orthodox Marxism also rejected the notion that Marx's social theory is to be associated with any kind of moral vision or ethical ideal. On the contrary it claimed itself to be a "scientific" account of human society and of human history, the purpose of which is explanatory rather than normative or evaluative.[27] Orthodox Marxism assumes that all morality is ideology—specifically "bourgeois" ideology—and that the idea of an "ethical Marxism" is a contradiction in terms. From this point of view, writers like Le Guin who think about human affairs in ethical terms are not and could not possibly be Marxists. Those who look at the world from Marx's point of view must eschew the employment of moral categories altogether.[28]

CLASSICAL ANARCHISM AND LEFT HEGELIANISM

So far as classical anarchism is concerned, both Proudhon and Bakunin might be classified as Left Hegelians. For example, George Woodcock has noted that for Proudhon in both science and society "progress," that is to say change, is "indefinite." It "has no end, nor, in the ordinary sense, does it appear to have a goal." Rather, it is the "negation of immutable forms and formulae, of all doctrines of eternity, permanence, or impeccability, of all permanent order, not excepting that of the universe, and of every subject or object, spiritual or transcendental, that does not change." Proudhon envisages a world in which "history loses all its rigidity in the interflow of the balancing forces," a world which "changes constantly and never reaches the stillness of perfection because imperfection is a cause and a consequence of its everlasting movement." Quite rightly, Woodcock associates Proudhon's attitude toward change with the philosophy of Heraclitus. "The formula," he says, "is almost Heraclitean." As such "it suggests the flux of a never ending change." Woodcock seems to me, however, to be quite wrong when he also suggests that this is an aspect of Proudhon's thought which might be contrasted with that of Hegel and Marx, or in Woodcock's words, "the dialectical forward movement of the Hegelians and the Marxists,"[29] at least on one reading of their respective philosophies. For both Hegel and Marx have also been interpreted as followers of Heraclitus. In the opinion of at least some commentators, Heracliteanism is something which Marx and Engels have in common with classical anarchists such as Bakunin and Proudhon, and indeed with contemporary postmodernism, the reason for this being that all of these strands of thinking share a common source of influence, namely the philosophy of Hegel, who on this reading is himself interpreted as a follower of Heraclitus.[30] Whatever their differences might be in other areas, then, this common intellectual debt to the philosophy of Hegel is not one of them. Their respective interpretations of Hegel, and their conclusion that his philosophy has potentially revolutionary political implications, are fundamentally the same. They are all what I have referred to as Left Hegelians.

Similarly, in the case of Bakunin we find not just an enthusiasm for the philosophy of Hegel but, more specifically for that particular interpretation of Hegel's philosophy which I have characterized as Left Hegelianism. For Bakunin, in an essay entitled "The Reaction in Germany" which he wrote in 1842, "contradiction and its immanent development," or the dialectical outlook, constitute the "keynote of the whole Hegelian system," and for this reason Hegel is "unconditionally the greatest philosopher of the present time," precisely because this category of contradiction is the "chief category of the governing spirit of our times."[31] Bakunin agrees with what he takes to be Hegel's view that contradiction alone, understood as the "embracing of its two one-sided members," is "true." One cannot, he says, reproach the principle of contradiction for being "one sided" and, therefore, "superficial." Following Hegel, Bakunin associates the notion of contradiction generally with the ideas of that which is "Positive," on the one hand, and that which is "Negative" on the other. He associates the principle of "positivity" with "what is" and what will remain as it is if it is not changed. The principle of "negativity," on the other hand, he associates with the idea of change, the criticism of what is and its alteration of transformation into something else, something radically new and different. Those who identify themselves with the principle of positivity Bakunin refers to as the "Positives," or what perhaps today we would refer to as the "Positivists." Those who identify themselves with the principle of "Negativity" he refers to as "the Negatives," or as perhaps we would say today the "Negativists." According to Bakunin, Hegel's philosophy generally, because it is a philosophy of contradiction, must recognize the validity of both of these principles together.

Bakunin notes that some of Hegel's interpreters, whom he refers to as "compromisers," use the Hegelian philosophy to defend the *status quo* by suggesting that, from Hegel's point of view, although existing society can and will, and indeed must, change, nevertheless the change in question ought to be a slow one, so as to preserve the identity of what is changing in and through the process of change which it undergoes. As Bakunin puts it, these compromisers say to the Positivists, "Hang on to the old, but permit the Negatives at the same time to resolve it gradually." On the other hand, however, they say to the Negativists, "Destroy the old, but not all at once and completely, so that you will always have something to do." In short, Bakunin maintains, the compromisers say to the advocates of each of the other two opposing interpretations of Hegel's philosophy, "each of you remain in your one-sidedness, but we, the elect, will prove the pleasure of totality for ourselves."[32] Hence, these compromisers, interpret Hegel's philosophy in such a way that, politically speaking, far from being revolutionary it leads to nothing more than a moderate program of social and political reform.[33]

In Bakunin's view, the particular way in which these compromisers present Hegel as a social and political reformer is by emphasizing that precisely because it is a philosophy of contradiction, and, therefore, embraces both the principle of the Positive as well as that of the Negative, Hegel's philosophy could not in principle ever lead to radical or revolutionary political conclusions. For a revolutionary political program would be one which focuses solely and exclusively on the idea of the Negative, and would ignore entirely that of the Positive, something which no properly dialectical approach could possibly do. Indeed, if it *were* to do so then it would immediately become partial and one sided, and, therefore, necessarily undialectical. The compromisers, therefore, Bakunin points out, "forbid that one of the two one-sided members be taken in the abstract" and require that "they be comprehended as a totality in their necessary union, in their inseparability." For they say that "either of its opposed members, taken by itself, is one-sided and thus untrue" and consequently insist that "we have to grasp the contradiction in its totality in order to have truth."[34]

It should be obvious that the interpretation of Hegel's philosophy which Bakunin associates with his compromisers is the one which I earlier referred to as the Centrist interpretation, and which in my view is basically correct. Not surprisingly, given that he was himself a Left Hegelian, a social and political revolutionary, Bakunin had little time for this particular interpretation of Hegel's philosophy and its practical political implications. Against it, therefore, he proposed an alternative. This alternative could not, of course, state explicitly that for Hegel the principle of Positivity is of no importance at all, as that would indeed be a partial, one-sided and undialectical reading of Hegel's philosophical outlook. Instead, Bakunin asserts that although Hegel certainly does attach importance to the principle of the Positive as well as that of the Negative, nevertheless he does not attach the *same* or as much importance to it. As Bakunin himself puts it, for Hegel "the Positive and the Negative do not, as the Compromisers think, have *equal* justification" (my emphasis). For Hegel, the principle of contradiction should not be associated with a state of "equilibrium" but rather with one in which there is a "preponderance of the Negative." Following a line of reasoning which is of dubious logical validity, Bakunin maintains that for Hegel because the Positive cannot exist without the Negative it follows that the Negative determines "the life of the Positive itself." Consequently it is the Negative alone which "includes within itself the totality of the contradiction," and which, there-fore, "has absolute justification."[35] In this way, then, Bakunin presents a radical and revolutionary interpretation of Hegel's philosophy which as-sociates that philosophy with Heracliteanism and with a commitment to the negation of what is, no matter what the nature of that is might be, and hence with the idea of constant and radical change, or permanent revolu-tion. Bakunin's interpretation of Hegel associates the idea of the Negative with that of "denial, destruction and passionate consumption" of the Pos-itive and hence with "the complete annihilation of the present social and political world."[36] From his point of view although it is true that the com-promisers "acknowledge the totality of contradiction, just as we do," nev-ertheless it is also true that they "rob it, or rather want to rob it, of its mo-tion of its vitality," of its "soul."[37] For Bakunin, then, the principle of Negativity is the "spirit of revolution." In a famous, indeed notorious, phrase he asserts that this principle is the "passion for destruction," which is also a "creative passion." As such, as in the case of the allusion to fire or a flame in the philosophy of Heraclitus, it is "the eternal spirit which destroys and annihilates only because it is the unfathomable and eternally creative source of life."[38]

ZAMYATIN'S *WE* AND LEFT HEGELIANISM[39]

In my view, the Left Hegelian reading of Hegel's philosophy which iden-tifies it with that of Heraclitus, is also subscribed to by both Nietzsche and Zamyatin. So far as Nietzsche's relation to Hegel is concerned,[40] Walter Kaufmann has stated that "Nietzsche and Hegel were at one in their high esteem of Heraclitus." Nor is this surprising. For "both thinkers admired the 'dark' philosopher for the same reason," namely because "their own absolute principles were not inert, or stable." Hegel and Nietzsche also "expressly denied," Kaufman goes on, "the peaceful self-identity of the basic cosmic force and considered *strife* a definitive feature of the 'Ab-solute.'"[41] Michael Inwood has noted Nietzsche's remark in *The Gay Sci-ence* (1882) that "we Germans are Hegelians even if there had never been any Hegel" precisely because we "instinctively assign a deeper sense and richer value to becoming, to development, than to what 'is.'"[42] According to Inwood, however, the understanding of Hegel's philosophy which un-derpins this remark is erroneous. For Nietzsche wrongly identifies the principle of Becoming as the *sole* principle upon which Hegel's philoso-phy is based.[43]

It is difficult to read what Bakunin has to say about Hegel and the rev-olutionary political implications of the Hegelian philosophy in "The Re-action in Germany" and *not* to think of what Zamyatin says about change and the idea of "permanent revolution" as the "law of life," both in his essays and in his novel *We*.[44] Moreover, it should be noted that, despite his general enthusiasm for the philosophy of Nietzsche, Zamyatin does also have a tendency to employ the categories of Hegel's philosophy in his writings. Like Nietzsche, he too interprets Hegel as being a straightforward exponent of the philosophy of Heraclitus. Thus, for example, when talking about "progress" in the history of science Zamyatin asserts that this always follows the same pattern: "yesterday the thesis; today, the antithesis; and tomorrow, the synthesis."[45] It is arguable, then, that Zamyatin's views on scientific progress, and on history generally, are informed as much by a Left Hegelian reading of Hegel's philosophy as they are by the ideas of Nietzsche. In other words, as Marx also occasionally does, Zamyatin might be said to endorse the Left Hegelian or revolutionary reading of Hegel which focus exclusively on the idea that all things are undergoing a process of constant change and consequently nothing, and especially no particular form of society, could ever be permanent or enduring. By implication, then, Zamyatin also thinks that there is a striking affinity between the views of Hegel and Nietzsche, two philosophers whose ideas are usually considered to be antithetical to one another. From Zamyatin's standpoint there is no significant difference at all between the philosophical beliefs of Heraclitus, Hegel, and Nietzsche. Moreover, given the fact that Marx also occasionally said things which indicate that he too was prepared, if only at times, to identify himself with the principles of Left Hegelianism, we might go even further than this and add the name of Marx himself to the list of philosophers with whose views Zamyatin might be associated. I note in passing that George L. Kline has linked Zamyatin with what he (Kline) refers to as a form of "Nietzschean Marxism" which existed in Russia in the early years of the twentieth century.[46] Unlike some commentators, Kline evidently does not think that the idea of a "Nietzschean Marxism" is a contradiction in terms.

It is clear, however, that Zamyatin has a very particular understanding of the views of Hegel and Marx, both of whom he interprets as being, like Nietzsche, perspectivists or relativists. According to Zamyatin, both Hegel and Marx were of the opinion that no particular framework of ideas or beliefs, in either philosophy or science, could ever be permanently "true," in the sense that they possess the kind of timelessness, universality, and objectivity which, from the time of Plato, have often been associated with genuinely philosophical or with "scientific" knowledge. In one of his essays, for example, Zamyatin cites Marx in support of his own view that what we need is "daring dialectics," that is to say "relativism." We must, Zamyatin insists, referring to the very words from Marx's *The Poverty of Philosophy* cited earlier, "contemplate every accomplished form in its

movement, that is, as something transient' (Marx)."[47] In particular, Zamyatin abandons the idea, which is often associated with the philosophy
of Hegel by those of a Right Hegelian persuasion, that there is an "end of
history," especially the history of philosophy or science, at which point
"absolute knowledge" will have been achieved and no further progress
will be either required or possible. For Zamyatin this view might be said
to represent the utopian dimension of both Right Hegelianism and of a
certain kind of Marxism. It is this utopianism which he satirizes in *We*.

I will end this section by observing that if Marx is interpreted as Zamyatin interprets him, as a Left Hegelian, then the distinction between
Marxism and anarchism collapses. I have argued elsewhere that Zamyatin's views are strikingly similar to those of Jean François Lyotard, and
that both thinkers might be associated with the anarchist tradition, or one
strand of it. It follows that if Zamyatin's understanding of Marx is accepted as being authentically "Marxist," then not only is there no significant difference between Marxism and anarchism, there is also no significant difference between Marxism and postmodernism. Thus it makes just
as much sense to talk about "postmodern Marxism" as it does to talk, as
Kline does, about "Nietzschean Marxism." To my mind this is a good reason for thinking that Zamyatin's understanding of Marx is not sound. It
must however be conceded that Marx does occasionally say things which
support it, or which at least appear to do so.[48]

LE GUIN'S ANARCHISM AND LEFT HEGELIANISM

To those familiar with both debates, the more recent debate between commentators regarding the interpretation of the philosophical outlook which
underpins Le Guin's *The Dispossessed*, has a striking affinity with the earlier debate over the issue of the interpretation of Hegel's philosophy
which took place in the nineteenth century. Olander and Greenberg, for
example, have argued that generally speaking Le Guin "projects the
essence of life not as unlimited change or process, but as quietude, stillness, and mystical union with Being."[49] This is an attitude which, presumably, Olander and Greenberg would associate with Le Guin's commitment to Taoism. On this reading Le Guin's philosophical outlook, as
illustrated by the views of the central character in the book, the physicist
Shevek, is exclusively that of an advocate or a Yin utopia or an exponent
of the Simultaneity Theory of Time. It is clear enough, however, that, this
assessment ignores completely the other dimension of Le Guin's (and
Shevek's) thinking, which strongly emphasizes the importance of "unlimited change or process," that is to say, not the Simultaneity but the Sequency Theory of Time; not the principle of Yin but that of Yang; not the

principle of Being, but rather that of Becoming; a principle which is just as much an element in Le Guin's thinking as the one isolated by Olander and Greenberg. Equally one sided, however, albeit in the opposite direction, is the remark of Peter Brigg cited earlier to the effect that in *The Dispossessed* the principle of *becoming* "dominates Odonian philosophy. Thus the *only* goal one may have is to remain open to change."[50] In short, as in the case of Hegel, so also in that of Le Guin, what is required is an interpretation which is properly dialectical, in the sense that it attaches due importance to each of these two opposing principles despite the fact that they stand in contradiction to one another.

It is this, in my view, which provides the key to understanding the relationship which exists between the views of Le Guin and those of Zamyatin regarding this fundamental problem of metaphysics, a problem which lies at the core of Le Guin's *The Dispossessed*. Irrespective of the issue of whether Zamyatin's views represent an accurate account of the philosophies of either Hegel or Marx, and taking those views solely on their own merits, Le Guin is of the opinion that what I have referred to as Zamyatin's Left Hegelianism is a philosophical outlook which is indeed partial and one sided. In her opinion it is an outlook which is associated exclusively with the Sequency Theory of Time. For this reason, although it certainly does grasp a part of "the truth," this outlook is nevertheless limited one, focusing as it does exclusively on the principle of Becoming and ignoring completely the opposite principle, which Le Guin associates with the Simultaneity Theory of Time, the principle of Being. It does not, therefore, grasp the whole of "the truth." Against Zamyatin, however, Le Guin, through her central character Shevek, does not reject the Sequency Principle outright. Nor does she simply oppose to it the Simultaneity principle. Rather she seeks to embrace Zamyatin's views within an overarching dialectical synthesis. She takes Zamyatin's philosophical beliefs up and incorporates them within her own philosophical outlook, whilst at the same time also going beyond them. In so doing Le Guin engages in a philosophical enterprise which exactly mirrors the strategy adopted by Hegel in relation to the views of Heraclitus, when dealing with this same problem of metaphysics in his own philosophical writings.

There is disagreement amongst commentators over the issue of Hegel's attitude toward the question of whether "contradictions" can or cannot be resolved in some higher synthesis. The poststructuralist critics of Hegel attribute such a view to him. In so doing they identify themselves with Left Hegelianism and attribute to Hegel himself the views which are associated with Right Hegelianism. Consequently, like Proudhon before them, they condemn Hegel for advocating "stasis" in Zamyatin's sense. From the standpoint of a certain kind of anarchism, as also for contemporary

postmodernism, this is, of course, profoundly "anti-life." It is arguable, however, that this is a misreading of Hegel. At least it is a highly selective "appropriation" of certain aspects of his philosophy taken out of their immediate context. There is nothing wrong with the notion of attributing the
notion of "synthesis" to Hegel, although some have taken issue with this.[51]
In my view, though, such higher "syntheses" in Hegel's philosophy should
not be thought of as resolving "contradictions" at a lower level in the sense
of dissipating them or making them go away, in such a way that what remains is a state of harmony and equilibrium. Rather, these contradictions
continue to exist even within the third position which has arisen as a consequence of their theoretical synthesis. For Hegel, then, contradictions
which exist at a lower level are creative and productive because they generate new tensions and new contradictions at a higher level. Gregor McLennan has said about this issue that it is quite wrong to think that Hegel seeks
to "escape" rather than fully "recognize" the "intractability of the stubborn
tensions which exist between the constitutive poles of the knowledge relation: subject/object, general/particular, self/other." According to McLennan, such a reading of Hegel is "highly idiosyncratic" because "the whole
point of Hegel's effort" was to "lodge within the very identity of each anti-
monial pole of consciousness its tense but indispensable relation with the
other, opposite pole." Hegel, then, in "unshrinkingly *recognizing* rather than
seeking to *escape* the tensions entailed by identity-in-difference" is "able to
claim that a new level of understanding has been reached" (my emphasis).[52]

Arguing along the same lines as Hegel's poststructuralist critics, Simon
Stow has also suggested that, generally speaking, "dialectic occurs when
some way is found to reconcile two *apparently* conflicting positions, by lo-
cating some *third* position that both accounts for and explains the apparent conflict in such a way as to make the conflict *disappear*" (my emphasis).[53] By implication, then, he too presents his readers with what is in
effect a Right Hegelian understanding of Hegel's philosophy. Interestingly, however, Stow also appears to attribute this way of thinking to Le
Guin. He maintains that her outlook is dialectical in just this sense. As a
characterization of the concept of dialectics as this is to be found in
Hegel's philosophy, Stow's account is not accurate. More to the point,
though, it is not accurate as an account of Le Guin's views on this subject
either. For these are much closer to those of Hegel, properly understood,
than they are to Stow's mistaken account of dialectics.

IS LE GUIN A POSTMODERN ANARCHIST?

The reading of Le Guin presented above brings me into disagreement
with Lewis Call, who has argued that Le Guin can and should be claimed

for the cause of what Todd May has described as "poststructuralist anarchism,"[54] what Saul Newman has characterized as "post-anarchism,"[55] and what Call himself refers to as "postmodern anarchism."[56] According to Call, the 1960s and 1970s was the moment when "anarchism took its 'postmodern turn'" and the writings of Le Guin were "instrumental in bringing about this transformation in anarchist thinking."[57] She "initiated a major postmodern move in her science fiction."[58] Call strongly objects to interpretations which present Le Guin as a "dialectical" thinker, and especially to any interpretation which suggest that her views on some issues have an affinity with those of Hegel. As Call himself puts it, "I find the dialectical interpretation of Le Guin difficult to sustain, and the specifically Hegelian form of that interpretation even more so."[59] His criticism of dialectical readings of Le Guin is that an "assault on binary thinking" is a "fundamental feature" of Le Guin's work, and his criticism of Hegelian readings is that Le Guin is an anarchist whereas, by contrast, Hegel is a "statist" or even a "totalitarian" thinker.[60] As Call puts it, "one cannot help but suspect that a theory which is built upon the Hegelian dialectic— surely one of the most totalizing grand narratives in the history of Western thought—is likely to remain totalitarian."[61]

So far as the first of these criticisms is concerned, it is arguable that in one sense at least an assault on "binary thinking" (by which I mean the "either-or" thinking of traditional logic) has been central to the dialectical tradition in philosophy from the time of Heraclitus onward. Moreover, such an assault is also clearly discernible in the writings of Hegel, who associates such thinking with the standpoint of "negative reason," and contrasts it first with the standpoint of "positive reason," then finally with that of "speculative reason."[62] Moreover, it is precisely because Le Guin is critical of "binary thinking," understood in this way, that some commentators have argued that her philosophical outlook is a dialectical one. This particular criticism of a Hegelian/dialectical reading of Le Guin seems to me, therefore, to be wide of the mark.

So far as the second criticism is concerned, to suggest that Le Guin's ideas could not possibly have an affinity with those of Hegel on the grounds that Hegel is a statist thinker also seems to me to be misguided. I agree with Call that there is a sense in which Hegel could be said to be a statist thinker. However, there is much more to Hegel's philosophy than this. And it is, of course, possible for someone to reject Hegel's statism whilst at the same time acknowledging that other aspects of his thinking are nevertheless of value. I argued earlier that there is evidence to support the view that this is precisely what the classical anarchists of the nineteenth century did. In particular, the attitude of Bakunin and Proudhon toward Hegel is not by any means one of complete rejection or outright hostility.[63] Moreover, it is arguable that a Left Hegelian "appropriation" of Hegel's philosophy could offer a valuable theoretical resource for contemporary postmodernist or poststructuralist anarchism.[64] Indeed, I think that a number of twentieth century philosophers and social theorists, especially in France, owe a great deal more to Hegel than they appear willing to admit. They have drunk deeply at the well of Hegelian philosophy in private even if they have explicitly rejected that same philosophy in public.[65] Consider, for example, Michel Foucault's oft cited remark that "any real escape from Hegel presupposes that we have an accurate understanding of what it will cost to detach ourselves from him; it presupposes that we know the extent to which Hegel, perhaps insidiously, has approached us; it presupposes that we know what is still Hegelian in that which allows us to think against Hegel; and that we can assess the extent to which our appeal against him is perhaps one more of the ruses he uses against us and at the end of which he is waiting for us, immobile and elsewhere."[66] Or Jacques Derrida's claim, also frequently cited, that "we will never be finished with the reading or rereading of Hegel, and, in a certain way, I do nothing other than attempt to explain myself on this point."[67] The importance of Hegel for poststructuralism is something which Call overlooks both in his paper on Le Guin and in his work generally, which seems to me to be far too hostile in general, and unnecessarily dismissive of certain aspects of Hegel's thought in particular. This is true especially of the Heraclitean dimension of Hegel's philosophy.

Like Stow, Call wrongly associates the view that paradoxes and contradictions can actually be *resolved* in some higher synthesis with the philosophy of Hegel, who he, therefore, interprets in a Right Hegelian manner. Call denies, however, that such a view can be found in the writings of Le Guin. This is his principal reason for thinking that Le Guin is not a Hegelian thinker. Calls understanding of Le Guin so far as this issue of the essential non-resolvability of paradoxes and contradictions is concerned is basically sound. In my view, though, Hegel's position with respect to this same issue, properly understood, is not significantly different from that of Le Guin. It is for this very reason that I think that Le Guin might be thought of as a Hegelian thinker. Call has mistakenly attributed to me the view that for both Hegel and Le Guin such contradictions are in principle resolvable. In fact I am of the opinion that neither Hegel nor Le Guin think that this is the case. In an earlier piece, which discusses Le Guin's relationship to Hegel, I was in fact agnostic about this issue, not because I do not have opinions about it, but rather because it was not directly relevant to the argument which I was developing at the time.[68]

Call rightly suggests that a major source of theoretical inspiration for contemporary postmodern anarchism is the philosophy of Nietzsche. In his opinion Nietzsche initiated a "new form of radical politics" which is both "anarchistic" and "postmodern."[69] One of the principal reasons for this is because Nietzsche is a philosopher of pure "becoming," whose philosophy suggests that "we are in a state of permanent and total revolution, a revolution against being."[70] In this regard Call thinks that Nietzsche's philosophy stands in direct opposition to that of Hegel. As Call puts it, "for Nietzsche the world has no teleology, no destination. The forces of history do not direct us towards a Zeitgeist named Hegel. Indeed, if Hegel was the preeminent philosopher of the state, Nietzsche's philosophy of perpetual becoming heralds the state's demise."[71] Thus, in contrast to the philosophy of Nietzsche, Call presents Hegel's philosophy as a form of Platonism, and Hegel as a philosopher of pure *Being*, for whom the principle of *Becoming* has no significance at all. This is an interpretation which completely ignores the importance which Hegel attaches to the philosophy of Heraclitus, something which he shared with Nietzsche. It also overlooks the radical potential which Left Hegelians from Bakunin and Marx until today have always seen in Hegel's thinking. Indeed, it might be suggested that, like Nietzsche and Zamyatin, the central figure of contemporary postmodernism and of postmodern anarchism, Jean-François Lyotard, is a "Left Hegelian" thinker in the very sense indicated earlier.[72] In my view, then, Call's interpretation of Le Guin is based on a double mistake. In effect Call endorses both the Right Hegelian misreading of Hegel's philosophy, on the one hand, and the Left Hegelian misreading of Le Guin's philosophy on the other. In fact, though, both Hegel and Le Guin should be associated with what I have referred to as Centrist Hegelianism.

To conclude, so far as questions of ethics and politics rather than metaphysics are concerned, it might be suggested that against the Left Hegelianism of earlier anarchists such as Proudhon, Bakunin and Zamyatin, Le Guin endorses views which might be associated with the Centrist reading of Hegel's philosophy referred to earlier. In effect, Le Guin is one of Bakunin's "compromisers." Despite the similarity which exists between the thinking of Le Guin and Bakunin in respect to a number of issues, therefore, there remains this one important difference. This is, of course, simply an alternative way of saying that Le Guin refuses to accept Bakunin's principle that in the sphere of morals and politics there are certain circumstances in which "the end justifies the means." It is this more than anything else which ensures that, viewed from the standpoint of Bakunin's anarchism, Le Guin's endorsement of a dialectical outlook which is strikingly similar to that of Hegel is nevertheless associated with a politics which is not radical or revolutionary, but conservative in terms of its political implications.

NOTES

1. Darko Suvin, "Parables of De-Alienation: Le Guin's Widdershin's Dance," in *Positions and Presuppositions in Science Fiction* (Kent: Kent State University Press, 1988), 134–50, cited 301; Douglas Barbour, "Wholeness and Balance: An Addendum," in *Science Fiction Studies: Selected Articles on Science Fiction 1973–1975*, eds. R. D. Mullen and Darko Suvin (Boston: Gregg Press, 1976), 151.

2. Lao Tzu, *Tao Te Ching: A Book About the Way and the Power of the Way*, a new English version, ed. Ursula K. Le Guin (Boston and London: Shambhala Books, 1998), 74.

3. Suvin, "Parables of De-Alienation: Le Guin's Widdershins Dance," 301.

4. Elizabeth Cogell Cummins, "Taoist Configurations: *The Dispossessed*," in *Ursula K. Le Guin: Voyager to Inner Lands and to Outer Space*, ed. Joe de Bolt (New York: Kennikat Press, 1979), 154.

5. Donald Theall, "The Art of Social-Science Fiction: The Ambiguous Utopian Dialectics of Ursula K. Le Guin," in *Science Fiction Studies: Selected Articles on Science Fiction 1973–1975*, eds. Mullen and Suvin, 293–94.

6. Theall, "The Art of Social-Science Fiction: The Ambiguous Utopian Dialectics of Ursula K. Le Guin," 293–94.

7. Le Guin, "A Response to the Le Guin Issue," *Science Fiction Studies*, 3, no. 8 (1976), 45.

8. Le Guin, "A Response to the Le Guin Issue," 45.

9. Le Guin, notes to Lao Tzu, *Tao Te Ching*, 38–39.

10. Ursula K. Le Guin, *The Lathe of Heaven* (London: Granada Books, 1984 [1971]), 28.

11. See Le Guin, "A Non-Euclidean View of California as a Cold Place to Be," in *Dancing at the Edge of the World: Thoughts on Words, Women, Places* (New York: Harper and Row, 1989), 89. Capra's views on science and on the similarities which exist between the outlook of the Copenhagen Interpretation of quantum physics and Eastern philosophy, is mentioned in connection with Le Guin in Cogell Cummins, "Taoist Configurations: *The Dispossessed*," fn. 19, 208; and Carol McGuirk, "Optimism and the Limits of Subversion in *The Dispossessed* and *The Left Hand of Darkness*," in *Ursula K. Le Guin*, ed. Harold Bloom (New York: Chelsea House, 1985), 258. I discuss that view of the part which paradox and contradiction have to play in science and scientific knowledge which underpins Le Guin's *The Dispossessed* in Tony Burns, "Science and Politics in *The Dispossessed*: Le Guin and the 'Science Wars,'" *The New Utopian Politics of Ursula K. Le Guin's The Dispossessed*, eds. Laurence Davis and Peter Stillman (Lanham, Md.: Lexington Books), 195–215.

12. Charlotte Spivack, *Ursula K. Le Guin* (Boston: Twayne, 1984), 78.

13. For this see Shlomo Avineri, *Hegel's Theory of the Modern State* (Cambridge: Cambridge University Press, 1970), 126; Isaiah Berlin, *Karl Marx* (London: Home University Library, 1965), 63–65; Sidney Hook, *From Hegel to Marx: Studies in the Intellectual Development of Karl Marx* (New York: Humanities Press, 1958); David McLellan, *Marx Before Marxism* (Harmondsworth: Penguin Books, 1972), 36; David McLellan, *Karl Marx: His Life and Thought* (London: Macmillan, 1973), 30–31; David McLellan, *The Young Hegelians and Karl Marx* (Harmondsworth: Pen-

guin, 1969); *The Young Hegelians: An Anthology*, ed. Steven Stepelevich (Cambridge: Cambridge University Press, 1983).

14. For this see Tony Burns, "Hegel's Interpretation of the Philosophy of Heraclitus: Some Observations," in *Contemporary Political Studies: 1997*, eds. G. Stoker and J. Stanyer (The Political Studies Association of Great Britain, 1997), Vol. 1, 228–39.

15. I discuss some of these in Tony Burns, "Hegel (1770–1831)," in *Interpreting Modern Political Philosophy from Machiavelli to Marx*, eds. Alastair Edwards and Jules Townshend (London: Palgrave, 2002), 162–79; and Tony Burns, "Hegel," in *Palgrave Advances in Continental Political Thought*, eds. Terrell Carver and James Martin (London: Palgrave, 2005), 45–58.

16. The erroneous suggestion that Hegel is a Platonist is not uncommon amongst commentators. I question this reading and argue that Hegel is not a Platonist but an Aristotelian in Tony Burns, "Metaphysics and Politics in Aristotle and Hegel," in *Contemporary Political Studies: 1998*, eds. A. Dobson and G. Stanyer (The Political Studies Association of Great Britain), Vol. 1, 387–99. I also question Jacques Derrida's Platonist reading of Hegel in Tony Burns, "The Purloined Hegel: Semiology in the Thought of Saussure and Derrida," *The History of the Human Sciences*, 13, 4 (2000): 1–24.

17. Hook, *From Hegel to Marx*, 32.

18. There are different possible readings of Heraclitus's "flux theory." For this and for the relationship between Hegel's philosophy and that of Heraclitus see Tony Burns, "Hegel's Interpretation of the Philosophy of Heraclitus: Some Observations."

19. Burns, "Hegel's Interpretation of the Philosophy of Heraclitus: Some Observations."

20. Frederick Engels, *Ludwig Feuerbach and the End of Classical German Philosophy*, in Karl Marx and Frederick Engels, *Selected Writings* in 2 volumes (Moscow: Foreign Languages Publishing house, 1958), Vol. II., 361–65.

21. Engels, *Ludwig Feuerbach and the End of Classical German Philosophy*, 364.

22. Engels, *Ludwig Feuerbach and the End of Classical German Philosophy*, 362.

23. Sidney Hook, *From Hegel to Marx*, 17.

24. Karl Marx, *The Poverty of Philosophy: Answer to "The Philosophy of Poverty"* by M. Proudhon (Moscow: Progress Publishers, 1973 [1846]), 96. Note that although this text is for the most part a severe critique of the ideas of Proudhon, and of Proudhon's understanding of the philosophy of Hegel, nevertheless with respect to this one issue at least Marx records his agreement with Proudhon and with what, on this occasion, appears to be Proudhon's interpretation of Hegel.

25. Karl Marx, "Afterword" to 2nd. German edition of *Capital: A Critical Analysis of Capitalist Production*, Vol. 1, ed. F. Engels, trans. Samuel Moore and Edward Aveling (London: Lawrence and Wishart, 1974 [1873]), 29.

26. See Vincent Geoghegan, *Utopianism and Marxism* (London: Methuen, 1987).

27. I discuss these issues in Tony Burns, "Karl Kautsky: Ethics and Marxism," in *Marxism's Ethical Thinkers*, ed. Lawrence Wilde (London: Macmillan, 2001), 15–50; and in "Whose Aristotle? Which Marx? Ethics, Law and Justice in Aristotle and Marx," *Imprints: Egalitarian Theory and Practice*, 8, no. 2 (2005), 125–55.

28. I have argued elsewhere that there is an affinity between Le Guin's approach to ethics and the theory of alienation which is to be found in the writings of the young Marx, and hence also with what Lawrence Wilde has referred to as the tradition of "ethical Marxism." See Tony Burns, "Marxism and Science Fiction: A Celebration of the Work of Ursula K. Le Guin," *Capital and Class*, 84 (2004): 141–50l. See also Lawrence Wilde, *Ethical Marxism and its Radical Critics* (London: Macmillan, 1998); *Marxism's Ethical Thinkers*, ed. Lawrence Wilde. For the Hegel-Marx connection generally see Tony Burns and Ian Fraser, "Introduction: An Historical Survey of the Hegel-Marx Connection," in *The Hegel-Marx Connection*, eds. Tony Burns and Ian Fraser (London: Palgrave-Macmillan, 2000), 1–33.

29. George Woodcock, *Anarchism* (Harmondsworth: Penguin Books, 1975), 26–27.

30. For Marx's relationship to Heraclitus see Howard Williams, *Hegel, Heraclitus and Marx's Dialectic* (London: Harvester, 1989). Paradoxical though it might seem, Marx's occasional enthusiasm for Heraclitus, and for a one-sided reading of the philosophy of Hegel, a reading which focuses exclusively on the notion of constant change or permanent revolution, brings him close to the reading of Hegel which is offered by contemporary postmodernists like Lyotard. For Marx and postmodernism generally see Terrell Carver, *The Postmodern Marx* (Penn State University Press, 1999).

31. Mikhail Bakunin, "The Reaction in Germany," in *Selected Writings*, ed. A. Lehning (London: Cape, 1973), 47.

32. Bakunin, "The Reaction in Germany," 52.

33. For the currently unfashionable view that Hegel is best interpreted as being some kind of conservative thinker, along these lines, see Tony Burns, *Natural Law and Political Ideology in the Philosophy of Hegel* (Aldershot: Ashgate, 1996); also Tony Burns, "The Ideological Location of Hegel's Political Thought," in *Contemporary Political Studies: 1995*, Vol. 3, eds. J. Lovenduski and J. Stanyer eds. (The Political Studies Association of Great Britain, 1995), 1301–1308.

34. Burns, "The Ideological Location of Hegel's Political Thought," 1301–1308.

35. Bakunin, "The Reaction in Germany," 49.

36. Bakunin, "The Reaction in Germany," 49, 55.

37. Bakunin, "The Reaction in Germany," 50.

38. Bakunin, "The Reaction in Germany," 56, 58.

39. For an earlier version of the argument presented in this section see Tony Burns, "Hegel and Anarchism" (paper presented at the annual meeting of the Political Studies Association of Great Britain, University of Bath, 11–13 April 2007).

40. For the complex relationship between Hegel and Nietzsche see Will Dudley, *Hegel, Nietzsche and Philosophy: Thinking Freedom* (New York: Cambridge University Press 2002); Stephen Houlgate, *Hegel, Nietzsche and the Criticism of Metaphysics* (Cambridge: Cambridge University Press, 1986); Elliot Jurist, *Beyond Hegel and Nietzsche: Philosophy, Culture and Agency* (Cambridge, Mass.: MIT Press, 2000); Walter Kaufmann, *Nietzsche: Philosopher, Psychologist*, Antichrist (Princeton: Princeton University Press, 1974 [1950]), 235–46, 329–32; and Karl Löwith, *From Hegel to Nietzsche: The Revolution in Nineteenth Century Thought* (London: Constable, 1965).

41. Kaufmann, *Nietzsche: Philosopher, Psychologist, Anti-Christ*, 241.

42. Michael Inwood, *A Hegel Dictionary* (Oxford: Blackwell, 1992), 44–45.

43. Inwood, *A Hegel Dictionary*, 44–45.

44. The affinity between the respective outlooks of Bakunin and Zamyatin has been noted by both Gorman Beauchamp and Phillip E. Wegner. See Gorman Beauchamp, "Zamyatin's *We*," in *No Place Else: Explorations in Utopian and Dystopian Fiction*, eds. Eric S. Rabkin, Martin H. Greenberg, and Joseph D. Olander (Carbondale: Southern Illinois University Press, 1983), 70, and Phillip E. Wegner, *Imaginary Communities: Utopia, the Nation and the Spatial Histories of Modernity* (Berkeley, Los Angeles, London: University of California Press, 2002), 162, 172.

45. Yevgeny Zamyatin, "Tomorrow," in Yevgeny Zamyatin, *A Soviet Heretic: Essays by Yevgeny Zamyatin*, ed. Mirra Ginsburg (Chicago: University of Chicago, 1991), 51; see also Zamyatin, "On Synthetism," in *A Soviet Heretic*, 81.

46. See George L. Kline, "Bogdanov, Aleksandr Alexandrovich," in *The Encyclopaedia of Philosophy*, Vol. 1 (New York: Macmillan, 1967); George L. Kline, "'Nietzschean Marxism' in Russia," in *Demythologizing Marxism*, ed. Frederick J. Adelman (The Hague: Martinus Nijhof, 1969), 166–83; George L. Kline, "Nietzschean Marxism in Russia," *Boston College Studies in Philosophy*, 2, (1969): 166–83; George L. Kline, "The Nietzschean Marxism of Stanisklav Volsky," in *Western Philosophical Systems in Russian Literature: A Collection of Critical Studies*, ed. Anthony M. Mlikotin (Los Angeles: University of Southern California Press, 1979), 177–95; George L. Kline, "Foreword" to Bernice Glatzer Rosenthal, *Nietzsche in Russia* (Princeton: Princeton University Press, 1986), ix–xvi; Bernice Glatzer Rosenthal, *New Myth, New World: From Nietzsche to Stalinism* (University Park, Pa.: Pennsylvania State University Press, 2002).

47. Yevgeny Zamyatin, "The New Russian Prose," in *A Soviet Heretic*, 92–106, cited 105.

48. For Zamyatin, Lyotard, and postmodernism see Tony Burns, "Zamyatin's *We* and Postmodernism." *Utopian Studies*, 11, no. 1 (2000): 66–90. For Marx and postmodernism see Terrell Carver, *The Postmodern Marx*.

49. Joseph D. Olander, and Martin Harry Greenberg, "Introduction" to *Ursula K. Le Guin*, eds. Joseph Olander and Martin Harry Greenberg (New York: Taplinger, 1979), 111–12.

50. See Peter Brigg, "The Archetype of the Journey in Ursula K. Le Guin's Fiction," in *Ursula K. Le Guin*, eds. Joseph Olander and Martin Harry Greenberg, 39. See also Jennifer Rodgers, "Fulfillment as a Function of Time: Or The Ambiguous Process of Utopia," in *The New Utopian Politics of Ursula K. Le Guin's The Dispossessed*, eds. Davis and Stillman, 181: "In *The Dispossessed*, Ursula K. Le Guin provides the reader with a working model for utopia as evolution—not a place, but a process of becoming."

51. See Gustav E. Mueller, "The Hegel Legend of 'Thesis-Antithesis-Synthesis,'" *Journal of the History of Ideas*, 19, no. 3 (1958): 411–14.

52. Gregor McLennan, "Sociology, Eurocentrism and Postcolonial Theory," *European Journal of Social Theory*, 6, no. 1 (2003): 69–86. For a reading of Hegel, which is similar to that of McLennan, see also Daniel Berthold-Bond, *Hegel's Grand Synthesis* (New York: SUNY, 1989).

53. Simon Stow, "Worlds Apart: Ursula K. Le Guin and the Possibility of Method," in *The New Utopian Politics of Ursula K. Le Guin's The Dispossessed*, eds. Davis and Stillman, 42.

54. Todd May, *The Political Philosophy of Poststructuralist Anarchism* (Pennsylvania: Pennsylvania State University Press, 1994); Todd May, "Is Poststructuralist Political Theory Anarchist?" *Philosophy and Social Criticism*, 15, no. 2 (1989): 275–84.

55. Saul Newman, *Power and Politics in Poststructuralist Thought: New Theories of the Political* (London: Routledge, 2005); Saul Newman, *From Bakunin to Lacan: Anti-Authoritarianism and the Dislocation of Power* (Lanham, Md.: Lexington Books, 2001).

56. Lewis Call, "Postmodern Anarchism in the Novels of Ursula K. Le Guin," *SubStance* 36, no. 2 (2007): 87–105; Lewis Call, *Postmodern Anarchism* (Lanham, Md.: Lexington Books, 2002), 11–12.

57 Call, "Postmodern Anarchism in the Novels of Ursula K. Le Guin," 88.

58. Call, "Postmodern Anarchism in the Novels of Ursula K. Le Guin," 91.

59. Call, "Postmodern Anarchism in the Novels of Ursula K. Le Guin," 90.

60. Call, "Postmodern Anarchism in the Novels of Ursula K. Le Guin," 90.

61. Call, *Postmodern Anarchism*, 11.

62. G. W. F. Hegel, *Logic: Being Part One of the Encyclopaedia of the Philosophical Sciences*, trans. William Wallace (Oxford University Press, 1975), §§79–81. For Hegel and Heraclitus see Tony Burns, "Hegel's Interpretation of the Philosophy of Heraclitus: Some Observations."

63. See Tony Burns, "Hegel and Anarchism."

64. I discuss this issue in Tony Burns, "Hegel, Identity Politics and the Problem of Slavery," *Culture, Theory and Critique*, 47, 1 (2006): 87–104; and "Hegel," in *Palgrave Advances in Continental Political Thought*, eds. Terrell Carver and James Martin (London: Palgrave, 2005), 45–58.

65. For discussion of Hegel in France see Bruce Baugh, *French Hegel: From Surrealism to Poststructuralism* (London: Routledge, 2003); Judith Butler, *Subjects of Desire: Hegelian Reflections in Twentieth Century France* (New York: Columbia University Press, 1999 [1987]); Michael Kelly, *Hegel in France* (Birmingham: Birmingham Modern Languages Publications, 1992); Michael S. Roth, *Knowing and History: Appropriations of Hegel in Twentieth Century France* (Ithaca: Cornell University Press, 1988); David Sherman, "The Denial of the Self: The Repudiation of Hegelian Self-Consciousness in Recent European Thought," in Leo Rauch and David Sherman, *Hegel's Phenomenology of Self-Consciousness* (New York: SUNY Press, 1999), 163–222; Robert R. Williams, "Recent Views of Recognition and the Question of Ethics," *Hegel's Ethics of Recognition*. (Berkeley: University of California Press, 1998), 364–412.

66. Cited Jon Marks, *Gilles Deleuze: Vitalism and Multiplicity* (London: Pluto Press, 1998), 17.

67. Jacques Derrida, *Positions*, trans. Alan Bass (Chicago: University of Chicago Press, 1981), 77–8.

68. See Lewis Call, "Postmodern Anarchism in the Novels of Ursula K. Le Guin," 102–03 and Tony Burns, "Science and Politics in *The Dispossessed*: Le Guin and the 'Science Wars,'" 202–03.

69. Call, *Postmodern Anarchism*, 40.

70. Call, *Postmodern Anarchism*, 51.

71. Call, *Postmodern Anarchism*, 50.

72. In Tony Burns, "Zamyatin's *We* and Postmodernism," I argued that there is a striking affinity between the views of Lyotard and those of Zamyatin in relation to science and politics and that, conceptually, the link between them is provided by the philosophy of Nietzsche, by whom they were both influenced. In that paper I distanced both Zamyatin and Nietzsche from Hegel. Now, however, I am more sympathetic to the view that the ideas of Nietzsche, Zamyatin, and Lyotard might all fruitfully be thought of in connection with Left Hegelianism.

4

Science and Progress in the Writings of Zamyatin and Le Guin

LE GUIN'S FAMILIARITY WITH THE WORKS OF ZAMYATIN

The fact that there are at least some similarities between the writings of Ursula K. Le Guin and those of Yengeny Zamyatin had not gone *entirely* unnoticed before Phillip Wegner recently drew our attention to them, although it could hardly be said to have received the treatment which it deserves. It has, for example, been remarked upon by both Leonard Fleck[1] (though only in passing), and Kingsley Widmer.[2] According to Widmer, Le Guin's *The Dispossessed* is derived, at least "in part," from Zamyatin's *We*, not only in its "larger spirit" but also "in some specifics, including the call to permanent revolution."[3] However, like Fleck, Widmer does not make very much of this idea or discuss the relationship at any great length. Nor have the vast majority of other commentators. For example, the name of Zamyatin, and the relevance of Zamyatin's work for Le Guin, is hardly mentioned in the most recent collection of essays devoted to Le Guin's *The Dispossessed*, and when it *is* mentioned, this is again only in passing, usually in the course of a discussion of the need to locate the general background for understanding *The Dispossessed* within the context of the history of dystopian literature in the twentieth century.[4]

It might be thought that the *lacuna* in the commentaries on the work of Le Guin regarding her relationship to Zamyatin is not too surprising, as Le Guin does not make very much of her own relationship to Zamyatin. For example, in the lists of the names of the sources for her understanding of anarchism which she occasionally provides for her readers, that of Zamyatin is conspicuous by its absence.[5] Nor does she mention Zamyatin when listing the authors of literary utopias who have inspired her.[6] Nor, finally, does she mention Zamyatin when listing the figures in the history of European literature who she considers to have been important influences on her own work. "My own list of 'influences,'" she tells us, would include "Shelley, Keats, Wordsworth, Leopardi, Hugo, Rilke, Thomas and Roethke in poetry, Dickens, Tolstoy, Turgenev, Chekhov, Pasternak, the Brontes, Woolf, E. M. Forster in prose."[7]

However, to suggest that Le Guin does not attach much significance to her relationship to Zamyatin, or to Zamyatin's *We*, as a source of influence for her own work, especially *The Dispossessed*, would be an exaggeration. For she does refer to Zamyatin on several occasions in her writings, and always favorably.[8] There are references to Zamyatin in Le Guin's short stories, in her essays, and in novels such as *The Dispossessed* and *The Lathe of Heaven*. One piece of evidence connecting Le Guin to Zamyatin, as Wegner has noted, is the fact that at one point Le Guin refers explicitly to Zamyatin's *We*, maintaining that in her view it is "the best single work of science fiction yet written."[9] It is, she says, a "subtle, brilliant and powerful book; emotionally stunning, and technically, in its use of the metaphorical range of science fiction, still far in advance of most books written since."[10] Another is that there is evidently a sense in which Le Guin *identifies* with Zamyatin politically, especially because and insofar as they were both the target of criticism from people Le Guin refers to variously as "orthodox Marxists" or "Stalinists,"[11] people who in her view are dogmatically opposed to the idea of an "open society"—and indeed an "open universe."[12] Thus in a symposium on Marxism and Science Fiction published in *Science Fiction Studies* in 1973,[13] Le Guin refers to Zamyatin as an "internal émigré," the very phrase which she uses to describe herself when objecting to what she considered to be the orthodox Marxist use of "smear" words such as "bourgeois" or "liberal" to characterize her own political beliefs. As Le Guin herself put it, "I do not like to see the word 'liberal' used as a smear word. That's mere newspeak. If people must call names, I cheerfully accept Lenin's anathemata as suitable. I am a petit-bourgeois anarchist and an internal émigrée."[14] It should be noted that by identifying her own position with that of Zamyatin here, Le Guin *suggests* at least (in my view quite rightly) that, like herself, ideologically speaking Zamyatin too is best thought of as an anarchist rather than as a liberal thinker.[15]

A third piece of evidence is that Le Guin gives an important essay, in which she locates her own work against the background of the utopian tradition of political thought and literature, has the title "A Non-Euclidean View of California as a Cold Place to Be."[16] This title clearly echoes Zamyatin's characterization of One State, the allegedly utopian society satirized in *We*, as being organized in accordance with the principles of Euclidean geometry. Like the world of Euclid, the world of the One State is "very simple."[17] It is based on the principle of the "straight line." Indeed, according to the engineer D-503, the novel's central character, the One State itself is nothing more than "a straight line."[18] This order and symmetry is reflected in the layout of its "straight, immutable streets."[19] Le Guin's characterization of her own approach as being "non-Euclidean" indicates that she has a certain sympathy with Zamyatin's critique of utopianism as it has traditionally been practiced and understood.

Fourthly, there is evidence that some of Le Guin's early short stories owed a debt to Zamyatin. For example, the central female character in a short story called "Nine Lives," which Le Guin first published in 1969, and which is reprinted in *The Wind's Twelve Quarters*, is called "Zayin."[20] Moreover, another of the short stories which Le Guin published in the 1960s (1963), "The Masters," is also evidently inspired by a reading of Zamyatin's work. This story deals with the theme of the scientist in society, or the "politics" of science. The central character in it is a scientist-mathematician named Ganil, who is significantly described by Le Guin as being a "heretic" (of "invention"),[21] a characterization which reflects a familiarity on Le Guin's part with Zamyatin's essays, especially an essay entitled "On Literature, Revolution and Other Matters," where Zamyatin discusses the part which such heretics have to play in the history of science. Ganil is not only a mathematician but, much like the character D-503 in *We* and Shevek in *The Dispossessed*, also a creative individual with new ideas which bring him into conflict with the entrenched conservatism of his own society.

In the preamble to "The Masters," which Le Guin added when it was re-printed in *The Wind's Twelve Quarters*, Le Guin says that "the figure of the scientist is a quite common one in my stories, and most often a rather lonely one, isolated, an adventurer, out on the edge of things."[22] In a clear reference to *The Dispossessed*, she also says that "the theme of this story is one I returned to later, with considerably better equipment."[23] In the same vein, Le Guin states in the introduction to "The Stars Below," a parallel story published in the second volume of *The Wind's Twelve Quarters*, that "as in the earlier story, 'The Masters,' I was telling a story" here "about science itself—the *idea* of science. And about what happens to the idea of science when it meets utterly opposed and powerful ideas, embodied in government, as when seventeenth century astronomy ran up against the Pope, or genetics in the 1930s ran up against Stalin."[24]

Although it is perhaps an exaggeration it seems to me that there is at least *some* truth in Peter Koper's suggestion that the role of science in society, or the politics of science, is "the issue in all Le Guin's fiction."[25] It is interesting to note in this connection that in "The Masters," when Le Guin is thinking of a historical example of a scientist who is such a "lonely, isolated adventurer," alienated from his own society then, as in the case of

Zamyatin, the name which immediately springs to her mind is that of Galileo.[26] This is made very clear by Ganil's suggestion in the story that the language of nature is mathematics,[27] and by references within it to papers written by, Ganil, which have titles such as "Trajectories," "Speed of Falling Bodies," and "The Nature of Motion."[28] The treatment meted out to Ganil in "The Masters" resonates strongly with the treatment of Galileo by the Catholic Church in the seventeenth century.

Fifthly, there is the issue of the source for Le Guin's employment of the metaphor of a *wall*, which occurs frequently in *The Dispossessed*, the very first sentence of which is, "There was a wall."[29] This has been noted by a number of commentators.[30] Phillip E. Smith, has rightly claimed that Le Guin "has woven the imagery and metaphor of walls throughout *The Dispossessed*."[31] It has been suggested more than once that Shevek's principal aim is to "break down walls," or the barriers which separate people from one another, at the various different levels of society. Smith points out that this idea that an anarchist society would "overthrow walls and frontiers" is to be found in the writings of Kropotkin.[32] He offers the conjecture, therefore, that it is "perhaps" from Kropotkin that Le Guin found "her inspiration" in this regard.[33] It seems to me, however, if there is indeed an outside source for this idea in Le Guin's writings, to be much more likely that Le Guin took this idea from Zamyatin.[34] For, of course, the metaphor of "walls" also lies at the heart of Zamyatin's *We*. For example, at one point Zamyatin has D-503 maintain that "walls are the basis of everything that's human."[35] And elsewhere, that "Oh, the great, divinely limiting wisdom of walls and barriers! The wall is, probably, the greatest of all inventions. Man ceased to be a wild animal only when he built his first wall."[36] Moreover, the motif of "breaking down the walls" or barriers which surround us, and divide us from others, and perhaps also even from ourselves, is also to be found in *We*. As the character I-330 puts it, toward the end of the novel, "the day has come for us to raze this Wall—all walls—so that the green wind may blow over all the earth, from one end of it to the other."[37]

Finally, there is an important passage in Le Guin's *The Lathe of Heaven* which indicates her continued engagement with Zamyatin's work, especially his views on energy and entropy, and which touches on the issue of time, and its association with the notions of *Being* and *Becoming*, a theme which is also central to Le Guin's *The Dispossessed*.[38] The passage in question is a dialogue between the novel's two central characters, George Orr and the "mad scientist" Dr. Haber. The passage is worth quoting at length. It runs as follows, with Orr speaking first:

> "I'm afraid of –." But he was too afraid, in fact, to say the pronoun. "Of changing things, as you call it."

"O.K. I know. . . . Why, George? You've got to ask yourself that question. What's wrong with changing things? . . . I want you to try to detach yourself from yourself and try to see your own viewpoint from the outside objectively. You are afraid of losing your balance. But change need not unbalance you; life's not a static object, after all. It's a process. There's no holding still . . . Nothing remains the same from one moment to the next, you can't step into the same river twice. Life – evolution – the whole universe of space/ time, matter/energy – existence itself – is essentially change."

"That is one aspect of it," Orr said. "The other is stillness."

"When things don't change any longer, that's the end result of entropy, the heat-death of the universe. The more things go on moving, interrelating, conflicting, changing, the less balance there is—and the more life. I'm pro-life, George. Life itself is a huge gamble against all odds! You can't try to live safely, there's no such thing as safety. Stick your neck out of the shell and live fully! It's not how you get there, but where you get to that counts. What you're afraid to accept, here, is that we're engaged in a really great experiment, you and I. We're on the brink of discovering and controlling, for the good of all mankind, a whole new force, an entire new field of anti-entropic energy, of the life force, of the will to act, to do, to change!"

"All that is true. But there is" –

"What, George?" He was fatherly, and patient, now: and Orr forced himself to go on, knowing it was no good.

"We're in the world, not against it. It doesn't work to try to stand outside things and run them, that way. It just doesn't work, it goes against life. There is a way, but you have to follow it. The world *is*, no matter how we think it ought to be. You have to be with it. You have to let it be."[39]

This passage is complex and interesting, for a number of reasons—some of which I will return to later. For present purposes let me emphasize that the echoes of Zamyatin and his influence on Le Guin are very clear in the passage in question, as is indicated by Le Guin's employment of Zamyatin's vocabulary, specifically the notions of energy and entropy. It is also interesting that in the passage in question Le Guin should place the expression of Zamyatin's views on change, and on life, in the mouth of her character Haber, of whose views (at least some of them) she evidently disapproves. Here, as later in *The Dispossessed*, Zamyatin's beliefs are presented as being partial and one-sided, as omitting something else which is also essential for our understanding not only of change and temporal development, but also of "life."

ZAMYATIN'S VIEWS ON TRUTH AND SCIENTIFIC PROGRESS

In this section I propose to lay the foundation for a discussion of Le Guin's views on science by first discussing those of Zamyatin, with which they may fruitfully be compared. I shall attempt to show that Le Guin is not only interested in the same questions as Zamyatin, but that with respect to a number of issues her views appear to have been directly inspired by a reading of and a critical engagement with those of Zamyatin. I shall also attempt to show that the suggestion that Le Guin responds to Zamyatin by rejecting outright what he affirms, or by affirming what he rejects, is far too simplistic. For Le Guin's strategy when dealing with Zamyatin is a properly dialectical one. She rarely rejects Zamyatin's ideas outright. Rather, she seeks to incorporate them into her own work, in a manner which retains their strengths but not what she considers to be their weaknesses. In short, in a manner similar to that of Hegel, the ideas of Zamyatin are "sublated" in the work of Le Guin. Le Guin takes these ideas up, incorporates and preserves them in her own work, whilst at the same time being critical of them and seeking to go beyond them, without actually leaving them behind entirely.

Let us first consider Zamyatin's views on the nature of scientific knowledge and, more specifically, the position which he adopts in the two major debates in the philosophy of science, that of "objectivism versus relativism" and that of "realism versus constructivism." Elsewhere I have argued that, with respect to these issues, Zamyatin is a follower of Nietzsche and holds views which, today, would be associated with postmodernism.[40] He therefore embraces the principles of relativism and constructivism and rejects those of objectivism and realism. A good illustration of this is provided by some remarks which Zamyatin makes in an essay entitled "On Synthetism."[41] "Take something," he says, "apparently very real and beyond question—your own hand. You see the smooth, pink skin, covered with delicate down. So simple, so unquestionable. And here is a little piece of this skin under the cruel irony of the microscope: ditches, pits, furrows; thick stems of unknown plants—once hair; a huge lump of earth, or a meteorite which dropped down form the infinitely distant sky—the ceiling—just recently a mere speck of dust; a whole fantastic world—perhaps a plain somewhere on Mars. Yet it is your hand. And who will say that the 'real' one is this hand, familiar, smooth, visible to all the Thomases, and not the other—the fantastic plain on Mars?"[42] In opposition to scientific realism, then, Zamyatin maintains that what scientists take to be real, and what they consider to be true statements about reality depends upon their theoretical perspective or point of view; and there is always more than one point of view from which scientists can look at the world. One cannot observe the world directly, but always "through a glass, darkly," or through a particular "lens," the choice of the level of magnification of which will influence considerably what is seen by a scientist in any particular act of experimental observation.

Given this, Zamyatin maintains, the only thing that any natural scientist can do when observing the world is to come to the task "with a complex assortment" of different lenses. And when the scientist does this then it becomes obvious that there is not just one world, or one reality, the nature of which is revealed to us by science, but many. There are "strange multitudes" of different worlds. Indeed, because for every such lens there is a corresponding world, it follows that there are as many worlds as there are lenses. This is an attitude which recognizes that, depending upon the power of magnification of the lens adopted, an individual human being might be said to constitute an entire "universe," whereas the sun might, in contrast, be thought to be nothing more than an "atom." It is, in short, an attitude which according to Zamyatin has discovered "the relativity of everything."[43] Like H. G. Wells before him,[44] then, Zamyatin shares Nietzsche's view that there is nothing "fixed in nature." There is no natural system of order. The only order that there is, is that which scientists themselves impose upon the flux of their experiences when they employ a certain framework of theoretical concepts. Zamyatin's debt to Nietzsche here is obvious. Indeed he tells us himself that he considers Nietzsche to be an important source for this way of thinking about truth: "If there *were* anything fixed in nature, if there *were* truths, all this would, of course, be wrong. But fortunately, all truths are erroneous. This is the very essence of the dialectical process: today's truths become errors tomorrow; there is no final number" (my emphasis). "*This* truth," Zamyatin goes on, "the *only* one" is "for the strong alone" (my emphais). For "weak nerved minds insist on a finite universe, a last number; they need, in Nietzsche's words, 'the crutches of certainty.'"[45] I have argued elsewhere that this way of thinking about science is similar to that developed by Thomas S. Kuhn in his *The Structure of Scientific Revolutions* and inherited by Jean-François Lyotard in his *The Postmodern Condition*.[46] Like Nietzsche, Zamyatin, and Lyotard, Kuhn too is a relativist who associates what Zamyatin refers to as the "lenses" of science with the different "paradigms" which are employed by practitioners of the various scientific disciplines.

A good way of illustrating this way of thinking about the notion of truth in science is to consider the example of Galileo and his dispute with the Catholic Church in the seventeenth century over the issue of whether the earth revolves around the sun or *vice versa*. According to Kuhn, within the discipline of astronomy at the time there were just *two* ways of looking at this. The first, that of Aristotle and the Church, maintained that the earth is stationary and the sun revolves around it. And the second, that of Copernicus and Galileo, maintains that it is the sun which is stationary and the earth which moves. Aristotle and Ptolemy maintained in effect that the earth is a "star" and the sun is a "planet," whereas Copernicus and Galileo contradicted this view and maintained that it is the sun which is a "star" and the earth which is a "planet."[47] Kuhn argues in his book that whether one considers the earth to be stationary and the sun to revolve around it, or *vice versa*, depends on one's point of view. In his opinion, each of these accounts is equally well supported by the available empirical evidence, or at least was so in the seventeenth century, when Galileo was writing.[48] Each has as much right to be considered to be "the truth" as the other. Students of astronomy today cannot, therefore, make their choice of paradigm rationally on the basis of empirical evidence alone. They do not have sufficient justification for preferring the later views of Copernicus and Galileo, on the grounds that they are true, to the earlier views of Aristotle and Ptolemy, because *they* are false. For if we base our judgment of their respective merits on some act of experimental observation, these two opposed accounts might be said to "reflect reality" or "fit the facts" equally well. In this respect Kuhn's ideas differ significantly from those which are usually associated with the world view of modern science. In recent times the latter is, perhaps, best exemplified in the writings of Sir Karl Popper, who endorses the more traditional "correspondence" theory of truth, which can be traced back to the writings of Aristotle, and who has criticized Kuhn's views precisely because of their reliance on the principle of epistemic relativism.[49]

But Zamyatin is in agreement with Kuhn here and not Popper. He accepts, therefore, that we cannot differentiate between the astronomical theories of Aristotle and Galileo by means of any rational decision making procedure of the kind which is usually associated with modern science. Indeed, Zamyatin maintains that one of the most significant recent developments in the philosophy of the natural sciences at the turn of the nineteenth and twentieth centuries was the suggestion that what appears to be true to one scientist, who is looking at a situation from one point of view, or through one particular "lens," might be considered to be false by another who is looking through a different "lens," or from the opposite point of view. Like Kuhn and Nietzsche, then, Zamyatin is a relativist and not an objectivist in the sphere of epistemology, just as he is a constructivist and not a realist in that of ontology. In his view, there is no order which might be said to inhere within the fabric of the universe. The only order that can be discerned by scientists is the order which they themselves impose upon the flux of their own experiences by means of language, specifically the language of science and scientific explanation. Crucially, however, this can be done in different (and indeed diametrically opposed) ways. It is this which creates the paradoxes and contradictions which lie at the very heart of the scientific enterprise, for example, that associated with the problem of the "star-planet" duality within the discipline of astronomy and (as we shall see) that associated with the problem of "wave-particle duality" within the discipline of physics. In Zamyatin's opinion these paradoxes and contradictions are not to be thought of as intrinsic to a "reality" which subsists independently of the conceptual frameworks employed by scientists. They are, rather, generated by the thought processes of scientists themselves when, in their different ways, they attempt to understand the natural world by imposing some conceptual order or other upon it.

According to Zamyatin, the opposing beliefs of Galileo and the Church might be thought of as "revolving" around one another within a particular "system" of explanatory beliefs in much the same way as the earth and the sun revolve around one another within the solar system which this framework of beliefs is attempting to explain. Moreover, for anyone located within this explanatory system, because each of these sets of beliefs is equally well supported by the available empirical evidence, it is not at all clear which of them is true. Although it does appear to the participants in this dispute that only one of them *could* be true, and indeed that one or the other of them *must* be true and, consequently, the other false.

In his essay "On Synthetism" Zamyatin suggests that natural scientists can and do undertake acts of empirical observation using a multiplicity of different lenses, and that for each of these there is a corresponding world associated with a definite body of beliefs which are considered by at least some scientists to be true. There is, therefore, not one "Truth" with a capital letter "T," so far as any particular scientific problem is concerned, but rather many "truths." However, what the example of the dispute between Galileo and the Church appears to show is that in disputes within any given scientific discipline at a given time, there are not many but rather just *two* different ways of looking at the problem at issue, the question it poses, and the answer which might be given to that question. To support his claim that in any particular discipline there is always going to be a *multiplicity* of "lenses" through which scientists can look at a given problem, it is necessary for Zamyatin to introduce a historical perspective into the discussion. This brings us to a consideration of his views on the history of science and on the notion of scientific progress.

Zamyatin's views on scientific progress are closely associated with his understanding of the notions of energy and entropy. As the character I-330 puts it in *We*, "there are two forces in this world—entropy and energy. The first leads to beatific quietism, to a happy equilibrium; the other to the destruction of equilibrium, to excruciatingly perpetual motion,"[50] that is to say, to "permanent revolution." In an important essay, significantly entitled "On Literature, Revolution, Entropy and Other Matters," Zamyatin states that when "the flaming, seething sphere (in science, religion, social life, arts) cools" then "the fiery magma becomes coated with dogma—a rigid, ossified, motionless crust." But "dogmatization in science, religion, social life, or art," he insists, "is the entropy of thought."[51] According to Zamyatin, then, the process of change in both science and in society is one which is permanent and never-ending. "Revolution is," Zamyatin says "everywhere, in everything. It is infinite. There is no final revolution, no final number. The social revolution is only one of an infinite number of numbers: the law of revolution is not a social law, but an immeasurably greater one. It is a cosmic, universal law—like the laws of the conservation of energy and of the dissipation of energy (entropy)."[52] This is the "law of life." As such either it is undeniably a "good" thing or, alternatively, could not possibly be said to be a "bad" one.

As in the case of the Left Hegelians, classical anarchists such as Proudhon and Bakunin, Nietzsche, and contemporary postmodernists like Lyotard, with his notion of "paralogy," at the very heart of Zamyatin's philosophical outlook is the "flux" theory associated with the philosophy of Heraclitus, the idea that all things are changing all of the time, and that this is not just inevitable but also a good thing. This just *is* "progress," both in science and in society. For again the law of change is the law of life. In Zamyatin's view, anyone who seeks to suppress or even slow down the pace of change, whether in science or in politics, can for that reason be considered to be not just opposed to progress but also profoundly "anti-life."

Because Zamyatin is a relativist he rejects entirely the notion of objective truth or "Truth" with a capital "T." In his view, there can be no scientific progress at all if by that expression one means, as for example Zamyatin thought that Hegel meant, a movement *toward* a final endpoint which could not possibly be improved upon, namely "The Truth," or what Hegel refers to in his *Phenomenology of Spirit* as "absolute knowledge."[53] There can, however, be scientific progress in a different sense from this. This is possible because all of the scientific disciplines have a history. Within each of them, change does undoubtedly occur. New ideas replace old ones and, periodically, there are even moments of revolutionary upheaval when one way of looking at the world and the ideas associated with it is entirely replaced by another, which is considered by scientists within a particular discipline to be an *improvement* on the view which it replaces.

In his essay "On Literature, Entropy, Revolution and Other Matters," Zamyatin associates change in science, or scientific progress as he understands it, with the activity of "heretics" whose views on truth flout the conventions of their own societies. As Zamyatin puts it, "heretics are the only (bitter) remedy against the entropy of human thought." Heretics are "necessary to health." Indeed, "if there are no heretics, they should be invented."[54] Zamyatin took the view that, not only are heretics necessary for scientific progress, they are also necessary for "life." "The world" generally, he says, "is kept alive only by heretics."[55] It is heretics who are the engineers of change generally, and, therefore, of all scientific progress, in the only sense of that term which Zamyatin is prepared to endorse. At the same time, however, these heretics have to pay a heavy price for their heresy, as they are invariably persecuted for their pains.

In the same essay Zamyatin refers explicitly to Galileo as one of these agents of scientific progress. As Zamyatin puts it, "what has become dogma" in science "no longer burns; it only gives off warmth—it is tepid, it is cool. Instead of the Sermon on the Mount, under the scorching sun, to up-raised arms and sobbing people, there is drowsy prayer in a magnificent abbey. Instead of Galileo's 'But still, it turns!' there are dispassionate computations in a well heated room in an observatory." "On the Galileos," Zamyatin continues, "the *epigones* build their own structures, slowly, bit by bit, like corals. This is the path of evolution—until a new heresy explodes the crush of dogma and all the edifices of the most enduring stone which have been raised upon it."[56] Zamyatin also uses Galileo as an example of this kind in his novel *We*. Consider, for example, the following passage, a dialogue between the characters D-503 (the male, scientific rationalist) and I-330 (the female defender of the principle of irrationality both in science and in the world generally):

> "And if throughout the universe all bodies are equally warm, or equally cool . . . You've got to smash them into each other—so there'll be fire, explosion, inferno. And we—we're going to smash them."
> "But I-330 - remember, just remember: That's just what our ancestors did - during the 200 Years War. . . "
> "Oh, and they were right, they were a thousand times right. They made only one mistake: Afterward, they got the notion that they were the final number—something that doesn't exist in nature. Their mistake was the mistake of Galileo. He was right that the earth revolves around the sun, but he didn't know that the entire solar system revolves around yet another centre; he didn't know that the real orbit of the earth as opposed to the relative orbit, is by no means some naive circle."[57]

As Zamyatin understands it, scientific progress might be said to involve a constantly repeating two-stage process. Although Zamyatin does not himself employ this terminology, in my opinion his views about this process are best characterized by employing the notions of "reversal" and "displacement." This can be illustrated by considering again the example taken from the discipline of astronomy referred to above. Zamyatin suggests that, just as the earth and the sun can be thought of as together constituting a particular solar system, so also it is fruitful to think of the opposed beliefs of Galileo and the Catholic Church as constituting some sort of intellectual "system." When discussing this example he suggests that if this situation is looked at from the point of view of someone who is located within this intellectual system then the empirical evidence appears *either* to support the views of the Church *or* those of Galileo. We are, therefore, presented with a straightforward choice between just two alternatives, each of which flatly contradicts the other, and each of which is considered by its proponents to be objectively true—or to be "The Truth" of the matter. In this system of beliefs, Galileo's way of looking at things is, chronologically speaking, the later of the two and might be said to constitute a simple "reversal" or "inversion" of the view adopted by Aristotle and the Church.

According to Zamyatin, however, if one were able to place oneself, or imagine that one is placed, *outside* of this system or in some way above it and looking down upon it, using a "lens" with a different degree of magnification, then one would then be able to appreciate that neither of these two ways of looking at things on its own, or even both of them together, could be said to capture "The Truth" of the matter, and indeed that there is no such "Truth" with a capital "T" to be captured. It will not then seem so evidently the case that either the Church's perspective or Galileo's perspective, that is to say, their particular versions of "the truth," are the only possible ones. And for Zamyatin this recognition constitutes a *third* way of looking at the situation, which might be said to be the necessary preliminary for the development at a later stage of a completely new way of looking at things, one which employs entirely new categories and which, therefore, does not simply reverse the beliefs associated with an earlier paradigm, but actually "displaces" those beliefs and the perspectives with which they are associated altogether.

As Zamyatin himself occasionally suggests, this way of thinking about change in the history of science owes at least *something* to the philosophy of Hegel. And it is certainly possible to offer an account of Zamyatin's views on scientific progress using what are (rightly or wrongly) traditionally thought to be the categories of Hegelian metaphysics, especially the notions of "thesis," "antithesis," and "synthesis."[58] However, Zamyatin's views are "Hegelian" only in an attenuated sense. Like Bakunin and Proudhon before him, Zamyatin's understanding of Hegel's philosophy is that of a Left Hegelian. As such it is based on a highly selective, partial and one-sided reading of Hegel's writings. It is based more on "appropriation" of just some of Hegel's views, taken out of context, than on an "interpretation" of Hegel's philosophy as a whole, taking into account all of its aspects.[59] Indeed, as we have seen, it might be suggested that Zamyatin's views on truth and scientific progress owe more to Nietzsche, or to his predecessor the pre-Socratic philosopher Heraclitus, than they do to Hegel.[60] Correctly understood it is in my view not only possible, but also highly desirable, to offer an account of Zamyatin's views on scientific development which does not employ the technical vocabulary of Hegel's philosophy.

Zamyatin's similar way of thinking about scientific progress in terms of the notions of reversal and displacement is illustrated very well by the following passage from his essay "On Literature, Revolution, Entropy and Other Matters," which characterizes Einstein as a scientist who came along after the dispute between Galileo and the Catholic Church had taken place, and who succeeded in placing himself outside or above the duality of the system of beliefs constituted by their opposed views. According to Zamyatin, then, if it was Galileo who reversed the views of Aristotle in the seventeenth century, nevertheless it was Einstein who was responsible for the displacement of the explanatory categories associated with this earlier dispute in the history of science altogether. As Zamyatin puts it: "The weak nerved lack the strength to include *themselves* in the dialectic syllogism. True, this is difficult. But it is the very thing that Einstein succeeded in doing: he managed to remember that he, Einstein, observing motion with a watch in hand, was also moving; he succeeded in looking at the movement of the earth from *outside*"[61] (my emphasis). Zamyatin goes on to say, in a telling phrase, that this is "precisely how a great literature, which knows no final numbers, looks at the movement of the earth."[62]

This way of thinking about scientific progress is also depicted in *We* when, in conversation with D-503, the character I-330 refers to "the mistake of Galileo," who "was *right* that the earth revolves around the sun," when, that is, he followed Copernicus and opposed Aristotle and the Catholic Church, but who nevertheless himself fell into *error* because he "didn't know that the entire solar system" itself "revolves around yet another centre"[63] (my emphasis). According to Zamyatin, then, although the views of Galileo rightly superseded those of Aristotle, by an act of reversal, nevertheless they were themselves (inevitably) superseded in their turn by a later act of displacement which was undertaken by Albert Einstein, and again rightly so. For that is change in science, and in science (as in politics) change is the law of life. In Zamyatin's view this is what scientific progress amounts to. For "progress" just *is* change; and *all* change is necessarily progressive. Change is something which is valuable for its own sake. Zamyatin has no conception of the idea that some change is retrograde; or that there might be situations in which change in a particular direction might be for the worse rather than for the better.[64]

So far as the example of the dispute between Galileo and the Church is concerned, then, Zamyatin maintains that it is possible for a *third* scientific observer to come on the scene at a later date, to reflect on the disagreement which has occurred, and to look at the situation in a completely new and different way by imaginatively placing themselves *outside* of the system within which the two disputants were locked. This third observer can, as it were, rise above this dispute and look at it afresh—by raising the level of magnification of the lens which is being used in the process of empirical observation.

Zamyatin's remarks about Einstein in the passage cited above indicate this very well. According to Zamyatin, when observing the motion of the earth, Einstein did succeed in placing himself *outside* of the system within which both the Catholic Church and Galileo were locked in this way. So far as the question of whether the earth revolves around the sun or the sun around the earth is concerned, then, Zamyatin's remarks imply that we only feel compelled to make an invidious "either-or" choice between one or the other of these two alternatives because we allow ourselves to be constrained by this particular conceptual system, or "strait-jacket," and the limited range of possibilities associated with it. As long as we remain at this level, then we will be confronted by the paradoxical situation that each of these *two* opposing accounts can legitimately be considered to be true, because they are both supported by relevant empirical evidence, despite the fact that they actually contradict one another. For Zamyatin, this is merely an indication that the world is not "in-itself" a rational, ordered, law-governed place. In a passage cited earlier, Zamyatin refers to Einstein's successful effort to deal with this problem by placing himself "outside" or "above" the system of opposed beliefs by which Galileo and the Catholic Church had previously been constrained. It is for this reason that Einstein's views might be said to constitute scientific progress in relation to those of his predecessors Aristotle and Galileo.

It is more or less inevitable that anyone who thinks about the example of Galileo and the Church will be led to ask the question of where, if anywhere, lies "the truth" between the two opposing sides in this dispute? At first sight there appears to be just two possible answers which might be given to this question, namely, "nowhere" or "somewhere." If we answer "nowhere" then we are in effect denying that there is any such thing as objective truth or "The Truth" so far as this dispute (or indeed any other scientific dispute) is concerned. If, on the other hand, we answer "somewhere" then we commit ourselves to the view that such a truth exists. In my opinion, because he is a relativist, the answer which Zamyatin would give to this question is "nowhere."

This question is especially significant for any attempt to understand the relationship which exists between the views of Zamyatin on truth and scientific progress and those which underpin Le Guin's *The Dispossessed*. For although her views are not by any means identical with those of Zamyatin, and indeed (as we shall see) differ from his in a number of significant respects, nevertheless Le Guin's thinking about this subject in the 1970s does appear to have been directly inspired by an engagement with Zamyatin's writings. As I pointed out earlier, there are a several reasons for thinking this, not least of which is the fact that Le Guin demonstrates a familiarity with the passages cited above. Indeed in an essay entitled "The Stalin in the Soul" Le Guin tells us that she wishes Zamyatin to have "the last word" on this subject, as he is someone who "understood something about truth."[65] I will consider the views on scientific truth which underpin Le Guin's *The Dispossessed* later in this chapter. First, however, I want to say something about the way in which Le Guin deals with the issues discussed above in one of her short stories, "Schrödinger's Cat," which was published in the same year as *The Dispossessed*.[66]

LE GUIN ON TRUTH AND SCIENTIFIC PROGRESS: "SCHRÖDINGER'S CAT"

"Schrödinger's Cat" deals with the theme of the nature of scientific truth and progress which is raised by Zamyatin in *We* and in his essay "On Literature, Revolution, Entropy and Other Matters." In this story Le Guin focuses on what she refers to as Erwin Schrödinger's (well known) "Gedankenexperiment."[67] The background required for any attempt to understand this story is a familiarity with the discipline of physics at the very beginning of the twentieth century, especially the developments associated with the emergence of quantum mechanics. One of the problems addressed by physicists at that time had to do with the nature of light, and of electromagnetic radiation more generally. This is the phenomenon usually referred to as "wave-particle duality." How can we best explain the movement of light through a medium? Should we think of the movement of light as being like that of a wave or like that of a particle? Traditional Aristotelian logic, a core element in the explanatory methodology of modern science, tells us that light *cannot* be both a wave and a particle at the same time, and yet the evidence available to us from the world of quantum physics suggests that paradoxical though it might seem (and might actually be) this is indeed the case. This idea is usually referred to as the principle of "complementarity" in physics. The attitude of mind which it expresses is also usually associated with Werner Heisenberg's well-known "uncertainty principle," according to which it is impossible for scientists to accurately measure both the location and the direction of any subatomic particle at the same time; for given the size of the particles in question, the act of measuring the value of one of these two variables inevitably alters the value of the other. For Niels Bohr and Werner Heisenberg, and the other advocates of what came to be called "The Copenhagen Interpretation," the world of quantum physics is a "topsy turvy" world in which Newton's Laws of Motion and the normal rules of explanatory procedure of modern science simply do not apply. For Zamyatin this is an indication of the "irrationality," or perhaps more accurately the "non-rationality," of both the world generally and of the scientific enterprise. It also demonstrates that the views which are traditionally associated with the explanatory procedures of what some would refer to as "modern" science are now, at the beginning of the twentieth century, significantly out of date.

One of the two main characters in "Schrödinger's Cat" is a "mail man" who is for some reason transformed into a talking dog called "Rover." In the story Le Guin portrays Rover as an enthusiastic supporter of the Copenhagen Interpretation of quantum physics, the basic philosophical assumptions of which are not objectivist and realist, but rather relativist and constructivist. In particular, Rover endorses Heisenberg's uncertainty principle. At one point, for example, Le Guin has Rover assert that "it is beautifully demonstrated," in Schrödinger's original thought experiment, that "if you desire certainty, *any* certainty," in science then "you must create it yourself."[68] She also has Rover maintain, against Albert Einstein, that it is in fact the case that "God plays dice with the world." If these remarks are intended to represent the views of Schrödinger, then they do not succeed. For Schrödinger agreed with Einstein's realist critique of the Copenhagen Interpretation. He accepted Einstein's view that any randomness, chaos, or disorder that might *appear* to exist within the world, even at the quantum level, is in fact a reflection of our own ignorance of the laws which are operating there. And he endorsed Einstein's assumption that, even at the quantum level, the world is fundamentally an ordered rather than a disordered place. Indeed, as James Bittner has noted, the purpose of Schrödinger's original thought experiment, which employs the image of "Schrödinger's Box," one which is also used by Le Guin in her story, was to offer a *reductio ad absurdum* of what Schrödinger took to be the logical paradoxes associated with the views of Bohr and Heisenberg.[69] On the other hand, however, the above cited remarks which Le Guin puts into the mouth of the character Rover *do* provide a good account of the views of Zamyatin, who basically endorses the principles associated with the Copenhagen Interpretation of quantum physics in his writings. Indeed, following Dostoevsky and Nietzsche, Zamyatin suggests that these principles apply, not just at the quantum level, but to the world generally at every level.

There is a striking analogy between the problem of wave-particle duality in quantum physics and the earlier problem of whether the earth revolves around the sun, or *vice versa*, or the problem of "star-planet duality" within the discipline of astronomy. For in both cases we have a system of beliefs which comprises of just *two* diametrically opposed, and indeed mutually contradictory, ways of looking at things, one of which is the reverse of the other. If someone asserts at a certain time that light is a particle then they must at that time deny that it is a wave, and *vice versa*. It seems that it cannot be the case that light is *neither* a particle *nor* a wave.

On the other hand, however, it is logically absurd to suggest, at one and the same time, that it can be thought of as being *both* a particle *and* a wave. But that is precisely what the adherents of The Copenhagen Interpretation and the principle of complementarity, as Schrödinger understood them, were in fact suggesting. To the rationalist Schrödinger, this is a logical absurdity. Such contradictions can have no part to play in science because scientific explanation is a quintessentially rational enterprise which must respect the traditional principles of reasoning and inference which were first laid down long ago by Aristotle.

The details of Schrödinger's thought experiment need not concern us at the present time. They are undoubtedly of importance for anyone who wishes to understand the physics which underpins Le Guin's *The Dispossessed*, especially the theoretical developments which lie behind the development of the "ansible," a telecommunications device which allows instantaneous communication between worlds which are light years apart. This, of course, could only occur if it were possible for the communication in question to travel faster than the speed of light. It requires what Le Guin refers to as "transillience," something the possibility of which Einstein denied.[70] But none of this is directly relevant to the immediate task at hand. It will suffice to say that in Schrödinger's thought experiment there is a point at which it must be said either that Schrödinger's cat is *both* dead *and* alive at the same time, or alternatively that it is *neither* dead *nor* alive at the same time—but in each case Schrödinger thought that the outcome is one which is logically absurd when considered from the standpoint of the conventional criteria of scientific explanation which he himself endorsed. In short, the point of Schrödinger's own story, with its invocation of the idea of the "cat" in the "box," was to debunk the claims of the advocates of the Copenhagen Interpretation that their way of thinking about the problems of atomic physics was "good science."

What is most important for present purposes is the question of how Le Guin deals with this issue in "Schrödinger's Cat," and whether her views on the subject bear any resemblance at all to those of Zamyatin, as presented earlier. And it seems to me that they *do*—although again that is not to say that their respective views are identical. Thus, for example, at one point in the story Le Guin inserts the following piece of dialogue between the narrator of the story and the character Rover. The narrator says to Rover, "'Do you mean,' I said carefully, 'that until you lift the lid of the box, the cat has *neither* been shot *nor* not been shot?' 'Yah,' Rover said, radiant with relief, welcoming me back to the fold. 'Or maybe, you know, *both*.'"[71] This is of course a logical paradox, but the existence of the paradox which is generated by Schrödinger's thought experiment is evidently only a problem for those who, like Schrödinger himself and Einstein, but unlike Nietzsche and Zamyatin, think that the world (at every level) just is or must be basically a law-governed and ordered place, the inner workings of which are in principle rationally apprehensible by natural scientists.

In a manner similar to that of Zamyatin before her, Le Guin suggests in "Schrödinger's Cat" that the question of what is going on inside her own story's equivalent of Schrödinger's box could be considered by two physicists with different points of view which flatly contradict one another. She also suggests that the ideas connected with these contradictory points of view might be said to be located within the same conceptual "system." To these two physicists, and anyone else looking at the situation from within this conceptual system, there *must* be a cat in the box. The point at issue in the dispute between these two physicists is *not* whether the box does or does not contain a cat. It is, rather, the further issue of whether this cat in question is dead or alive. In other words, although they do disagree about some things, specifically whether the cat in the box is alive or dead, nevertheless the two physicists involved in this particular dispute also share a number of the basic assumptions. This is reflected by the fact that they employ the same conceptual categories and vocabulary (e.g., the words "cat," "dead," "alive"). In their dispute the one simply affirms what the other denies, and because this is the nature of their dispute they might be said to stand on the same conceptual terrain. The views of the one might be said to constitute an inversion or a reversal of the views of the other, and nothing more.

Let us now consider the attitude which Le Guin adopts toward logical paradoxes and their role in the discipline of physics, and by implication in science more generally. Like Zamyatin, in "Schrödinger's Cat" Le Guin takes the view that the first system of beliefs referred to above, which contains two ways of looking at things which stand diametrically opposed to one another, constitutes some kind of conceptual strait jacket or "box." She has her narrator suggest that if physicists allow themselves to remain locked into the assumptions made by those who work within this first system of beliefs, then they will inevitably be confronted with a paradox of the kind envisaged by Schrödinger. They will be presented with a problem for which there is no logical or rational solution. Nonetheless Le Guin suggests, through her narrator, that even if there is no such solution to these problems, given the terms in which they are presently formulated, nevertheless there is always some way of dealing with them. Moreover, although Le Guin does not refer explicitly to him by name, the strategy for dealing with them which she proposes is strikingly similar to that proposed by Zamyatin.

In our earlier discussion of the astronomical problem of "star-planet duality" we saw that Zamyatin invokes the metaphor of the lenses of a microscope and their varying powers of magnification, in order to deal with such problems. He allows for the possibility of the introduction of a new way of looking at things associated with a process of displacement rather than inversion. In "Schrödinger's Cat" Le Guin makes what is in effect the same point by employing a different metaphor, that of "nesting boxes." She alludes to the possibility of a second thought experiment, one which brings in to question the assumptions made by Schrödinger when he carried out the first. If this second experiment were carried out it would become clear that there is more than one possible conceptual system to which scientists might appeal when attempting to characterize this situation. Physicists would then be able to envisage the possibility that there might be a second system or conceptual box which overarches and contains the first. They could imagine the possibility of a *third* point of view, operating at a higher level than either of the contradictory viewpoints which are associated with this first conceptual system. This would be a new theoretical perspective based on different assumptions from those envisaged by Schrödinger. It would, therefore, stand on another conceptual terrain and employ different explanatory categories. The theoretical perspective of someone who looks at the situation from this third point of view might, therefore, be thought of as constituting a displacement rather than a simple reversal of either of the two perspectives associated with that first system. Like Zamyatin, then, Le Guin suggests that when dealing with logical problems of this nature it is always going to be possible for scientists to place themselves above any situation and look down upon it from a new and different point of view. They will always be able to go higher by raising the level of magnification of the lens through which they look at a given situation. They can think about any situation or problem in a completely new way. In short, they can always step outside of the particular conceptual box which is currently constraining their thoughts—as, according to Zamyatin, Einstein did when considering the problem addressed by Aristotle and Galileo.

In principle, of course, the process of inversion and displacement which we have just envisaged is one which could continue *ad infinitum*, as one conceptual box in the history of any scientific discipline such as physics is replaced by another. As the narrator of Le Guin's story puts it, "I said, 'but really we should use larger boxes.' He gazed about him in mute bewilderment, and did not flinch even when the roof of the house was lifted off just like the lid of a box, letting in the unconscionable, inordinate light of the stars. He had just time to breathe, 'Oh, wow!'"[72]

I will end this section by saying something about Le Guin's understanding of the notion of "uncertainty," and the part which it has to play in quantum physics and in science more generally. At one point in "Schrödinger's Cat," Le Guin puts into the mouth of the character Rover the following assertion: "Certainty. All I want is certainty. To know for *sure* that God *does* play dice with the world" (my emphasis).[73] Paradoxically, then, Le Guin presents the character Rover in her story as someone who wishes to be absolutely certain that there are *no* beliefs at all in science which can be known with certainty, that is to say, no beliefs at all which are objectively true. Rover wishes to know for sure that there are no "Truths" with a capital "T." Similarly, toward the end of the story, she presents the character of the narrator as being unable to cope with the "terrible uncertainty" associated with the logical paradox which is associated with the thought experiment which was envisaged by Schrödinger.[74] The narrator assumes that there *must* be a cat inside the story's equivalent of Schrödinger's box and wishes to know with certainty whether this cat is dead or whether it is alive. The narrator also assumes that the cat in question *must* be either one or the other because it makes no sense, and is inimical to the fundamental assumptions of the scientific world view, to say that it is neither one nor the other, or that it is both one and the other.

In "Schrödinger's Cat" Le Guin associates Schrödinger's quest for certainty with a quite traditional way of thinking about science. This view of science is associated with three basic principles. The first of these is a commitment to the notion of objective truth. The second is an endorsement of the "correspondence theory of truth," which goes back to Aristotle. And the third is an acceptance of the "either-or" thinking of Aristotelian logic. The narrator of the story, like all "good scientists," is driven by a desire to achieve certainty, understood in just this sense. It is in order to satisfy that desire, to know with certainty which of the two contradictory statements, "The cat in the box is alive" and "The cat in the box is dead," is in fact true and which is false, that toward the end of the story the narrator finally throws open the lid of the box—only to find, of course, neither a live cat nor a dead cat, but an empty box, and, therefore, no cat at all. As the narrator puts it, just like the traditional way of thinking about truth in science for which it is a metaphor, "'the cat, of course, was not there.'"[75]

LE GUIN ON TRUTH AND SCIENTIFIC PROGRESS: *THE DISPOSSESSED*[76]

James Bittner has claimed that "the message of 'Schrödinger's Cat' is the message of Le Guin's 'ambiguous utopia' *The Dispossessed*."[77] It is not clear to me that either text actually has a "message" in any straightforward sense. However, that aside, I agree that the view of science and scientific progress which underpins these two works is basically one and the same. Let us now turn, therefore, to consider Le Guin's novel. One passage from *The Dispossessed* is especially interesting because it alludes to the dispute between Galileo and the Catholic Church over the issue of whether the earth revolves around the sun or *vice versa*, an example which, as we have seen, is also referred to by Zamyatin both in *We* and in his essays. Early in the novel, whilst still on Anarres, the young Shevek and his friends are sitting at night contemplating the moon (that is to say, the planet Urras), and the character Tirin says, "I never thought before" of the fact that "there are people sitting on a hill, up there, on Urras, looking at Anarres, at us and saying, 'Look, there's the Moon.' Our earth is their Moon; our Moon is their Earth." To which the character Bedap immediately responds, "where, then, is Truth?"[78] A moment's reflection indicates that, so far as its intrinsic logic is concerned, this is the very same problem as that posed by the dispute between Galileo and the Catholic Church which is referred to by Zamyatin, both in his essays and in *We*. It is also the problem which is addressed by Le Guin in "Schrödinger's Cat."

I suggested earlier that there are just two possible answers to Bedap's question, "Where, then, is Truth?"—namely, "nowhere" and "somewhere." If we were to answer "nowhere" then, in effect, we would be denying that there is any such thing as objective truth or "The Truth" and embracing the principles of relativism and constructivism. This, in my opinion, is how Zamyatin answers this particular question. If, on the other hand, we were to answer "somewhere" then we would be distancing ourselves from relativism and constructivism, and committing ourselves to the principles of objectivism and scientific realism and to the idea that science is indeed a quest for "The Truth." Those who say "somewhere" in answer to Bedap's question are of the opinion that the aim of all scientists is to uncover or discover certain truths about the causal mechanisms which operate within the order of nature; mechanisms which exist quite independently of the thought processes of scientists, and which would continue to do so even if there were no science or scientists.

In my view Le Guin's answer to Bedap's question is not "nowhere," but "somewhere." This is an important difference between her views on science and those of Zamyatin, despite the similarities which exist between their thinking about other issues. So far as it touches on Le Guin, I have presented the evidence and developed the argument which supports this claim elsewhere and do not propose to repeat myself here.[79] I will, however, cite just one important passage, from one of Le Guin's essays, which I think illustrates the difference between her views on science and those of Zamyatin very well. In it Le Guin says that the world "is orderly, *not* chaotic." Moreover, "its order is not one imposed by man or by a personal or humane deity. The true laws—ethical and aesthetic, as surely as scientific—are not imposed from above by any authority, but exist in things and are to be found—discovered."[80] This is not the view of Zamyatin or Nietzsche. Nor, *pace* Lewis Call, is it the understanding of natural science adopted by "postmodernist" thinkers such as Jean-François Lyotard, or

Paul Feyerabend.[81] It is, indeed, a way of thinking which is typically "modern" rather than "postmodern."

This is not to say, of course, that the view of scientific truth and progress which underpins Le Guin's *The Dispossessed* is *entirely* conventional. Far from it. For it differs from what is usually considered to be "the modern scientific world view," which again I will assume is represented by the writings of Karl Popper, in one fundamentally important respect. Why this is so will become clear if we look again at the dispute between Galileo and the Catholic Church from the standpoint of Bedap's question in *The Dispossessed*, "Where, then, is truth?" For although both Popper and Le Guin would answer "somewhere" to this question, they would nevertheless have quite different things in mind when doing so.

Popper's approach exemplifies that of the modern scientific world view referred to earlier. He endorses the notion of objective truth and the traditional correspondence theory of truth. Moreover, Popper also endorses the "either-or" thinking of Aristotelian logic and has no time at all for a "dialectical" outlook which accepts that there might be "some truth" in the views held by "both sides" in this or any other dispute in science. Indeed, Popper rejects the notion of "dialectics" out of hand as "unscientific."[82] In his opinion, therefore, if we ask "Where, then, is the Truth?" in relation to the dispute between Galileo and the Church what we are attempting to establish is which of the views associated with the two "sides" in this dispute is true and which, in consequence, is false.

Le Guin's position regarding this particular issue is quite different from that of Popper. For although she is not a relativist, Le Guin is nevertheless sympathetic to the idea that there is indeed something to be said for the views of both "sides" in this particular dispute. There is at least *some* "truth" in the views held by Galileo, just as there is at least *some* "truth" in the views held by the Catholic Church. Each of these two ways of looking at the situation, and the beliefs associated with them, might be said to be a part of "the Truth." Le Guin suggests, however, that the ability of scientists to apprehend this truth depends on the extent to which they can distance themselves from any direct involvement in this system of contradictory beliefs, to place themselves above it, and appreciate that there is something to be said for *both* of the positions associated with it, despite the fact that they contradict each other.

As in the case of Le Guin's story, "Schrödinger's Cat," it is difficult to read this extract from *The Dispossessed* and *not* think of the passages in Zamyatin's *We* and in his essays cited earlier. Once again, though, despite these similarities, there are also important differences between Le Guin's views and those of Zamyatin. For, as we have seen, in the case of Zamyatin the paradoxes and contradictions of science are generated by the thought process of scientists, who choose to look at the natural world in different and contradictory ways, whereas for Le Guin, just as for Hegel, they are inherent in the natural order of things. In Le Guin's opinion, then, the world itself really is an intrinsically contradictory place. Consequently when scientists are compelled to engage with logical paradoxes, and to embrace them in thought, what they are doing in effect is gaining insight into objective truths which reflect the way in which the "real" world actually works.

To summarize the preceding discussion, the views on scientific truth and progress which are associated with Le Guin's *The Dispossessed* differ from both those of Zamyatin and those of a representative of the more traditional way of thinking about science which can be found in the writings of Karl Popper. They differ from those of Zamyatin because Le Guin is an objectivist and a scientific realist, whereas Zamyatin is a relativist and a constructivist. They differ from those of Popper because although Le Guin shares both Popper's commitment to the idea of objective truth and (in a manner of speaking) his endorsement of the idea of truth as "correspondence" to reality, she nevertheless distances herself from the "either-or" thinking of traditional Aristotelian logic and is willing to accept that the principles of paradox and contradiction have an important part to play in science, precisely because the world just is an inherently contradictory place. For this reason I have suggested elsewhere that there is a striking affinity between the views of Le Guin and those of Hegel, not Nietzsche or Zamyatin. In my view both Hegel and Le Guin are "dialectical" thinkers who are willing to embrace both "sides" of a contradiction, at the same time, because they are committed to the principle that "The Truth is the whole." In the case of *The Dispossessed* the most striking example of this attitude is to be found in the way in which Le Guin deals with the Sequency and the Simultaneity theories of time, both of which the central character Shevek incorporates into his General Temporal Theory, despite the fact that they not only appear to flatly contradict one another, but may in fact actually do so.[83]

The reader will not need reminding that the subtitle of *The Dispossessed* is "An Ambiguous Utopia." Setting aside for the time being a discussion of the idea of utopia, what does Le Guin have in mind when she employs the notion of "ambiguity" in connection with science and scientific knowledge? Rightly or wrongly, Le Guin associates the notion of ambiguity with that of "uncertainty," as indicated above. In order to understand her position it is helpful to look at this issue from the standpoint of the particular view of science which she is criticizing, as again it is represented by the work of Karl Popper. Advocates of that view would distinguish between the notions of meaning and truth. They would maintain that it is *concepts* in science which can be said to be either meaningful or meaningless, whereas it is the explanatory *propositions* or hypotheses of science which can be said to be either true or false. Additionally, they would claim that it might be said of *both* concepts and propositions (hypotheses) that they can be either certain or uncertain. However, on this Popperian view, what is meant when a *concept* is said to be uncertain is different from what is meant when an explanatory *proposition* or hypothesis is said to be uncertain. For concepts are uncertain when their meaning is unclear or imprecise, whereas propositions are uncertain when their truth is open to doubt, which according to Popper must always be the case.

Popper would argue that if there is a connection at all between the notion of "ambiguity" and that of "uncertainty' in science, then this is so only in the case of concepts and not that of explanatory propositions or hypotheses. On this view although there will always be some uncertainty about the issue of whether a particular scientific theory is true this is not because of any ambiguity surrounding the meaning of the theoretical concepts with which that theory is associated. This uncertainty occurs, rather, because of the philosophical problem of induction. It occurs because the explanatory hypotheses of science take the form of universal generalizations which connect "effects" to their underlying "causes," of the form "All As are B," or "If A, then B." If we are to be justified in concluding that these generalizations are true then we must be certain that they apply in *all* possible cases, including all possible future cases. We must be certain that they could never be falsified. According to Popper, though, we could never be certain of this. It is always possible that new evidence, at some point in the future, might be discovered which shows that a hypothesis which we thought was true because it had passed all of our "tests" is actually false.[84]

According to Popper, then, although scientists might be uncertain as to whether or not a particular explanatory hypothesis is in fact true or false, they are nevertheless justified in claiming to know with certainty that it *must* be either one or the other. If there is any uncertainty surrounding a given hypothesis, this uncertainty does not relate to the truth status which that proposition possesses in reality, that is to say, its being true or its being false. For it is *certainly* either the one or the other. If the proposition is indeed true then it is objectively true and could not possibly be false. Moreover, its truth status is what it is, and will continue to be what it is, quite independently of what scientists happen to think about it. Rather, the uncertainty surrounding hypotheses has to do with the *knowledge* which scientists have of their truth status. For they cannot be sure, in any given case, which of these two mutually incompatible possibilities (a hypothesis being true or its being false) actually holds. It is for this reason that Popper suggests that the good scientist is someone who thinks of explanatory hypotheses as being tentative *conjectures* only. They must be advanced cautiously, with a certain degree of skepticism as to their truth, and an acceptance that they might possibly be false, even though nobody has as yet succeeded in falsifying them. Indeed, the principal aim of the scientist is to establish, not that these hypotheses are true (an impossibility, because of the problem of induction), but rather that they are false. It is to attempt to falsify them. For it is the replacement of one false theory by another, better one, which Popper associates with scientific progress and the growth of knowledge in any particular scientific discipline.[85]

Let us now turn to consider the notion of "ambiguity" in relation to Le Guin's understanding of science and scientific knowledge. One thing which Le Guin appears to have in mind when she uses the word "ambiguity" in this context is simply the fact that the meaning of the concepts which are employed by scientists might be vague or imprecise, and, therefore, in that sense "uncertain." More importantly though, unlike Popper, Le Guin also employs this term when talking about the truth or falsity of the explanatory propositions of science. She suggests that these, too, might be said to be "ambiguous," precisely because there is some "uncertainty" which surrounds them. Here, however, Le Guin's views differ significantly from those of Popper. For Le Guin disagrees with Popper's view that, if we cannot know with certainty whether or not a particular hypothesis is true, we can at least know with certainty that it must be "either true or false." Rather, as we have seen, she maintains that even if two explanatory hypotheses flatly contradict one another they could nevertheless *both* be said to possess some truth or constitute a "part" of "The Truth." In her view, then, the truth in science is Janus faced. It always looks both ways, and to grasp this properly it is necessary to abandon the "either-or" thinking which Popper associates with the "logic of scientific discovery."

Citing Shevek's opposition to the claim, made by the character Dearri in *The Dispossessed*, that one "can't assert two contradictory statements about the same thing," D. G. Williams has suggested "like a good Taoist" Shevek (and by implication Le Guin) is "comfortable with ambiguity and paradox." It is not surprising, then, Williams continues, that Dearri should protest "when Shevek views time as *both* sequency and simultaneity," despite the logical contradiction involved in doing so. Williams notes the affinity, in this regard, between Le Guin's attitude toward problems of quantum physics, especially the problem of "wave-particle duality" ("What is light? Particle or wave?"[86]), on the one hand, and her enthusiasm for Taoism on the other. He also notes that the *Tao Te Ching* of Lao Tzu "points at truth using similar ambiguities and contradictions,"[87] and that the "Taoist sage" is "the person who understands the Tao, the way in which the Universe works, the order of Nature," which is the way of paradox and contradiction.[88] Williams is right I think to suggest here that, unlike the case of Popper, from the standpoint of Le Guin's philosophy of science, "ambiguities" and "paradoxes," or "contradictions," are actually the same thing.

However, it might be suggested that Le Guin does not need to argue that because in science there is no partial or one-sided truth which can be known with "certainty," it follows that we must accept that the notion of "ambiguity" is of fundamental importance for any adequate understanding of the scientific enterprise. It would rather, in my view, have been better if she had argued that, with respect to any given problem in a particular scientific discipline at a particular time, there *is* indeed one unambiguous and certain (though contradictory) "Truth," a truth which can, in principle at least, be grasped by those who are prepared to think "holistically" or "dialectically" and to embrace the principle of contradiction. For Le Guin, as also for Hegel, it is only the beliefs of those who "see things" in this way which accurately reflect the inherently contradictory nature of reality.[89]

As Williams suggests, the fact that Le Guin incorporates Zamyatin's views on change and the desirability of change, both in science and in society, into *The Dispossessed* is evident in what she says about the nature of time, and the various theories of time there. Zamyatin's views on change are, in effect, identical with what Le Guin refers to as the Sequency Theory of Time in *The Dispossessed*, the most appropriate metaphors for the understanding of which are the "river of time" and the "arrow of time." This way of thinking about time is much the same as that which is associated with the extreme interpretation of Heraclitus's "flux" theory, which considers things to be constantly changing in all respects all of the time. It is valuable as a corrective to any metaphysics which attaches no importance at all to the idea of change (for example that of Parmenides or Plato). It is clear, however, that Le Guin thinks that this way of thinking about time is limited because it only tells one-half of the story. In particular, it cannot account for the fact that the very things which undergo a process of change nevertheless remain in existence, or retain their identity, in and through such a process of change—in other words, that there is a sense in which they remain the same and hence do not and cannot be said to change at all. To capture this other aspect of any process of change, we need to supplement the Sequency Theory with the Simultaneity Theory. Any theory of time which has pretensions to being comprehensive, such as Shevek's General Temporal Theory in *The Dispossessed*, must include *both* of these ways of thinking, despite the fact that they contradict one another. Important as Zamyatin's views on change are, therefore, Le Guin thinks that they are inadequate precisely because they are partial and one-sided. For this reason they are of limited value and require supplementation by beliefs which tell the other half of the story. In my view this is another reason for not associating Le Guin with the outlook of postmodernism. We shall see later that Le Guin adopts exactly the same approach to the problems of ethics and politics.

NOTES

1. Leonard M. Fleck, "Science Fiction as a Tool of Speculative Philosophy: A Philosophical Analysis of Selected Anarchistic and Utopian Themes in Le Guin's *The Dispossessed*," in *Selected Proceedings of the 1978 Science Fiction Research Association National Conference*, ed. Thomas J. Remington (Cedar Falls, Iowa: University of Iowa Press, 1979), 138.

2. Kingsley Widmer, "Utopian, Dystopian, Diatopian Libertarianism: Le Guin's *The Dispossessed*," *The Sphinx*, 4, 1 (1981): 55–66.

3. Widmer, "Utopian, Dystopian, Diatopian Libertarianism: Le Guin's *The Dispossessed*," 56.

4. Laurence Davis and Peter Stillman. eds. *The New Utopian Politics of Ursula K. Le Guin's The Dispossessed* (Lanham, Md.: Lexington Books, 2005). See especially Chris Ferns, "Future Conditional or Future Perfect? *The Dispossessed* and Permanent Revolution," 252–53; Claire Curtis, "Ambiguous Choices: Skepticism as a Grounding for Utopia," fn. 1, 280; Everett L. Hamner, "The Gap in the Wall: Partnership, Physics and Politics in *The Dispossessed*," 228; Laurence Davis, "The Dynamic and Revolutionary Utopia of Ursula K. Le Guin," 16.

5. See Ursula K. Le Guin, "The Day Before the Revolution," *The Wind's Twelve Quarters*, Vol 2 (London, Granada, 1980 [1975]), 121, where Le Guin refers to the work of Goldman, Goodman, Shelley, and Kropotkin; Ursula K. Le Guin and Jonathan Ward, "Interview," *Dreams Must Explain Themselves* (New York: Algol Press, 1975), 35, where she mentions only Paul Goodman; and Ursula K. Le Guin and Larry McCaffery, "An Interview with Ursula K. Le Guin," in Larry McCaffery, *Across the Wounded Galaxies* (Chicago: University of Chicago Press, 1990), 166, where she refers to Kropotkin and Goldman "and the rest."

6. Ursula K. Le Guin, "Science Fiction and Mrs. Brown," in *The Language of the Night: Essays on Fantasy and Science Fiction*, ed. Susan Wood (New York: Perigee Books, 1979), 111, where Le Guin refers to the work of Thomas More, H. G. Wells, W. H. Hudson and William Morris. Interestingly, in the same passage Le Guin also cites the names of "Engels, Marx, Godwin, Goldmann, Goodman, and above all Shelley and Kropotkin" as being sources for her understanding, not of anarchism, but of "utopia."

7. Ursula K. Le Guin, "A Response to the Le Guin Issue," *Science Fiction Studies*, 3 (1976): 43–46.

8. Ursula K. Le Guin, "A Non-Euclidean View of California as a Cold Place to Be," in *Dancing at the Edge of the World: Thoughts on Words, Women, Places* (New York: Harper and Row, 1989), 85; Le Guin, "Science Fiction and Mrs. Brown," 118; Ursula K. Le Guin, "The Stalin in the Soul," in *The Language of the Night*, 211–21; Ursula K. Le Guin, "Surveying the Battlefield," contribution to a symposium on "Change, Science Fiction and Marxism: Open or Closed Universes?" *Science Fiction Studies*, 1, no. 2 (Fall 1973), 89.

Chapter 4

9. Ursula K. Le Guin, "The Stalin in the Soul," 212.

10. Le Guin, "Science Fiction and Mrs. Brown," *The Language of the Night*, 101–19, 105.

11. See for example Ursula K. Le Guin, "Surveying the Battlefield," *Science Fiction Studies*, 1, no. 2 (1973), 90, where Le Guin maintains "Marxism" can be "accepted as an open system (Marx) or a closed one (Stalin)." Note that Le Guin does not associate Marx himself with either "orthodox Marxism" or with Stalinism. This suggests that she is sympathetic to the idea of an "open Marxism."

12. Ursula K. Le Guin, "Escape Routes," *The Language of the Night*, 206. See also Susan Wood, "Introduction," to Le Guin, *The Languages of the Night*, 34.

13. "Symposium on Change, Science Fiction and Marxism: Open or Closed Universes?" *Science Fiction Studies*, 1 (1973): 84–98; reprinted in R. D. Mullen and Darko Suvin. eds. *Science Fiction Studies: Selected Articles on Science Fiction 1973–1975* (Boston: Gregg Press, 1976), 48–58.

14. Ursula K. Le Guin, "A Response to the Le Guin Issue," 45; see also Wood, "Introduction," to *The Language of the Night*, 13.

15. For the claim that Zamyatin's views on science and politics in *We* are best characterized as anarchist see Tony Burns, "Zamyatin's *We* and Postmodernism." *Utopian Studies*, 11, no. 1 (2000): 79–81.

16. Ursula K. Le Guin, "A Non-Euclidean View of California as a Cold Place to Be," 80–100.

17. Yevgeny Zamyatin, "On Literature, Revolution, Entropy and Other Matters," in *A Soviet Heretic: Essays by Yevgeny Zamyatin*, ed. Mirra Ginsburg (Chicago: University of Chicago, 1991), 112. See also 105, 107, 111.

18. Yevgeny Zamyatin, *We*, trans. Bernard Gilbert Guerney (Harmondsworth: Penguin, 1970 [1924]). I, 19.

19. Zamyatin, *We*, II, 23.

20. Ursula K. Le Guin, "Nine Lives," in *The Wind's Twelve Quarters*, Vol. 1 (London: Granada, 1978 [1969]), 128–57.

21. Ursula K. Le Guin, "The Masters," in *The Wind's Twelve Quarters*, Vol. 1, 56.

22. Le Guin, "The Masters," 46.

23. Le Guin, "The Masters," 46.

24. Le Guin, "The Stars Below," in *The Wind's Twelve Quarters*, Vol. 2, 60.

25. Peter T. Koper, "Science and Rhetoric in the Fiction of Ursula Le Guin," in *Ursula K. Le Guin: Voyager to Inner Lands and Outer Space*, ed. Joseph de Bolt (New York: Kennikat Press, 1979), 67.

26. Zamyatin, "On Literature, Revolution, Entropy and Other Matters," in *A Soviet Heretic*, 108; Zamyatin, *We*, XXX, 170.

27. Le Guin, "The Masters," 54.

28. Le Guin, "The Masters," 62. See also Koper, "Science and Rhetoric in the Fiction of Ursula Le Guin," 67.

29. Le Guin, *The Dispossessed*, I, 9.

30. Phillip E. Smith, "Unbuilding Walls: Human Nature and the Nature of Evolutionary and Political Theory in *The Dispossessed*," in *Ursula K. Le Guin*, eds. Joseph Olander and Martin H. Greenberg (New York: Taplinger, 1979), 77–96; Mark Tunick, "The Need for Walls: Privacy, Community and Freedom in *The Dispossessed*," in *The New Utopian Politics of Ursula K. Le Guin's* The Dispossessed, eds.

Davis and Stillman, 129–48; Winter Elliott, "Breaching Invisible Walls: Individual Anarchy in *The Dispossessed*," in *The New Utopian Politics of Ursula K. Le Guin's* The Dispossessed, eds. Davis and Stillman, 149–66; Everett L. Hamner, "The Gap in the Wall: Partnership, Physics and Politics in The Dispossessed," in *The New Utopian Politics of Ursula K. Le Guin's* The Dispossessed, eds. Davis and Stillman, 219–32.

31. Smith, "Unbuilding Walls: Human Nature and the Nature of Evolutionary and Political Theory in *The Dispossessed*, 87.

32. Smith's article appears to have had some impact, and is frequently cited in the literature, his claim that the most significant influence on Le Guin is Kropotkin being widely accepted. To cite just one example, Dan Sabia, "Individual and Community in Le Guin's *The Dispossessed*," in *The New Utopian Politics of Ursula K. Le Guin's* The Dispossessed, eds. Davis and Stillman, fn. 2, 125, maintains that Smith "plausibly argues that it is Kropotkin's ideas which seem most to inform *The Dispossessed*." This seems to me to be an oversimplification.

33. Smith, "Unbuilding Walls: Human Nature and the Nature of Evolutionary and Political Theory in *The Dispossessed*, 87.

34. Since writing this I have since discovered that this point is also made by Phillip Wegner, *Imaginary Communities: Utopia, the Nation and the Spatial Histories of Modernity* (Berkeley, Los Angeles, London: University of California Press, 2002), 175. See also Peter Ruppert, "The Ambiguous Utopia: A Third Alternative," *Reader in a Strange Land: The Activity of Reading Literary Utopias* (Athens, Georgia: University of Georgia Press, 1986), 141: "As in Zamyatin's *We*, the ambiguity of all boundaries is the central theme of Le Guin's novel."

35. Zamyatin, *We*, VIII, 53.

36. Zamyatin, *We*, XVII, 99–100. See also II, 21. This is also, of course, a *motif* to be found in the writings of Dostoevsky, an important source for many of Zamyatin's ideas. See especially Fyodor Dostoevsky, *Notes from the Underground*, trans. Jessie Coulson (Harmondsworth: Penguin, 1973), 20–23.

37. Zamyatin, *We*, XXVII, 154.

38. Ursula K. Le Guin, *The Lathe of Heaven* (London: Granada, 1984 [1971]), 119–20.

39. Le Guin, *The Lathe of Heaven*, 119–20.

40. See Burns, "Zamyatin's *We* and Postmodernism."

41. Zamyatin, "On Synthetism," *A Soviet Heretic*, 81–91. See also Zamyatin, "Contemporary Russian Literature," *A Soviet Heretic*, 41–42.

42. Zamyatin, "On Synthetism," 85.

43. Zamyatin, "On Synthetism," 85–86.

44. See H. G. Wells, "Skepticism of the Instrument," Appendix to *A Modern Utopia*, in *A Modern Utopia and Tono Bungay* (London: Odhams Press, n.d. [1905]). See also H. G. Wells, "Metaphysics," Book I of *First and Last Things: A Confession of Faith and Rule of Life* (London: Watts, 1930 [1929]), 1–42, especially §4, "Skepticism of the Instrument," 9–11; §8, "Logic Static and Life Kinetic," 21; §13, "Nominalism and Realism," 38–40; and §15, "The General and the Individual," 41–42. I discuss Wells's views on these issues and their influence on Zamyatin in Tony Burns, "Zamyatin's *We* and Postmodernism," 84–85, fns 20, 23, 24, 25.

45. Zamyatin, "On Literature, Revolution, Entropy and Other Matters," 110–11.

46. For a discussion of the views of Zamyatin and Le Guin on science in relation to Kuhn and postmodernism see Burns, "Zamyatin's *We* and Postmodernism" and

"Science and Politics in *The Dispossessed:* Le Guin and the 'Science Wars.'" See also Ziauddin Sardar, *Thomas Kuhn and the Science Wars* (London: Icon Books, 2000), published in a series entitled *Postmodern Encounters.*

47. T. S. Kuhn, *The Structure of Scientific Revolutions,* 2nd ed. (Chicago: University of Chicago Press, 1970 [1962]), 128–29: "The Copernicans who denied its traditional title 'planet' to the sun were not only learning what 'planet' meant or what the sun was. Instead they were changing the meaning of 'planet' so that it could continue to make useful distinctions in a world were all celestial bodies, not just the sun, were seen differently from the way they had been seen before."

48. Kuhn, *The Structure of Scientific Revolutions,* 128–29, 149–50.

49. See, for example, Karl Popper, "The Theory of Objective Truth: Correspondence to the Facts," in *Conjectures and Refutations: The Growth of Scientific Knowledge* (London: Routledge, 1972 [1963]), 223–28; also Karl Popper, "Facts, Standards and Truth: A Further Criticism of Relativism," Addendum I, *The Open Society and Its Enemies,* Vol. 2, *Hegel and Marx* (London; Routledge, 1966 [1945]), 369–96; Karl Popper, "Normal science and its Dangers," in Imre Lakatos and Alan Musgrave, eds., *Criticism and the Growth of Knowledge* (Cambridge: Cambridge University press, 1974 [1970]), 51–58.

50. Zamyatin, *We,* XXVIII, 161; also XXX, 170.

51. Yevgeny Zamyatin, "On Literature, Revolution, Entropy and Other Matters," 108.

52. Zamyatin, "On Literature, Revolution, Entropy and Other Matters," 108. See also Zamyatin, *We,* XXX, 168–69.

53. G. W. F. Hegel, *Phenomenology of Spirit,* trans. A. V. Miller (Oxford: Clarendon Press, 1977), 479–93.

54. Yevgeny Zamyatin, "On Literature, Revolution, Entropy and Other Matters," 108–09.

55. Yevgeny Zamyatin, "Tomorrow," in *A Soviet Heretic,* 51–52.

56. Zamyatin, "On Literature, Revolution, Entropy and Other Matters," 108.

57. Zamyatin, *We,* XXX, 170.

58. For the view that Hegel rarely, if ever, employs the notions of "thesis," "antithesis," and "synthesis" see Gustav E. Mueller, "The Hegel Legend of 'Thesis-Antithesis-Synthesis,'" *Journal of the History of Ideas,* 19, no. 3 (1958): 411–14.

59. For the distinction between a "reading," an "interpretation," and an "appropriation" of a text see Tony Burns, "Hegel and Anarchism" (paper presented at the annual meeting of the Political Studies Association of Great Britain, University of Bath, 11–13 April 2007).

60. This issue is made more complicated by the fact that, like Nietzsche, Hegel too was a great enthusiast for the philosophy of Heraclitus. For this see Tony Burns, "Hegel's Interpretation of the Philosophy of Heraclitus: Some Observations," in G. Stoker and J. Stanyer eds., *Contemporary Political Studies: 1997* (The Political Studies Association of Great Britain, 1997), Vol. 1, 228–39.

61. Zamyatin, "On Literature, Revolution, Entropy and Other Matters," 110–11.

62. Zamyatin, "On Literature, Revolution, Entropy and Other Matters," 110–11.

63. Zamyatin, *We,* XXX, 170.

64. I attempt to show elsewhere that, in this respect, there is an affinity between the views of Zamyatin and the way of thinking about the notions of truth and sci-

entific progress adopted by Jean-François Lyotard and contemporary "postmodernism." See Burns, "Zamyatin's *We* and Postmodernism." There is also an affinity between these ideas and the "anarchist" view of science developed by Paul Feyerabend in his *Against Method: Outline of an Anarchistic Theory of Knowledge* (London: Verso, 1978 [1975]).

65. Le Guin, "The Stalin in the Soul," 220–21.

66. Ursula K. Le Guin, "Schrödinger's Cat," in *Universe 5*, ed. Terry Carr (New York: Random House, 1974), 26–34. One of the few commentators to discuss this story is James Bittner. See James W. Bittner, *Approaches to the Fiction of Ursula K. Le Guin* (Ann Arbor: UMI Press, 1984), 77–82 and fn 45, 139–40.

67. Le Guin, "Schrödinger's Cat," 31. For other references by Le Guin to such *Gedankenexperimenten* see Ursula K. Le Guin, "Introduction to *The Left Hand of Darkness*," in *The Language of the Night*, 156; and Ursula K. Le Guin, "Is Gender Necessary?" *The Language of the Night*, 163.

68. Le Guin, "Schrödinger's Cat," 32.

69. Bittner, *Approaches to the Fiction of Ursula K. Le Guin*, 139–40.

70. For an accessible account of the physics involved here see John Gribbin, *In Search of Schrödinger's Cat: Quantum Physics and Reality* (New York: Bantam Books, 1988), 113, 118–19, 121, 160–61, 165, 170–73, 204–05; John Gribbin, *Schrödinger's Kittens and the Search for Reality* (London: Phoenix Books, 1995), 11–12, 15, 19–21, 24, 28–30; and Peter Nicholls ed., *The Science in Science Fiction* (New York: Alfred Knopf, 1983), 98–101.

71. Le Guin, "Schrödinger's Cat," 32.

72. Le Guin, "Schrödinger's Cat," 34.

73. Le Guin, "Schrödinger's Cat," 34.

74. Le Guin, "Schrödinger's Cat," 32.

75. Le Guin, "Schrödinger's Cat," 33.

76. The interpretation of Le Guin presented here is developed at greater length in Tony Burns, "Science and Politics in *The Dispossessed:* Le Guin and the 'Science Wars.'"

77. Bittner, *Approaches to the Fiction of Ursula K. Le Guin*, 82.

78. Le Guin, *The Dispossessed*, II, 41.

79. Tony Burns, "Science and Politics in *The Dispossessed:* Le Guin and the 'Science Wars.'"

80. Ursula K. Le Guin, "Dreams Must Explain Themselves," *The Language of the Night*, 49.

81. Lewis Call, "Postmodern Anarchism in the Novels of Ursula K. Le Guin," *SubStance* 36, no. 2 (2007): 87–105.

82. Karl Popper, "What is Dialectic?" *Conjectures and Refutations: The Growth of Scientific Knowledge*, 312–35.

83. I discuss this issue in more detail in Burns, "Science and Politics in *The Dispossessed:* Le Guin and the 'Science Wars,'" 201–03.

84. Karl Popper, *The Logic of Scientific Discovery* (London: Routledge, 1959), 27–29, 40, 59–60; also Karl Popper, "Back to the Presocratics," in *Conjectures and Refutations: The Growth of Scientific Knowledge*, 151–52; Sir Karl Popper, "The Problem of Induction," in *A Pocket Popper*, ed. D. A. Miller (London: Fontana Books, 1983), 103–5. As Popper himself puts it in *The Open Society and Its Enemies*, Vol. 2,

262–63: "We can never rationally establish the truth of scientific laws; all we can do is to test them, severely, and to eliminate the false ones."

85. See Karl Popper, *The Open Society and Its Enemies*, Vol. 2, 263, 363, 370, 375, 377, 386; Karl Popper, "Truth, Rationality and the Growth of Knowledge," *Conjectures and Refutations: The Growth of Scientific Knowledge*, 225–26; Karl Popper, "Back to the Presocratics," *Conjectures and Refutations*, 152.

86. D. G. Williams, "The Moons of Le Guin and Heinlein," *Science Fiction Studies*, 21, no. 2 (1994), 170.

87. Williams, "The Moons of Le Guin and Heinlein," 170.

88. Williams, "The Moons of Le Guin and Heinlein," 169.

89. For a discussion of Hegel and the "Correspondence Theory of Truth," or the "Reflectionist Theory of Knowledge," see Lucio Colletti, "Hegel and the 'Theory of Reflection,'" in Lucio Colletti, *Marxism and Hegel* (London: Verso Books, 1973), 52–67; and H. S. Harris, "Hegel's Correspondence Theory of Truth," in *Hegel's Phenomenology of Spirit: A Reappraisal*, ed. Gary K. Browning (Dordrecht: Kluwer, 1997), 11–22. It should be noted that Engels also attributes a "reflectionist" theory of knowledge to Hegel in *Ludwig Feuerbach and the End of Classical German Philosophy*, in Karl Marx and Frederick Engels, *Selected Writings* in 2 volumes (Moscow: Foreign Languages Publishing House, 1958), Vol. II, p. 370; also 363, 377, 387.

5

Le Guin's *The Dispossessed* and Utopian Literature

LE GUIN AND THE UTOPIAN TRADITION

I will begin this chapter by making a few preliminary remarks about how a familiarity with Le Guin's dialectical philosophical outlook helps us to better understand her views on literature, and especially the relationship which exists between her own work and the utopian/ dystopian literary tradition, an issue to which I shall return in the next chapter. Le Guin discusses this in an essay entitled "A Non-Euclidean View of California as a Cold Place to Be," both the title and the contents of which indicate that it was inspired by her reading of Zamyatin. Interestingly, she appears to think of Zamyatin here as being a utopian and not a dystopian writer, presumably on the grounds that his intention in *We* was to criticize present society by depicting an alternative, imaginary society with which the author's own society might be compared and be found wanting, which is what all utopian writers do. In what appears to be both a reference to and a partial critique of Zamyatin, Le Guin maintains in this essay that up until the present, "utopia has been Yang." From Plato onward, she continues, utopia "has been the big Yang motorcycle trip. Bright, dry, clear, strong, firm, active, aggressive, lineal, progressive, creative, expanding, advancing" and above all "hot."[1] Overlooking the fact that in *We* Zamyatin himself is critical of utopianism precisely because of the "Euclidean" thinking which he associates with it, Le Guin suggests that hitherto utopian speculation, including that of Zamyatin, "has been Euclidean, it has been European, and it has been masculine."[2]

It is obvious that there is a close association in Le Guin's mind between the form of utopian thinking which she considers here to be inadequate and the Sequency Theory of Time to which she refers in *The Dispossessed*. Against this type of utopian thinking, she opposes "another kind," which she says has yet to be developed. In contrast to the ideas associated with earlier utopian writing, Le Guin refers to a new "Yin utopia" which has not yet come into existence but which, she says, "would be dark, wet, obscure, weak, yielding, passive, participatory, circular, cyclical, peaceful, nurturant, retreating, contracting" and above all "cold."[3] Again it is clear that there is a close association between this alternative form of utopianism and, on this occasion, the Simultaneity Theory of Time which is referred to in *The Dispossessed*. This characterization suggests of course that for Le Guin, when considered from the standpoint of this new kind of "Yin utopia," what has hitherto been considered to be a utopian ideal should in fact be thought of as a *dystopian* state of affairs.

An unwary reader might think that Le Guin herself unequivocally endorses or identifies with this second form of utopian theorizing. This, however, would almost certainly be a mistake. That this is so is indicated by the fact that in *The Dispossessed* the General Temporal Theory which is developed by Shevek involves some kind of theoretical synthesis of these two opposed theories of time and of the underlying principles associated with them. In other words, Le Guin suggests in this text that although each of these two opposed ways of looking at the world is necessary, neither on its own is sufficient, either for an adequate account of the nature of time, or for an adequate account of the nature of utopia. In short, in Le Guin's opinion, we need *both*. To this end, inspired by her reading of the anthropological theories of Claude Lévi-Strauss, Le Guin suggests that in utopian writing there is a need for a "progressive integration of the best of the 'hot' with the best of the 'cold.'"[4]

For this reason I find it difficult to accept Donna R. White's assertion that Le Guin "admits that *The Dispossessed* is mostly a Yang utopia."[5] This is so partly because I do not think that Le Guin considers *The Dispossessed* to be a utopia at all (of which more later), and partly because it is clear from this *novel* that, throughout, Le Guin emphasizes the importance of the *interaction* between the two principles of the Yang and the Yin, each of which necessarily relies for its very existence upon the other. To be precise, what Le Guin actually says about this issue is that there are occasions in the novel when "its *excess* Yang shows" (my emphasis).[6] For the same reason I disagree with Naomi Jacobs's claim that *The Dispossessed* is an example of an approach which in "A Non-Euclidean View of California as a Cold Place to Be,"[7] Le Guin characterizes as "Western, linear and rational"—or, as White has put it, that it is *itself* "an example of the Euclidean utopia," or the Yang utopia, which Le Guin criticizes so strongly in this essay.[8]

On the other hand, however, in my view, both Jacobs and Donna Glee Williams go too far in the opposite direction when they suggest that, in the words of Williams, the "governing principles" of *The Dispossessed* are in effect exclusively those of a Yin utopia and "might be described as feminist, communal, centrally coordinated, anarchist, and Taoist."[9] For as Le Guin states in her "Introduction" to *Planet of Exile*, "Yin does not occur without Yang, nor Yang without Yin."[10] Indeed, Le Guin associates the idea of the separation of these two principles, Yin and Yang, with what she refers to as "alienation," something which she evidently considers to be undesirable. "Our curse," she says, "is alienation, the separation of Yang from Yin."[11] According to Le Guin, the drive to separate the two is connected not with the "search for balance and integration" but with a "struggle for dominance."

In short, as Le Guin herself understands it, *The Dispossessed* is neither a Yin utopia nor a Yang utopia. This raises the question of whether the third kind of thinking to which Le Guin alludes in the passage just cited, the one which constitutes the dialectical "integration" of the Yang and the Yin forms of utopian speculation, either should or even *could* itself be considered to be a new form of "utopian" writing. In my view there are good reasons for thinking that the answer to both of these questions is "no." One such reason is that Le Guin maintains that each of Yang and the Yin approaches can legitimately be said to be "utopian," despite the fact that they stand diametrically opposed to one another. This implies, however, that from the point of view of the Yang approach the Yin utopia is in fact not a utopia at all, but on the contrary a dystopia; and *vice versa*. In other words, each of these two forms of writing is *both* utopian *and* dystopian, depending on the point of view from which one considers them. Consequently, it could be said of neither of them that it is simply or solely *either* utopian on the one hand *or* dystopian on the other. But it follows from this that insofar as *The Dispossessed* incorporates each these two ways of thinking within itself, which it evidently does, given that Shevek's General Temporal Theory constitutes some kind of synthesis of them both, then it, too, could not be said to be either a literary utopia or a literary dystopia. Rather, it embraces within itself both forms of thinking and writing, together with the tension or contradiction which exists between them. What is required, therefore, is an appropriate label with which to characterize the character of Le Guin's text in this particular regard; and in my view the best way to do this is to say that *The Dispossessed* is a *novel* the main theme of which is precisely this tension between two different forms of utopian/dystopian thinking and writing, as it is played out in the lives of its individual characters, and especially its central character, Shevek. It is arguable, then, that the appropriate conclusion to draw from Le Guin's attempt to situate herself against the background of the utopian literary tradition in this essay is that *The Dispossessed* is not a literary utopia at all. It is rather a *novel* about utopianism in politics.

Toward the end of "A Non-Euclidean View of California as a Cold Place to Be," echoing similar remarks made by Wells in *A Modern Utopia*, Le Guin makes the following extremely interesting observation: "We're in a rational dilemma, an either/or situation as perceived by the binary computer mentality, and neither the either nor the or is a place where people can live."[12] This suggests that she considers it to be her task in *The Dispossessed* to portray a situation where admittedly "imaginary" (and yet in some extremely important sense nevertheless "real" or "realistic") people could and do live. This is another way of saying that for Le Guin the imaginary individuals who inhabit the two worlds of *The Dispossessed* are indeed genuine characters, or "real" people, with all that this involves, rather than mere vehicles for the expression of the abstract ideas associated either with utopian/dystopian theorizing, or with any political ideology, including anarchism. Again, however, this implies that Le Guin does not think of *The Dispossessed* as being either a utopia or a dystopia at all—of either the Yang or the Yin variety. For each of these two forms of speculation might be said to be an abstraction from that "real world," which is always her main concern. Each taken in isolation fails to capture something which is captured by the other, and which Le Guin considers to be of fundamental importance for anyone who is interested in confronting, in and through a work of literature, the ethical dilemmas with which people have to deal in that real world.

It is in the light of this, I think, that we should interpret Le Guin's remark, made in the same essay, that "the major *utopic element* in my novel *The Dispossessed* is a variety of pacifist anarchism, which is about as Yin as a political ideology can get" (my emphasis).[13] Laurence Davis appeals to the remark of Le Guin's cited above in order to justify his claimed that *The Dispossessed* is indeed a literary utopia. It seems to me, though, that in fact Le Guin's remark does not justify this claim at all. For what Le Guin actually says is that her text, which she characterizes as being not a literary utopia but a novel, contains a "major utopic *element*" (my emphasis). To my mind this indicates that Le Guin thinks that her novel also contains *another* element which is *not* utopic or utopian. But if that is so then it seems inappropriate to characterize *The Dispossessed* as a literary utopia. It would be much more accurate to say that it is a *novel*. As such it is a complex or articulated whole which contains both utopian and dystopian elements within itself. Consequently it cannot be simply identified with either one or the other of these two component elements. One of these elements might be said to be a type of utopia, namely that of the Yin variety referred to above. It is evident that, personally, Le Guin has a great deal of sympathy with this particular form of utopian speculation; but that is not to say that, as a novelist, she simply identifies herself with it. For she appreciates that, considered in isolation, it has definite limitations. It, too, presents, and could only ever present, just one-half of the story.

Nor again, therefore, despite Le Guin's statement in this same essay that "in these areas anarchism and Taoism converge," and hence her connection of this form of pacifist anarchism with Taoism, of which of course she approves, does Le Guin go so far as to actually *identify* Taoism with the type of thinking which she associates with her notion of a Yin utopia. Such a conclusion would not be justified, as it suggests, undialectically, that the principle of the Yin could be entirely separated from that of the Yang, and that the two principles of Yin and Yang, and the forms of life associated with them, might actually be capable of existing independently of one another—and hence that it makes sense to consider the practical possibility of a life, or a society, that is to say a sociological as opposed to a literary utopia, organized entirely in accordance with Yin principles, within which those aspects of human existence which Le Guin associates with the notion of Yang are entirely absent.

As Le Guin herself suggests in this same essay, to be "utopian" in this sense is to be "unrealistic." It is to envisage, not a state of affairs which though possible is not yet actual, but rather a state of affairs which is "impractical" precisely because it is not empirically *possible* for such a state of affairs ever to occur. From this point of view, which is in fact a quite traditional way of thinking about the idea of utopia and that which is utopian, a "utopian" society is by definition one which could never actually exist. At the same time however, as H. G. Wells suggests in his *A Modern Utopia,* the political struggle which is an attempt to achieve or create such a society certainly can, and does exist; and it is this real life struggle which is what Le Guin seeks to dramatize in her novel. For despite the fact, or perhaps even because of the fact, that it is inevitably doomed to failure, this struggle to create a better world constitutes a core element in the tragedy which is human life. On this reading of her work Le Guin would agree with Lyman Tower Sargent's observation that the quest for utopia might be said to be the "ultimate tragedy of human existence, constantly holding out the hope of a good life and repeatedly failing to achieve it."[14]

It is precisely by writing a *novel* dealing with this particular theme that Le Guin seeks to transcend the "either-or" type of thinking which she associates with all forms of utopian/dystopian theorizing and embrace a thoroughgoing dialectical approach when seeking to understand and dramatically portray the ethical dilemmas which are associated with human existence. There is, therefore, a great deal to be said for James Bittner's assertion that, generally speaking, Le Guin "wants to teach" (though I think "encourage" is a better word) her reader to think "dialectically," or, as Bittner puts it, "to think *both-and* rather than *either-or*" when it comes to the fundamental problems of morality and politics.[15] This is, of course, yet another reason for associating Le Guin with the name of Hegel. This is not to claim that Le Guin's thinking has been influenced directly by a reading of Hegel, but simply that it is in some respects quite similar to that of Hegel—the link being provided, perhaps, by the fact that the views of them both have something in common with Taoist philosophy, properly understood.

LE GUIN AND THE IDEA OF AN AMBIGUOUS UTOPIA

The subtitle of *The Dispossessed* when it was first published was *An Ambiguous Utopia*. The fact that Le Guin gave her work this subtitle is obviously significant. It is not clear, however, exactly what its significance is. As Simon Stow has rightly observed, the meaning of the subtitle is "perhaps, as ambiguous as the utopia itself."[16] One reason for this has to do with the fact that the word "utopia" might refer *either* to the anarchist society on Anarres which Le Guin portrays within the novel *or* to the novel itself. Consequently, if one asks "Is *The Dispossessed* a Utopia?" it is not entirely clear whether one has in mind the question "Is Anarres a utopian society, a sociological utopia?" or the somewhat different (though obviously related) question, "Is *The Dispossessed* a utopian text, a literary utopia?" Patrick Parrinder has expressed surprise that some "political scientists" seem "quite innocent of the idea that a utopia is a particular kind of text rather than a kind of society."[17] However, this remark is not entirely accurate. It would be more accurate to say that the word "utopia" is used to designate a particular kind of text *as well as* (rather than *instead of*) a particular kind of society. However, that aside, Parrinder's observation is sound. Moreover, it does not just apply to some political scientists. I would say that it also applies to the vast majority, if not all, of those who have commented on the work of Le Guin.

There is also some confusion surrounding the issue of whether Le Guin's own views with respect to these two questions is a privileged one. It is not entirely clear whether we simply want to know what Le Guin, as the author of the text in question, thinks about them, or whether we are seeking answers which, although they take Le Guin's opinions into account, are nevertheless also independent ones—answers which could in principle, and might in fact, disagree with Le Guin's stated views. However, even if we sought to clarify matters by first focusing on the views of Le Guin herself and second conceptually separating the question "Is Anarres a utopia (a utopian society)?" from the question "Is *The Dispossessed* a utopia (a utopian text)?" a lack of clarity would still remain. For the answer which Le Guin gives to each of these questions is itself ambiguous. In the case of the first question, it is not at all clear whether Le

Guin thinks that the society on Anarres is an example of a utopian society and intends to present it to her readers as such. Nor, in the case of the second question, is it clear whether Le Guin thinks that *The Dispossessed* is a literary utopia and wishes to present it to her readers as such.

To illustrate this confusion we can cite the work of Brennan and Downs, and that of Tom Moylan. At one point, for example, Brennan and Downs maintain that the society on Anarres in *The Dispossessed* "is *unambiguously a utopia*" (my emphasis).[18] Elsewhere, however, they suggest that as a text, considered from the point of view of its aesthetic form, *The Dispossessed* is not a literary utopia at all, but a novel. It is, they say, "novelistic" rather than "visionary," in the sense in which utopian texts are usually thought to be "visionary."[19] At the same time, however, Brennan and Downs do not make an explicit distinction between these two different senses of the meaning of the word "utopia." Consequently, in their work the difficulties associated with making these apparently contradictory statements are left unresolved. Similarly, Moylan states that in *The Dispossessed* "a *utopia* is in full operation on the first page of the text, in this case the *utopian society* of Anarres" (my emphasis).[20] Moylan also maintains that as a text *The Dispossessed* can be straightforwardly thought of as an example of a literary utopia, albeit of a new kind, a "critical utopia." Considered as a "critical utopia," he says, *The Dispossessed* "does not negate or transform the utopian mode as much as it preserves and revitalizes it."[21] Elsewhere, however, Moylan also asserts the contrary view that in *The Dispossessed* Le Guin "constructs a narrative that goes *beyond* utopian and dystopian exposition" (my emphasis).[22] In my view, the latter assessment is preferable to the former. It is much better to say that *The Dispossessed* is a *novel* about utopianism than it is to say that it represents a new kind of literary utopia. Moreover, this claim is compatible with Moylan's perceptive comment that in *The Dispossessed* Le Guin "preserves, negates and transforms the utopian mode" of writing, *provided* this is taken to mean that the utopian principle, together with its opposite, the dystopian principle, is a component element, or "moment" in the Hegelian sense, of the structure of the novel as a whole. From this point of view, the utopian principle is "sublated" or *aufgehoben* within Le Guin's text, which might in consequence be thought of as going beyond it, whilst at the same time incorporating its essential features within itself.

There are two quite different ways of interpreting the significance of Le Guin's employment of the notion of ambiguity in the subtitle of *The Dispossessed*. It might be suggested, first, that in Le Guin's view *The Dispossessed* is undoubtedly a literary utopia. There is no doubt at all about its status *as* a utopia—no ambiguity of *that* kind. However, on this reading, there are certain respects in which *The Dispossessed* is obviously different from other works of literature which have in the past been characterized as utopias. For example, it does not unequivocally depict any ideal or perfect society, or even what is obviously a better society than the one inhabited by its author. Moreover, unlike earlier utopian works, *The Dispossessed* is a novel. And as we shall see there is at least some doubt that it is possible for a text to be both a literary utopia and a novel at the same time. From the standpoint of this first reading, then, *The Dispossessed* has an ambiguous status because it is associated with a new departure in the genre of utopian fiction, precisely because it is a "utopian novel"—just as on occasion Le Guin suggests that Zamyatin's *We* was the first "dystopian novel."[23] What its subtitle indicates, therefore, is the existence of a certain degree of uncertainty in Le Guin's mind. However, this uncertainty does not have to do with the status of *The Dispossessed* as a literary utopia. It has, rather, to do with Le Guin's understanding of what it is for any work to *be* a literary utopia. It has to do with the meaning of the concept of a literary utopia. Employing the terminology of Gottlöb Frege, a proponent of this reading would say that when she wrote *The Dispossessed* in the 1970s Le Guin was absolutely certain in her own mind about the "reference" of the term "utopia" and its applicability to *The Dispossessed*. What she was uncertain about was the term's "sense."[24]

In the second place, however, the employment of the notion of ambiguity in the subtitle of *The Dispossessed* might be read as suggesting that at this time Le Guin was doubtful about whether it is legitimate to consider this text to be a literary utopia in the strict sense of the term at all, precisely because it differs from earlier texts which have been characterized as utopias in the two respects indicated above. It might be interpreted as an admission on Le Guin's part that she was uncertain in her own mind whether it is appropriate to think of *The Dispossessed* as being a literary utopia, as opposed to a novel, precisely because it appeared to her then to be logically impossible that it could be both. Again employing the terminology of Frege, we might say that on this second reading that although Le Guin was at this time certain about the "sense" of the term "utopia," she was nevertheless uncertain about its "reference," that is to say its applicability to *The Dispossessed*.

It is interesting to at least consider the possibility that *The Dispossessed* might be thought of as not being a literary utopia *at all* precisely because it is a *novel*, and that Le Guin might actually have been right about this issue in the 1970s, if only because this is a view which is not commonly found in the secondary literature on Le Guin. For the vast majority of those who have commented on Le Guin's work do consider *The Dispossessed* to be at least *some* kind of literary utopia. Moreover, the minority of commentators who do not read the text in this way have a tendency to do the opposite. They merely invert (rather than displace) this more popular reading and argue that the text should be read as an example of a literary *dystopia* rather than as a utopia. It is rare indeed to find a commentator suggesting that it is neither one of these things, or that it is both at the same time. My argument in this chapter has two components. First I shall address the issue of whether Le Guin considers the society on Anarres which is portrayed in *The Dispossessed* to be a utopian society, a sociological utopia. I shall argue that she does not. Second I will turn to consider the issue of the status of *The Dispossessed* as a literary production. Here I shall argue that when she wrote *The Dispossessed* in the 1970s Le Guin thought of herself as being primarily a novelist who was writing about utopianism rather than the author of a literary utopia.

IS ANARRES A UTOPIAN SOCIETY?

Le Guin concedes that it could not straightforwardly be asserted that the society on Anarres is an example of a sociological utopia, because that society is neither perfect nor ideal. Indeed, there are respects in which it is not even "better" than the society on Urras. It is, in short, only a utopia for those who look at the world from the standpoint of the Anarresti and the values associated with their particular version of anarchism. It might be said that as a *political activist*, of course, given that she too is an anarchist, Le Guin agrees with those who take this view. As a *novelist*, however, she appreciates that others will not. In order to emphasize this point, Le Guin refuses to depict the society on Anarres *au couleur de rose*. She does not present it to her readers *as* a utopia, but only as a society inhabited by people who do consider it to be one. At least they consider Anarres to be on the whole preferable to Urras (more accurately A-Io) despite the obvious drawbacks associated with living there. For example, as numerous commentators have observed, life is extremely hard on Anarres, which is depicted by Le Guin as a dry and barren planet capable of sustaining only a low material standard of living in comparison with that available to the inhabitants of Urras.[25]

The account of the views of Zamyatin and Le Guin regarding the nature of scientific knowledge presented in chapter 4 has a direct bearing on the question of whether Le Guin thinks that the society on Anarres is best characterized as a utopia, or a dystopia, or as something else. As we saw earlier, when discussing the problem of "star-planet duality" within the discipline of astronomy, in Le Guin's view both Anarres and Urras could be described as being either the earth or the moon, depending on one's point of view. The inhabitants of Anarres and Urras will "see" things differently from one another. They are locked into a "system" which comprises these two contradictory sets of beliefs and their respective judgments regarding "the Truth" of the matter will flatly contradict one another. For someone who appreciates this, as Le Guin does, it makes no sense for someone who is located within this particular system to claim that objectively speaking Anarres is either *"the* moon" or that it is *"the* earth," and similarly for Urras. This is so because from the standpoint of the Anarresti, it is Anarres which is the earth and Urras which is the moon; whereas from the standpoint of the Urrasti the opposite is the case. We also saw that the conclusion which Le Guin draws from this is not the "relativist" one that there is no such thing as objective truth. It is rather that the objective "Truth" in this case is associated with the perspective of an observer who is able to place her or himself outside or above this belief system and "see" that there is at least something to be said for each of these points of view despite the fact that they contradict one another. For Le Guin, as for Hegel, truth lies in the "totality" or the "whole."

Exactly the same thing might be said, however, of the social systems of Anarres and Urras within *The Dispossessed,* and of the moral values associated with them. For here also the two planets and their respective societies (in the case of Urras, the society of A-Io) might be thought of as being placed together within the same ethical system, which is the analogue of the solar system referred to by both Zamyatin and Le Guin when discussing scientific truth within the discipline of astronomy. Each, therefore, represents a moral "truth" the validity of which the other denies. If one were to characterize these societies by the labels "utopia" and "dystopia," then by an analogous line of reasoning to that presented in the preceding section, one might conclude that what the inhabitant of one society considers to be a utopia, the inhabitants of the other society consider to be a dystopia, and *vice versa.* Here also, therefore, Le Guin suggests, the conclusion at which one arrives depends upon one's point of view. For the Anarresti, of course, their own society is a utopia and that of A-Io on Urras a dystopia. But for the Urrasti, who have different (indeed opposed) ethical and political values, the society on Anarres is a dystopia, whereas it is their own society that is a utopia.

It is presumably for this reason that, as a number of commentators have noted, Le Guin takes such great pains to present the negative aspects of life in Anarresti society as well as the positive ones. So much so that, as we shall see, some of them have drawn the conclusion that in fact Le Guin's intention must have been to portray the society on Anarres as being not utopian at all but rather, on the contrary, *dystopian.* Barbara Bucknall has rightly observed in respect to this issue that "each of the planets is the other's moon, and how things look depend on where you stand."[26] She also maintains, however, that "this does not mean" that Le Guin herself "does not have preferences."[27] Bucknall expresses surprise that some students who have read *The Dispossessed* have drawn the conclusion either that its purpose was to promote "the capitalist society" on Urras, or alternatively to demonstrate that "one man's utopia was another man's dystopia."[28] To my mind, however, this is an indication that no matter what her preferences as an anarchist political activist might be, Le Guin did her job very well as a *novelist* when she wrote *The Dispossessed*.

According to this line of reasoning, it is impossible to characterize absolutely the societies on Anarres and Urras as being either utopias or dystopias. We cannot say of Anarres that it is obviously *the* utopia and of Urras that it is obviously *the* dystopia within this particular ethical system. For anyone who remains locked into the system of ethical beliefs of which they are the component parts, there is no possibility of achieving any kind of objectivity in respect to this issue. That does not mean, however, Le Guin suggests, that all objectivity is impossible. For here again it is possible for a third person, a detached observer, to place themselves outside this particular conceptual "box," to rise up above it and look down upon it, and to see "the Truth" which lies within the whole. Indeed, for Le Guin the principal task of the novelist is to embrace and dramatically portray paradoxes of this kind, that is to say moral dilemmas, without simplistically taking either one side or the other, or making the mistake of thinking that the contradiction between them could be reconciled or resolved.

Susan Wood has rightly stated that "Anarres is neither a utopia, an impossible no-place, nor a dystopia." It is, rather, "a functioning, and convincing, society."[29] Similarly, Neil Easterbrook has suggested that Urras and Anarres might be thought of as being "dialectical binary opposites."[30] And James Bittner has correctly remarked that "not only is the dystopia on Urras a necessary precondition for the utopian society on Anarres, they are complementary, for they both orbit around a common centre of gravity."[31] The two planets, Anarres and Urras, are indeed both essential component parts of the same *ethical* as well as the same solar system. Where Bittner seems to me to go wrong, however, is when he suggests that for Le Guin it is the planet Anarres which is (or must be) the utopian society within this system, and Urras which is (or must be) the dystopian society. It would be more accurate to say that Anarres and Urras each possess both utopian and dystopian aspects.

In much the same vein, Warren G. Rochelle has argued that, for Le Guin, given that Anarres and Urras are *both* "utopias *and* dystopias" (my emphasis) at the same time, "depending on one's perspective," they present to the reader of *The Dispossessed* "not constant extremes," but rather "the ambiguity of human life."[32] Rochelle associates this idea with what he claims is Le Guin's "inversion" of the "conventions" of the traditional literary utopia. In my view, however, this is an indication that Le Guin's *The Dispossessed* should not be regarded as a literary utopia at all, but, rather, as a *novel* about utopianism in politics. As such it represents, not an inversion of the conventions of the traditional utopia, but their displacement altogether.

Winter Elliott has said that "in their own ways" *both* of the two worlds portrayed in *The Dispossessed* are "attempts at utopia," or might be thought of as being utopias, depending on one's point of view. He also states that Le Guin's text offers some kind of "mediation" between these "two utopias." Elliott rightly claims that in Le Guin's view each of these worlds "is essential to the survival of the other" and suggests that in her novel Le Guin "is not ultimately interested in which world has the best, or even better, political system," but rather in her central character Shevek and his "role within those worlds."[33] These remarks seem to me to offer a fairly accurate assessment of what Le Guin is up to in *The Dispossessed*. However, Elliott does not distinguish between the idea of a *sociological* utopia and that of a *literary* utopia. Nor does he consider the possibility that the word "dystopia" might have been substituted for "utopia" throughout these remarks. In other words, it could be said with as much justification that both Anarres and Urras in *The Dispossessed* might be considered to be *dystopian* societies, again depending on one's point of view. In my opinion, this supports the claim that *The Dispossessed* is best thought of as being neither a literary utopia nor a literary dystopia, but rather a *novel* about utopianism/dystopianism in politics. It should also be noted that Elliott confuses matters somewhat by also saying, without noticing the logical inconsistency involved, that *The Dispossessed* is not merely a "*discussion* of utopia," as it were, but *also* "a *representation* of an idealized utopia" (my emphasis). In other words in his view it might legitimately be said to be a literary utopia after all.

More than one commentator has considered the geographical or spatial location of Le Guin's alleged "utopian" society in *The Dispossessed*. Everett L. Hamner, for example, has emphasized that "it is worth noting how unusual Le Guin's fiction is in its *equal* attention to utopian and dystopian spaces. Generally utopian and dystopian novels focus on one world or the other."[34] From the standpoint of the present reading, Hamner's employment of the word "novel" is inappropriate here. So also is the spatial metaphor associated with the uses of the expression "utopian dystopian spaces." In my view it would be better to talk about utopia and dystopia as two *principles* which might be conjoined in the *same* space (or even in the same character or person) rather than in distinct and separate geographical spaces.

The views of Bulent Somay on this subject are of particular interest. Somay's starting point is the assumption that *The Dispossessed* contains a literary depiction of a sociological utopia. Somay is aware, however, that Le Guin portrays the society on Anarres in a bad light, in at least some respects—just as she portrays the society on Urras in a good one. But this immediately raises the question: If *The Dispossessed* does contain a portrayal of a utopian society, where is this utopia spatially located? Is it to be placed on Anarres, or on Urras, or if not either of these, then where? According to Somay, given Le Guin's somewhat negative depiction of life on the planet Anarres, it would seem that the utopia in question must be placed somewhere else. Somay claims, for example, that Le Guin "is try-ing to place" what he refers to as the "utopian horizon" *not* on Anarres "but elsewhere."[35] He also states that because "Anarres does not pretend to be a utopia" it follows that the utopia with which Le Guin's work deals "must be located *somewhere*,"[36] (my emphasis) that is to say somewhere *else*. But where? Somay is unclear what the answer to this question is. At one point he suggests that Le Guin's utopia is in fact located "in the void between Anarres and Urras," or in "the fantasy space" between them "which has no actuality."[37] If this amounts to suggesting no more than that for Le Guin the notions of utopia and dystopia, being dialectically re-lated, must necessarily stand or fall together; and that, consequently, in order to spatially locate utopia within *The Dispossessed* one must consider the system which is formed by the conjunction of the two planets, Anar-res and Urras, as being an ethical totality or whole, then as we have seen there is something to be said for this view. On another occasion, however, Somay also says that "the much needed 'third element' through which the enclosure of the Anarres/Urras binary system can be transcended," is nothing less than "the whole universe." According to Somay, for the pur-poses of such a "transcendence" one "planet" is "not enough." Indeed, "not even a solar system could serve." For, as H. G. Wells once observed (transposing Trotsky's opposition to the Stalinist notion of "Socialism in One Country" into the much more ambitious slogan of "Utopianism in One Universe"), "utopia is either everywhere at the same time, filling all the space within an absolute limit, or it cannot exist at all."[38]

It might be suggested, however, that this problem concerning the spa-tial location of utopia in *The Dispossessed* is one to which there is no an-swer. The reason for this is that the problem is generated by the *assump-tion*, made by Somay at the outset, that *The Dispossessed* is indeed a literary utopia which depicts an ideal or a "better" society somewhere or other. For if this is indeed the case then it follows that the utopian society in question *must* indeed have a definite geographical or spatial location. In my view, the appropriate way to deal with this problem is not to actually solve it, by pointing out the actual location of Le Guin's "utopia" within the text, but rather to "dis-solve" by pointing out that *The Dispossessed* is not a literary utopia at all, but rather a *novel* about utopianism in politics. On this reading *The Dispossessed* does not even attempt to depict a utopian society, and consequently to ask the question where in the work this al-leged utopian society is spatially located makes no sense at all. For Le Guin, the idea of utopia has to do more with an ethical and/or psychic principle than with any spatially located society. Moreover, because *The*

Dispossessed is a novel, rather than attempt to portray an ideal society or even a better society than the author's own, its task is to dramatically portray the ethical dilemmas confronted by its individual characters, especially of course the physicist Shevek, who are involved in an attempt to create what *they* consider to be a "better" society in an imperfect world.

IS *THE DISPOSSESSED* A LITERARY UTOPIA?

Most of those who have written about Le Guin's *The Dispossessed* are of the opinion that it is *obvious* that it is a literary utopia of *some* kind. Laurence Davis, for example, has maintained that "*The Dispossessed* is a utopia and it is intended as such."[39] And there is, of course, support for this view in the writings of Le Guin herself. For example, there is the fact that Le Guin gave *The Dispossessed* the subtitle *An Ambiguous Utopia,* which at first sight seems to be unambiguous enough. Then there is the fact that in her interview with Jonathan Ward, when asked about the status of the work, Le Guin replies by saying "I think it is what you would *have* to call a utopia; an ambiguous utopia" (my emphasis).[40] There is also the fact that in her essay "Science Fiction and Mrs. Brown," Le Guin states quite clearly that *The Dispossessed* "is a utopia of sorts."[41] And in the same essay she refers to Shevek as being "a citizen of Utopia."[42] Given these remarks of Le Guin, it is perhaps not too surprising that Davis has argued that Le Guin herself "has consistently referred to the novel as a utopia."[43] Nor is it at all surprising that other commentators on the work of Le Guin have also taken this view.

Those who think that *The Dispossessed* is a literary utopia fall into two categories. The first includes those who think that Le Guin's work represents a return to the writing of traditional literary utopias which occurred in the 1970s after a period during which this form of writing had become unfashionable, and in which the dominant literary form had been that of the dystopia. From this point of view, there is nothing especially new about the stylistic form of *The Dispossessed* and Le Guin makes no contribution to the historical development of this particular genre of writing.[44] The second category includes those commentators who think that although *The Dispossessed* is indeed a literary utopia, nevertheless it is one of a quite new type. Le Guin has, therefore, made a significant contribution to the evolution of this particular literary genre. Commentators who take this view have characterized *The Dispossessed* in different ways, for example, as a "flawed utopia,"[45] an "open ended" utopia,[46] or a "post dystopian utopia."[47] Of particular interest in this connection are the writings of Tom Moylan, whose views have been influential.[48] In Moylan's opinion *The Dispossessed* is best characterized as a new kind of literary utopia. It is, he claims, a "critical utopia," but a utopia nonetheless. Consequently, by writing this book Le Guin did indeed make a significant contribution to the historical evolution of the utopian genre. It is not always clear, however, what exactly, according to Moylan, this contribution is supposed to have been; or what in his opinion is new about *The Dispossessed* which differentiates it from earlier literary utopias. Nor is it always clear what it is that makes *The Dispossessed* "critical" when it is compared with traditional literary utopias. As we shall see, Moylan says different things about these issues at different times. For the time being, however, we may note that at least one of the things which Moylan has in mind here is the fact that the allegedly utopian society on Anarres which is portrayed in this work is not by any means an ideal or perfect, but a society which is flawed in a number of significant ways.

The view that *The Dispossessed* is indeed a literary utopia, either a traditional one or one which for some reason must be considered to be of a new kind, is one which is widely held in the secondary literature on Le Guin.[49] It is also occasionally held by Le Guin herself, something which if it has not led commentators on her writings to hold this view, will have no doubt at least reinforced the convictions which they hold about it. But that does not mean, of course, that Le Guin's judgment about this issue is obviously correct, or that simply to consider what Le Guin herself occasionally thinks about this issue is the end of the matter. For although Le Guin does undeniably suggest at times that *The Dispossessed* is a literary utopia, nevertheless this view is not consistent with some of the other things which she says elsewhere.

Indeed, a number of commentators have taken the opposite view and insisted that far from being a utopia *The Dispossessed* is in fact the opposite, a literary dystopia. George Turner, for example, has claimed that *The Dispossessed* "is *totally* anti-utopian, dystopian"[50] (my emphasis). Chris Ferns has stated that *The Dispossessed* "has much in common with the dystopian parodies of the utopian ideal," like Zamyatin's *We*, which "emerge in the twentieth century."[51] Brennan and Downs have claimed that Le Guin's intention when she wrote the novel was to offer a "penetrating critique of all utopian experience."[52] Keith Booker has argued, more cautiously, that *The Dispossessed* is one of the most "important feminist texts" of recent times which have been "significantly informed by dystopian energies."[53] And Ken MacLeod has maintained that it is the "relentless presence of morality" in *The Dispossessed* which makes the "communism of Anarres" so "oppressive."[54]

Of particular interest in this context are the views of Gerard Klein, who has argued that a "specter" haunts science fiction, a specter which more than any other author of science fiction "Le Guin helps to exorcise," namely that of "the ideal society."[55] This specter, Klein goes on, "ridiculously clothes itself in scientific hand-me-downs or rather in pseudo-scientific metaphor appropriated from the natural sciences. If we are to believe these zealots, from their various ideological perspectives, there exists a precise solution to all human problems, in particular social ones: the main question is to utilize the science which would supply these solutions."[56] All these propositions are, Klein maintains, "based on the hypothesis of the objectivity of the social realm." Thus they "exhibit a strong odor of metaphysics."[57] According to this view, "the world is understood to have been made in a certain manner whose laws it would suffice to know and respect in order to gain mastery over it."[58] In Klein's opinion, in the realm of science fiction Philip K. Dick "did much to shake such a confidence in 'reality,'" but "it was" above all Ursula K. Le Guin "who introduced the consequences of its destruction into the practice of conjectural literature."[59]

Klein's assessment seems to me to ignore completely the contribution made by Zamyatin to the process of challenging the influence of "realism" in the natural sciences, and the ethical ideal of "utopia" with which that realist attitude is associated once it is transferred either to the social sphere or to the world of literature. It also, it seems to me, gets completely wrong Le Guin's understanding of the nature of science and scientific knowledge, which differs from that of Zamyatin precisely because it is objectivist and realist rather than relativist and constructivist. Klein's remarks here imply that there is no significant difference at all between Zamyatin and Le Guin, both so far as their views on natural science is concerned and so far as their views on ethics and the desirability or undesirability of political "utopianism" is concerned. Le Guin is presented as a straightforwardly dystopian writer whose concerns are much the same as those addressed by Zamyatin in his novel *We*. We have seen, however, that no matter how much Le Guin might have been inspired by the views of Zamyatin with respect to some issues, it would nevertheless be a mistake simply to *identify* them as, by implication at least, Klein's reading of Le Guin does here. This is not an accurate way of thinking about the complex relationship which exists between Zamyatin and Le Guin. Hence also it is not an accurate way of characterizing the views of Le Guin independently of those of Zamyatin.

Given the existence of a sizable minority of commentators who take the view that *The Dispossessed* is a *dystopian* text, Avery Plaw is right to observe that "critics have been divided over whether its intention is utopian or dystopian."[60] Focusing on the issue of Le Guin's intentions, Plaw's view is that Le Guin did not consider the society on Anarres to be a utopian society when she wrote *The Dispossessed*, and his conclusion is that it would be inappropriate, for this very reason, to classify this text as a literary utopia. Le Guin's "depiction of Anarres," he says, was "not meant to be utopian, at least in the conventional sense of a perfect (and usually static) political society."[61] What then, in his view, *was* it meant to be? Plaw is not clear in his own mind about this. He states that he is "not really sure whether such a *society* would be properly described as utopian or "ambiguously utopian" or as "anti-utopian" because of Le Guin's rejection of "any vision of final perfection."[62] These remarks elide the question of whether the society on Anarres is a (sociological) utopia and the different (though related) question of whether *The Dispossessed* is a (literary) utopia. Plaw's uncertainty over the issue of whether *The Dispossessed* is either a literary utopia or a dystopia arises from his implicit assumption that it *must* be either one or the other, and that there is no third alternative. But there *is* a third alternative—which is to say that it is a *novel* which deals with the tension between the utopian and the dystopian impulses, as this is played out in the lives of individual characters who inhabit two different societies which might be characterized as being either utopian or dystopian, depending on one's point of view.

The fact that some commentators believe Le Guin to be a dystopian writer and *The Dispossessed* to be, like Zamyatin's *We*, an example of a literary dystopia, is enough to indicate that the question of what is "the Truth," so far as the status of *The Dispossessed* as a literary production is concerned, can itself be answered in diametrically opposed ways. We need, therefore, to be cautious when addressing this question and not simply assume at the outset that *The Dispossessed must* be a literary utopia simply because Le Guin herself sometimes says so. For to say that the text is a literary utopia, as opposed to a dystopia, or to assume that it must be either one or the other, is to think "undialectically." Such a view is not consistent with Le Guin's views on truth generally, with her views regarding truth in the natural sciences, or with her views regarding truth in the sphere of morality and politics.

But if *The Dispossessed* is not a literary utopia, then what is it? I have already suggested that the answer to this question is that it is best thought of as a *novel* the main theme of which is the moral dilemmas generated by the workings of the utopian impulse in politics. Such a reading relies heavily on the view that Le Guin does at times make a clear distinction between literary productions which are *novels* and those which are *utopias*. My next task, therefore, is to explain just what Le Guin has in mind when she makes this distinction. A useful preliminary to this is to say something about Le Guin's views on science fiction as a literary genre before turning to consider the relevance of her views about that subject for her understanding of utopian literature.

LE GUIN AND THE IDEA OF A SCIENCE FICTION NOVEL

Like Zamyatin, one of the questions that Le Guin has an interest in is, "Can a science fiction writer write a *novel*?" This is a question which she discusses in an important essay entitled "Science Fiction and Mrs. Brown," first published in 1976.[63] This question is related to two others, which seem similar but should not be confused with one another. The first is "what is the aim of science fiction?" What is it that science fiction authors write about, or should write about? The second is "can the author of a work of science fiction be a 'good' writer?" Or are all works of science fiction necessarily "pulp fiction," and, therefore, by their very nature not to be taken seriously as works of literature? Before turning to consider Le Guin's views I shall say a little more about these two issues.

So far as the issue of what it is that works of science fiction are supposed to do, a number of commentators have held the view that works of this kind are *not* novels. These are quite distinct genres of writing, each with its own stylistic conventions, which differ fundamentally from one another. For novelists are primarily interested in such things as character and plot rather than scientific ideas and the technological inventions associated with them, whereas for the authors of works of science fiction the reverse is the case. For example, in *New Maps of Hell* Kingsley Amis cites favorably Edmund Crispin's view that "characters in science fiction stories are *usually* treated rather as representatives of their species rather than as individuals in their own right. They are matchstick men and matchstick women."[64] According to Amis, "science fiction shows us human beings in their relations not with one another, but with a thing, a monster, an alien, a plague, or a form of society."[65] In works of science fiction then, unlike works of "ordinary fiction," much less attention is paid to "matters of human situation or character." Rather it is a particular "idea" which is "the hero of the story."[66] Amis argues that if this notion of the "idea as hero" is not the basis for all science fiction, it is nevertheless the basis for "a great deal" of it.[67] It is this more than anything else which distinguishes science fiction from "general fiction." For the "whole tenor" of a book which was intended to be a work of science fiction would be "set awry" if its author were to indulge in "the kind of specifying, distinguishing, questioning form of characterization to which general fiction has accustomed us."[68] Similarly, J. O. Bailey has observed that "the interest of science fiction is chiefly in things, *ideas* and discoveries, rather than in *people*. For this reason, perhaps, though a few characters found in this fiction are memorable, many are not even individuals, but *types*" (my emphasis).[69] In words which echo those of Zamyatin in his essay on H. G. Wells, Bailey argues that although "occasionally" in a work of science fiction "a character *develops*, grows more mature," for the most part "characters in science fiction are *static*" (my emphasis).[70]

There is, then, a widespread popular belief that the intentions of the authors of works of science fiction are quite different from those of novelists. And it is this belief which has led some commentators to take the view that the former are not "good" writers, or that they do not have the right to be considered as the authors of serious works of "literature." However, the fallaciousness of the reasoning which lies behind this judgment is readily apparent. For if the intentions of the authors of works of science fiction are quite different from those of novelists then it is obviously unreasonable to criticize science fiction writers for not writing good novels, as if they had tried to do so but had not succeeded.

The context required for understanding Le Guin's views on the subject of whether it is possible for a particular text to be categorized as both a work of science fiction and a novel at the same time is precisely this widely held assumption that science fiction is necessarily "pulp fiction" and, therefore, could not possibly be thought of as serious literature, and that generally speaking the authors of works of science fiction are not good writers. This is an issue which has an obvious application to *The Dispossessed* and it is not at all surprising that Le Guin has always had an interest in it. In "Science Fiction and Mrs. Brown," which is an important contribution to the debate over this issue, like Zamyatin, Le Guin makes a very clear distinction between literary productions of this implicitly "inferior" kind and a novel, or more accurately a good novel. In works of "science fiction," which are of an inferior kind, there is indeed a tendency for the ideas (usually relating to some scientific discovery or invention) to take over. In such works, the development of character is very weak. The authors of such texts tend to treat their own creations, not as individuals, but as "cardboard cutout" figures that are merely a mouthpiece for the expression of the abstract ideas which are what the text is really about. As Le Guin understands it, however, a *novel* ought to attempt not to do this; and a good novel will, in fact, refrain from doing it. Following Virginia Woolf, whose essay "Mr. Bennett and Mrs. Brown," published in 1924,[71] provides the inspiration for the title of her own essay, Le Guin insists that the specific literary form known as the novel is primarily about *character*, and it is this, above all, which makes the classical novels of the nineteenth century associated with European Realism the "good" works of literature which they are.[72]

This conceptual distinction which Le Guin makes between those literary productions which are novels and those which are works of science fiction clearly implies that, whatever her views might be now, at the time that she wrote *The Dispossessed* in the 1970s, Le Guin took very seriously the possibility that the idea of a "science fiction *novel*" might be a contradiction in terms.[73] Some of Le Guin's remarks about this issue in "Science Fiction and Mrs. Brown" suggest that in her view it is actually impossible, logically speaking, for there to be such a thing as a "science fiction novel," or a work of science fiction which is also serious literature or a "work of art." It is true, of course, Le Guin is prepared to concede, that some novelists have chosen as their theme, developments which have taken place in science and technology. But this does not (and could not) mean that their novels are works of science fiction. They are rather works of fiction, specifically novels, which deal with the theme of scientific and technological development and the impact which they have on the lives of their imaginary characters. A logical implication of some of the things which Le Guin says in this essay, then, is that those novelists who choose to write about this theme remain "novelists," in the strict sense of the term, rather than writers of science fiction, precisely because "they say what they have to say through a *character*—not a mouthpiece, but a fully realized secondary creation." For Le Guin then, in a novel, properly so called "character is primary."[74] It is the focus on character which differentiates between novels and works of "science fiction," *all* of which, from this point of view, might be said to be inferior works of literature because they lack the qualities required in a novel.

Franz Rottensteiner has suggested that "science fiction is a minor branch of fiction, minor at least in artistic terms." For "any writer who would write *only* science fiction can only be a minor writer."[75] This implies that in his view works of science fiction generally are indeed by their very nature "inferior" and not to be taken seriously as works of literature, a view which Rottensteiner also appears to endorse in his review of Le Guin's *The Language of the Night*, which touches on the issues discussed by Le Guin in "Science Fiction and Mrs. Brown."[76] If this were true of all science fiction, then that would be damning judgment, not just of science fiction generally, but also, of course, of the work of Le Guin. Nevertheless it seems to me that at one time Le Guin herself also appears to have endorsed this view. It is for this very reason that Le Guin has in the past aspired to be a novelist rather than a writer of science fiction.

Somewhat inconsistently, however, Rottensteiner also maintains that his assessment of the aesthetic merits of works of science fiction does not apply to *all* works of that kind. This is so because, as he puts it, "the greatest works of science fiction have all been written by people who were good writers anyway, choosing the form of science fiction only when it was the best expression for the things they had to say."[77] Rottensteiner, then, differentiates between "good" and "bad" science fiction, the former category containing those works which not only deal with abstract ideas but which will also withstand scrutiny as works of literature—in short, which are good novels.[78] This is a view which is, I think, shared by Le Guin today. However, it is not a view which was held unequivocally by Le Guin in the 1970s. For Le Guin *did* say things at this time which suggest that in her view novelists who write about the impact of science and technology on society, and the ethical dilemmas which this creates, should not be thought of as the authors of works of science fiction at all. Such writers have chosen the aesthetic form of the *novel* rather than that of science fiction. They write novels about the moral and political implications of developments in science and technology, rather than works of "science fiction."

In connection with this issue, George Woodcock has shrewdly described Le Guin as "a highly accomplished fantasist and allegorist" who is far more interested in issues of "ethical and spiritual" concern than she is with "scientific development" as such.[79] Given Le Guin's remark in "Science Fiction and Mrs. Brown" that "if Mrs. Brown is dead, you can take your galaxies and roll them up into a ball and throw them into the trash can, for all I care,"[80] there is evidently something to be said for this view. It is arguable, then, that in "Science Fiction and Mrs. Brown" Le Guin did not think of herself as being primarily (or indeed at all) a writer of "science fiction" in the sense outlined above. Rather, in this essay she thought of herself as a *novelist*. As such she wished to be a creative writer who is concerned with the "human condition" and the moral dilemmas associated with it, and who also happens to have an interest in the ethical and political implications of developments in science and technology. Barry Pegg has rightly said of both Le Guin's *The Left Hand of Darkness* and *The Dispossessed* that they "address the usual set of concern of the traditional *novel*—human relations at both the individual and the social level—but in a technologically extrapolated society." "Technological innovations are present," Pegg continues, "but they are *not* emphasized in the bulk of the novel, whose business is more with *human* traffic" (my emphasis).[81]

It must be conceded however that, like Rottensteiner's, Le Guin's own views on this subject are not entirely consistent, even in "Science Fiction and Mrs. Brown." For there Le Guin also appears to accept that it is possible to write a "science fiction novel" after all. Indeed, she suggests that this has already been done, and that it was done for the first time not by H. G. Wells but by Zamyatin. It was Zamyatin, she insists, who when he wrote *We* was "the author of the first science fiction *novel*," properly so called. Zamyatin was, she says, the first author to show that "when science fiction uses its limitless range of symbol and metaphor *novelistically*, with the subject at the centre, it can show us who we are, and where we are, and what choices face us, with unsurpassed clarity, and with a great and troubling beauty."[82] Indeed, it is quite striking that when seeking to illustrate her views on the importance of *character* for a work of good literature, or a novel properly so called, in this essay Le Guin chose, not any of the works of H. G. Wells, but rather Zamyatin's *We* as her decisive example that it *is* possible for a literary production which deals with the impact of science and technology on society to achieve such a high standard of literary achievement. For despite the fact that he is designated by an abstract "number," and is, therefore, not presented as an individual, Zamyatin's D-503 evidently does possess "character" in Le Guin's sense of the term.[83]

If Le Guin's views on this subject were inconsistent in the 1970s, today she is very clear in her own mind that it certainly *is* possible for a text to be both a work of science fiction and not just a novel but also a good novel. She is clear that the fact that a text is a work of science fiction is not necessarily an indication that it should not be taken seriously as a work of literature. And she is also clear that those who write works of science fiction which are also good novels have a right to be considered as the authors of serious works of "literature." Consequently, they ought not to be ashamed of the fact that they write science fiction. Moreover Le Guin has criticized other writers, for example Jeanette Winterson, who appear not to share these views.[84] Nevertheless this has not always been the case. For Le Guin does say things in "Science Fiction and Mrs. Brown" which suggest that in the 1970s she was quite concerned about this issue and was, in consequence, somewhat uncertain both about the literary status of *The Dispossessed* and her own status as an author.

LE GUIN AND THE IDEA OF A UTOPIAN NOVEL

Bearing the above remarks about science fiction and the novel in mind, let us now consider whether it is best to think of Le Guin's *The Dispossessed* as being either a literary utopia, on the one hand, or a novel about utopianism on the other. Discussion of this issue is connected to the question of whether it is possible for the author of a work of literature which might correctly be described as being "utopian" to write a *novel*, in the strict sense of the term, as opposed to a traditional literary utopia. As in the case of our discussion of the idea of a "science fiction novel" in the preceding section, what lies behind this question is the assumption (which Le Guin also appears to have taken seriously in the 1970s) that, just like works of pulp science fiction, and for much the same reasons, traditional literary utopias do not pass the test for being considered "good" works of literature. They too are not "novels" in the sense in which the great works of European literature in the nineteenth century are novels. Thus, for example, like works of pulp science fiction, traditional literary utopias are weak so far as characterization and plot are concerned. They too are didactic works which are given over to the communication of abstract ideas. As such they have a tendency to oversimplify things, to see things straightforwardly in "black-and-white" or "either-or" terms. Consequently, they do not handle satisfactorily the complexities of the ethical dilemmas with which a novel, or a "good" work of literature, has to deal.

The above account of the difference between a novel and a traditional literary utopia suggests that it is not logically possible for a particular text to be both a novel (or at least a good novel) and a literary utopia at the same time, because as in the case of science fiction the stylistic conventions associated with these two genres and the intentions of the authors associated with them are quite different from one another. But are there any good reasons for attributing such an assumption to Le Guin? In my view there are. At least Le Guin said things in the 1970s which support this reading, even if her views on this issue have changed since. For example, in "Science Fiction and Mrs. Brown" Le Guin cites favorably Virginia Woolf's claim that "there are *no* Mrs. Browns in Utopia" (my emphasis).[85] In other words, there are no individual "characters" in those productions which are usually characterized as literary utopias. In "Mr. Bennett and Mrs. Brown," the essay which provided the source of inspiration for Le Guin's thinking on this subject, Virginia Woolf tells her readers that she believes that all novels "deal with character," and that "it is to express character—not to *preach doctrines*, sing songs, or celebrate the glories of the British Empire, that the form of the novels, so clumsy, verbose, and undramatic, so rich, elastic, and alive, has been evolved" (my emphasis).[86] All the "great novelists," Woolf claims, "have brought us to see whatever they wish us to see through some character. Otherwise they would not be novelists at all "but poets, historians, or *pamphleteers*" (my emphasis).[87] Woolf, then, draws a clear contrast in this essay between what she considers to be a (good) novel, understood in this sense, and a literary utopia, and it is for precisely this reason that she claims that "there are no Mrs. Browns in Utopia."[88] According to Woolf (as Le Guin understands and agrees with her), then, a major defect in the utopian literary tradition is that their authors do not attach sufficient value to "the individual."

I note in passing that this was also the opinion of the early H. G. Wells whose writings, apart from those of Virginia Woolf, may well have provided Le Guin with a source of inspiration for her own views on this subject. Writing in 1911, thirteen years before Woolf, Wells argued that "the distinctive value of the *novel* among written works of art is in *characterization*, and the charm of a well conceived character lies, not in knowing its destiny, but in watching its proceedings" (my emphasis).[89] Wells also noted that a number of "competent critics" have examined this supreme importance of individualities, in other words of 'character' in the fiction of the nineteenth century and early twentieth century."[90] It is this understanding of what it is to be a creative writer which led Wells to the conclusion that there is an important difference between being a novelist and a preacher or a teacher. "I do not mean for a moment," Wells's states at one point, "that the novelist is going to set up as a *teacher*, as a sort of a priest with a pen, who will make men and women believe and do this and that. The novel is *not* a new sort of *pulpit*" (my emphasis).[91] Needless to say, as Wells himself was very well aware, when judged by this criterion his own later writings could not be taken seriously as "works of art." Indeed, in "Mr. Bennett and Mrs. Brown" Woolf cites Wells as an example of someone who writes, not novels, but "literary utopias." Woolf evidently thought that Wells had by then (1924) ceased to be a novelist and had become nothing more than a political *doctrinaire* or a pamphleteer. We can see from this that it was only the *later* Wells who, quite deliberately, *chose* to stop being a novelist and become a political propagandist. It is, therefore, somewhat ironic, as Krishan Kumar has noted, that Woolf's views regarding the importance of characterization for the form of the novel were first developed by Wells himself and could even have been inherited from works which he wrote at the beginning of the twentieth century.[92]

Similar ideas can also be found in Wells's *A Modern Utopia*, where at one point Wells states that in the early literary utopias there are "no individualities, but only generalized people." "One sees," Wells continues, "handsome but characterless buildings, symmetrical and perfect cultivations, and a multitude of people, healthy, happy, beautifully dressed, but without any personal distinction whatever."[93] This important passage helps us perhaps to understand not only the views of H. G. Wells but also those of Le Guin. For example, it is cited by Robert Elliott, in his *The Shape of Utopia: Studies in a Literary Genre*,[94] a work which is significant because Le Guin tells us that it was an important source of information for her when she was developing her own views on the utopian literary tradition and her relationship to it.[95]

According to Krishan Kumar, Wells "accepts" that this lack of sensitivity to the importance of individual character "is probably an inevitable limitation of the utopian literary form."[96] And again there is at least some evidence that in the 1970s Le Guin agreed with this view. This is a reason for thinking that Le Guin thought of herself at that time as attempting to break free from the constraints which association with this particular literary genre would place upon her. As Le Guin has one of her characters in *Always Coming Home* say, "I never did like smartass utopians. Always so much healthier and saner and sounder and fitter and kinder and tougher and wiser and righter than me and my family and friends. People who have the answers are boring, niece. Boring, boring, boring."[97] When writing in this vein, Le Guin was broadly sympathetic to the view, which according to Richard Gerber is held by a number of commentators, that a literary utopia "is not considered to be a *novel* in the proper meaning of the word," precisely because works of this kind are "concerned with *ideas* instead of characters"[98] (my emphasis).

In the 1970s, then, Le Guin was of the opinion that, like the authors of works of science fiction, so too the authors of traditional literary utopias tend to think in terms of abstract categories or classes of person, each of which, for precisely this reason, *lacks* character and is merely a mouthpiece for the expression of abstract ideas. Literary utopias are vehicles for the expression of abstract ideas and nothing more. They are in effect works of political theory, akin to political pamphlets. Their primary purpose is didactic, or educational in the limited or "bad" sense that they are a means for their authors to tell their readers what they ought to think. In short, Le Guin agreed with Virginia Woolf's judgment that the authors of literary utopias have a tendency to be dogmatic, doctrinaire, and ideological. In "Science Fiction and Mrs. Brown" she maintains that Woolf is "absolutely right" about this.[99] In her view, therefore, there is a significant difference between a literary utopia, on the one hand, and a *novel* which has political utopianism as its central theme on the other.

If this analogy between works of science fiction and literary utopias is a helpful one, then it raises the possibility that, just as she is not a writer of science fiction in the derogatory sense referred to above, so also, specifically in the case of *The Dispossessed,* Le Guin should not be thought of as being a writer of literary utopias, at least as the notion of utopia has been traditionally understood; as it is understood by Zamyatin in his essay on H. G. Wells; and as it is still often understood today. Le Guin is best thought of as being first and foremost a *novelist.* She is a creative writer who, in the case of *The Dispossessed,* has written, not a literary utopia, but rather a novel about the trials and tribulations of utopian politics.

The origins of *The Dispossessed,* Le Guin tells us, lay not in the fact that she is an anarchist with a definite political ideology and framework of beliefs which she wishes to "embody," in the sense of advocating them to her readers in a particular literary form by providing them with a spokesperson, or a mouthpiece. It is not to educate her readers in *that* sense. It is not to tell them what she thinks they ought to think. For that, in Le Guin's view, would not be a genuine education at all. Rather, it lay in the development of a character. "It began with a person."[100] It is true, of course, that the character in question, Shevek, is an anarchist, and consequently someone who has definite political beliefs. Consequently Shevek would not be the person he is, with the character he has, unless he did subscribe to those beliefs. But there is much more to Shevek than simply the fact that he subscribes to those beliefs. And as novelist rather than a political theorist Le Guin is, consequently, also interested in these other things about Shevek which make him the character that he is.

In this respect once again it might be said that *The Dispossessed* has something in common with Zamyatin's *We.* As we have seen, in "Science Fiction and Mrs. Brown," Le Guin expresses her claim that Zamyatin's *We* is indeed a *novel* by stating that although it certainly *is* an example of a literary dystopia, nevertheless it is a peculiar one because it is "a dystopia which contains a hidden or implied utopia."[101] It would however have been more accurate, given what she says elsewhere in this same essay about the differences which exist between literary utopias/dystopias and novels, if she had said that Zamyatin's *We* should not be thought of as an example of a literary dystopia at all, but rather, as Zamyatin himself implies in his essay on H. G. Wells, as a *novel* about political utopianism and the potential pitfalls of utopianism in politics. For this, it seems to me, is what Le Guin actually thought at the time. From this point of view, given what Le Guin says about the importance of character in Zamyatin's *We*, that work is just as little a literary dystopia as *The Dispossessed* is a literary utopia. For *both* texts are novels which deal with the political implications of the utopian impulse on individual characters in a natural scientific context.[102]

A number of commentators have argued that a distinction needs to be made between the stylistic conventions associated with the utopian literary tradition and those associated with the form of the novel. Edward James, for example, has argued that traditional literary utopias "offer no fictional excitement," whereas the "perpetual and unending struggle for a better world offers plenty of plot opportunities" for someone seeking to write something quite different, namely a *novel* about utopianism.[103] According to James, one of the standard objections to the "classic utopia" as an aesthetic form "rests on purely literary grounds." "Most classic utopias," he says, "fall short of the standards expected of a novelist." Again, James notes that within them "characterization is often non-existent: the protagonists merely fulfill their necessary roles, as visitor-listener, as utopian-lecturer or as token female." Moreover, the "plot development" is all too often "perfunctory." Once the visitor to a utopian society "has arrived, he is shown or merely told about one aspect of the society after another."[104]

Similarly, Gary Saul Morson has suggested that "the interpretive conventions of *utopias* are radically *different* from those of *novels*" (my emphasis).[105] According to Morson there are two reasons for this. First, "in the novel, unlike the utopia, the narrative is taken as representing a plausible sequence of events."[106] Second, "in a novel, the statements, actions, and beliefs of any principal character (or the narrator) are to be understood as a reflection of his or her personality, and of the biographical events and social milieu that have shaped it."[107] In Morson's opinion an "important corollary" of this is that "the sort of unqualified, *absolute truths* about morality and society that constantly occur in utopias have no place in novels" (my emphasis).[108] It is true, of course, Morson notes, that a "novelistic character" may in fact make such categorical statements. However, Morson insists, insofar as we interpret the work "as a novel," then we must "take such statements differently from the way we would take them if they were made by the delineator of a utopia."[109] This is so because literary utopias "make the sort of categorical claims about ethics, values and knowledge that novels do not admit." In short, a literary utopia depicts an "ideal society" which is associated with "timeless and absolute standards" which might be used "not only as a guide to building a new society but also as a sure measure of the justice of existing ones."[110] For this reason a literary utopia "surveys and describes a world that is not as complex as it has been thought to be, a world where psychology, history and social problems are a Gordian knot to be immediately cut rather than laboriously untied."[111]

Finally, Robert C. Elliott has claimed that there is a "major difference" between a literary utopia and a novel. For, as Elliott puts it, "at the heart of any literary utopia there must be detailed, serious discussion of political and sociological matters." Citing the literary critic F. R. Leavis in his support, Elliott claims that "Leavis is surely right to insist on the elementary distinction to be made between the *discussion* of problems and ideas and what we find in the great novelists'" (my emphasis). For "the novelist's art is to metamorphose ideas into the idiosyncratic experience of complex human beings," whereas the writer of literary utopias "has rarely been able to accomplish this translation." Indeed, "instead of *incarnating* the good life dramatically, novelistically, the characters of utopia *discuss* it." Elliott notes that "because they are subject to the laws of politics, morality, sociology, economics and various other fields," the issues dealt with by the authors of literary utopias "require discursive treatment." For this reason they might be said to "belong to a reality" which is "foreign to that enacted in a novel." For these issues are "not literary issues." Nor, therefore, can the "work" which elicits them "be judged" in terms of the aesthetic criteria which are "applicable" to a "novel."[112]

It is clear that James, Morson, and Elliott are in substantial agreement with one another about this issue. In my opinion, however, there is evidence to support the claim that the views expressed in the passages cited above were also held by Le Guin in the 1970s. These remarks seem to me to capture very well the implicit assumptions which Le Guin does sometimes make about her task as a *writer*, which in the case of *The Dispossessed* was to write a novel about utopianism rather than a literary utopia. In this connection it is worth comparing Le Guin's views specifically with those of Elliott. The reason for this is because Le Guin's essay "A Non-Euclidean View of California as a Cold Place to Be" is the most explicit and detailed attempt by Le Guin to relate herself and her work to the utopian literary tradition. As Le Guin acknowledges, however, one of her main sources for this particular essay is Elliott's *The Shape of Utopia: Studies in a Literary Genre*. Indeed, she tells us that she wrote "A Non-Euclidean View of California as a Cold Place to Be" specifically to honor Elliott's memory after his death in 1981.[113] Moreover, Elliott's suggestion that it is necessary to distinguish clearly between the form of the traditional literary utopia and that of the novel seem to me to capture very well the attitude which

Le Guin has at times adopted toward her own work, especially *The Dispossessed*, which in the 1970s she did consider to be a novel rather than a literary utopia, at least as that notion had until then traditionally been understood. Elliott's use of the word "incarnating" in the passages cited above is strikingly similar to Le Guin's suggestion that when she wrote *The Dispossessed* she was "embodying" anarchism in a novel. It has not, however, been noticed by commentators on Le Guin's work that if we understand what she means by "embodying" anarchism in a novel in the way indicated by Elliott's use of the similar word "incarnating" in his *The Shape of Utopia* then it follows that *The Dispossessed* should not be classified as an example of a literary utopia at all. Nor, therefore, should it be thought of as a literary production the author of which has primarily a didactic intention, namely, to persuade the reader of the superiority of anarchism and the anarchist way of life.

Le Guin concedes at one point in "Science Fiction and Mrs. Brown" that there are times when *The Dispossessed* is indeed "didactic" and "idealistic." The "sound of axes being ground," she tells us, "is occasionally audible." It might, therefore, she suggests, for that very reason or to that extent, legitimately be considered to be, not a *novel* as Le Guin understands it, but rather an example of a traditional literary utopia, although not a very good one, because the qualities which it possesses as a novel obstruct the didactic purpose which it should have and would have if it were a good example of a traditional literary utopia. Although other readings are, of course, possible, this I take it is what Le Guin had in mind when she described *The Dispossessed* as being a "utopia, of sorts." But in Le Guin's opinion any didacticism which it might possess is a definite aesthetic *weakness* in *The Dispossessed*, if it is considered as a serious "work of literature." It is a weakness precisely because its author has aspirations for it to be, not a literary utopia in the traditional sense, but a *novel*, a work of art. Nevertheless, despite this undoubted weakness, Le Guin goes on to conclude that, on the whole, "I do believe that it *is* basically a *novel*," rather than a literary utopia, "because at the heart of it you will not find an idea, or an inspirational message, or even a stone ax, but something much frailer and obscurer and more complex: a *person*" (my emphasis).[114]

THE EVOLUTION IN LE GUIN'S THINKING ABOUT THE LITERARY STATUS OF *THE DISPOSSESSED*

In "Science Fiction and Mrs. Brown" Le Guin evidently did think that there is a tension or contradiction either in *The Dispossessed* itself, or alternatively in her own understanding of its status. She could not decide whether it is a literary utopia on the one hand or a novel on the other.

When she wrote this essay in the 1970s Le Guin found this question difficult to answer because at that time she felt compelled to choose either one
or the other of these two alternatives in a situation where she actually
wanted to say that it is both. At that time, however, she felt unable to say
that it is both because she thought that it just *could not* be both, or that
there is a logical difficulty involved in claiming that it is both. In short, her
remarks in this essay at least, if not elsewhere,[115] indicate that she was of
the opinion that the idea of a "utopian novel" is a contradiction in terms.
For if it is true that literary utopias are primarily vehicles for the didactic
expression of abstract ideas, whereas novels, on the other hand, are concerned primarily with such things as characterization and plot, this does
suggest, as Wells notes in *A Modern Utopia*, that it is not possible for a
work to be both a literary utopia and a novel at the same time.

There is, therefore, at least some evidence to support the view that in
the 1970s Le Guin did not even attempt to challenge but actually *accepted*
the quite traditional way of thinking about those works of literature
which might be said to be utopias, a view which as we have seen is expressed forcefully by Zamyatin in his essay on H. G. Wells. In effect, she
agreed with Zamyatin that literary utopias are indeed didactic works, the
purpose of which is simply to present abstract ideas in a pseudo-literary
form; that they lack that emphasis on character which is necessary in a
novel or any text which has aspirations to be considered as a good work
of literature; and that so far as their literary form is concerned they are
not, therefore, "dynamic" texts in the specifically non-sociological sense
in which Zamyatin employs that term in his essay on Wells.

Since she wrote "Science Fiction and Mrs. Brown," however, Le Guin
has changed her mind on this subject, although it remains just as much of
interest to her today as it was thirty years ago. Indeed, Le Guin thinks that
this issue remains the most important one to be addressed by anyone
seeking to interpret *The Dispossessed*. This is clear from her reply to the papers collected together in the most recent (indeed the only) collection devoted to *The Dispossessed*, which was published in 2005.[116] In my view it is
highly significant that in reassessing the significance of *The Dispossessed*
three decades after it was first published, Le Guin should choose this very
issue as the main focus for discussion.

In her most recent comments Le Guin insists that *The Dispossessed* is a
novel in the strict sense of the term. Referring once more (and again using
the very same expression) to the view which sees her as some kind of political "ax grinder," which she evidently has no desire to be, Le Guin tells
her readers that she has often, in response to this accusation, been "driven
to deny that there is any didactic intention at all" in her fiction." Readers,
she says, "are often led astray by the widespread belief that a novel springs
from a single originating 'idea,' or that it is a "rational presentation of

ideas" which are "completely accessible to intellect" by means of an "essentially ornamental narrative." Because *The Dispossessed* is "not only concerned with politics, society and ethics but approaching them *via* a definite political theory," it has in the past, she says, "given me a lot of grief," precisely because it has "generally, not always but often, been discussed as a *treatise*, not a *novel*" (my emphasis). Le Guin concedes in this recent text that this is "*its* own damn fault" (by which she evidently means it is *her* "own damn fault"). After all what could it expect by "announcing itself as a *utopia*, even if an ambiguous one?" For "everyone knows that utopias are to be read *not* as novels but as blue prints for social theory or practice" (my emphasis). The justification which Le Guin gives for this "fault" in *The Dispossessed* is simply that she herself has always "read utopias as novels." Consequently, "when I came to write a utopia of course I wrote a novel."[117] On *this* occasion, however, Le Guin is much more positive than she was in "Science Fiction and Mrs. Brown," or at least much *clearer* in her own mind than she was then, about the idea that it makes perfect sense to describe a literary production as being both a literary utopia *and* a novel at the same time. In other words, what she once thought might well be a contradiction in terms, namely, the very idea of a "utopian novel," she is now convinced is not so. What in the 1970s was for Le Guin an ambiguity has now been transformed into a certainty.

To employ Frege's terminology yet again, we might say that today Le Guin is now much clearer in her own mind about the meaning of the term "literary utopia" than she was thirty years ago, both with respect to its sense and with respect to its reference. So far as the latter is concerned, she is now of the opinion that *The Dispossessed* is one of the many texts which are legitimately denoted by this term. Similarly, with respect to the former issue, she now has a much clearer understanding that the fact that *The Dispossessed* is a *novel* and not a political pamphlet or similar didactic text is *not* an obstacle to its being characterized as a literary utopia. Her understanding of the sense of the term "literary utopia" has, therefore, altered significantly since 1974 and she is no longer concerned that the idea of a utopian novel might be a contradiction in terms. It is, therefore, understandable that Le Guin should have dropped the subtitle *An Ambiguous Utopia*, which she appended to the first edition of her book, from later reprintings of *The Dispossessed*. Le Guin's most recent opinions on this subject now reflect the general trend amongst commentators on her work, which considers *The Dispossessed* as representing a significant turning point in the history of the concept of a literary utopia. It is a "critical utopia" in Moylan's sense.

Setting aside Le Guin's most recent views about this issue, however, my conclusion in this chapter is that, at least when she first wrote it, Le Guin considered *The Dispossessed* to be neither a traditional literary utopia nor a new type of utopian text, that is to say a "critical utopia" or a "utopian novel." Rather, she thought of it as being a novel dealing with the theme of utopianism in politics. And it follows from this that it could not be said that, at the time, *The Dispossessed* was intended by Le Guin either to initiate or even contribute to the reinvigoration of the utopian literary tradition which, according to a number of commentators, occurred in the 1970s.

AUTHORIAL INTENTIONALISM AND THE INTERPRETATION OF LE GUIN'S *THE DISPOSSESSED*

The reference to Le Guin's intentions in the preceding paragraph raises the issue of how much importance should be attached to the intentions of an author by those seeking to interpret the meaning of any literary text. This is an issue which has been the focus of a great deal of discussion within the disciplines of political theory and the history of ideas in the last few decades, and is usually associated with the work of Quentin Skinner. Commentators such as Chad Walsh, Lyman Tower Sargent, Tom Moylan, and Ruth Levitas have all embraced what is now widely considered to be Skinner's notion of "authorial intentionalism" as an important guiding principle for the interpretation of works of utopian literature and/or science fiction. Chad Walsh, for example, writing as early as 1962 (seven years before Skinner's first major article in this area, "Meaning and Understanding in the History of Ideas," first appeared) forcefully argued that "the intent of the author is crucial" when interpreting or classifying any text.[118] According to Walsh, "anyone skimming through *Brave New World* with a bare minimum of literary acumen will know after twenty pages that the author loathes that idiotically happy world of feelies, Malthusian belts and prenatal happiness engineering. *Brave New World* is not a utopia but a dystopia. Always a writer's *intention* is what counts. It is up to the reader to read between the lines and discern that intention."[119]

I am broadly sympathetic to this approach to the interpretation of texts. However, it seems to me that there are problems involved in any attempt to apply it to Le Guin's *The Dispossessed*. This is so because in the case of this particular text its author did not have a clear or unambiguous intention when she wrote it. She was herself at the time unsure whether she had written a literary utopia, on the one hand, or a novel on the other. This evidently makes it difficult for commentators who subscribe to the principle of authorial intentionalism to interpret this particular text. If Le Guin's uncertainty in the 1970s regarding the status of *The Dispossessed*, as to whether it should be thought of as a novel or a literary utopia, does not actually undermine the claim that when considering such questions the commentator ought to attach exclusive importance to the *intentions* of the author of a text, then it does at least demonstrate how difficult it is on occasion to apply this principle in practice.[120]

NOTES

1. Ursula K. Le Guin, "A Non-Euclidean View of California as a Cold Place to Be," in *Dancing at the Edge of the World: Thoughts on Words, Women, Places* (New York: Harper and Row, 1989), 90.

2. Le Guin, "A Non-Euclidean View of California as a Cold Place to Be," 88.

3. Le Guin, "A Non-Euclidean View of California as a Cold Place to Be," 90.

4. Le Guin, "A Non-Euclidean View of California as a Cold Place to Be," 91.

5. Donna K. White, "The Great Good Place," in *Dancing with Dragons: Ursula K. Le Guin and the Critics* (New York: Camden House, 1999), 96.

6. Le Guin, "A Non-Euclidean View of California as a Cold Place to Be," 93.

7. Naomi Jacobs, "Beyond Stasis and Symmetry: Lessing, Le Guin, and the Remodelling of Utopia," *Extrapolation*, 29, no. 1 (Spring 1988): 40–41.

8. White, "The Great Good Place," 98.

9. D. G. Williams, "The Moons of Le Guin and Heinlein," *Science Fiction Studies*, 21, no. 2 (1994), 165.

10. Le Guin, "Introduction" to *Planet of Exile*, in *The Language of the Night: Essays on Fantasy and Science Fiction*, ed. Susan Wood (New York: Perigee Books, 1979), 143.

11. Le Guin, "Is Gender Necessary," in *The Language of the Night*, 159.

12. Le Guin, "A Non-Euclidean View of California as a Cold Place to Be," 98.

13. Le Guin, "A Non-Euclidean View of California as a Cold Place to Be," 93.

14. Lyman Tower Sargent, "The Problem of the 'Flawed Utopia': A Note on the Costs of Eutopia," in *Dark Horizons: Science Fiction and the Dystopian Imagination*, eds. Tom Moylan and Raffaella Baccolini (London: Routledge, 2003), 226. It should be noted that Tower Sargent associates the belief that the fact that the quest for utopia is doomed to failure, and, therefore, one of the tragic aspects of human existence, not so much with utopianism, but with *anti*-utopianism. It is in this connection that he discusses Le Guin's short story, "The Ones Who Walked Away from Omelas," *The Wind's Twelve Quarters*, Vol. 2, (London: Granada, 1980 [1975]), 112–20. Tower Sargent, therefore, identifies a distinct dystopian (in the sense of an anti–utopian) dimension to Le Guin's work, which is also a critique of certain aspects of a particular type of anarchism (especially that of Bakunin). For commentary relating to this story see the articles in the special issue of *Utopian Studies*, 2, nos. 1–2 (1991) devoted to it.

15. James W. Bittner, *Approaches to the Fiction of Ursula K. Le Guin* (Ann Arbor: UMI Press, 1984), 35.

16. Simon Stow, "Worlds Apart: Ursula K. Le Guin and the Possibility of Method," in *The New Utopian Politics of Ursula K. Le Guin's* The Dispossessed, eds. Laurence Davis and Peter Stillman, (Lanham, Md.: Lexington Books, 2005), 48. See also Judah Bierman, "Ambiguity in Utopia, *The Dispossessed*," in *Science Fiction*

Studies: Selected Articles on Science Fiction 1973–1975, eds. Mullen and Suvin (New York: Gregg Press, 1975), 279–85.

17. Patrick Parrinder, "Utopia and Meta-Utopia," in *Shadows of the Future: H. G. Wells, Science Fiction and Prophecy* (New York: Syracuse University Press, 1995), 98, fn. 3.

18. John P. Brennan and Michael C. Downs, "Anarchism and Utopian Tradition in *The Dispossessed*," in *Ursula K. Le Guin*, Eds. Joseph Olander and Martin Harry Greenberg, (New York: Taplinger, 1979), 144.

19. Brennan and Downs, "Anarchism and Utopian Tradition in *The Dispossessed*," 151.

20. Tom Moylan, "Beyond Negation: The Critical Utopias of Ursula K. Le Guin and Samuel R. Delany," *Extrapolation*, 21 (1980), 238; also 241: "Le Guin's vision of Anarres is a totally conceived social construct well within the traditional utopian mode."

21. Moylan, "Beyond Negation: The Critical Utopias of Ursula K. Le Guin and Samuel R. Delany," 243.

22. Moylan, "Beyond Negation: The Critical Utopias of Ursula K. Le Guin and Samuel R. Delany," 242.

23. For some interesting remarks about the rise of the "utopian novel" within the tradition of utopian literature more broadly conceived, see Richard Gerber, *Utopian Fantasy: A Study of English Utopian Fiction Since the End of the Nineteenth Century* (London: Routledge, 1973 [1955]), especially chapter 4, "Towards the Novel," 113–19, and chapter 5, "Literary Achievement," 120–32.

24. Gottlöb Frege, "On Sense and Reference," in *Translations from the Philosophical Writings of Gottlöb Frege*, trans. Peter Geach and Max Black (Oxford: Basil Blackwell, 1977), 56–78.

25. See Bierman, "Ambiguity in Utopia: *The Dispossessed*," 280; Claire Curtis, "Ambiguous Choices: Skepticism as a Grounding for Utopia," in *The New Utopian Politics of Ursula K. Le Guin's* The Dispossessed, eds. Davis and Stillman, 265–82; Moylan, "Beyond Negation: The Critical Utopias of Ursula K. Le Guin and Samuel R. Delany," 248; David Porter, "The Politics of Le Guin's *Opus*," in *Science Fiction Studies: Selected Articles on Science Fiction 1973–1975*, eds. Mullen and Suvin, 274; Warren Rochelle, *Communities of the Heart: The Rhetoric of Myth in the Fiction of Ursula K. Le Guin* (Liverpool: Liverpool University Press, 2001), 75; Mark Tunick, "The Need for Walls: Privacy, Community and Freedom in *The Dispossessed*," in *The New Utopian Politics of Ursula K. Le Guin's* The Dispossessed, eds. Davis and Stillman, 131; Victor Urbanowicz, "Personal and Political in *The Dispossessed*," in *Ursula K. Le Guin*, ed. Harold Bloom (New York: Chelsea House, 1985), 147; Raymond Williams, "Science Fiction and Utopia," in *Science Fiction: A Critical Guide*, ed. Patrick Parrinder (London: Longman, 1979), 64.

26. Barbara J. Bucknall, *Ursula K. Le Guin* (New York: Ungar, 1981), 102.

27. Bucknall, *Ursula K. Le Guin*, 102.

28. Bucknall, *Ursula K. Le Guin*, 103.

29. Wood, "Discovering Worlds: The Fiction of Ursula K. Le Guin," in *Ursula K. Le Guin*, ed. Bloom, 204.

30. Neil Easterbrook, "State, Heterotopia: The Political Imagination in Heinlein, Le Guin and Delany," in *Political Science Fiction*, eds. Donald Hassler and Clyde Wilcox (Columbia: University of South Carolina Press, 1997), 56.

31. Bittner, *Approaches to the Fiction of Ursula K. Le Guin*, 114.

32. Rochelle, *Communities of the Heart: The Rhetoric of Myth in the Fiction of Ursula K. Le Guin*, 74. See also Krishan Kumar, *Utopia and Anti-Utopia in Modern Times* (Oxford: Blackwell, 1991 [1987]), 414: "In the end, utopia and anti-utopia both find a place in *The Dispossessed*"; and Peter Ruppert, "The Ambiguous Utopia: A Third Alternative," *Reader in a Strange Land: The Activity of Reading Literary Utopias* (Athens, Georgia: University of Georgia Press, 1986), 140. Ruppert claims that when it comes to answering the question "which of the two planets is a utopia and which a dystopia?" Le Guin "leaves this task up to the reader."

33. Elliott, "Breaching Invisible Walls: Individual Anarchy in *The Dispossessed*," in *The New Utopian Politics of Ursula K. Le Guin's* The Dispossessed, eds. Davis and Stillman, 150.

34. Hamner, "The Gap in the Wall: Partnership, Physics and Politics in *The Dispossessed*," in *The New Utopian Politics of Ursula K. Le Guin's* The Dispossessed, eds. Davis and Stillman, 228.

35. Somay, "From Ambiguity to Self-Reflexivity: Revolutionizing Fantasy Space," in *The New Utopian Politics of Ursula K. Le Guin's* The Dispossessed, eds. Davis and Stillman, 239.

36. Somay, "From Ambiguity to Self-Reflexivity: Revolutionizing Fantasy Space," 242.

37. Somay, "From Ambiguity to Self-Reflexivity: Revolutionizing Fantasy Space," 242.

38. Somay, "From Ambiguity to Self-Reflexivity: Revolutionizing Fantasy Space," 241.

39. Laurence Davis, "The Dynamic and Revolutionary Utopia of Ursula K. Le Guin," in *The New Utopian Politics of Ursula K. Le Guin's* The Dispossessed, eds. Davis and Stillman, 3.

40. Ursula K. Le Guin and Jonathan Ward, "Interview," *Dreams Must Explain Themselves* (New York: Algol Press, 1975), 34.

41. Le Guin, "Science Fiction and Mrs. Brown," *The Language of the Night*, 112.

42. Le Guin, "Science Fiction and Mrs. Brown," 111.

43. Davis, "The Dynamic and Revolutionary Utopia of Ursula K. Le Guin," fn. 3, 32.

44. We may include in this category: Bierman, "Ambiguity in Utopia: *The Dispossessed*," 280; Bucknall, *Ursula K. Le Guin*, 119; Carl Freedman, *Critical Theory and Science Fiction* (Hanover and London: Wesleyan University Press, 2000), xvii, 114; Peter T. Koper, "Science and Rhetoric in the Fiction of Ursula Le Guin," in *Ursula K. Le Guin: Voyager to Inner Lands and Outer Space*, ed. Joseph de Bolt (New York: Kennikat Press, 1979), 81; Frederick Jameson, "World Reduction in Le Guin," in *Archaeologies of the Future: The Desire Called Utopia and Other Science Fictions* (London: Verso, 2005), fn. 8, 278; Patrick Parrinder, "Science Fiction and the Scientific World View," *Science Fiction: A Critical Guide*, 86; and Robert Scholes, "The Good Witch of the West," in *Ursula K. Le Guin*, ed. Harold Bloom, 45.

45. Lyman Tower Sargent, "The Problem of the 'Flawed Utopia': A Note on the Costs of Eutopia"; Lyman Tower Sargent, "Anarchism: Social and Political Ideas in Some Recent Feminist Utopias," in *Women and Utopia: Critical Interpretations*, ed. Marleen Barr (New York: University Press of America, 1983), 10, 13; Lyman Tower Sargent, "Eutopias and Dystopias in Science Fiction: 1950–75," in *America as Utopia*, ed. Kenneth M. Roemer (New York: Burtt Franklin, 1981), 348, 355, 354.

46. Bulent Somay, "Towards an Open Ended Utopia," *Science Fiction Studies* 11 (1984), 25–38. See also Somay, "From Ambiguity to Self-Reflexivity: Revolutionizing Fantasy Space," 234–35.

47. Donna R. White, "The Great Good Place," 82.

48. Tom Moylan, "The Locus of Hope: Utopia Versus Ideology," *Science Fiction Studies*, 9, 2 (1982): 163–65. See also Tom Moylan, *Demand the Impossible: Science Fiction and the Utopian Imagination* (London: Methuen, 1986), 44, 91; Tom Moylan, *Scraps of the Untainted Sky: Science Fiction, Utopia, Dystopia* (Boulder, Colo.: Westview Press, 2000), 31, 78, 82–83, 194, 303; Raffaella Baccolini and Tom Moylan, "Introduction: Dystopia and Histories," in *Dark Horizons: Science Fiction and the Dystopian Imagination*, eds. Baccolini and Moylan, 2.

49. For the suggestion that because Le Guin characterizes an imperfect society in *The Dispossessed* we may conclude that she has written, or even invented, a new kind of literary utopia, see also the following works, many of which employ Moylan's notion of a "critical utopia" in this context: Brennan and Downs, "Anarchism and Utopian Tradition in *The Dispossessed*," 151; Curtis, "Ambiguous Choices: Skepticism as a Grounding for Utopia," 280; Freedman, *Critical Theory and Science Fiction*, 8–83, and "Science Fiction and Utopia: A Historico-Philosophical Overview," in *Learning from Other Worlds: Estrangement, Cognition and the Politics of Science Fiction and Utopia*, ed. Patrick Parrinder (Durham: Duke University Press, 2001), 90–93; Edward James, "Utopias and Anti-Utopias," in Edward James and Farah Mendelsohn, eds., *The Cambridge Companion to Science Fiction* (Cambridge: Cambridge University Press, 2003), 226; Frederic Jameson, "How to Fulfill a Wish," in *Archaeologies of the Future: The Desire Called Utopia and Other Science Fictions*, 80; Krishan Kumar, *Utopianism* (Milton Keynes: Open University Press, 1991), 105; Krishan Kumar, *Utopia and Anti-Utopia in Modern Times*, 412–14; Donna R. White, "The Great Good Place," 82, 90; Raymond Williams, "Utopia and Science Fiction," 63; and Hoda Zaki, *Phoenix Renewed: The Survival and Mutation of Utopian Thought in North American Science Fiction: 1965–1982* (San Bernadino, Calif.: Borgo Press, 1988), 37–38, 98.

50. George Turner, "Paradigm and Pattern: Form and Meaning in *The Dispossessed*," *Science Fiction Commentary* 41/42 (February 1975), 65.

51. Chris Ferns, "Future Conditional or Future Perfect? *The Dispossessed* and Permanent Revolution," in *The New Utopian Politics of Ursula K. Le Guin's* The Dispossessed, eds. Davis and Stillman, 252.

52. Brennan and Downs, "Anarchism and Utopian Tradition in *The Dispossessed*," 117.

53. Keith Booker, *The Dystopian Impulse in Modern Literature: Fiction as Social Criticism* (Westport, Conn.: Greenwood Press, 1994), 23, fn. 16.

54. Ken MacLeod, "Politics and Science Fiction," in *The Cambridge Companion to Science Fiction*, eds. Edward James and Farah Mendelsohn, 230.

55. Gerard Klein, "Le Guin's 'Aberrant' Opus: Escaping the Trap of Discontent," in *Ursula K. Le Guin*, ed. Bloom, 88.

56. Klein, "Le Guin's 'Aberrant' Opus: Escaping the Trap of Discontent," 88.

57. Klein, "Le Guin's 'Aberrant' Opus: Escaping the Trap of Discontent," 88.

58. Klein, "Le Guin's 'Aberrant' Opus: Escaping the Trap of Discontent," 88.

59. Klein, "Le Guin's 'Aberrant' Opus: Escaping the Trap of Discontent," 88.

60. Avery Plaw, "Empty Hands: Communication, Pluralism and Community in Ursula K. Le Guin's *The Dispossessed*," in *The New Utopian Politics of Ursula K. Le Guin's* The Dispossessed, eds. Davis and Stillman, 291.

61. Plaw, "Empty Hands: Communication, Pluralism and Community in Ursula K. Le Guin's *The Dispossessed*," 302.

62. Plaw, "Empty Hands: Communication, Pluralism and Community in Ursula K. Le Guin's *The Dispossessed*," 302.

63. Le Guin, "Science Fiction and Mrs. Brown," 103.

64. Kingsley Amis, *New Maps of Hell* (London: Ayer, 2000 [1960]), 128.

65. Amis, *New Maps of Hell*, 128.

66. Amis, *New Maps of Hell*, 137.

67. Amis, *New Maps of Hell*, 137.

68. Amis, *New Maps of Hell*, 127.

69. J. O. Bailey, *Pilgrims Through Space and Time: Trends and Patterns in Scientific and Utopian Fiction* (Westport, Conn.: Greenwood Press, 1972 [1947]), 212.

70. Bailey, *Pilgrims Through Space and Time: Trends and Patterns in Scientific and Utopian Fiction*, 212.

71. See Virginia Woolf, "Mr. Bennett and Mrs. Brown," in Virginia Woolf, *The Captain's Bed and Other Essays* (New York: Harcourt Brace Jovanovich, 1978 [1924]), 94–119.

72. For some criticisms of Le Guin on this subject, see also Carl D. Malmgren, "Self and Other in SF: Alien Encounters." *Science Fiction Studies*, 20 (1993): 15–33; Patrick Parrinder, "The Alien Encounter: Or, Ms. Brown and Mrs. Le Guin," in Patrick Parrinder ed., *Science Fiction: A Critical Guide*, 148–161; Franz Rottensteiner, "Le Guin's Fantasy: Review of Ursula K. Le Guin. *The Language of the Night: Essays on Fantasy and Science Fiction*," *Science Fiction Studies*, 8, no. 1 (1981): 87–90; and Scott Sanders, "Invisible Men and Women: The Disappearance of Character in Science Fiction," in Parrinder ed., *Science Fiction: A Critical Guide*, 137–147.

73. As I argue below, Le Guin's views on this subject have changed. See the remarks which Le Guin made recently in "Head Cases: A Review of Jeanette Winterson's *The Stone Gods*," *The Guardian*, Saturday, 22 September, 2007.

74. Le Guin, "Science Fiction and Mrs. Brown," 108.

75. Franz Rottensteiner, "European Science Fiction," in Darko Suvin, *Positions and Presuppositions in Science Fiction* (Kent: Kent State University Press, 1988), 204.

76. See Rottensteiner, "Le Guin's Fantasy: Review of Ursula K. Le Guin. *The Language of the Night: Essays on Fantasy and Science Fiction*," 87–90.

77. Franz Rottensteiner, "European Science Fiction," 204.

78. I feel obliged to note that in "Le Guin's Fantasy: Review of Ursula K. Le Guin. *The Language of the Night: Essays on Fantasy and Science Fiction*," 87–90, Rottensteiner places Le Guin firmly in the latter category, and consequently has a low opinion of her merits as a novelist. Rottensteiner notes, correctly, that Le

Guin's "preference and love in literature, including SF, is definitely the great traditional novel of character that helps to understand human nature." However, despite making a distinction between "good" and "bad" science fiction elsewhere, on this occasion he insists that although "there exist some SF novels that are quite decent as novels of ideas," there are *none* at all, including, therefore, Le Guin's *The Dispossessed*, which "would make the grade as novels of character." Indeed if Le Guin's merits as an author are evaluated by reference to her own aesthetic standards, or her own aspirations to be a novelist, then in Rottensteiner's opinion she "comes off as at best second-rate." According to Rottensteiner, not even Le Guin's "best" science fiction is exceptional, and "her celebrated and award-winning longer and shorter stories," though they are "ethically and morally commendable," are nevertheless "first and foremost banal" and "essentially shallow." Rottensteiner claims that Le Guin may be a "decent person and a respectable writer," indeed a "shining exception in the desolate wastelands of SF," but she is "not a great writer." He concludes what I think is an uncharitable and intemperate review of Le Guin's book by arguing that as an erstwhile "aesthetics of SF," the views expressed by Le Guin in her essay on "Science Fiction and Mrs. Brown" could only "further the self-deception to which SF and SF criticism tend anyway: the pretension that mediocre but popular works are first-rate works of literature."

79. Woodcock, cited by James Bittner, "A Survey of Le Guin Criticism," in *Ursula K. Le Guin: Voyager to Inner Lands and Outer Space*, ed. De Bolt, 46.

80. Le Guin, "Science Fiction and Mrs. Brown," 116.

81. Barry Pegg, "Down to Earth: Terrain, Territory and the Language of Realism in Ursula K. Le Guin's *The Left Hand of Darkness* and *The Dispossessed*," *Michigan Academician*, 27, 4 (1995), 482.

82. Le Guin, "Science Fiction and Mrs. Brown," 118.

83. It should be noted, however, that elsewhere in the same essay Le Guin also endorses there the traditional view that *We* is a literary dystopia.

84. Ursula K. Le Guin, "Head Cases: A Review of Jeanette Winterson's *The Stone Gods*."

85. Le Guin, "Science Fiction and Mrs. Brown," 104; Woolf, "Mr. Bennett and Mrs. Brown," 106.

86. Woolf, "Mr. Bennett and Mrs. Brown," 101.

87. Woolf, "Mr. Bennett and Mrs. Brown," 103.

88. Woolf, "Mr. Bennett and Mrs. Brown," 106.

89. H. G. Wells, "The Contemporary Novel" (1911), in *Henry James and H. G. Wells: A Record of Their Friendship, Their Debate on the Art of Fiction and Their Quarrel*, eds. Leon Edel and Gordon N. Ray (London: Rupert Hart Davis, 1958), 137; and Wells, "Digression About Novels," *Henry James and H. G. Wells*, eds. Edel and Ray, 222.

90. H. G. Wells, "Digression About Novels," in *Henry James and H. G. Wells*, eds. Edel and Ray, 222.

91. Wells, "The Contemporary Novel," in *Henry James and H. G. Wells*, eds. Edel and Ray, 154,

92. Kumar, "Science and Utopia: H. G. Wells and *A Modern Utopia*," in *Utopia and Anti-Utopia in Modern Times*, 193.

93. H. G. Wells, *A Modern Utopia*, in *A Modern Utopia and Tono Bungay* (London: Odhams Press, n. [1905]), 317.

94. Robert C. Elliott, *The Shape of Utopia: Studies in a Literary Genre* (Chicago: University of Chicago Press, 1970), 116.

95. Note, also, that Le Guin does this in "A Non-Euclidean View of California as a Cold Place to Be," an essay with a clear reference to Zamyatin in its title.

96. Kumar, *Utopia and Anti-Utopia in Modern Times*, 193.

97. Ursula K. Le Guin, *Always Coming Home* (London: Grafton Books, 1988), 316.

98. Richard Gerber, *Utopian Fantasy: A Study of English Utopian Fiction Since the End of the Nineteenth Century*, 120–21.

99. Gerber, *Utopian Fantasy: A Study of English Utopian Fiction Since the End of the Nineteenth Century*, 120–21.

100. Le Guin, "Science Fiction and Mrs. Brown," 111.

101. Le Guin, "Science Fiction and Mrs. Brown," 105.

102. I disagree, therefore, with Phillip Wegner's claim that Zamyatin's *We* and Le Guin's *The Dispossessed* are *both* literary utopias. In my view, neither one of them is. See Phillip Wegner, "A Map of Utopia's 'Possible Worlds': Zamyatin's *We* and Le Guin's *The Dispossessed*," in *Imaginary Communities: Utopia, the Nation and the Spatial Histories of Modernity* (Berkeley, Los Angeles, London: University of California Press, 2002), 147–82.

103. James, "Utopias and Anti-Utopias," 222.

104. James, "Utopias and Anti-Utopias," 222.

105. Gary Saul Morson, "Utopia as a Literary Genre," in *The Boundaries of Genre: Dostoevsky's Diary of a Writer and the Traditions of Literary Utopia* (Evanston, Ill.: Northwestern University Press, 1981), 77.

106. Morson, "Utopia as a Literary Genre," 77.

107. Morson, "Utopia as a Literary Genre," 77.

108. Morson, "Utopia as a Literary Genre," 77.

109. Morson, "Utopia as a Literary Genre," 77.

110. Morson, "Utopia as a Literary Genre," 77.

111. Morson, "Utopia as a Literary Genre," 77.

112. Elliott, *The Shape of Utopia: Studies in a Literary Genre*, 110–11.

113. Le Guin, "A Non-Euclidean View of California as a Cold Place to Be," 80–81.

114. Le Guin, "Science Fiction and Mrs. Brown," 111–12. I am unable to agree with Peter Fitting's suggestion that Le Guin's work is to be associated with a form of "didactic and committed art," at least in one sense of the word "committed" (there are others). See Peter Fitting, "Positioning and Closure: On the "Reading Effect" of Contemporary Utopian Fiction, *Utopian Studies*, I (Lanham, Md.: University Press of America, 1987), 26.

115. Note that in her interview with Jonathan Ward, Le Guin characterizes *The Dispossessed* as both a "utopia" *and* a "novel." See Ursula K. Le Guin and Jonathan Ward, "Interview," 34. See also Le Guin, "Science Fiction and Mrs. Brown," 112.

116. Ursula K. Le Guin, "A Response, by Ansible, from Tau Ceti," in *The New Utopian Politics of Ursula K. Le Guin's* The Dispossessed, eds. Davis and Stillman, 305–08.

117. Le Guin, "A Response, by Ansible, from Tau Ceti," 305–06.

118. Chad Walsh, *From Utopia to Nightmare* (Westport: Greenwood Press, 1962), 25–26.

119. Chad Walsh, *From Utopia to Nightmare*, 25–26. For a similar view see also Lyman Tower Sargent, "Utopia: The Problem of Definition," *Extrapolation* 16 (1975), 137–48, especially 142–43; Lyman Tower Sargent, "The Three Faces of Utopianism Revisited," *Utopian Studies*, 5, 1 (1994), 1–38, especially 6; Ruth Levitas, *The Concept of Utopia* (Syracuse: Syracuse University Press, 1990), 165; and Moylan, *Scraps of the Untainted Sky*, 73, 155, 303.

120. For discussion of this issue in general see J. H. "Intention, Words and Meaning: The Case of More's *Utopia*," *New Literary History*, 6, 3, (1975), 529–41, and the persuasive criticisms of Hexter's version of "authorial intentionalism" advanced by Gary Saul Morson, *The Boundaries of Genre*, 69–72, 174–75.

6

Politics and Literature in the Writings of Le Guin

POLITICS AND THE FORM OF THE NOVEL

If it is true that Le Guin's *The Dispossessed* is a novel in the sense indicated earlier and not a literary utopia then this has definite political implications. For if a traditional literary utopia can and does present a radical critique of existing society, a novel, as Le Guin understands this term, cannot do so. The literary form of the novel is necessarily "conservative" in terms of its political implications. Why? Like Hegel and his disciple Georg Lukács, Le Guin thinks that the human condition is always one of dramatic tension between opposites or, to be more precise, of contrasting moral forces in conflict or "collision" with one another.[1] It is irresolvable moral conflicts or conflicts of this kind which, in the modern era, provide the subject matter for the novelist, especially the "great" novelists writing within the tradition of European realism in the nineteenth century. For those familiar with both, it is obvious that this way of thinking about the novel is one which suggests an interesting parallel between the concerns of the novelist in modern times and those of the dramatists of ancient Greece, especially those associated with the tragic drama of fifth-century Athens. That is why, on this view, the moral insights of ancient Greek tragedy continue to be of relevance today.

Drawing his inspiration from Hegel rather than from the writings of Marx, Lukács has made the extremely interesting, though also somewhat surprising, remark that "the contradictoriness of social development" and the "intensification of these contradictions to the point of *tragic collision*" (my emphasis) has to do not so much specifically with the capitalist mode of production, but is rather a "general fact of life,"[2] or a feature of all human existence. Lukács takes this notion of a "tragic collision" from Hegel's aesthetics. Like Hegel, Lukács associates it with the parallel notion of a fundamental ethical dilemma.[3] Moreover, also like Hegel (and as we shall see Le Guin) Lukács considers the classic example of such a tragic collision to be the works of Sophocles, especially the *Antigone*.[4] Hegel's views on this subject have been neatly summarized by F. L. Lucas who maintains that, so far as the moral conflict depicted by Sophocles in this play is concerned, Hegel is of the opinion that both of the play's two central characters, Antigone and Creon, "were right." At the same time, however, Hegel *also* insists that they were "both wrong," because they were "not right enough," or rather because they were "too *one-sided* in their righteousness" (my emphasis).[5]

We may note in passing that this way of thinking about the relationship which exists between Hegel's philosophy and ancient Greek tragedy reverses, and amounts to a theoretical "inversion" of a more traditional view. According to that view if anyone is seriously interested in studying ancient Greek tragedy, then it is necessary that they acquaint themselves with Hegel's philosophy, especially but not only the *Lectures on Aesthetics*. This is so because, despite the employment of the technical jargon of his metaphysical system there, Hegel's understanding of ancient Greek tragedy is nonetheless a profound one. Whether one likes or dislikes Hegel's analysis, then, it is arguable that no serious student of tragedy can afford to ignore it; although some scholars have, of course, dismissed it.[6] On this traditional reading, then, Hegel's views on tragedy are *central* for anyone wishing to understand ancient Greek tragedy. However, that is not to say they are of any great significance for anyone seeking to understand Hegel's own philosophy. On the contrary, they might be said to be peripheral to that particular enterprise. This is so because one can perfectly well understand Hegel's philosophy, broadly understood (including, therefore, his social and political thought) without engaging with his aesthetics— either his philosophy of aesthetics in general, or his views on tragedy in particular. The understanding of the relationship between Hegel's philosophy and his views on tragedy presented here, however, is different from this. This is so because it maintains that Hegel's views on tragedy are not peripheral but *central* for any adequate understanding of his philosophy as a whole, at least insofar as that philosophy incorporates a social theory which touches specifically on human existence and the ethical and political problems associated with "the human condition," problems which, by their very nature, are to be found in all societies everywhere, and not just in ancient Greece in the fifth century BCE.

Una Ellis-Fermor has made the interesting claim that the moral outlook associated with Greek tragedy is associated with an attempt on the part of the dramatist to maintain an "equilibrium" between two "opposite readings of life, to neither of which the dramatist can wholly commit himself."[7] This seems to me to capture very well, not only the outlook of Greek tragic drama as understood by Hegel, but also that of the novelist writing in the tradition of European realism. It also captures very well the outlook of Le Guin insofar as she thinks of herself as a novelist working within that tradition. It is arguable that in the history of European literature there has been, at least from the time of Sophocles and the other Greek tragic dramatists onward, a tendency for the creative writer (who in modern times is, of course, often a novelist)[8] to attempt *not* to "take sides." There has been an unwillingness on the part of some authors to make moral judgments about the ethical dilemmas which they depict in their writings. Indeed, rather like the good scientist discussed earlier, they have attempted to rise above them, to place themselves *au dessus de la mêlée*, and simply to dramatize the tragedy associated with these moral events as they unfold.

In the case of ancient Greek drama, D. D. Raphael has rightly said that "although tragedy does not have a directly moral purpose," it is nevertheless for this reason "deeply concerned with morality."[9] For although, Raphael goes on, the tragic author is not a preacher or a propagandist, and his aim is not an overtly didactic one, to provide some "proof" or "demonstration" which will actually solve the fundamental moral problem being dramatized in the play for his audience, nevertheless tragic drama can be seen as an attempted "exploration" of such fundamental moral problems.[10] According to Raphael, it is in this sense only that it could be said that tragic drama "was the moral philosophy of fifth-century Athens."[11]

These remarks seem to me to have a direct application to Le Guin and her understanding of the novel and of the task of the novelist today. And it is in this sense only, I think, that Le Guin might be said to conform to the judgment of Lukács that in the novel generally "the *ethical intention* is visible in the creation of every detail and hence is, in its most concrete content, an effective structural element of the work itself" (my emphasis).[12] In this regard Le Guin's views also have an affinity with those of more recent commentators such as Antony Arblaster and Martha Nussbaum. According to Arblaster it is works of literature rather than the abstract reasoning of moral philosophers which are best suited to portraying the practical moral problems of everyday life, precisely because these problems so often take the form of a fundamental ethical dilemma.[13] Similarly, for Nussbaum it is works of literature, more specifically tragic drama, which can best express "the existence of conflicts" among the ethical "commitments" of "complex characters"; or what Andrew Gibson, speaking of the novel, has referred to as "contradictions between significant systems of value."[14] Gibson appears to associate the idea of "the inescapability of paradox in ethics" specifically with a "postmodern" approach to reading works of literature.[15] In my view, however, anyone who made such an identification would be making a mistake. Nussbaum for example, as an advocate of Aristotelian "essentialism," has no great sympathy for postmodernism.[16] But in any case this way of thinking about the novel might be said to stand in a long tradition which goes back, through the work of Lukács on the novel to Hegel and thence to the ancient Greeks. And it is within this tradition that Nussbaum must be located.

On this view, it is the task of the novelist to capture and evince the complex and contradictory nature of the ethical dilemmas which lie at the very heart of all human existence, not to attempt to resolve them. Indeed, from this standpoint, being genuine moral dilemmas, they just cannot be resolved as there is no rational solution to them. To think that there *is* to indulge in the "good/bad, yes/no moralizing that," in Le Guin's opinion, "denies fear" and "ignores" the "mystery" which surrounds the human condition.[17] As Le Guin herself puts it, in human existence "*tragedy* is the truth, and truth is what the very great artists, the absolute novelists, tell" (my emphasis). Moral "truth," she says, always "encompasses tragedy" because, unflinchingly, it embraces "life." For this reason it "partakes of the eternal joy" which Le Guin associates with the order of the Cosmos.[18] According to Le Guin, then, a good novelist must engage with the ethical dilemmas of human existence without preaching, moralizing or "taking sides." The novelist must be able to present "both sides of the story" evenhandedly.

It is obvious that considered from this standpoint a novelist is not and cannot be a utopian writer, or a writer of literary utopias, at least as the notion of a literary utopia has traditionally been understood. For utopian texts are "one-sided," whereas on this view a good novel could not possibly be. Indeed, from this standpoint, the form of the novel is necessarily associated with a *critique* of utopianism, on both aesthetic as well as moral grounds. According to Frederic Jameson, Lukács maintains that although it is true that the novel "has ethical significance," the reason for this is because the form of the novel is that of "concrete narration" rather than that of the "abstract thought" traditionally engaged in by the authors of works of utopian literature. In Jameson's opinion, the "great novelists" of the nineteenth century were, therefore, even in the "very formal organization of their styles" engaged in a *critique* of utopian thought and writing, which from their point of view offered what is merely a "pallid and abstract dream" or an "insubstantial wish-fulfillment." By adopting the form of the novel the nineteenth century realists offered a "concrete demonstration of the problems of Utopia."[19]

So far as the status of *The Dispossessed* as a literary production is concerned, then, it is arguable that insofar as it does seek to rise up above the situation and see "both sides of the story," evenhandedly, to capture the dramatic tension between the two types of society on Anarres and Urras and their respective values, both at a macro and at the micro level of the personal experiences of just one individual character, then, as Le Guin herself has indicated, it is indeed again best thought of as a *novel* about the trials and tribulations of utopianism, and *not* as an example of a literary utopia, as until quite recently this notion has traditionally been understood.

In this connection John P. Brennan and Michael C. Downs have argued that "only a biased or inattentive reader of *The Dispossessed* could possibly conclude that the novel presents Ioti society as healthier or more desirable than Anarresti society." Le Guin, they continue, "doesn't intend that we read the novel as either an attack on anarchism or a plea for tolerance of diversity in social organization." On the contrary, she "indicates that her motivation for writing *The Dispossessed* was to embody anarchism in a novel." Thus, in their view, "the contrast between Anarres and A-Io," which is the "chief utopian dialectic of the novel, must," if it is to be resolved at all, "be resolved in favor of Anarres."[20] But this wrongly assumes that to seek to embody anarchism in a *novel* necessarily involves espousing the cause of anarchism, which, of course, it does not. It also assumes, again wrongly, that Le Guin thinks that there *is* a need to resolve the dialectical tension between the two worlds of Anarres and Urras. It seems to me, though, that the whole point of the philosophical outlook which informs Le Guin's self-understanding as a *novelist* is precisely that such tensions and contradictions cannot be resolved. It is to attempt to get away from the "either-or" thinking of commentators like Brennan and Downs who think that they can be, and should be, resolved one way or another. And if Le Guin thinks that such ethical dilemmas cannot be resolved, then, of course, the issue of which particular way she would like to resolve them evidently does not arise. If *The Dispossessed* is a novel about the human condition then it must embrace *both* principles at the same time without seeking to resolve, rationally, the contradiction which exists between them.

In this regard, a remark which Hegel makes when discussing the collision of moral forces in Sophocles' *Antigone* seems to me to have a direct application for any attempt to understand Le Guin's *The Dispossessed*. Speaking about the conflicting moral perspectives of Antigone and her uncle, Creon, Hegel states that neither of these "ethical powers" has "any advantage over the other," such that it should be considered to be "a more essential moment of the subtance common to both." For they are "equally and to the same degree essential," and indeed possess "no separate self." Thus, according to Hegel, to portray "the victory of one power and its character, and the defeat of the other side," would be to produce a merely partial and "incomplete work." For it is "in the equal subjection of both sides that absolute right is first accomplished."[21]

Nevertheless, I do agree with Brennan and Downs when they say that "the primary source of ambiguity in *The Dispossessed*, with respect to its claim to "being a utopian work," lies "in the fact that it is a *novel* and not the simple stylized vision of a perfected society usually dealt with by utopian visionaries" (my emphasis). As such, "it must deal with suffering, conflict and discovery, with becoming rather than with essence or perfection"[22] Brennan and Downs quite rightly maintain here that *The Dispossessed* is indeed "*novelistic* rather than visionary"[23] (my emphasis). Where they go wrong, in my view, is when they go on to suggest that the fact that *The Dispossessed* is a *novel* is not an obstacle to our thinking of it as being *also* a literary utopia. Brennan and Downs maintain that "the Odonian planet is 'ambiguous' because it is not perfect, because it is a utopia that comes to terms with man as he is—mortal, weak, and potentially spiteful— rather than with man as he would be were he angelic."[24] Against this it might be argued that insofar as *The Dispossessed* does, as Brennan and Downs rightly maintain, succeed in dealing "with suffering, conflict and discovery, with becoming rather than with essence or perfection," then rather than think of it as an ambiguous literary *utopia*, as even Le Guin herself occasionally suggests, it would be much more accurate to think of it as being *unambiguously* a *novel* which deals with the theme of political utopianism and with the ethical dilemmas which are inevitably associated with it.

Lyman Tower Sargent has claimed that science fiction is "first and foremost designed to *entertain*" (my emphasis).[25] However, as Tower Sargent himself acknowledges, this description hardly fits the case of Le Guin, either in general or specifically in the case of *The Dispossessed*. For Le Guin is a moralist who writes with a serious concern about fundamental ethical issues. At the same time, however, just like the author of a classical realist novel, Le Guin tries to write about such issues *without* moralizing or being didactic.[26] Le Guin's views on the novel and the role of the novelist in society might fruitfully be compared with those of H. G. Wells, Jean-Paul Sartre, and George Orwell. So far as H. G. Wells is concerned, both Jack Williamson and Lovat Dickson have noted that one of the main points of disagreement between H. G. Wells and Henry James in their interchange over the novel as an art form in the early years of the twentieth century had to do with the issue of whether a novel can serve as a work of social criticism. According to Williamson, James was an artist who "wanted to render life objectively, as he saw and felt it, without conscious manipulation." In contrast to this, the later Wells "didn't even care about rendering life; he wanted to change it."[27] In a similar vein, Dickson has noted that "the more or less placid life of the successful novelist was uncongenial" to the later Wells's "reforming temper."[28] According to Dickson, Wells "wanted to alter things" in and through his writings. He "profoundly believed that the novel was an instrument of education" because it "enlarged the mind and understanding." In Dickson's opinion, however, what Wells "overlooked" is that very "few people submit to education" in that sense of the term, and that a novel "has to succeed first as a novel," or as a work of art, before it could possibly undertake such "additional functions."[29] In my view Le Guin's views on the novel and the social function of the novelist are much closer to those of Henry James in this debate than they are to those of H. G. Wells.

Insofar as she is a novelist Le Guin is, therefore, opposed to the idea of a "committed" literature, or a *"littérature engagée,"* at least in the sense of that expression as it is employed by Jean-Paul Sartre.[30] According to Sartre, it would be "inconceivable" that the reader "could enjoy his freedom while reading a work which approves or accepts or simply *abstains from condemning* the subjection of man by man"[31] (my emphasis). In Sartre's view, this tendency to "abstain from condemning" is the "error of realism" in literature.[32] Sartre insists that he can imagine a "good novel" being written, for example, by an American negro "even if hatred of the whites were spread all over it, because it is the freedom of the race that he demands through his hatred."[33] Unlike Le Guin, then, Sartre thinks that being partial and "one sided" is not an obstacle which lies in the way of the production of a good work of literature, a good novel, provided, of course, that the author is on the "right" side.

Views similar to those of Le Guin are also held by Iris Murdoch, who has explicitly criticized Sartre's notion of "commitment in literature" on aesthetic grounds.[34] For Murdoch an important issue is whether Sartre's commitment "helps or hinders him as an *artist*"[35] (my emphasis). Murdoch maintains that key questions, for Sartre, are "Can art liberate without being itself committed? Can it be committed without degenerating into *propaganda*?" (my emphasis).[36] One cannot help thinking that in Murdoch's opinion the answer to the second of these questions just has to be "no." Consequently Murdoch considers Sartre's notion of "commitment" in literature to be a weakness rather than a strength. In her view it demonstrates Sartre's obvious "limitations as a novelist."[37] Sartre, she maintains, all too often "by-passes the complexity of the world of ordinary human relationships" in his novels.[38] Because of Sartre's endorsement of the principle of "commitment" in literature, Murdoch describes him as a "sincere propagandist," but a *propagandist* nonetheless. She insists that Sartre is a far better dramatist than he is a novelist. He a "natural playwright (and an excellent one) rather than a novel writer."[39] It is clear from the text that Murdoch thinks that one reason for this is because Sartre is too much of a "rationalist." Whatever Le Guin's views regarding Sartre and his qualities as a novelist might be, it is difficult to imagine her disagreeing with Murdoch about the general issue of "commitment in literature" here. Le Guin would wholeheartedly endorse the broad thrust of Murdoch's remarks so far as they touch on the issue of what a good novel is and does.

Le Guin would also be sympathetic toward George Orwell's observation that "when a writer engages in politics he should do so as a citizen, as a human being, but not as a *writer*," (my emphasis) for in that capacity he "should make clear that his writing is a thing apart."[40] She would, therefore, be inclined to agree with John Mander's suggestion that for Orwell "a writer can never become a good party-liner." For "if he introduces politics into his writing he will become" nothing more than "a *pamphleteer*" (my emphasis).[41] Mander maintains that in a number of his essays Orwell "seems to be arguing that art should never *preach*, have nothing to do with politics, and, like Orwell's Shakespeare, be content "merely to love the surface of the earth and the *process of life*" (my emphasis).[42] The sentiments attributed here to Orwell by Mander seem to me to accord exactly with those of Le Guin. However, for Le Guin the problem is not so much *whether* "politics" is introduced into one's writing, or into a novel, but rather *how* this is to be done. Le Guin wishes to introduce politics, and the debates and conflicts associated with it, which are always ethical in nature, into her work *without* transforming herself into a pamphleteer. She wants *The Dispossessed* to be a novel rather than a pamphlet or an item of political propaganda.

In his criticism of Orwell, Max Adereth maintains that the "main danger" which the "committed writer" must "guard against is that of bias, one-sidedness and dogmatism." Adereth insists, however, that it is possible for a novelist to do this whilst at the same time *remaining* in some sense politically "committed."[43] Le Guin would, I think, endorse this sentiment, but only if one means something quite specific by the notion of being "committed." To properly understand Le Guin's attitude toward this issue, it is necessary to make a distinction between someone who is a "moralist," on the one hand, and someone who is a "moralizer" on the other. The former is someone who is deeply concerned about the fundamentally important moral and political problems of human existence, as these are portrayed in and through the lives of the central characters of a novel. The latter is someone who attempts to instruct the reader concerning the "correct" solutions for those problems. Both the moralist and the moralizer might be said to be committed in some sense of the term, though in different ways. Le Guin is committed in the first of these senses, and not in the second. She is a moralist and not a moralizer. So far as her own work is concerned, therefore, a crucially important question is whether it is possible for a text to be a *novel*, and, therefore, the work of someone who is committed in the *first* of these two senses only (as a moralist) whilst at the same time *also* being an example of the genre of the literary utopia. As I have attempted to show, there is at least some evidence to support the view that in the 1970s Le Guin was of the opinion that this is not possible. At that time Le Guin took the view that literary utopias are written by moralizers. It is tragic dramas and novels in the realist tradition which are written by moralists.

Charles Nicol has stated that "Le Guin writes to *persuade* the reader of a particular moral view"[44] (my emphasis). In my opinion this is actually the reverse of the truth. Rather, as a novelist, Le Guin invites her readers to think for themselves about the complexities of particular moral dilemmas, which have no obviously right or objectively correct answer. At the same time, given that she is herself not just a novelist but also an anarchist, no doubt Le Guin would be delighted if her readers should, after serious consideration of the issues and through their own free choice, also come to embrace the values associated with anarchism. Alternatively, paradoxical though it may appear, one could say that by deliberately *not* seeking to persuade her readers, Le Guin is hopeful that they might be somehow inspired, and therefore, in a quite different sense of the term, persuaded by the views being dramatically represented in the text. This would fit in very well with the Taoist notion of *wu wei*—to "act without acting"— toward which Le Guin is evidently sympathetic. For example, in the notes to her edition of the *Tao Te Ching*, she emphasizes that "over and over Lao Tzu says *wei wu wei:* Do not do. Doing not-doing. To act without acting." This, she goes on, is "not a statement susceptible to logical interpretation." It is, however, "a concept that transforms thought radically, that changes minds. The whole book [the *Tao Te Ching*] is both an explanation and a demonstration of it."[45] Similarly, in *The Left Hand of Darkness* Le Guin has one of her characters state that "to oppose something" is in effect "to maintain it."[46]

In Le Guin's opinion, then, novelists qua *novelists* preach no solutions to political problems and have no political programme of their own. To employ an expression which Le Guin frequently uses in her essays, insofar as one is a novelist, as opposed to a political activist, one can have no particular "ax to grind." There is an important sense, therefore, in which a successful novel must, by its very nature, "leave everything as it is." But such a way of thinking about the novel is inevitably in some sense conservative in terms of its political implications. For it amounts to saying that a good novelist positively embraces the tragic dilemmas of human existence as being the very stuff of life, or a part of the cosmic order of things, and this must at the same time involve also *accepting* them, in what some would consider to be a politically quietistic manner. To employ the terminology of the Hegelian philosophy, which is close to Taoism in this regard, this amounts to adopting an attitude of *resignation* toward them. Indeed, as Georg Lukács has noted, the writings of Hegel might be thought of as providing a rational or philosophical justification not only for this attitude of mind generally, but for this way of thinking about the political significance of works of literature, and of the novel in particular.[47]

In my view, then, there is much truth in Mark Tunick's claim that Le Guin's "project" is best thought of as being "Hegelian" rather than "utopian."[48] According to Tunick, if Le Guin offers a "political solution" at all to the conflicts, tensions, and ethical dilemmas portrayed in this work then this "may be" a solution which is best thought of as a "dialectical mediation," in the Hegelian sense, between the "conflicting ideals" associated with the societies on Anarres and Urras (specifically, A-Io). It is not entirely clear what Tunick means by this remark, which, as his employment of the expression "may be" indicates, is a cautious one. But one possible response to Tunick's suggestion that Le Guin's approach is similar to that of Hegel because both of them offer their readers a dialectical "solution" to the fundamental moral or political problems with which they deal is to deny that this is the case. From this point of view, although it is true that Le Guin's project in *The Dispossessed* might be said to be a Hegelian one, this is not so for the reason given here by Tunick. For neither Hegel nor Le Guin offer their readers solutions in this sense, not even solutions of a rather special, "dialectical" kind. It would be more accurate to suggest that, just like Hegel, Le Guin does not offer her readers any solutions at all. Nor does she consider it to be her business to do so, insofar as she is the author of a *novel* dealing with the themes of scientific development and political utopianism, and with the ethical dilemmas and the tragic outcomes associated with them. This is the attitude which is best associated with Le Guin's "dialectical" outlook. Indeed, this is something which Tunick himself appears to acknowledge, a little later in his text, when he shows that he is well aware that in *The Dispossessed* Le Guin might *not* be "*advocating* an anarchist-communist libertarian society," (my emphasis) or offering any "political solutions" to complex moral problems and that, as in the case of Greek tragic drama, this work is perhaps better seen as "an *exploration* of the complex tensions one faces in building a community in which," (my emphasis) to employ the terminology of Hegel, one can be "at home and free."[49] Here at least, then, Tunick appreciates that *The Dispossessed* is indeed a *novel* and not a political pamphlet.

From the standpoint of this particular reading of Hegel (there are of course others), there is no actual society which might be said to be perfect or ideal; and thus no utopia as this notion has often been understood. What we have before us, our own society, is "all that there is"— the suggestion being, of course, that we can do nothing more than make the best of it, and must find a way of reconciling ourselves to it, either through religion (Taoism) or through philosophy (Hegel). Applied to the person in the street, this attitude implies that there is no point in trying to change things fundamentally, for in that sense things just never *could* be changed. Applied to the writer of political pamphlets or literary utopias, this attitude suggests either that they are simply wasting their time, or that they are misleading their readers into thinking that existing society could be dramatically otherwise than it is. That is not to say, however, that creative writers or novelists could not take as their chosen subject matter the fact that there are 'utopians' in their own society who do not agree with this view; people who think that things *can* be fundamentally changed, and who are interested in promoting practical programs in pursuit of such change.

Avery Plaw has claimed that "far from being one-sided or didactic, the worlds that Le Guin presents in *The Dispossessed* are genuinely pluralistic, realizing different but equally ultimate human goods at different, but similarly heavy, human costs."[50] It seems to me, however, that it would be more accurate to say that, so far as questions of morality and politics are concerned, Le Guin's outlook in the novel and more generally is dialectical or *dualistic* rather than pluralistic. In this connection, there is at least something to be said for the claim made by Brennan and Downs that *The Dispossessed* "is itself 'two faced' (as perhaps all novels are)," because it "refuses to resolve the tensions" associated with the various "dualities" with which it deals. Brennan and Downs maintain that in *The Dispossessed* Le Guin has *not* presented her readers with "a utopian vision," that is to say a work with a final outcome in which "all opposites are united, all contradictions overcome." This, they maintain, must be an "unsatisfactory conclusion" for any reader of the text who is "hungering for certainty," but it is a conclusion which, in their view, is almost inevitable given that Le Guin "accepts ambiguity heroically" rather than retreating from it or ignoring it."[51] In my view, however, it would be better to say that, rather than accepting "ambiguity" heroically in *The Dispossessed*, what Le Guin actually does is reject the notion of ambiguity and embrace that of a certainty— namely the certainty that "the Truth" in both science and politics possesses a paradoxical character. As far as the sphere of ethics and politics is concerned, like Hegel, Le Guin associates "the Truth" in this area with the tragedy which is human existence. It is this moral "Truth" which, in her view, all novelists must seek to portray.

According to Bulent Somay Le Guin "is by no means ambiguous toward the Anarres/Urras dichotomy" in *The Dispossessed*. On the contrary, she is "wholeheartedly for Anarres, or at least what the Anarresti are trying to do, as she makes amply clear throughout the novel as well as in a later essay, in which she suggests that the whole enterprise was an effort "to embody [anarchism] in a novel."[52] However, against this it might be argued that to seek to "embody" anarchism in a *novel*, given Le Guin's understanding of the meaning of the terms "embodying" and "novel," is not

at all (and could not be) the same as being "wholeheartedly" for the anarchist values which provide a part of the subject matter of that novel. At
least this is true insofar as we think of Le Guin as a *novelist* as opposed to
a political activist. Somay's remarks are accurate insofar as they are an account of Le Guin as a political activist. They are, however, inaccurate to
the extent that they do not distinguish, as Le Guin herself does, between
her two identities of political activist on the one hand and novelist on the
other.

Earlier I cited Laurence Davis's claim that *The Dispossessed* has "radical
political implications" which have as yet not been explored. Against Davis
it might be suggested, that to the extent to which it actually succeeds as a
novel, as Le Guin herself understands that term (at least on occasion), *The
Dispossessed* has no radical political implications at all, nor could it have. In
Le Guin's opinion there are obvious limitations regarding the extent to
which *The Dispossessed*, or indeed any novel, could change the world by
transforming the level of political consciousness of its readers. Nor indeed,
in her view, is that the point of writing a novel. Again, therefore, there is an
important sense in which the literary form which is that of the novel is inherently and inevitably conservative in terms of its political implications. If
there is anything to be said for this reading, then Le Guin is not by any
means a conventional utopian writer. Nor should we think of her advocating in any naïve or straightforward sense a positive utopia to her readers.
She is as cautious about such things as anarchists like Zamyatin. She is also
just as cautious about it as any conservative thinker from Aristotle, through
to Burke and Hegel. There is something in George Slusser's observation
that "Le Guin is not competing with Orwell or Hemingway. Her social
analysis is acute, but its purpose is not indignation or reform. She has no social program, offers no panaceas."[53]

If Le Guin's literature generally, and *The Dispossessed* in particular, do
possess a conservative dimension this is not because, as some commentators have suggested, Le Guin's views as a *novelist* as opposed to a political activist can be identified, one-sidedly, with those of the "Yin utopia"
to which she refers in her essay "A Non-Euclidean View of California as a
Cold Place to Be." Nor is it because they can be identified with the views
of George Orr in *The Lathe of Heaven*. Nor, finally, is it because they can be
identified with the "circular" (as opposed to "linear") thinking associated
with the Simultaneity Theory of Time in *The Dispossessed*. Rather, the reason for this is because insofar as she is indeed a novelist, and not a political propagandist, Le Guin considers it to be her task (indeed her duty) to
portray the ethical dilemmas of human existence in a way that involves
not writing didactically. She does not wish to "take sides" and makes an
effort to tell the "story" in all of its ethical complexity—portraying the

paradoxical nature of the ethical dilemma in question just "as it is." Le Guin does not, therefore, consider it to be her task as a novelist, as opposed to a political activist or an ideologist, to morally condemn existing society and its social relations. It is inevitable, therefore, that if, like Jean-Paul Sartre, one takes the view that those who refuse to condemn existing society necessarily condone it, one will think that Le Guin's opinions concerning the task of the novelist are politically conservative.[54]

LE GUIN AND THE REALIST TRADITION IN EUROPEAN LITERATURE

Paradoxical though it may seem given that she writes works which are usually considered to be "science fiction," Le Guin is best thought of as a novelist working within the realist tradition of European literature. There is a great deal to be said for Darko Suvin's suggestion that Le Guin is "the most European" and "the most *novelistic* writer in present day American SF," (my emphasis) her work having an affinity with "nineteenth century Realism."[55] This is also the view of Tom Moylan and Deirdre Burton, although as in the case of Suvin this is an idea which is not adequately developed in their work. Moylan has rightly suggested that Le Guin "seems to prefer the attitudes of the realist novel or the tragedy rather than the utopia."[56] And Burton has argued that *The Dispossessed* is "a rather gripping story (far less didactic than *Herland*) whose central characters engage our sympathies, concern, anxieties, and so on, in just the manner of the classic realist novel."[57]

Far from being escapist, because it is science fiction, Le Guin's work is best thought of as a form of literary realism. It is "realist" because it encourages her readers to engage with important moral problems, even if it does not actually solve these problems for them. After all, how could it? For in Le Guin's view there are no right answers to these problems; and it is her readers who must try to solve these problems for themselves, or at least find some way of dealing with them. It is for this reason that Le Guin claims that the world which she portrays in both her fantasy literature and in her science fiction, which is often wrongly thought to be an attempt to escape from reality, is in fact a world where "joy, *tragedy* and morality exist" (my emphasis). Consequently it is an "intenser" world and an "intenser reality" than the so-called "real" world of the present. It is not, she maintains, as if she was attempting in her fiction to escape from "a complex, uncertain, frightening world of death and taxes into a nice simply cozy place where heroes don't have to pay taxes, where death only happens to villains, where Science plus Free Enterprise, plus the Galactic Fleet in black and silver uniforms, can solve all problems – where human suffering is something that can be cured, like scurvy." This is what science fiction as it is often understood attempts to do, but escapist or "pulp" fiction of that kind is *not* what Le Guin wishes to write. Such fiction is, she says, "no escape *from* the phoney," but rather "an escape *into* the phoney" (my emphasis). It is a "rejection of reality" rather than what Le Guin refers to as that "intensification of the mystery of the real" that one finds, and must always find, in a good novel.[58] Le Guin's use of the word "mystery" in this context is interesting, and suggests an affinity between her own attitude and that of Gabriel Marcel.[59] As D. D. Raphael has noted, [60] Marcel distinguishes between a "mystery" and a "problem." The latter is something which *can* be solved by some kind of logical argument, theoretical analysis, or appeal to the available empirical evidence, whereas the former cannot be, presumably because engaging with a "mystery," in Marcel's sense of the term, necessarily involves embracing a logical contradiction.

Again it is interesting to compare Le Guin's views on this subject with those of Jean-Paul Sartre. Iris Murdoch has contrasted the works of Sartre with those of the realist tradition in European literature, as this is exemplified by the novels of Tolstoy. Sartre's characters, she argues, are little more than the vehicles for the expression of abstract ideas or one-sided ideological positions rather than "characters" of the kind that one finds in a good realist novel. Sartre's writings tend to be based on "issues" rather than on individual "characters" or real "people."[61] According to Murdoch, because he is little more than a political propagandist, Sartre lacks that perception, held by the great writers within the realist tradition, that "the human person," as a concrete individual as opposed to a theoretical abstraction, is something which is both "precious and unique."[62] Again Murdoch contrasts this attitude with that of Tolstoy, who, she maintains, held the view that "the novelist has his eye fixed on what we *do*, and not on what we *ought* to do" (my emphasis). Within the realist tradition, the novelist is "a *describer* rather than an explainer" (my emphasis). Tolstoy's novels portray "a picture of, and a comment upon, the human condition."[63] According to Murdoch, novels of this kind exhibit a "freedom from rationalism" which we do *not* find in Sartre's writings, even in his novels. Interestingly, Murdoch also says that an important difference between Sartre and the novelists working within the realist tradition is that in the case of Sartre human society is a world of "ideological battles" where certain "conflicts" are "inevitable" and "reconciliations are impossible." Consequently, unlike Tolstoy and the other realist authors, for Sartre literature ought not to be associated with a process of "*reconciliation through appropriation*" (my emphasis).[64]

One difficulty associated with the claim that Le Guin's *The Dispossessed* is best located against the background of the tradition of European realism in literature is the fact that there are occasions when Le Guin appears to dissociate herself from that tradition. So far as this issue is concerned, once again it is fruitful to compare Le Guin's views with those of Zamyatin. Unlike Le Guin, Zamyatin is opposed to all forms of realism. Consequently he rejects literary realism just as he does scientific and moral realism, and for the same reason. In all three cases what we have, he suggests, is an attempt to offer an account which its author considers (wrongly) to be objectively true. Thus, for example, speaking specifically about literary rather than either scientific or moral realism, Zamyatin maintains that its exponents seek to offer a "bare depiction of daily life."[65] He also claims that, just as scientific realists think of themselves as holding up a "mirror" to nature,[66] so also literary "realists" think of themselves as holding up a "mirror" to society. They too, Zamyatin says, "have a mirror in their hands."[67] Given that he is a relativist and a constructivist in science and a nihilist in ethics, and that he rejects the principles of objectivism and realism, it is not too surprising that Zamyatin should also object to the idea of literary realism, as he thinks that the philosophical assumptions upon which the notion of literary realism is based are the same as those associated with scientific and moral realism.

I suggested earlier, and have argued more fully elsewhere, that so far as questions of science and ethics are concerned, Le Guin is a realist.[68] She rejects Zamyatin's Nietzschean commitment to relativism and constructivism. One would expect, therefore, that Le Guin would be sympathetic to the idea of literary realism in *some* sense of that term; and indeed she is. On the other hand, though, it is undeniable that there is also some apparent evidence which might be thought of as counting against this claim. For example, in one of her essays, when discussing the idea of literary realism, Le Guin states that the literary realists of the past have thought that "an artist is like a roll of photographic film, you expose it and develop it and there is a reproduction of Reality in two dimensions. But that is all wrong, and if any artist tells you 'I am a camera,' or 'I am a mirror,' distrust him instantly, he's fooling you, pulling a fast one. Artists are people who are not at all interested in *the facts*—only in *the truth*. You get the facts from *outside*. The truth you get from *inside*"[69] (my emphasis). In these remarks Le Guin appears to be rejecting the idea of literary realism outright; and if we make Zamyatin's assumption that there is a connection between one's attitude toward literary realism and one's attitude toward scientific realism; then this suggests that Le Guin rejects the principles of scientific realism outright also. So how might we respond to these remarks? How can we defend the claim that not only is Le Guin a scientific and a moral realist, she is a literary realist also?

One possible response would be to suggest that although Le Guin is indeed a scientific realist and a moral realist, nevertheless she does not

consider this to be a reason for being a literary realist as well. Consequently, the rejection of literary realism which she appears to be making
here is in fact quite consistent with my earlier claim that she is sympathetic to other forms of realism. However, this does not seem to me to be
the best response to make to the remarks cited above because this counter-
argument simply assumes that these remarks are indeed best interpreted
as being a rejection by Le Guin of the principles of literary realism.

An alternative response, which in my view is to be preferred, would
be to say that when making these remarks what Le Guin is objecting to
is not literary realism *per se*, but rather literary realism as it has existed
in the past; just as her own views on science, although definitely in some
sense realist, also reject the idea of scientific realism as it has existed in
the past. In the case of scientific realism Le Guin thinks that her predecessors have had a tendency to think, somewhat naively, that establishing the truth or falsity of a theory or explanatory hypothesis in science
is a matter of seeing whether it or one of its competitors is or is not supported by the available empirical evidence—whether it "fits the facts"—
and that this can easily be done by performing some experiment, the
outcome of which will be the production of evidence which can conclu-
sively determine the matter one way or the other. Like Zamyatin, Le
Guin objects to scientific realism, understood in this particular sense. As
we have seen, in any given case, she thinks that it is necessary for natural scientists to appreciate that there will always be at least two opposed
ways of "looking at things," each of which is equally well supported by
the available empirical evidence. Disputes in science regarding the truth
of one or other competing theories are in consequence not so easily resolved. This does not mean, however, that Le Guin should be considered
to be a relativist. For Le Guin *does* think that there is such a thing as "*the
Truth*" which can be associated with disputes of this kind. In her view,
if one wishes to grasp this truth then it is necessary that one be able to
embrace the ideas associated with both sides in such a dispute, despite
the fact that they contradict one another. If one does this then one *has*
succeeded in getting at "the (objective) Truth" of the matter. For one's
views *do* then succeed in accurately "reflecting" the way things truly are
in the world. The world itself just is a paradoxical and contradictory
place and if the beliefs which natural scientists hold about it are *also* paradoxical and contradictory, then according to this line of reasoning that
is not an indication that those beliefs must be "false." It is rather a reason for thinking that they are objectively "true," precisely because they
accurately reflect the paradoxical nature of reality as well as the paradoxical reality of nature.

Similarly, so far as literary realism is concerned, one might say that Le
Guin objects to the idea that a creative writer, say the author of a novel,

might possess a privileged insight into the "truth" of the matter so far as any of the ethical dilemmas which are portrayed in the novel is concerned. For in the case of each of these ethical dilemmas, also, there will be two sides to a complex and contradictory story. For Le Guin it is not the task of the novelist to "take sides" in such disputes, or to moralize or preach to their readers, regarding the question of who is right and who is wrong—whose beliefs are true and whose false—in relation to these complex moral problems. But here again, as in the case of disputes in science, Le Guin seems to think that, even so there *is* such a thing as "the (objective) Truth" of the matter, and that it is the task of the novelist to attempt to grasp this truth and portray it dramatically in and through the lives and actions of her or his characters. It is in *this* sense, then, that I think that Le Guin's style of writing generally, and specifically in *The Dispossessed*, might legitimately be said to constitute a form of literary realism the aim of which is to dramatically portray "the Truth."

Again it is illuminating to consider the views of Le Guin about this issue against the background of the debate between H.G. Wells and Henry James over the nature of the novel and the social role of the novelist in the early years of the twentieth century. According to Wells, James took the view that a novel is "an end in itself" rather than a "means to an end." In short, he subscribed to the principle of "art for art's sake." This attitude, Wells maintains, is closely associated with James's commitment to the principle of "realism" in literature. Because James "has never discovered that a novel isn't a picture" of contemporary society he is, Wells insists, far too "eager" to "accept things" just as they are.[70]

On the other hand, however, it is clear that there are also significant *differences* between the attitude of Henry James (as H. G. Wells understood it) toward the novel and that of Le Guin. This is so because, as characterized by Wells, James had a tendency to write about "trivial" issues rather than the great moral and political problems of the day. This could not be said of Le Guin even though, as we have seen, like James (and indeed Wells himself on occasion), she makes an effort to avoid didacticism and preaching about them.

Le Guin's attitude here might be thought of as an attempt to steer a middle course between the views of the later Wells and of James. The later Wells wrote about the moral and political issues of his time, but he did so didactically, as a propagandist or as a journalist rather than as a novelist. James, on the other hand, was a novelist, or an artist, a creative writer who wished to avoid didacticism in his writing. According to Wells, however, he was only able to this by avoiding altogether writing about any matters of moral or political importance. We may now say that, like Wells but not James, Le Guin also wishes to write about such important matters. However, like James but not Wells, she wishes to do so as an artist and not as a political propagandist. She is concerned to raise these problems in her writing, and present them to her readers in a dramatic or literary form, whilst avoiding the temptation to tell her readers what they ought to think about them, or to persuade her readers that there is, objectively speaking, only one right answer which could be given to them.

DOSTOEVSKY, LE GUIN, AND THE POLITICAL NOVEL

Maurice Baring has made an interesting remark about Dostoevsky. He says that Dostoevsky is a "realist" who "sees things as they are all through life."[71] As such, "he is free from cant, either moral or political, and absolutely free from all prejudice of caste or class."[72] It is, Baring goes on, impossible for Dostoevsky to think that "because a man is a revolutionary he must, therefore, be a braver man than his fellows, or because a man is a Conservative he must, therefore, be a more cruel man than his fellows, just as it is impossible for him to think the contrary, and to believe that because a man is a Conservative he cannot help being honest or because a man is a Radical he must inevitably be a scoundrel."[73] Rather, Dostoevsky "judges men and things as they are, quite apart from the labels which they choose to give to their political opinions." It is for this reason, Baring maintains, that "nobody who is by nature a *doctrinaire* can appreciate or enjoy the works of Dostoyevsky" who "sees and embraces everything as it really is."[74]

A similar assessment of Dostoevsky, and specifically his novel *The Possessed*, is also offered by Irving Howe,[75] who discusses Dostoevsky in the context of a wider thesis concerning the nature of the "political novel." Howe defines a "political novel" as follows: "By a political novel," he says, "I mean a novel in which political ideas play a dominant role or in which the political milieu is the dominant setting."[76] In its ideal form "the political novel," Howe continues, "is peculiarly a work of internal tensions. To be a novel at all, it must contain the usual representation of human behavior and feeling; yet it must also absorb into its stream of movement the hard and perhaps insoluble pellets of modern ideology. The novel deals with moral sentiments, with passions and emotions; it tries, above all, to capture the quality of concrete experience. Ideology, however, is abstract, as it must be, and, therefore, likely to be recalcitrant whenever an attempt is made to incorporate it into the novel's stream of sensuous impression." In Howe's opinion this conflict is "inescapable." At the same time, however, "it is precisely from this conflict that the political novel gains its interest and takes on the aura of high drama."[77] For "no matter how much the writer intends to celebrate or discredit a political ideology, no matter how didactic or polemical his [sic] purpose may be, his novel cannot finally rest on the idea "in itself." To the degree that he [*sic*] is really a novelist, a man [*sic*] seized by the passion to represent and to give order to experience, he must drive the politics of or behind his novel into a complex relation with the kinds of experience that resist reduction to formula." Howe maintains that it "would be easy to slip into a mistake here," namely, to endorse the view that "abstract ideas invariably contaminate a work of art and should be kept at a safe distance from it."[78]

With respect to the issue of "didacticism versus art," Howe concludes his discussion with the following interesting remarks about Dostoevsky and *The Possessed*. He says that "while a political novel can enrich our sense of human experience, while it can complicate and humanize our commitments, it is only very rarely that it will alter those commitments themselves. And when it does so, the political novel is engaged in a task of persuasion which is *not* really its central or distinctive purpose" (my emphasis). For example, Howe maintains, "I find it hard to imagine" someone who is "a serious socialist being dissuaded from his belief by a reading of *The Possessed*, though I should like equally to think that the quality and nuance of that belief can never be quite as they were before he read *The Possessed*."[79] According to Howe, Dostoevsky's *The Possessed* is "the *greatest* of all political novels."[80] For despite his own political commitments, his hostility toward anarchism, nevertheless Dostoevsky "could not suppress his "artistic side," for "whatever else it does, *The Possessed* proves nothing of the kind that might be accessible to proof in "a mere pamphlet."[81]

It is not at all clear to me that, as a creative writer, Dostoevsky did in fact live up to this rather flattering picture which is painted of him here by Baring and Howe; and of no work is this more true than *The Possessed*, the very work which provided one of the sources of inspiration for Le Guin's own novel, *The Dispossessed*, which might indeed be read as a response to the earlier work of Dostoevsky. E. H. Carr's assessment of *The Possessed*, for example, is quite different from that of Baring and Howe, and much less eulogistic. According to Carr, "the glaring defects of *The Devils* are a serious bar to the enjoyment of it."[82] In *The Possessed*, Carr maintains, "the tortured questionings of *Crime and Punishment* are replaced by crude dogmatic assertion."[83] Peter Verchovenski, Carr goes on, is not "even a caricature; he is the walking embodiment of a *theory*. He is drawn with as little wit as understanding, and remains totally unconvincing" (my emphasis).[84] Indeed, Howe provides evidence which suggests that Dostoevsky was aware of the limitations of his novel if it is considered as a work of art, as opposed to a political pamphlet, the purpose of which is to present a tirade against anarchism and anarchists. Despite the praise lavished upon *The Possessed* by some critics, Dostoevsky was well aware of the artistic weaknesses of *The Possessed*, precisely because of the overtly hostile attitude of its author toward anarchism and hence also because of its tendency at times to become doctrinaire. "I mean to utter certain thoughts," wrote Dostoevsky about *The Possessed*, "whether all the *artistic* side of it goes to the dogs or not." Even "if it turns into a mere *pamphlet*," Dostoevsky continues, "I shall say all that I have in my heart" (my emphasis).[85]

It is interesting to consider whether the assessment of Dostoevsky's novel which is offered by Baring and Howe might have an application, if not to Dostoevsky and *The Possessed*, then to Ursula K. Le Guin and *The Dispossessed*. For it might be suggested that the praise which is perhaps unjustifiably given to Dostoevsky's novel by Baring and Howe might legitimately be accorded to that of Le Guin, which might in consequence be said to be a *better* example of a good "political novel," in Howe's sense of the term, than the work by Dostoevsky to which it is a response. David L. Porter has rightly said that for Le Guin a novelist, and hence also a good science fiction writer, must possess "moral seriousness, *without* moralizing and preaching" (my emphasis).[86] And it is clear that Le Guin agrees with him. In Le Guin's own words, the novelist "works as an *artist*" (my emphasis) and, in consequence, simply "tries to engage us" to think about important political issues rather than tell us what we ought to think about them.[87] According to Le Guin, novelists who allow their own ideological beliefs to influence their work could not possibly be "good" writers. Indeed, Le Guin has said of herself that "if I forced myself to" do this then "I would write dishonestly and badly." "Am I," she continues, "to sacrifice the ideal of truth and *beauty* in order to make an *ideological* point?" (my emphasis).[88]

It is clear from these remarks that Le Guin thinks that all writers who seek to proselytize or to promote directly any particular political cause, whether or not this happens to be the cause of anarchism, are necessarily "bad" writers. Moreover, for this very reason, it is likely that they will be unsuccessful in their efforts to make political converts. Rather, their writing will be ineffective in this regard because of its tendency to alienate their readers. Paradoxically, Le Guin thinks that the harder one tries as a *writer* to influence others so far as questions of ethics and politics are concerned; to "put them right"; to make them see things correctly, that is to say in one's *own* way; then the more likely it is that one's efforts will be considered by one's readers to be doctrinaire; and the more likely it is that they will be unsuccessful. It is for this very reason that Le Guin thinks that one should actually adopt the opposite strategy to this, to simply write well rather than to seek converts, and if one succeeds in this then in her view it is actually more likely that one's readers will, in this *indirect* manner, be inspired to come to embrace the author's outlook themselves of their own free choice. Although, of course, Le Guin appreciates that it is also possible that this will not happen, and that the reader will make a different choice. This strategy is associated with Le Guin's "humanism"—something which she has in common with the "realist" literary tradition. It is also, as we have seen, associated with her commitment to pacifism and with the Taoist notion of *wu-wei*, or of "acting without acting."

Perhaps Le Guin herself would not welcome this comparison with Dostoevsky, but it seems to me that insofar as Howe's characterization of a good "political novel" does apply to her, and to *The Dispossessed*, then what this shows is that her effort *not* to be a doctrinaire, if it were successful, could only result in a position which is in some sense politically conservative. This is a paradox, and indeed an indication of the tragic dimension to her own life and work. Le Guin wants to be both a good novelist and a political activist (an anarchist) at the same time, but it might be suggested that, as Le Guin herself understands them, these two social roles are actually incompatible with one another. For the novelist in Le Guin leans toward conservatism, not anarchism; and the anarchist in her leans toward didacticism, not good literature. The character of Le Guin herself, of course, might be seen as the totality of these two contradictory principles. Indeed, if it is true that Le Guin has no desire to preach or moralize, and that she has no desire to be doctrinaire or ideological, insofar as she is the creator of a "work of art," then it is evident that this must be her attitude toward *all* political projects and the ideologies associated with them including of course, paradoxically, that of anarchism. From this point of view, as Le Guin is well aware, her own personal commitment to anarchism as a political philosophy is likely to get in the way of her efforts as a novelist to produce a work which is a work of literature *about* anarchism and not a political pamphlet which espouses the cause of anarchism. To the extent that she succeeds as a novelist, this can only be at the expense of diluting, as it were, any political message that *The Dispossessed* might be thought to contain.

It should be noted that Le Guin has sometimes been criticized for her didacticism in *The Dispossessed*. Susan Wood, for example, has said of *The Dispossessed*, that "Shevek's speculations on government and on human relations, too, often become uncomfortably didactic." *The Dispossessed*, Wood maintains, "relies too heavily on the idea expressed and analyzed rather than embodied and shown."[89] Similarly, D. G. Williams has said of both *The Dispossessed* and Robert Heinlein's *The Moon is a Harsh Mistress* that "both books have strong didactic intentions, teaching, explaining, moralizing, and exemplifying in favor of their own versions of 'anarchism.'"[90] What is especially interesting about these remarks is that Le Guin is on occasion inclined to *agree* with them. Like Dostoevsky, Le Guin concedes that all too often she inclines toward didacticism in her work generally, and in *The Dispossessed* in particular. She acknowledges that there is a tendency in her own work to preach or to moralize, and hence to be doctrinaire. Indeed, in my view, her concern about this issue leads her to be excessively modest about the merits of *The Dispossessed* as a work of art—its status as a novel as opposed to a traditional literary utopia.

Le Guin recognizes not only the limitations of *The Dispossessed* as a work of art, but also the internal contradiction within her own character between the political activist who is an anarchist, on the one hand, and the artist who has aspirations to be a novelist in the great tradition of European Realism on the other. For example, in her interview with Jonathan Ward, Le Guin says that *in general* "my social activism is *separate* from my writing. *Except,* perhaps, for this last book, *The Dispossessed*, in which being *utopian*, I am trying to *state* something which I think desirable" (my emphasis).[91] And in another interview Le Guin notes: "I have found, somewhat to my *displeasure*, that I am an extremely moral writer. I am always *grinding axes* and making points. I wish I wasn't so moralistic, because my interest is *aesthetic*. What I want to do is make something beautiful, like a good pot or a good piece of music, and the ideas and moralism keep getting in the way" (my emphasis). There is, Le Guin concludes, "a definite battle on."[92]

These remarks suggest that with respect to this issue, also, there is an affinity between the views of Le Guin and those of George Orwell. According to Orwell, someone who is a "creative writer" can and occasionally must "split his life" and his [*sic*] "self" into "two compartments." For example the individual concerned might be thought of as being *both* a writer and a political activist at the same time. Moreover there can be and occasionally will be occasions when if someone who is a writer "is honest" then "his [*sic*] writings and his political activities may actually contradict one another." Orwell suggests that in such situations *"one* half" (my emphasis) of the person who is *both* "writer-*and*-activist" (my emphasis) will necessarily be "condemned to inactivity," although the *other* half of him is not. Interestingly, Orwell also maintains that it is the *writing* rather than the political activity of such a person which might be thought of as "the product of the *saner* self" (my emphasis).[93]

There are times, then, when Le Guin appears to *agree* with her critics that *The Dispossessed* is indeed an excessively didactic work. Avery Plaw has claimed that "one point on which *most* critics are agreed" is that *The Dispossessed* "is, in one way or the other, 'didactic,' 'moralizing,' and 'monistic.'"[94] If this criticism were valid then it would have to be said that *The Dispossessed* is a failure as a *novel* when evaluated by the aesthetic criteria which Le Guin herself endorses. However, even though Le Guin is occasionally sympathetic toward it, I do not myself think that this criticism is justified.

NOTES

1. For Hegel's theory of tragedy see the selection from Hegel's writings collected together in *Hegel on Tragedy*, eds. Anne Paolucci and Henry Paolucci (New York: Doubleday, 1962). This includes as an appendix A. C. Bradley's "Hegel's Theory of Tragedy," 367–88. See also Walter Kaufmann, "Hegel's Ideas About Tragedy," in *New Studies in Hegel's Philosophy*, ed. Warren E. Steinkraus (New York: Holt, Rinehart and Winston, 1971), 201–20. For Lukács see Georg Lukács, *The Historical Novel* (Harmondsworth: Penguin, 1976 [1936]), chapter 2, 101–22.

2. Lukács, *The Historical Novel*, 113: "The contradictoriness of social development, the intensification of these contradictions to the point of tragic collision is a general fact of life." see also 123: "At this point one might ask: granted that all these facts of life (whose artistic reflection we take dramatic form to be) are real and important – are they not in fact general facts of life? Must not epic also reflect them? The question is perfectly justified. Indeed in this general and therefore too abstract form, it must be answered in the affirmative."

3. See Hegel, *Hegel on Tragedy*, 280–81. D. D. Raphael has stated, *The Paradox of Tragedy* (London: Allen and Unwin, 1960), 25, that "tragedy always presents a conflict. The proposition needs no defense. It is familiar enough." Despite Raphael's dismissal of Hegel's views on tragedy, this view is so familiar in modern times largely because of the influence of Hegel's *Lectures on Aesthetics*. Raphael's own account of what the "conflict" dealt with by tragedy is about is different from that of Hegel. Surprisingly, it makes no reference to what Hegel considered to be essential, the notion of a moral dilemma.

4. Lukács, *The Historical Novel*, 105–13, 108–09. For the relationship between political theory and Greek tragedy generally see Tony Burns, "Sophocles' *Antigone* and the History of the Concept of Natural Law," *Political Studies*, 50, 3 (2002): 545–57; Peter J. Euben ed., *Greek Tragedy and Political Theory* (Berkeley and Los Angeles: University of California Press, 1988); and Peter J. Euben, *The Tragedy of Political Theory: The Road Not Taken* (Princeton: Princeton University Press, 1990); Christopher Rocco, *Tragedy and Enlightenment: Athenian Political Thought and the Dilemmas of Modernity* (Berkeley and Los Angeles: University of California Press, 1997).

5. F. L. Lucas, *Tragedy: Serious Drama in Relation to Aristotle's Poetics*, 2nd ed. (London: Chatto and Windus, 1972 [1927]), 64.

6. For example, see D. D. Raphael's somewhat contemptuous remarks about Hegel in his significantly entitled *The Paradox of Tragedy*, 19–20, 23–24, 37, 109–10. Despite being so dismissive of Hegel at times, Raphael's debt to him is evident throughout this book.

7. Una Ellis-Fermor, *The Frontiers of Drama* (London: Methuen, 1945), 17–18, cited Raphael, *The Paradox of Tragedy*, 39.

8. As Lukács puts it, *The Theory of the Novel: A Historico-Philosophical Essay on the Forms of Great Epic Literature* (London: Merlin Press, 1978), 93, the novel is "the representative art form of our age." See also Lukács, *Studies in European Realism: A*

Sociological Survey of the Writings of Balzac, Stendhal, Zola, Tolstoy, Gorki and Others (London: Merlin Press, 1972), 2: "[T]he novel is the predominant art form of modern *bourgeois* culture."

9. Raphael, *The Paradox of Tragedy*, 57.

10. Raphael, *The Paradox of Tragedy*, 101–02.

11. Raphael, *The Paradox of Tragedy*, 89–90. See also Martha Nussbaum, *The Fragility of Goodness: Luck and Ethics in Greek Tragedy and Philosophy* (Cambridge: Cambridge University Press, 1986), 12: "[E]pic and tragic poets were widely assumed to be the central ethical thinkers and teachers of Greece."

12. Lukács, *The Theory of the Novel*, 72.

13. Antony Arblaster, "Literature and Moral Choice," in *Literature and the Political Imagination*, eds. John Horton and Andrea T. Baumeister (London: Routledge, 1996), 129–44. See also Alasdair MacIntyre, "Moral Dilemmas," *Ethics and Politics: Selected Essays*, Volume 2 (Cambridge: Cambridge University Pres, 2006), 85–100. MacIntyre's interest in moral dilemmas is associated with his idea of a "virtue ethics," or a morality without rules. This idea also informs his appeal to what he takes to be Sartre's "situation ethics" in his critique of R. M. Hare, whose moral philosophy is a defense of the traditional way of thinking about morality as involving the impartial application of general rules. See chapter 7.

14. See Nussbaum, *The Fragility of Goodness: Luck and Ethics in Greek Tragedy and Philosophy*, 13; and Andrew Gibson, *Postmodernity Ethics and the Novel: From Leavis to Levinas* (London: Routledge, 1999).

15. Gibson, *Postmodernity Ethics and the Novel*, 4.

16. See Martha Nussbaum, *Frontiers of Justice: Disability, Nationality, Species Membership* (Cambridge, Mass, and London: Bellknap Press, 2006); and Martha Nussbaum, "Human Functioning and Social Justice: In Defense of Aristotelian Essentialism," *Political Theory*, 20, non. 2 (1992), 202–46.

17. Le Guin, notes to Lao Tzu, *Tao Te Ching: A Book About the Way and the Power of the Way*, a new English version, ed. Ursula K. Le Guin (Boston and London: Shambhala Books, 1998), 29.

18. Le Guin, cited Susan Wood, "Introduction," Ursula K. Le Guin, *The Language of the Night: Essays on Fantasy and Science Fiction*, ed. Susan Wood (New York: Perigee Books, 1979), 22.

19. Frederic Jameson, "The Case for Georg Lukács," in *Marxism and Form: Twentieth Century Dialectical Theories of Literature* (Princeton, N.J.: Princeton University press, 1974 [1971]), 173–74.

20. John P. Brennan and Michael C. Downs, "Anarchism and Utopian Tradition in *The Dispossessed*" in *Ursula K. Le Guin*, eds. Joseph Olander and Martin Harry Greenberg (New York: Taplinger, 1979), 123.

21. Hegel, *Hegel on Tragedy*, 280–81.

22. Brennan and Downs, "Anarchism and Utopian Tradition in *The Dispossessed*," 144.

23. Brennan and Downs, "Anarchism and Utopian Tradition in *The Dispossessed*," 151.

24. Brennan and Downs, "Anarchism and Utopian Tradition in *The Dispossessed*," 151.

25. Lyman Tower Sargent, "Eutopias and Dystopias in Science Fiction: 1950–75," in *America as Utopia*, ed. Kenneth M. Roemer (New York: Burtt Franklin, 1981), 356.

26. Tower Sargent, "Eutopias and Dystopias in Science Fiction: 1950–75," 356. Interestingly, writing in 1911, H. G. Wells was also critical of what he took to be the then dominant view that "the novel is wholly and solely a means of relaxation." See H. G. Wells, "The Contemporary Novel," in *Henry James and H. G. Wells: A Record of Their Friendship, Their Debate on the Art of Fiction and Their Quarrel*, eds. Leon Edel and Gordon N. Ray (London: Rupert Hart Davis, 1958), 132.

27. Jack Williamson, *H. G. Wells: Critic of Progress* (Baltimore: Mirage Press, 1973), 36.

28. Lovat Dickson, *H. G. Wells: His Turbulent Life and Times* (London: Macmillan, 1971), 214.

29. Dickson, *H. G. Wells: His Turbulent Life and Times*, 257. For the debate between Wells and James on the novel as an art form generally see the texts collected together in *Henry James and H. G. Wells*, eds. Edel and Ray.

30. According to Edel and Ray, the later H. G. Wells was also an advocate of "*littérature engagée*." See Edel and Ray, *Henry James and H. G. Wells*, 11.

31. Jean-Paul *What is Literature?* (London: Methuen, 1967 [1948]), 45.

32. Sartre, *What is Literature?* 44.

33. Sartre, *What is Literature?* 46.

34. Iris Murdoch, *Sartre: Romantic Rationalist* (London: Collins, 1967 [1953]), 9–10, 32, 49, 58, 111–12, 116–20.

35. Murdoch, *Sartre: Romantic Rationalist*, 10.

36. Murdoch, *Sartre: Romantic Rationalist*, 49.

37. Murdoch, *Sartre: Romantic Rationalist*, 117.

38. Murdoch, *Sartre: Romantic Rationalist*, 32.

39. Murdoch, *Sartre: Romantic Rationalist*, 119.

40. George Orwell, "Writers and Leviathan," in *The Collected Essays, Journalism and Letters of George Orwell*, in 4 volumes, Vol. 4, *In Front of Your Nose: 1945–50*, eds. Sonia Orwell and Ian Angus (Harmondsworth: Penguin, 1970 [1948]), 468. The issue of "art versus propaganda" is one to which Orwell returned on several occasions. See also George Orwell, "Inside the Whale," in *Collected Essays*, Vol. 1, *An Age Like This: 1920–1940* (Harmondsworth: Penguin, 1971 [1968]), 557–60, 568, 572; George Orwell, "Review of *The Novel Today*, by Phillip Henderson," *Collected Essays*, Vol. 1, 288–91; George Orwell, "The Frontiers of Art and Propaganda," in *Collected Essays*, Vol. 2, *My Country Right or Left: 1940–1943* (Harmondsworth: Penguin, 1970 [1968]), 149–53; George Orwell, "Tolstoy and Shakespeare," in *Collected Essays*, Vol. 2, 157; George Orwell, "Literature and Totalitarianism," in *Collected Essays*, Vol. 161–64; George Orwell, "Literature and the Left," in *Collected Essays*, Vol. 2, 334–37; George Orwell, "Why I Write," in *The Decline of the English Murder and Other Essays* (Harmondsworth: Penguin, 1980 [1965]), 183–86. Orwell's views on this subject are discussed by Max Adereth, "What is *Littérature Engagée*"? in *Commitment in Modern French Literature: A Brief Study of "Littérature Engagée" in the Works of Péguy, Aragon and Sartre* (London: Victor Gollancz, 1967), 25; John Mander, *The Writer and Commitment* (London: Secker and Warburg, 1961), 112; and by

Alan Swingewood, "George Orwell, Socialism and the Novel," in *The Sociology of Literature* (London: Paladin Books, 1972), 250.

41. Cited by John Mander, *The Writer and Commitment*, 112.

42. Mander, *The Writer and Commitment*, 82.

43. Adereth, "What is *Littérature Engagée*"? 27.

44. Charles Nicol, "The Good Witch of the West Processed: A Review of Warren G. Rochelle, *Communities of the Heart: The Rhetoric of Myth in the Fiction of Ursula K. Le Guin*," *Science Fiction Studies*, 29, no. 1 (2002), 127–28.

45. Lao Tzu, *Tao Te Ching*, 6.

46. Ursula K. Le Guin, *The Left Hand of Darkness* (London: MacDonald, 1991 [1969]), 11, 132.

47. Lukács, *The Historical Novel*, 67: "[Hegel] states theoretically those principles which determine [Sir Walter] Scott's historical practice."

48. Mark Tunick, "The Need for Walls: Privacy, Community and Freedom in *The Dispossessed*," in *The New Utopian Politics of Ursula K. Le Guin's* The Dispossessed, eds. Laurence Davis and Peter Stillman (Lanham, Md.: Lexington Books, 2005), 129.

49. Tunick, "The Need for Walls: Privacy, Community and Freedom in *The Dispossessed*," 141.

50. Avery Plaw, "Empty Hands: Communication, Pluralism and Community in Ursula K. Le Guin's *The Dispossessed*," in *The New Utopian Politics of Ursula K. Le Guin's* The Dispossessed, eds. Davis and Stillman, 295.

51. John P. Brennan and Michael C. Downs, "Anarchism and Utopian Tradition in *The Dispossessed*, 118.

52. Bulent Somay, "From Ambiguity to Self-Reflexivity: Revolutionizing Fantasy Space," in *The New Utopian Politics of Ursula K. Le Guin's* The Dispossessed, eds. Davis and Stillman, 236.

53. George Edgar Slusser, *The Farthest Shores of Ursula K. Le Guin* (Chapbook: Borgo Press, 1976), 20.

54. Sartre, *What is Literature?* 44–48.

55. Darko Suvin, "Parables of De-Alienation: Le Guin's Widdershin's Dance," in *Positions and Presuppositions in Science Fiction* (London: Macmillan, 1988), 149.

56. Tom Moylan, *Demand the Impossible: Science Fiction and the Utopian Imagination* (London: Methuen, 1986), 103.

57. Deirdre Burton, "Linguistic Innovation in Feminist Utopian Fiction," *Journal of English Language and Literature*, 29, no. 1 (1983), 35.

58. Le Guin, "Escape Routes," in *The Language of the Night: Essays on Fantasy and Science Fiction*, 205.

59. Gabriel Marcel, *Being and Having*, trans. Katherine Farrer (Boston: Beacon Press, 1951 [1935]), 117–18, 170–71. See also Gabriel Marcel, *The Mystery of Being*, Vol. I, *Reflection and Mystery*, trans. G. S. Fraser (Chicago: Regnery, 1950), 204–05, 211–16.

60. D. D. Raphael, *The Paradox of Tragedy*, 90–91.

61. Iris Murdoch, *Sartre: Romantic Rationalist* , 118.

62. Murdoch, *Sartre: Romantic Rationalist*, 120.

63. Murdoch, *Sartre: Romantic Rationalist*, 9–10.

64. Murdoch, *Sartre: Romantic Rationalist*, 51.

65. Yevgeny Zamyatin, "The New Russian Prose," in *A Soviet Heretic: Essays by Yevgeny Zamyatin*, ed. Mirra Ginsburg (Chicago: University of Chicago Press, 1991), 105.

66. Zamyatin's critique of the "mirror" metaphor, and the arguments and beliefs which he associates with the "realist" employment of it, prefigure in a striking way the views of Richard Rorty. See Richard Rorty, *Philosophy and the Mirror of Nature* (Oxford: Blackwell, 1980).

67. Yevgeny Zamyatin, "Contemporary Russian Literature," in *A Soviet Heretic*, 36.

68. Tony Burns, "Science and Politics in *The Dispossessed*: Le Guin and the 'Science Wars,'" in *The New Utopian Politics of Ursula K. Le Guin's* The Dispossessed, eds. Davis and Stillman, 195–215.

69. Ursula K. Le Guin, "Talking About Writing," in *The Language of the Night*, 198.

70. H. G. Wells, "Of Art, of Literature, of Mr. Henry James," in *Henry James and H. G. Wells*, eds. Edel and Ray, 244–45.

71. Maurice Baring, *Landmarks of Russian Literature* (London: Methuen, 1960 [1910]), 158–9.

72. Baring, *Landmarks of Russian Literature*, 158–59.

73. Baring, *Landmarks of Russian Literature*, 158–59.

74. Baring, Landmarks of Russian Literature, 158–59.

75. Irving Howe, "The Idea of the Political Novel," in *Politics and the Novel* (London; New Left Books, 1961). See also Joseph L. Blotner, *The Political Novel* (New York: Doubleday, 1955); John Horton and Andrea Baumeister eds., *Literature and the Political Imagination* (London: Routledge, 1996); and *Reading Political Stories: Representations of Politics in Novels and Pictures*, ed. Maureen Whitebrook (Lanham, MD: Rowman and Littlefield, 1991).

76. Howe, *Politics and the Novel*, 17.

77. Howe, *Politics and the Novel*, 20.

78. Howe, *Politics and the Novel*, 21.

79. Howe, *Politics and the Novel*, 22.

80. Howe, *Politics and the Novel*, 22.

81. Howe, *Politics and the Novel*, 22.

82. E. H. Carr, "Ethics and Politics: *The Devils*," in *Dostoevsky: 1821–1881* (London: Unwin Books, 1962 [1931]), 172.

83. Carr, "Ethics and Politics: *The Devils*," 175.

84. Carr, "Ethics and Politics: *The Devils*," 175.

85. Carr, "Ethics and Politics: *The Devils*," 175.

86. David Porter, "The Politics of Le Guin's Opus," in *Science Fiction Studies: Selected Articles on Science Fiction 1973–1975*, eds. R. D. Mullen and Darko Suvin (Boston: Gregg Press, 1976), 277.

87. Le Guin, "On Norman Spinrad's *The Iron Dream*," *Science Fiction Studies*, 1 (1973), 43.

88. Le Guin, "Introduction" to *Planet of Exile*, in *The Language of the Night*, 141.

89. Susan Wood, "Discovering Worlds: The Fiction of Ursula K. Le Guin," in *Ursula K. Le Guin*, ed. Harold Bloom (New York: Chelsea House, 1985), 204–5.

90. D. G. Williams, "The Moons of Le Guin and Heinlein," *Science Fiction Studies*, 21, no. 2 (1994), 164.

91. Jonathan Ward, "Interview With Ursula K. Le Guin," in Ursula K. Le Guin, *Dreams Must Explain Themselves* (New York: Algol Press, 1975), 34–5.

92. Win McCormack and Ann Mendel, "An Interview with Ursula K. Le Guin: Creating Realistic Utopias," in *The Language of the Night*, 128.

93. Orwell, "Writers and Leviathan," 469–70,

94. Plaw, "Empty Hands: Communication, Pluralism and Community in Ursula K. Le Guin's *The Dispossessed*," 284.

7

Ethics in the Writings of Ursula K. Le Guin

INTRODUCTION

In this chapter I shall discuss Le Guin's attitude toward questions of ethics. As a preliminary to this it should be noted that Le Guin makes a conceptual distinction between the standpoint of "ethics" and that of "morality." In this regard her thinking falls within a well-established tradition which goes back at least to Hegel, if not even further. For the time being, however, I will consider the meaning of the terms "ethics" and "morality" to be synonymous, and I will employ these two terms interchangeably unless I state explicitly my intention not to do so.

It should be remembered that earlier I distinguished between two "Le Guins," or between the two different component elements which make up the complex and contradictory character of the one, unified person who is Ursula Le Guin. I distinguished between the Le Guin insofar as she is a "private" individual and Le Guin insofar as she possesses a "public" *persona*. When I first introduced this distinction I suggested that it is the first of these "Le Guins" who is an anarchist, whereas the second is a novelist. But if we do make this distinction then it is clear that the question "what is Le Guin's attitude toward the problems of ethics?" might be answered in different ways, depending on whether one is talking about Le Guin the anarchist, on the one hand, or Le Guin the novelist on the other. Later I shall discuss each of the answers that might be given to this question in turn, focusing on the differences between them. This should not, however, be taken to imply that the attitude of these two "Le Guins" toward ethics are *entirely* different from one another. For there are similarities as well as differences between the ethical vision of Le Guin insofar as she is an anarchist and that of Le Guin insofar as she is a novelist.

WHAT IS ETHICS?

To discuss Le Guin's attitude toward questions of ethics involves relating her views to the various traditions of thought which have emerged historically within the discipline of moral philosophy from the time that philosophers first started speculating about such questions in ancient Greece. I have in mind such doctrines as ethical "eudaimonism," "consequentialism," "deontologism," "virtue ethics," "postmodern ethics," and the like. First of all, though, I wish to say something about the notion of "morality" and "the moral point of view," as these expressions have traditionally been understood by moral philosophers from the time of Plato and Aristotle until today.

There is a traditional way of thinking about ethics, which is first explicitly articulated in the writings of Plato and Aristotle. This view is sometimes wrongly identified with the moral philosophy of Immanuel Kant and for that reason, though again wrongly, considered to be exclusively "modern." This traditional view is based on the assumption that ethics has to do with moral duties or obligations, and that ethical relationships are grounded in some version or other of the principle of reciprocity. Ethical decision making, or deciding what one ought to do in a certain situation, requires a commitment to the principles of rationality and logical consistency. Moral reasoning, or the kind of practical reasoning which is required for the making of such decisions, necessarily invokes the principle that "equals are to be treated equally" in relevantly similar circumstances, or that "like cases are to be treated alike." Consequently, acting morally is always a law governed activity. It is a matter of following moral principles or rules, which by their nature must possess a general validity. It involves an attempt to apply such rules to the circumstances associated with a particular case or situation. Above all, moral reasoning is associated with the notion of equity or fairness and not making an exception in one's own case. This way of thinking assumes, therefore, that if one ethical subject is to be able to stand in an ethical relationship with another at all then there must be at least *some* similarities between them. There must be at least some respects in which they might be said to be *equals*. When deciding what one ought to do in any ethical situation the guiding principle for any moral agent is that one should not claim that the rule which one is invoking is a "moral rule" whilst at the same time claiming that it applies only to others (who are assumed to be one's equals) and *not* to oneself. On this view anyone who argued in this way would be making two kinds of "mistake," a practical one and a logical one. Practically speaking, this person will "fail" to act morally, something which for the purposes of the argument we may assume it is their intention to do. Logically speaking, such a person would demonstrate that they have not properly grasped the "logic of moral argument." They have not understood what is involved in looking at a given situation from "the moral point of view."[1]

According to this traditional way of thinking, then, it is legitimate to talk about such a thing as *the* moral point of view, which is assumed to be the same in all societies and cultures everywhere.[2] Those who do wish to act "morally" in relation to others, whether these others are members of their own society or culture, or whether they are from a different society and culture, most consider the situation in which they find themselves from this point of view. They must apply this line of reasoning and, of course, act accordingly. Those philosophers who have talked about "the moral point of view" in this way, from Plato onward, have not been ignorant of the differences which exist between different cultures so far as their moral values are concerned. They have, however, insisted that behind or beneath this diversity there are also certain common features which are present in all societies everywhere, and that by focusing upon these common features it is possible for us to uncover or discover the very essence of notions of "morality," "justice," and "law." In particular, especially in the case of Aristotle, they have noted that the above account of morality, or what is involved in looking at the world from "the moral point of view," is associated with principles of conduct which possess a highly "abstract" or "formal" character. For example, the principle that "like cases ought to be treated alike," or that "equals ought to be treated equally," does not state who exactly are equals, or how these equals are to be treated.

The fact that this is so has two extremely important consequences. In the first place, as we have seen, it implies that there is room for considerable diversity between different societies and cultures when it comes to the practical application of these very general principles of morality to the circumstances of particular cases. At the same time, however, adherents of this traditional way of thinking about ethics have also insisted (rightly or wrongly) that no society could exist without some system of morality, and that in all societies what is involved in "acting morality" is pretty much the same thing, although it is possible, of course, that those who do act morally in this way are not self-consciously aware that they are doing so. Not all moral agents are moral philosophers. And although the theoretical understanding of what is involved in "acting morally" was an intellectual discovery, arguably first made by Plato, that does not mean that nobody acted in this way before then.

In the second place, this way of thinking about ethics helps us to understand the nature of moral conflict, or how and why moral disagreements occur. For given this account it is always going to be possible for two individual agents, who may be from the same or different societies or cultures, both of whom are committed to "doing the right thing" or to "acting morally" in this sense, to look at the same situation conscientiously and yet nevertheless disagree fundamentally with one another over the issue of who are to be considered equals, how ought these equals to be treated, which particular moral rules should be applied, how exactly they should be applied, what exactly ought to be done or not done, whether or not a particular action should be performed or not performed, and so on. Similarly it is possible for one and the same individual, possessing more than one *persona,* to be placed in a situation within which she or he is confronted with a conflict of duties, such that the performance of one duty is necessarily associated with the nonperformance of another. When such disagreement occurs we get the moral dilemmas or "collisions" which Hegel considered to be the very essence of tragic drama—collisions which are, of course, as much internal as they are external, and as much psychological as they are moral. For example, in Sophocles' *Antigone,* Antigone is as much in conflict with herself as she is in conflict with her uncle Creon.

On this traditional view, moral action always involves obeying *some* moral law or other, or doing one's duty. If this is not a sufficient, it is at least a necessary condition for "acting morally," or for an action to be characterized as "moral." Moreover, moral action is usually (although not necessarily) associated with the notion of restraint or constraint, whether this is internally or externally imposed; freely undertaken or a consequence of some threat of coercion. If such action is freely undertaken it is associated with the notion of altruism or acting from, rather than simply in accordance with, the "sense of duty." Individuals who act in this way are thought of as being not complete "egotists," but as having a concern for the well-being of others and the wider community. Consequently, action of this kind can be contrasted with action which is *not* "moral" action, precisely because it involves disobedience to some moral law, it being assumed that such actions are motivated, not by a sense of duty, but by "self-interest."

The attitude which this traditional way of thinking about ethics associates with the "moral point of view" might be contrasted with that of "immoralism" or moral "nihilism." This is the attitude of those who refuse to look at the world from this "moral point of view," who refuse to accept that there are any moral duties or obligations which are binding, at least upon them, and who insist that the only thing which is going to motivate their own conduct is, not a concern for what is right and wrong, or a concern for the well-being of others, but exclusively their own self-interest. For immoralists or nihilists nothing matters more than their own "freedom," using this term in a specifically nonmoral sense. Freedom could certainly be said to be a "value" for the nihilist. It is not, however, according to this traditional view, a *moral* value.

Perhaps the best classical example of immoralism or nihilism in this sense is the contribution which the "Sophist" Callicles makes to the ancient debate concerning the respective merits of "nature versus convention" in Plato's dialogue *Gorgias*, although there are echoes of this attitude also in the *Melian Dialogues* of Thucydides.[3] This is the attitude of mind which is central to the "realist" perspective in the theory of international relations today.[4] On one reading of his views, it is also the approach to questions of ethics adopted by Friedrich Nietzsche, who was familiar with and admired the doctrines espoused by Callicles and the Athenian envoys at Melos. Both Nietzsche and his follower Zamyatin associate this attitude with the notion of "life." Hence, in their view, like freedom "life" is a value. Again, though, it is not a *moral* value. Those who value "life," understood in this way, must reject morality, just as they must reject all society and all law, for all of these things are profoundly "anti-life." More importantly, for present purposes, this attitude of mind can also be associated in modern times with the history of anarchism, or one particular strand of anarchist thought which emerged in the nineteenth century and is usually associated with the philosophy of Max Stirner, and again with that of Nietzsche. It is this type of anarchism which is celebrated by Zamyatin in his novel *We*, and which was the main target of criticism for Dostoevsky who, in his novel *The Possessed*, gives his readers the erroneous impression that *all* anarchists think in this way. These are the beliefs which have lent support to the popular misconception of the "anarchist," fueled by Dostoevsky in the nineteenth century, as a "bomb throwing" advocate of mindless violence—a person who believes that violence is valuable for its own sake, not as a means to an end, but as an end-in-itself. Finally these are the beliefs which, because of the influence of Nietzsche's philosophy in twentieth-century France, have until very recently been associated with postmodernism or poststructuralism.[5]

LE GUIN'S ETHICS

The starting point for understanding Le Guin's attitude toward questions of ethics is to appreciate that, both insofar as she is a political activist who is an anarchist *and* insofar as she is a creative writer who is a novelist, she rejects the doctrine of immoralism or nihilism and embraces what has traditionally been considered to be "the moral point of view," as outlined above. In both cases, like the ancient Greeks, Le Guin thinks that humans are by nature ethical animals. James Bittner and Gerard Klein are, therefore, in one sense at least, absolutely right to claim that for Le Guin "man" [*sic*] is an "ethical animal."[6] In consequence she has an overriding interest in the ethical dimension of human existence. Le Guin is, of course, familiar with the doctrine of nihilism, the strand of anarchist thinking which is associated with it, and the particular understanding that anarchists of this kind have of the notion of "freedom." And she rejects them all. This is very clear both from her essays and from her novels. In *The Dispossessed* the ideas associated with this way of looking at things are expressed by the female character Vea, and they are strongly criticized by the "hero" of the novel, Shevek, who we may consider on this occasion to be the mouthpiece for Le Guin's own views insofar as she is an anarchist.

Let us now turn to consider the ethical vision which is associated with Le Guin's outlook, again insofar as she is an anarchist. Contrary to contemporary postmodernists, who follow Nietzsche and maintain that, whether we are talking about the natural world or the social world, science or ethics, the only order that there is in the universe is that which human beings themselves impose upon it, Le Guin maintains that in both science and in ethics the world is intrinsically an orderly and not a chaotic place. She insists that the order which is to be discerned in the world is *not* "one imposed by man or by a personal or humane deity." On the contrary, there are "true laws - ethical and aesthetic, as surely as scientific" which "are not imposed from above by any authority, but exist in things and are to be found – discovered."[7] This is the attitude of someone who has been strongly influenced by the philosophy of Taoism.[8] But it is also the attitude of someone who is a humanist and a moral realist, as well as a scientific realist.[9]

In short, it is the attitude of someone who holds views which are currently unfashionable amongst those who have been influenced by the philosophies of postmodernism and poststructuralism. Le Guin's remarks on this subject indicate that she is committed to the idea that there is a universally valid ethical order, a moral law which applies to all human beings, a law which is in some sense "natural" rather than a purely social "construction," and which is, therefore, *discovered* by human beings rather than made by them.

In one of her essays, Le Guin tells us that what underpins her commitment to this ethical vision is the assumption, which she considers to be "essential," that "we" human beings "are not objects" but "subjects." Hence, "whoever among us treats us as objects is acting inhumanly, wrongly, against nature."[10] She insists that "if you deny any affinity with another person or kind of person, if you declare it to be wholly different from yourself" then you inevitably deny its "spiritual equality" and hence also its "human reality." In her view, "the only possible relationship" we could have with an "other" thought of in this way is "a power relationship" and not an ethical one.[11] Ethically speaking, the adoption of such an attitude is in her view undesirable. In words which echo the sentiments expressed by the young Marx in the *Paris Manuscripts* and, more recently, by "ethical Marxism,"[12] Le Guin states that the main reason for this is because it results in that "alienation" of ourselves from another human being or person which is an inevitable consequence of our attempting to enslave them or reduce them to the status of a "thing." For Le Guin, if you have alienated another person in this way then you have also in effect "alienated yourself," and have in consequence "fatally impoverished your own reality" as a human being, as a moral being.[13]

In *The Dispossessed* Le Guin describes this attitude as "propertarian." Much in the manner of Erich Fromm,[14] a onetime member of the Frankfurt School, Le Guin considers this to be the attitude of someone who seeks to "have" or "possess" another, to treat them as an item of property, a slave, rather than respect them as a free being, a fellow human being, equal to themselves in the cosmic order of things.[15] Expressed in terms of the philosophy of Taoism, those who seek to objectify or enslave others in such a manner have most definitely departed from the "way." This is the ethical vision which Le Guin had in mind when she wrote *The Dispossessed*, and with which she associates anarchism properly understood. It is the ethical vision of the central character in the novel, Shevek, who is both a brilliant physicist and an anarchist.

In *The Dispossessed* Shevek acknowledges only "one law," the principle of equity or fairness. This is the only law "he had ever acknowledged."[16] For Le Guin, as for Kropotkin and the classical anarchist tradition in the nineteenth century, with their assumption that in the cosmic order of things all human beings are by nature equal, this one moral law amounts to a commitment to the principle of equality. It is the law of human equality,[17] which is also the law of solidarity or of "mutual aid between individuals."[18] It is his commitment to this one law which leads Shevek to criticize the political system of the state of A-Io because it will "admit no morality outside the laws"[19] and which prevents him, unlike the inhabitants of A-Io, from "looking at foreigners as inferior, as less than fully human."[20] It is by reference to this moral law that Le Guin has Shevek criticize the various hierarchical social institutions which he encounters on the planet Urras. For example, he is quick to notice that "status" and the establishment in social relationships of who is "superior" and who "inferior" is a "central" issue in Ioti life.[21] Shevek first observes this when traveling from Anarres to A-Io at the beginning of the book. At one point he refers to the doctor who attends him as "brother," but after the doctor's departure he realized that he had spoken to him in Pravic, "a language he could not understand."[22] On another occasion, when speaking to an Ioti physicist Pae, Shevek expresses dismay that Pae seems unable to recognize him as an equal and insists on referring to him by the title "doctor," which in A-Io is a badge of social superiority. Pae's response to this admonition is to apologize for having offended Shevek by referring to him as "doctor," but also to point out that in A-Io *not* to do so would be offensive, as "in our terms, you see," this "seems disrespectful." For Pae, to treat another Ioti as one's own equal "just doesn't seem right."[23]

Last but by no means least, as in the case of Le Guin's *The Left Hand of Darkness* and *The Word for World is Forest*,[24] this is the ethical vision which underpins Le Guin's personal commitment to feminism and Shevek's attitude toward gender relationships in *The Dispossessed*. Shevek is not long in contact with Urrasti society before he reflects how wrong it is that in order to "respect himself" the doctor Kimoe "had to consider half the human race as inferior."[25] Moreover, once again he is dismayed when he discovers that some Urrasti women actually support the system of gender relationships in A-Io by apparently consenting to the reduction of themselves to the status of a "thing," an object to be used by others, in this case by men for the purposes of sexual gratification. At one point, for example, he notes that the character Vea "was so elaborately and ostentatiously a female body that she seemed scarcely to be a human being"[26] and that, as such, "in the eyes of men" she was "a thing owned, bought, sold."[27] This is Le Guin's approach to questions of ethics insofar as she is an anarchist. It is clear enough, I think, that this ethical vision is based on a quite traditional understanding of the nature of morality and a commitment on Le Guin's part to "the moral point of view" outlined earlier.

Now let us consider how she approaches the same questions as a novelist. Here her attitude is basically the same, although it does differ from the account just offered in one or two respects. Here also we may say that the assumption that by nature human beings are ethical or moral beings is central to Le Guin's basic outlook as a creative writer. It is clear from Le Guin's essays and her early fantasy literature, especially *The Earthsea Quartet*,[28] that she considers works of literature to be a vital element in the education (which is always for Le Guin the *moral* education) of those who read them, especially children. As Le Guin herself puts it in "The Child and the Shadow" all of the great children's "fantasies" possess a "practical" value, and this value is *"ethical"* (my emphasis). That is to say, they are works of literature which encourage the "growth" of children as *moral* beings.[29] This is a key *motif* in Le Guin's fantasy literature, but it is also to be found in her science fiction, especially *The Dispossessed*. It might indeed be said to be the core thematic element which links Le Guin's fantasy literature to her science fiction.

For Le Guin, however, a vital element in this process of moral education is that of encouraging the growth and development of her readers as autonomous moral agents who are capable of thinking and acting "morally" for themselves. As a novelist Le Guin wishes to stimulate her readers to engage with fundamental moral dilemmas, even if in the end it should turn out that they make substantive ethical judgments which are different from her own. For pedagogic as much as for aesthetic reasons, then, Le Guin wishes to avoid didacticism in her work. She is not a "moralizer" intent on preaching simplistic solutions to irresolvable ethical dilemmas, but rather a "moralist" whose aim is to encourage her readers to think about the problems posed by the existence of such dilemmas for themselves.

As we have seen, Le Guin is a profoundly "dialectical" thinker, whether one is talking about the natural world or the social world, the world of ethics and politics.[30] So far as the latter is concerned, and again insofar as she is a novelist, it is her dialectical outlook which leads her to take an interest in the conflicts or dilemmas which are an integral element in the ethical life of human beings. She is especially interested in those situations where two individuals might agree that it is good to act "morally," and even about what formally or abstractly this involves, but nevertheless still disagree with one another about what, in the situation in question, ought to be done, what is "good" and "evil," or what is "right" and "wrong." As a novelist with a dialectical outlook she is acutely aware that what is thought of as "acting morally" in a concrete sense, when considered by one moral agent from one point of view, may not simply be *different* from but actually the *reverse* of what is thought of as "acting morally" when considered by someone else from the opposite point of view.

Le Guin's attitude toward such ethical dilemmas, so far as she is a creative writer, is to resist the temptation to "take sides," to refuse to commit herself to just one of these two opposed points of view, or to think in simplistic "either-or" terms about the situation in question. For in her view, in ethics as in science, each of these two diametrically opposed ways of looking at things constitutes an important part of the "Truth." Rather, once again, Le Guin encourages her readers to think for themselves, and to engage with the complexities or the contradictions associated with the ethical dilemmas in question. Le Guin enjoins her readers to rise above each of these limited and partial perspectives of what is good and evil or right and wrong and to see the strengths and weaknesses associated with "both sides" of the moral dilemma being portrayed. In this respect, as I have noted, the vision which inspires her creative writing has a striking resemblance to that of the ancient Greek tragedians, especially Sophocles, of whose *Antigone* Hegel thought so highly.[31] Insofar as she is a novelist, it is the ethical dilemmas confronted by her central characters and the conflicts of moral duty with which these are associated which interest Le Guin most.

From this point of view, the best way to read *The Dispossessed* is to see Shevek, not as an anarchist, or not just as an anarchist, but as an erstwhile "tragic" hero who is placed by Le Guin in a situation where he is confronted by two conflicting moral duties, duties which on the surface appear irreconcilable; one as a citizen of Anarres to uphold the values of his own society, the other as a scientist, and hence a citizen of the world, to pursue "the Truth" in science come what may, for the benefit of all human kind, even if this brings him into conflict with the established authorities and conventional wisdom of his own society. It is, of course, not without irony that this society is supposed to be an anarchist society and, therefore, in theory, one which ought to value individual freedom and creative self-expression.

**LE GUIN AND THE DISTINCTION BETWEEN
ETHICS AND MORALITY**

I said earlier that Le Guin makes a distinction between the concept of "morality" and that of "ethics." In so doing she writes in a tradition which goes back at least as far as Hegel, who also distinguishes between the notions of "morality" (*Moralität*) and "ethics" (*Sittlichkeit*) in his *Philosophy of Right*.[32] The most influential representative of that tradition writing today is Jurgen Habermas.[33] Habermas uses the term "morality" to refer to practical reason insofar as it touches on the fundamental questions of right and wrong, that is to say, what Le Guin refers to as "ethics." As Habermas understands it, the principles of *morality* are universally valid and, as such, are obligatory for all human beings.[34] The principles of morality are, therefore, what are usually characterized as being principles of natural law. According to Habermas, the examination of these principles is the proper concern of *moral philosophy*. The term "ethical," on the other hand, refers to questions of the "good life" for particular human beings living in a particular society at a particular time; the life which will bring them *eudaimonia* or make them truly "happy," in what Habermas (in my view wrongly) takes to be Aristotle's sense of this term.[35] Habermas indicates that he considers the terms "ethics" and "ethical" to refer solely to empirically ascertainable norms of conduct which are specific to particular societies at particular times, and hence to the common good or collective self-interest of their individual members, rather than to any rationally apprehensible universally valid principles which apply to or within all societies at all times, which he considers to fall within the purview of *morality* rather than that of *ethics*. Understood in this way "ethical questions,"

Habermas insists, "point in a different direction from moral questions."[36] According to Habermas, it is important that philosophy should be in a position "to differentiate specifically *moral* questions from *ethical* ones" (my emphasis) and to give each of them "their proper due."[37]

We are now in a position to consider this distinction as it is to be found in the writings of Le Guin. It should be emphasized, at the outset, that Le Guin does not always distinguish between these two notions. As we have seen, there are times when Le Guin uses the terms "morality" and "ethics" interchangeably. For example, she does this in a passage from one of her essays, "The Child and the Shadow," which I cited earlier. And she also does it in her essay "Science Fiction and Mrs. Brown" when she says of Stanislaw Lem's novel *The Invincible* that "the book's theme is *moral*. And its climax is an extremely difficult *ethical* choice made by an individual"[38] (my emphasis). Similarly she maintains elsewhere that "most great fantasies contain a very strong, striking *moral* dialectic, often expressed as a struggle between the Darkness and the Light, but that makes it sound simple, and the *ethics* of the unconscious—of the dream, the fantasy, the fairy tale—are *not* simple at all. They are, indeed, very strange" (my emphasis).[39] In these passages, and others like them, Le Guin makes no distinction at all between "morality" and "ethics." She considers the two terms to be synonymous in meaning, and she has a positive attitude toward both. It is true that she objects to "moralism" or simplistic "moralizing," but that is not the same as objecting to "morality" itself, properly understood.

Elsewhere, however, like Hegel and Habermas, although not in exactly the same way, Le Guin does draw a sharp conceptual distinction between the concept of "ethics" and that of "morality." According to this distinction, as Le Guin understands it, the concept of ethics is associated with a "set of rules or rational theories" relating to a certain framework of duties or obligations. It is, in short, associated with the "moral point of view," and the traditional way of thinking about morality discussed earlier in this chapter. The concept of morality on the other hand, Le Guin tells us, "refers to *character*, to the person*" (my emphasis). From the standpoint of morality" a "moral choice" is "an act performed by one person" in a particular situation at a particular time, an act which "may or may not conform to *law*," (my emphasis)[40] and which, therefore, may or may not be ethical.

Le Guin has a tendency to associate the notion of ethics with the empire of "reason," with rules or laws, with *coercion*, and with patriarchal authority. On those occasions when she does distinguish between ethics and morality, therefore, because she is an anarchist, she is critical of "ethics" and the ethical attitude of mind. On the other hand, she is much more positive about "morality" and moral conduct, which she tends to associate with the absence of coercion and respect for individual moral choice, or individual conscience. She also suggests on occasion that, in contrast to ethics, the idea of morality is associated with that of the "feminine" and with that of "care," in the sense in which that notion is understood in the writings of Carol Gilligan.[41] On the occasions when Le Guin does distinguish between the notions of ethics and morality, she calls for a "new morality" which will in some way transcend the limitations of ethics, as this has traditionally been understood. She suggests that this proposed new way of thinking about morality would be different from the traditional account of "the moral point of view" presented earlier.

As we have seen, for Le Guin this new morality would be associated with the absence of coercion and with respect for conscience and individual moral choice. What is not readily apparent, however, is whether Le Guin also thinks that such a new morality would be associated with the absence of *all* moral rules or laws—whether it would be a *complete* departure from the traditional account of morality offered earlier. The problem here is that it is not entirely clear whether Le Guin thinks that moral rules or laws are necessarily coercive. Sometimes she suggests that she thinks that they are, as when she distinguishes ethics and morality. Elsewhere, however, when she does not make this distinction, she indicates that she does not think this at all. Moreover, given Le Guin's rejection of nihilism and her commitment to a certain kind of moral anarchism, one would expect Le Guin *not* to think this. One would expect her to acknowledge not only that noncoercive moral rules are possible, but also that such rules are a necessary precondition for the existence of any society based on anarchist principles.

With her enthusiasm for "morality" as opposed to "ethics," and for "character" rather than moral rules, on those occasions when Le Guin does make a clear distinction between "morality" and "ethics" her thinking has a striking similarity to what is today referred to as "virtue ethics," as this is to be found in the writings of Alasdair MacIntyre.[42] For example, when discussing fairy tales Le Guin rejects what she describes as "simplistic *moralism*"[43] (my emphasis) and maintains that in traditional "fairy tales" there is no obvious "right" and "wrong."[44] "Evil," she says, "appears in the fairy tale not as something diametrically opposed to good, but as inextricably *involved* with it, as in the Yang-Yin symbol. Neither is greater than the other, nor can human reason and virtue separate one from the other and choose between them" (my emphasis).[45] In this situation it is the hero or heroine who, she says, "sees what is appropriate to be done, because he or she sees the *whole*, which is greater than either evil or good. Their heroism is, in fact, their certainty. They do not act by *rules*; they simply know the way to go" (my emphasis).[46] Despite the different terminology employed, the affinity here between Le Guin's understanding of "morality" and that of "virtue ethics" as MacIntyre understands it is really quite striking.[47]

On the other hand, however, it would, I think, be an exaggeration to argue that what Le Guin refers to as "morality," attaches *no* importance at all to moral rules. Nor in consequence would it be correct to argue that her moral vision is identical with that of MacIntyre's version of "virtue ethics." For it seems that what Le Guin has in mind, and what she really objects to in the outlook which she describes as "ethical," is the idea that there is a catechism of such rules which, in any given situation, might be inflexibly or mechanically applied, so as to give an obviously "correct" result, or *the* "right answer," to the question of where an individual moral agent's duty lies. She rejects the idea that there is a manual of ethics which will tell the individual in question what it is that he or she ought to do because that is what *anyone*, and, therefore, *everyone*, ought to do in such situations. This way of thinking is, she rightly claims, far too simplistic and could never do justice to the complexities of the moral dilemmas which lie at the heart of human existence.[48] It takes away from individuals the moral responsibility for deciding for themselves, in the light of their own consciences, what they ought to do in any given situation. But this is not at all the same thing as saying, of course, that there are no moral rules *at all* which might serve as a guide to individuals when making such decisions. All it means is that the rules in question must be applied sensitively, having due regard for the circumstances of the particular case. This idea is, of course, a very old one. It is closely associated with the philosophy of Aristotle, and with what Aristotle refers to in the *Nicomachean Ethics* as *"phronesis"* or "practical wisdom"—something which can come to us only after we have undergone a process of education and have cultivated a certain maturity in our moral outlook, or when a certain level of the development of our "character" has been achieved.[49]

We should not, therefore, make too stark a contrast between a moral outlook which attaches importance to character and an ethical outlook which attaches importance to rules. It would indeed be a strange kind of morality which attached exclusive importance to character and none at all to rules, just as it would be a strange kind of ethics which attached exclusive importance to rules and none at all to character. For the former would evaluate individuals by focusing entirely on the issue of their motivation, without paying any attention at all to what they actually did; whereas the latter would evaluate them on the basis of their deeds alone, and would attach no importance at all to their motives or their character. Nor do I think that Le Guin does make the mistake of drawing too sharp a distinction between the moral and the ethical in this way. For despite her enthusiasm for a morality of character and her antipathy toward an ethics of rules in the essay cited above, it seems evident that Le Guin *does* attach importance to moral rules. In short for Le Guin, as for Hegel and Habermas, the standpoint of "ethics" and that of "morality" should not be thought of as standing in direct opposition to one another. It would be more accurate to think of them as mutually supplementing one another.

Once again, this is a situation which calls not for an "either-or" choice between these two different modes of thought, but for some kind of theoretical synthesis based on the principle of "both-and." It requires the dialectical outlook which we find in the writings of both Hegel and
Habermas which deal with this issue.

Le Guin's unwillingness to think about moral conduct as having to do
entirely with questions of motivation and character is made very clear in
The Dispossessed, where Shevek says, speaking of the society on Anarres,
"We have no law, *but* the single principle of mutual aid between individuals" (my emphasis).[50] In my opinion Le Guin's use of the word "but" in
this sentence is of the utmost significance. It indicates that, in her view,
even an "anarchist society" (given that for Le Guin this notion is not a
self-contradictory one) must be associated with the notion of *law* in at
least one sense of the term. This is the one law, the moral law, which
Shevek follows in all of his dealings with others—the principle of equity,
reciprocity, or reciprocal freedom.[51] According to Le Guin it is this one
moral law of reciprocal freedom which, in an anarchist society, would be
voluntarily obeyed by all individuals in the absence of repression and coercion. Thus for Le Guin anarchism is associated with a moral attitude
which is not opposed to the notions of "law" or "order" *per se*, but only to
coercive law and to coercive order. It is for this reason, of course, that Le
Guin is a *social* anarchist and not a nihilist.

It is arguable that despite her occasional flirtation with the idea of a
"virtue ethics" in Alasdair MacIntyre's sense, or in her terms a "morality"
without rules, Le Guin's moral vision actually has a good deal in common
with what is usually referred to as "deontological" ethics. This means
that, so far as the various perspectives discussed by moral philosophers
are concerned, her views have a certain affinity with those of Kant. Although Kant is not, of course, the only ethical deontologist and, as we
have seen, Le Guin is critical of certain aspects of the kind of moral theory which is often attributed to Kant. In particular, Le Guin is critical of
any moral theory which maintains that acting "morally" is solely a matter of following moral rules "mechanically," or "doing the right thing,"
and has nothing at all to do with "virtue," or the "character" of the individual moral agent.

Moreover, as is made very clear in her short story "The Ones Who
Walked Away from Omelas," and like all ethical deontologists, Le Guin is
also of the opinion that there are certain actions or modes of conduct (for
example the torture of an innocent) which are intrinsically wrong and
which could never be justified no matter what the circumstances within
which they are performed are, and no matter what the consequences of
performing them might be.[52] In this respect, despite their disagreement
about other issues, Le Guin's views are much the same as those of Dosto-

evsky. Both Lyman Tower Sargent and George Kateb have observed that the question of whether torturing an innocent might in certain circumstances be morally justified, which Le Guin writes about in "The Ones Who Walked Away from Omelas," is also dealt with by Dostoevsky in *The Brothers Karamazov*. At one point, for example, Ivan Karamazov asks his brother Alyosha the following question: "Imagine that you are creating a fabric of human destiny with the object of making men happy in the end, giving them peace and rest at last, but that it was essential and inevitable to torture to death only one tiny creature . . . and to found that edifice on its unavenged tears, would you consent to be the architect of those conditions?" Like Dostoevsky/Alyosha, Le Guin's answer to this question is a decisive "No!"[53]

This suggests that Le Guin might well have had Dostoevsky in mind when she was inspired to write this story. It would appear, however, that this is not the case. For in her introductory remarks to "The Ones Who Walked Away from Omelas," Le Guin points out that although she had read Dostoevsky many years before, nevertheless when she wrote her own story she had entirely forgotten about this particular episode. According to Le Guin, the immediate source of inspiration for her own treatment of this issue was in fact the writings of William James.[54] It is, I think, somewhat ironic that despite her efforts to distance herself from Dostoevsky, who she considers to be a "violent reactionary," here as elsewhere Le Guin does not quite succeed in doing so. Her critique of "ethical consequentialism," in this its "utilitarian" version, is a case in point, but there are other examples also.

Although an emphasis on the importance of moral rules is not by any means absent from Le Guin's moral vision, nevertheless it remains true that Le Guin *does* attach a great deal of importance to "character" so far as questions of morality are concerned, just as she does in the sphere of aesthetics and literature. For example, when writing about Stanislaw Lem's *The Invincible*, Le Guin maintains that at the end of the book neither "reward nor punishment ensues" for its central character Rohan. Rather, "all that we," the readers and Rohan "have learned is something about himself."[55] In my view this idea also has an application to Le Guin's own work. Indeed, it lies at the heart of her fantasy literature. More to the point however, in the present context, it is also central to *The Dispossessed*. At one point in the novel, for instance, Le Guin suggests that an anarchist society would require people who possess a certain type of "character." Such people might be said to be "free spirits." For "you cannot buy the Revolution. You cannot make the Revolution. You can only be the Revolution. It is in your spirit or it is nowhere."[56]

James Bittner has claimed that *The Dispossessed* "is at bottom a book on ethics."[57] There is much truth in this remark. However, given the fact that

Le Guin does at times make a clear distinction between the notion of "ethics" and that of "morality," and that she actually disapproves of the attitude which she associates with the former, it would be more accurate to say that she is a "moralist" rather than an "ethicist," and that in consequence *The Dispossessed* is best thought of as a book which deals with problems of morality rather than problems of ethics, as Le Guin understands these terms. It must be said, however, that from the standpoint of the history of moral philosophy it would have been much better, and more accurate, if Le Guin had chosen to use the word "morality" to capture what she means by the word "ethics," and *vice versa*. For the negative associations which the notion of "ethics" has in Le Guin's mind are much the same as those which are often associated with that of "morality," whilst the positive associations which Le Guin associates with the notion of morality are, in contrast, often associated with that of ethics.

LE GUIN, EXISTENTIALISM, AND SITUATION ETHICS

It is worth comparing Le Guin's views on morality with the existentialist philosophy of Jean-Paul Sartre, both of whom seem to have been influenced, albeit in different ways, by an engagement with ideas first presented in the writings of Dostoevsky and Nietzsche. Here we must distinguish between the views expressed by Sartre in *Being and Nothingness* and those which he develops in his later essay *Existentialism and Humanism*. Le Guin rejects the approach to ethics which Sartre adopts in the first of these texts. A good case could be made out, however, for the view that she endorses the views which Sartre puts forward in the second. In the earlier of these two works Sartre suggests that there is nothing more important to each individual than his or her own freedom. Like Nietzsche, Sartre associates the freedom of the individual with the *life* of that individual, understood as a free being. However, like Dostoevsky's Kirilov, Sartre thinks that moral duties act as an unwelcome constraint on that freedom. There is, therefore, a strong flavor of moral nihilism in the writings of the early Sartre, especially in *Being and Nothingness*.[58] This is something which Le Guin rejects, for the same reason that she rejects the arguments of Kirilov in *The Possessed*.

In the later *Existentialism and Humanism*, however, Sartre moves away from this nihilist position. He attempts to develop a new way of thinking about questions of ethics of his own, which is sometimes referred to as "situation ethics."[59] Le Guin's views are strikingly similar to those advanced by Sartre in this later work, provided these are properly understood. This "situation ethics" is often wrongly characterized as being an ethics without moral rules. John Mander, for example, cites the remarks made by a character in one of Sartre's plays who "cries out," obviously, Mander argues, "with his author's full approval," that "'there are no rules!'"[60] And there is at least some evidence in Sartre's *Existentialism and Humanism* which appears at least to support this view. At one point, for example, Sartre claims there that "no rule of general morality can show you what you ought to do" in any situation, as "no signs are vouchsafed in this world."[61]

Nevertheless, in my opinion, Mander's characterization of Sartre's views on ethics is not accurate. For elsewhere in the same text Sartre argues, not that there are no moral rules at all which can guide us, but rather that although such rules *do* undeniably exist they are far "too *abstract* to determine the *particular, concrete case* under consideration" (my emphasis) in any given ethical situation.[62] For example, Sartre notes, "Christian doctrine" says that one ought to "act with charity, love your neighbour, deny yourself for others, choose the way which is hardest, and so forth." But, Sartre continues, "which *is* the harder road? To *whom* does one owe the more brotherly love, the patriot or the mother?"[63] The fundamental point which Sartre makes in this text, then, is not so much that there are no moral rules at all which we ought to follow but, rather, that these rules are relatively "unhelpful" precisely because they possess an abstract or a formal character. As Sartre himself puts it, although "a certain *form*" of morality is indeed *universal*, nevertheless "the *content* of morality is *variable*" (my emphasis).[64] This leads Sartre to criticize the moral philosophy of Kant, in particular. For Kant, he maintains, "thinks that the formal and the universal *suffice* for the constitution of a morality" (my emphasis).[65] Against Kant, Sartre argues that "principles that are too abstract," such as Kant's famous "Categorical Imperative," break down "when we come to defining action."[66] Thus in the case of the often discussed example of the moral "situation" of a student who has to choose between caring for his mother and joining the resistance, Sartre asks "by what authority, in the name of what golden rule of morality, do you think he could have decided, in perfect peace of mind, either to abandon his mother or to remain with her? There are no means of judging." The moral "content" of this situation, Sartre insists, is "always concrete, and therefore unpredictable." It has "always to be invented."[67]

For the later Sartre, then, existentialist or situation ethics is *not* an ethics without rules. On the contrary, it is an ethic which does have rules, or at least *one* "golden rule," which in Sartre's words is the principle that as a free individual "I am obliged to will the liberty of others at the same time as mine." I cannot, Sartre argues, "make liberty my aim unless I make that of others equally my aim." Consequently, when I recognise that man is a "free being who cannot, in any circumstances, but will his freedom," at the same time I must also "realize that I cannot *not* will the freedom of others."[68] Sartre insists, however, that this one moral rule cannot be applied mechanically. In his view, individuals should be left free to interpret and apply this one rule for themselves depending on the circumstances of the particular moral situation within which they find themselves at any given time.

This way of thinking about ethics was also later endorsed by Simone de Beauvoir, in a work significantly entitled *The Ethics of Ambiguity*.[69] The reader will recall that the subtitle of Le Guin's *The Dispossessed* is *An Ambiguous Utopia*. In this work, de Beauvoir argues that "morality resides in the painfulness of an indefinite questioning." It will, she concedes, be said of this approach to morality "that these considerations remain quite *abstract*" (my emphasis). For in any given moral situation we must always ask ourselves "What must be done, practically? *Which* action is good? *Which* is bad?" According to de Beauvoir, however, even "to ask such a question" is to "fall into a naïve abstraction," as ethics "does not furnish recipes any more than do science or art." There must, therefore, de Beauvoir argues, always "be a trial and *decision* in each case" (my emphasis). It is obvious that the moral outlook defended by de Beauvoir in this work resembles very closely that of Sartre's *Existentialism and Humanism*. For present purposes there are two things about this work of de Beauvoir which are especially interesting. The first of these is the fact that its title resonates so closely with the sub-title of Le Guin's *The Dispossessed*. The second is that, for de Beauvoir as for Sartre, situation ethics is *not* an ethics which attaches no importance at all to moral rules. It is, rather, an approach to ethics which recognizes the limited value of moral rules for an individual moral agent who, in a given situation, is trying to decide, perhaps not so much what generally ought to be done in that situation, but rather what it is that she or he in particular ought to do.

If we take the notion of "ambiguity" here, understood specifically in the ethical sense in which Sartre and de Beauvoir understand it, then it is evident that anyone who holds such views about ethics would find it difficult, indeed impossible, to be either a utopian thinker or a utopian writer in the commonly accepted sense of these terms. For utopian thought and literature in that sense is associated with a form of moral and political rationalism which is different from, and indeed alien to, the type of reasoning associated with situation ethics. Utopian moral reasoning is not usually thought of as recognizing the complexity, indeed irresolvability, of the ethical dilemmas which lie at the heart of human existence; the sheer irreducibility of complex moral problems and their resistance to any attempt to provide them with a "rational" solution. It is a form of reasoning which fails to appreciate how moral problems of this kind defiantly resist the efforts of those who, when addressing them, assume from the outset that there must be just *one* objectively "correct" answer to the questions which they pose.

LE GUIN, POSTMODERN ETHICS, AND SCIENCE FICTION

Because of the profound influence of the philosophy of Nietzsche on French philosophy and social theory in the second half of the twentieth century,[70] and because the traditional reading of Nietzsche presents him as a nihilist or an "immoralist," it has in the past been assumed that there could not be any such thing as a positive "postmodern ethics." Postmodern thinkers can have no interest in developing an ethical system of their own. Their interest in ethics could only be a sociological one. On this understanding, although postmodernists can and do talk about ethics, they do not themselves make ethical judgments. Rather, they "debunk" ethical judgments by associating them with disguised self-interest and with an attempted rhetorical manipulation of others. Their approach to questions of ethics is, therefore, a "negative" or "destructive" one. We have already seen that although Le Guin is familiar with such ideas, and even incorporates them into *The Dispossessed,* where voice is given to them by the female character Vea, nevertheless there is good reason to suppose that Le Guin herself rejects them. Le Guin is a "moralist" through and through, and if she is an anarchist she is certainly not an anarchist of this kind.

In the last ten years or so this first understanding of the postmodern attitude toward ethics has been challenged, notably by Zygmund Bauman and Simon Critchley, who argue that the basis for a constructive postmodern ethics is to be found in the writings of Emmanuel Levinas and Jacques Derrida.[71] In order to clarify whether Le Guin's approach to ethics is that of postmodernism of this second kind it is fruitful to compare her views with those of Levinas[72] and Derrida,[73] who I shall take to be exemplars of what has come to be called "poststructuralist" or "postmodern" ethics. To see what is supposed to be distinctive about this allegedly new way of thinking about ethics, one which is claimed to be appropriate for the postmodern era, we must compare it with the traditional account of ethics outlined above, for it is intended to be a critique of that account.

As we have seen, according to the traditional account it is legitimate to talk about such a thing as *the* moral point of view, which is assumed to be the same in all societies and cultures everywhere. Those who wish to act "morally" in relation to "others," whether these others are members of their own society or culture, or whether they are from a different society and culture, most consider the situation in which they find themselves from this point of view. It is obvious that this traditional account of what is involved in acting morally relies on the assumption that the moral agents who are making decisions of this kind and the "others" who stand in an ethical relationship with them are *equals* in at least some morally relevant respects. For the basic principle which underpins all morality and law, just as it underpins all logical reasoning, is that of "consistency," that "equals are to be treated equally," provided their circumstances are relevantly similar. On this view the moral agents involved share certain characteristic features, their common possession of which makes it possible for the same general principles, or moral rules, to apply impartially to them all. It is these shared characteristics which bind all concerned together as members of the same moral community who participate in the same system of law—whether this be the *polis* of Plato and Aristotle or the *cosmopolis* of Kant and the Stoics. In short, for this way of thinking about ethics to "work" it has to be the case that although those involved might be in certain respects different from one another, they cannot be different from one another in *all* respects. They cannot be *completely* different from one another. For if they were then they could not possibly share the same system of law or be members of the same moral community. If the notion of that which is "other" has an important part to play here, then, nevertheless this other is not, and could not be, something which is *absolutely* other. Any presumption of absolute otherness would undermine this traditional way of thinking about ethics completely.

However, it is precisely such a presumption that "the Other" is an entity which is *absolutely* different which lies at the heart of contemporary poststructuralism/postmodernism, so far as it has a bearing on questions of ethics. Given this presumption, there are only two lines of reasoning which postmodern philosophers could possibly adopt in relation to ethical problems. The first involves arguing that in practice, precisely because of the presumption of absolute otherness, it follows that ethical life in the traditional sense is impossible. Those who argue in this way reject completely "the moral point of view" and, like the character Callicles in Plato's *Gorgias* and his follower Nietzsche (at least on one reading), become nihilists or "immoralists."[74] Paradoxically, however, although they reject the traditional understanding of ethics in practice, those who argue in this way might nevertheless be said to accept it in theory. For what they do *not* do is attempt to provide an alternative way of thinking about ethics based on different assumptions. This is the attitude of negative or destructive postmodernism. It is the approach to ethics which, until recently, has been associated with poststructuralism, largely because of the influence of the philosophy of Nietzsche in France at the end of the last century.[75]

The second response shares with the first the view that, precisely because of the presumption of absolute otherness, ethical life in the traditional sense is not possible. Those who respond in this way, however, also reject nihilism and immoralism. Instead they attempt to develop a new way of grounding ethical relationships which does not make the allegedly out-moded assumptions of the traditional account. This is the attitude of positive or constructive postmodernism. Following a lead provided by Emmanuel Levinas and Jacques Derrida, advocates of this new approach, such as Zygmund Bauman and Simon Critchley, maintain that the basic insight of such a postmodern ethics is that moral agents should be thought of as standing in an ethical relationship to something which is "other," not *despite* the differences which exist between them, but precisely *because* of these differences. This kind of ethics, therefore, involves the *celebration* of difference. It is this which distinguishes this new kind of ethics, in the postmodern age, from the traditional way of thinking about ethics presented earlier.

As an example of this attitude we may consider further the views of Emmanuel Levinas, whose approach to ethics is based on the notion of "absolute alterity," "absolute otherness," or "absolute difference." For Levinas others are unique "individuals" who must be valued as such. We must value others because they are "infinitely transcendent, infinitely foreign" to us. Levinas maintains, then, that we must value others not *despite* the differences which exist between ourselves and them, or because we are in some respects "the same," but precisely *because* of those differences.[76] It is obvious that this is a way of thinking about ethics which can have no place for moral "rules" or "laws." As Andrew Gibson has noted, an ethics of this kind "can have nothing to do with any transcendental sanction, any abstract principles or rules."[77] This is so because, as we have seen, an ethics of rules is based on the principle that one ought to "treat like cases alike." But for Levinas no two cases, no two individual moral agents, and no two ethical situations will ever *be* exactly or even sufficiently "alike" for any moral rule to apply to both of them.[78]

This aspect of Levinas's thought has been well captured by Hilary Putnam who has drawn an interesting contrast between Levinas's outlook and that of Kant. Putnam argues that Levinas's ethics is "very far from Kant." This is so because for Kant "ethics is fundamentally a matter of principles and of reason," whereas for Levinas, "the indispensable experience is the experience of responding to another person, where neither the other person nor my response are seen at that crucial moment as instances of universals." The "other," for Levinas, "is not an instance of any abstraction, not even 'humanity.'" Consequently, my ethical response to another "is not an instance of an abstract rule, not even the categorical imperative." It is simply a matter of "doing what I am 'called on' to do then and there," in the situation in which I find myself. For Levinas then, Putnam concludes, "one must respect the 'alterity' of the other, the other's manifold difference."[79]

Putnam rightly observes that Levinas "stresses the *asymmetry* of the fundamental moral relation" (my emphasis). One consequence of this

asymmetry is that ethical relationships cannot be grounded on the principle of equity or reciprocity, as the traditional understanding of ethics inherited by Kant maintains. As Putnam puts it, Levinas insists that ethics
must come "before reciprocity." On this view, "to seek to base ethics on
reciprocity," as the traditional approach does, is once again "to seek to
base it on the illusory 'sameness' of the other person," an alleged "sameness" which according to Levinas does not in fact exist.[80] My ethical relationship to the "other" is, therefore, to employ a phrase of Simon Critchley's, one which is "infinitely demanding."[81] It is a relationship within
which I might be said to have "duties" but no corresponding rights. In effect, as Robert Bernasconi has noted, Levinas transforms those duties
which moral philosophers usually refer to as "superogatory" into the *normal* duties of everyday ethical life.[82] It is clear, however, that the "duties"
in question, if they exist at all, must be of a very unusual and nontradi-
tional kind, precisely because they are not associated with any correlative
rights, and are not defined by any moral rule or law.

The issues discussed by both of the above mentioned strands of poststructuralist thought in relation to ethics have found their way into the
writings of those who have an interest in philosophy, politics, and literature.[83] In the case of the second strand, for example, Hilary Putnam has
noted that if one asks the question "Why act morally?" then "ninety nine
times out of a hundred the answer you will be given is 'Because the other
is fundamentally the same as you.'" According to Putnam, however, "the
limitations of such a 'grounding' of ethics only have to be mentioned to
become obvious." Following Levinas, Putnam has argued that "the danger in grounding ethics in the idea that we are all 'fundamentally the
same' is that a door is opened for a Holocaust." This is so because "one
only has to believe that some people are *not* 'really' the same to destroy all
the force of such a grounding." Somewhat surprisingly, and in my view
wrongly, the writings of Le Guin being a case in point, Putnam argues that
"*every* good novelist rubs our noses in the extent of human *dissimilarity*,
and many novels pose the question 'If you really knew what other people
were like, could you feel sympathy with them at all?'"[84]

An interest in issues of this kind is evidently not unique to the genre of
science fiction. However, we do also find these issues being dealt with by
science fiction writers. Nor is this too surprising. For works of science fiction are, of course, traditionally thought to have as one of their core
themes the relationship in which a particular subject subjects stands to
something (some "thing") which at first sight *appears* to be (and may indeed actually be) entirely "alien" or "other." To some extent, therefore, the
concerns of those philosophers who have been influenced by poststructuralism (whether or not they are associated with the recent effort to develop a new constructive approach to ethics) and those authors who have

contributed to the development of the new subgenre of "postmodern science fiction" have been one and the same.[85]

Now let us turn to consider Le Guin's views on ethics and, in particular, the way in which her science fiction deals with what postmodernists refer to as the problem of "the Other," in the light of the above.[86] Thomas J. Remington has maintained, in relation to Le Guin's *Planet of Exile,* that the novel's two main characters Jakob and Rolery are "bound together" ethically precisely *"because* of their differences, and not *in spite* of them" (my emphasis).[87] According to Remington, this is important for understanding Le Guin's moral outlook. For in Le Guin's vision "differences in human relationships are not to be ignored or minimized." Rather, they "should be embraced and cherished," presumably, in Remington's view, for their own sake.[88] This assessment seems to me to be leading in the direction of a Levinasian or poststructuralist reading of Le Guin's moral outlook. However, in my view, such a reading overlooks the significance which Le Guin attaches to the notions of identity, sameness, and indeed equality for those making moral judgments in any given situation.

For example, the entire thrust of Le Guin's *The Left Hand of Darkness* is to invite her male readers to engage in the moral equivalent of a "thought experiment" in physics, an experiment which involves putting themselves in the situation of "others" (women) who, although they are in *certain* respects different from themselves (biologically), are nevertheless, in other important respects, assumed by Le Guin to be "the same" as themselves (as human beings). But if there were no similarities at all between men and women, as in the situation envisaged by Levinas, then the thought experiment in question, and the kind of moral reasoning associated with it, could not possibly do its work. This is not at all to suggest that Le Guin does not value the principle of "difference." All I am claiming is that, unlike Levinas and contemporary postmodern ethics, she does not attach *exclusive* importance to that principle. Indeed, like Hegel, Le Guin values identity *and* difference, and suggests that these two principles complement rather than conflict with one another. Both principles, therefore, have an important part to play in Le Guin's anarchist moral vision.

I pointed out earlier that the fundamental principle which underpins Le Guin's ethical outlook is the assumption, which she considers to be "essential," that "we" human beings "are not objects" but "subjects." Hence, "whoever among us treats us as objects is acting inhumanly, wrongly, against nature."[89] In an essay significantly entitled "American SF and the Other," and in words which might have had postmodern ethics directly in mind, Le Guin insists that "if you deny any affinity with another person or kind of person, if you declare it to be *wholly* different from yourself" then you inevitably deny its "spiritual equality" and hence also its "human reality." In her view it is not actually possible for human beings to stand in an ethical relationship with something which is totally different from themselves. Indeed, rightly or wrongly, she argues that "the only possible relationship" they could have with an "other" thought of in this way is a "power relationship" and not an ethical one.[90] Unlike Levinas, then, Le Guin thinks that the outcome of any argument that "others" are so different from ourselves as to be considered *entirely* "alien" would be, not a rethinking of what is meant by "ethics," or a regrounding of the basis upon which moral status is granted to that which is different. Rather, in the manner of Robert Heinlein's *Starship Troopers*, such an argument would lead (it is not clear whether Le Guin thinks that this is inevitable) to a denial that an "other" who is thought of in this way, in this case Heinlein's "bugs," could have any moral standing at all.[91]

In my view, then, both insofar as she is an anarchist and insofar as she is a novelist, Le Guin's moral vision is definitely not "postmodern." Indeed, it is much closer in certain respects to that of Rousseau, Kant, Hegel and arguably Marx than it is to that of Levinas and Derrida. Moreover, as in the case of Le Guin's views on science, it is also much closer to the classical anarchism of the nineteenth century than it is to the "postmodern anarchism" of today. This is especially evident if we compare the views of Le Guin with those of Bakunin. According to Bakunin, liberty "is a feature, not of isolation but of interaction, not of exclusion but rather of connection." For "the liberty of any individual is nothing more or less than the reflection of his humanity and his human rights in the awareness of all free men – his brothers, his equals." I am, Bakunin continues, "human and free only to the extent that I acknowledge the humanity and liberty of all my fellows." For "it is only by respecting their human character that I respect my own." When, for example, "a cannibal treats his prisoner like an animal, he himself is not a man but an animal." Most tellingly of all, however, Bakunin concludes, in words which echo quite forcefully those of Le Guin cited earlier, and which also fall within that tradition which runs from Rousseau, through Kant to Hegel and beyond, that "a slave master is not a man but a master." Thus, by "ignoring his slave's humanity, he ignores his own."[92]

We may conclude from this that Le Guin does not write works of postmodern science fiction. This is very clear, for example, in the case of *The Left Hand of Darkness*. There Le Guin is concerned with exploring the ethical issues generated by the problem of "the other." This "other," however, is not by any means the *absolute* "other" associated with poststructuralist philosophy. Indeed, the moral outlook which informs this novel, as it does all of Le Guin's work, is precisely the traditional one outlined earlier. Although I am not entirely happy with the employment of temporal categories as a way of categorizing Le Guin's beliefs, we might provisionally state that her basic mind-set is what is often referred to (rightly or wrongly) as that of a "modernist" rather than a "postmodernist." If one wishes to call this traditional way of thinking about ethics (as for example it is to be found in the writings of Kant and his followers) "modern" then this implies that Le Guin is best thought of once again as a "modern" and not a "postmodern" thinker and writer. It is for this reason that some of Le Guin's critics have questioned the theoretical assumptions upon which Le Guin's commitment to feminism is based. In particular they have objected to her endorsement of the principle of essentialist humanism, and to her suggestion that it is not possible for us to celebrate "difference" along Levinasian lines because we are unable to relate ethically to something which is absolutely "other" to ourselves.[93]

Le Guin has been criticized on more than one occasion precisely because she does not write science fiction of this kind. As an example of this type of criticism we may consider the views of Carol McGuirk.[94] Following Stanislaw Lem, McGuirk criticizes Le Guin's way of dealing with the problem of "the other" in science fiction for being anthropocentric. She maintains that in Le Guin's science fiction "there is no *true* 'other' because "all intelligent life has a common origin and a common humanity."[95] For Le Guin, therefore, "otherness" is always merely apparent and never real. Although a concern with the problem of 'the other' is a central concern in Le Guin's fiction, nevertheless "the final message always seems to involve the ultimate *bridgeability* of difference" (my emphasis).[96] For this reason McGuirk maintains that Le Guin's outlook is basically an "optimistic" one. As McGuirk puts it, "Le Guin's vision of the alien works in a more optimistic direction, seeing beyond *apparent* 'otherness' to a connectedness—she sometimes calls it 'human solidarity'—that goes beneath and beyond apparent difference" (my emphasis).[97] Because Le Guin is intent on "denying the ineluctable difference of the *truly* alien" (my emphasis) she ensures that a central feature of the "heroic behaviour" of all of her central characters is precisely "a refusal to be alien-ated." Le Guin's heroes "insist on the negotiable status of difference." McGuirk maintains that the plot lines of both of *The Dispossessed* and *The Left Hand of Darkness* involve a "successful negotiation" of this kind. Above all, the universe which is depicted in Le Guin's writings is an ethical one, "designed to provide a setting for the drama of human choice."[98] According to McGuirk, then, Stanislaw Lem's critique of American science fiction generally "does suggest a troubling limitation" if it is applied specifically to the work of Le Guin. It indicates a definite weakness in Le Guin's "vision," namely an "optimism that too easily tames the universe by denying its perilous otherness."[99]

McGuirk thinks that the assumptions which lie behind Le Guin's writing are traditional, tame, "liberal," "pacifistic," and over "optimistic," rather than being truly radical or "subversive."[100] It is not always clear when McGuirk uses this last term whether she has in mind questions of ethics and politics on the one hand or questions of aesthetics on the other. In particular, McGuirk strongly objects to Le Guin's humanism, a doctrine which in her view is tainted by its associations with the principle of "essentialism." "The real limit to subversion in Le Guin," she maintains, is "her tendency to an unexamined humanism."[101] According to McGuirk, it is Le Guin's commitment to humanism which is the source of all of the weaknesses, both aesthetic as well as political, which can be found in her science fiction. To be more specific, McGuirk claims that Le Guin's universe only "achieves its balance and coherence through a diminished emphasis," not on the unknown but on "the unknowable, the alien."[102] In McGuirk's opinion science fiction writers today ought to be far more ambitious than this. For "with its potentially powerful imagery of voyages into the unknown and encounters with the alien," science fiction is "probably better designed to subvert than to validate human-centered norms and values."[103]

McGuirk argues that Le Guin's science fiction is "content to dwell on the knowable," whilst "never striking into the heart of true darkness," which, again, is the realm not merely of the unknown but of the "unknowable." For McGuirk this is a realm which might contain entities which, precisely because they are truly alien and unknowable, are at least potentially threatening to human beings. This is the *possible* world which ought to be depicted by science fiction writers today, and it is not the rather cozy and unthreatening world of Ursula Le Guin. Rather, it is a "dark" world which "poses" what are "literally unimaginable dangers." In McGuirk's opinion, the world depicted in Le Guin's science fiction lacks entirely "these dark intonations." In consequence, Le Guin's "human centered, progressive vision" all too easily degenerates into sentimentality.[104]

It is worth noting that, in the case of *The Dispossessed*, McGuirk connects what she takes to be these limitations in Le Guin's writing, so far she might be thought of as contributing to the genre of science fiction, with the fact that *The Dispossessed* is (in her judgment) a literary utopia. The genre of utopian writing is no longer, she maintains, "the avant-garde literary form that it was in 1516." Moreover, just like Le Guin's science fiction, it too is tainted with the outmoded assumptions of "enlightened humanism." It too presupposes not just the "reasonableness of human nature" but also the "intelligibility of the cosmos," a presupposition which, once again, "detracts from some of the more powerfully *subversive* symbolic possibilities of the science fiction genre" (my emphasis).[105] For McGuirk, like that of Le Guin, the style of writing associated with the traditional literary utopia is "inherently anthropocentric." This is not, therefore, "a genre that encourages its practitioners to use all the symbolic capacities of science fiction."[106] It is for this very reason that, as we have seen, McGuirk maintains that because of their "emphasis on the innate rationality and altruism of human character," the views of Odo, the founder of the anarchist community on the planet Anarres in Le Guin's *The Dispossessed*, "sound very much like" those of Thomas More, something which in McGuirk's opinion makes the society on Anarres a much "less ambiguous utopia than the subtitle of *The Dispossessed* would suggest."[107] When she made these remarks McGuirk was talking about science fiction in general. However, if we connect McGuirk's views to the account presented earlier, then what they amount to is the claim that it is the fact that Le Guin is a utopian writer which prevents her from being the author of works of postmodern science fiction.

McGuirk's essay on Le Guin indicates that, in her opinion, there are two contrasting literary genres, each of which can be associated with a certain cluster of descriptive labels. The first is that of utopian literature, which as McGuirk suggests is traditionally humanistic, altruistic, rationalistic, optimistic, moralistic, communitarian, pacifistic, and so on. This is a style of writing which emphasizes all of the human character traits which utopian writers have traditionally considered to be "good." The second is its opposite, *avant garde* science fiction, or what I have referred to as "postmodern science fiction," which McGuirk thinks is both aesthetically and politically more "subversive" than the writing of Le Guin. As McGuirk appears to understand it, this second genre is the very opposite of the first, focusing as it does on that about the absolutely "other" which might be potentially dangerous or threatening to human beings. The list of terms which McGuirk uses to describe this second type of fiction includes such words as "dangerous," "perilous," and "dark." Unlike utopian literature, then, the outlook of those who write in this way, and that of the entities about which they write, is not "liberal," "humane" or "pacifistic," and so on. However it is obvious that the characteristic features which McGuirk associates with the absolutely "other" are in fact human character traits. It is arguable, therefore, that despite her professed intentions, even McGuirk does not succeed in distancing herself entirely from anthropocentrism.

In my view it is not possible to locate Le Guin's fiction neatly into either one or the other of these two categories. The first of these two forms of writing, associated with the principle of utopianism, *does* have a place in Le Guin's work. In *The Dispossessed* it might be associated with the anarchist society on the planet Anarres. But, of course, to say this is to tell only one-half of the story. Furthermore, contrary to McGuirk's suggestion that Le Guin is a utopian writer, the second kind of writing and the features associated with it *also* have a place in *The Dispossessed*. They might be associated with the social organization of the society on the planet Urras. Although, of course, being "anarchic" in the "bad" sense, if they were developed to the

extreme, these principles would be inimical to *any* form of social organization. Again, however, if we were to focus exclusively on this dimension
of Le Guin's work, we would be telling only one-half of the story, the other
half. For *The Dispossessed* is a novel in the realist tradition and Le Guin's
novelistic form of writing, at its best, attempts to steer a *via-media* between
these two extremes, or at least to give both of them their due. It seeks to
embrace both of these principles at the same time without rejecting either
of them. In particular, as we shall see, and notwithstanding McGuirk's
criticism of her, Le Guin does not ignore altogether the "darker" side of
human nature, of human existence, or of the world generally. On the contrary, she is aware of it and seeks it incorporate it into her work. In my
view, then, McGuirk is wrong to suggest that Le Guin is straightforwardly
a writer who works within the utopian tradition. *The Dispossessed* is neither a work of utopian literature, nor a work of postmodern science fiction, but a *novel* in the tradition of European realism. There is a sense,
therefore, in which Franz Rottensteiner is absolutely correct when he
claims that Le Guin's "understanding of literature" is similar to that of the
great European novelists of the nineteenth century, though of course Rottensteiner considers this to be a weakness rather than a strength in Le
Guin's work. It is, he suggests, an attitude which is "more appropriate for
the nineteenth than the twentieth century" than it is for science fiction
writers today.[108]

NOTES

1. The reader will no doubt recognize the affinity which exists between this account and the moral philosophy of Kant. In recent times this way of thinking
about ethics is, perhaps, best exemplified in the writings of R. M. Hare. See R. M.
Hare, *The Language of Morals* (Oxford: Oxford University Press, 1991 [1952]); R. M.
Hare, *Freedom and Reason* (Oxford: Oxford University Press, 1990 [1963]); also Kurt
Baier, *The Moral Point of View: A Rational Basis of Ethics* (New York: Random House,
1966 [1958]). For criticism of this view, as it is to be found specifically in the writings of R. M. Hare, see especially Alasdair MacIntyre, "What Morality is Not," in
Alasdair MacIntyre, *Against the Self Images of the Age: Essays on Ideology and Philosophy* (Notre Dame: University of Notre Dame Press, 1978), 136–56.
    2. For the suggestion that, given the diversity of moral beliefs associated with
different cultures, there is no such thing as *the* "moral point of view" see Alasdair
MacIntyre, *A Short History of Ethics*, 2nd ed. (London: Routledge, 1998 [1967]), 1 et
seq. and Terence Ball, *Transforming Political Discourse* (Oxford: Blackwell, 1988), 2,
4, 6, 21, 145–49. For a thoughtful response to this line of reasoning see G. J.
Warnock, *The Object of Morality* (London, 1971), 3–10.
    3. I write about this in Tony Burns, "Aristotle and the *Nomos* Versus *Physis* De-
bate in Ancient Greek Political Thought" (paper presented to a panel on Ancient

Greek Political Thought at the Annual Conference of the American Northeastern Political Science Association, Philadelphia, Pa., United States, 17–19 November, 2005).

4. For this issue generally see *International Relations Through Science Fiction*, eds. Martin Harry Greenberg and Joseph D. Olander (New York and London: Franklin Watts, 1978).

5. For this see, inter alia, Alan D. Schrift, *Nietzsche's French Legacy: A Genealogy of Poststructuralism* (London and New York: Routledge, 1995), which explores the influence of Nietzsche on the work of Jacques Derrida, Michel Foucault, Gilles Deleuze, and Hélène Cixous.

6. James Bittner, "A Survey of Le Guin Criticism,"*Ursula K. Le Guin: Voyager to Inner Lands and to Outer Space*, ed. Joseph De Bolt (New York: Kennikat Press, 1979), 39; "For Le Guin, man is an *ethical* animal" (my emphasis); Gerard Klein, "Le Guin's 'Aberrant' Opus: Escaping the Trap of Discontent," in *Ursula K. Le Guin*, ed. Harold Bloom (New York: Chelsea House, 1985), 89–90: "Man is "naturally" for Le Guin an *ethical* animal" (my emphasis).

7. Ursula K. Le Guin, "Dreams Must Explain Themselves," in *The Language of the Night: Essays on Fantasy and Science Fiction*, ed. Susan Wood (New York: Perigee Books, 1979), 49.

8. In 1997 Le Guin published a "translation" of the *Tao Te Ching*. See Ursula K. Le Guin, *Tao Te Ching: A Book about the Way and the Power of the Way*. A new English version. by Ursula K. Le Guin with the collaboration of J. P. Seaton (Boston and London: Shambhala Press, 1997). For Le Guin and Taoism see Dena C. Bain, "The *Tao Te Ching* as Background to the Novels of Ursula K. Le Guin," *Ursula K. Le Guin*, ed. Harold Bloom, 211–224; Elizabeth [Cogell] Cummins, "Taoist Configurations: *The Dispossessed*," *Ursula K. Le Guin: Voyager to Inner Lands and Outer Space*, ed. Joseph de Bolt (New York: Kennikatt Press 1991 [1979]), 153–79.

9. John Fekete, "Circumnavigating Ursula Le Guin: Literary Criticism and Approaches to Landing: A Review of Joe De Bolt. ed. *Ursula K. Le Guin: Voyager to Inner Lands and to Outer Space*," *Science Fiction Studies*, 8, no. 1 (1981), 97–98, refers to Le Guin's philosophical commitment to "realism" in the passage just cited. He claims, however, that this is something which sets Le Guin against "the entire Kantian, Hegelian rationalist tradition." In the case of Kant, this seems to me to be correct, but not in that of Hegel, who in my view offers a critique of Kant along "realist" lines. The fact that Hegel is a philosophical idealist does not mean that he is not or could not be at the same time a "realist." For this issue see Tony Burns, "Metaphysics and Politics in Aristotle and Hegel," in *Contemporary Political Studies: 1998*, Vol. 1, eds. A. Dobson and G. Stanyer (The Political Studies Association of Great Britain, 1998), 387–99.

10. Ursula K. Le Guin, "Science Fiction and Mrs. Brown," *The Language of the Night*, 116.

11. Ursula K. Le Guin, "American SF and the Other," *The Language of the Night*, 99.

12. See *Marxism's Ethical Thinkers*, ed. Lawrence Wilde (London: Palgrave, 2002).

13. Ursula K. Le Guin, "American SF and the Other," 99.

14. Erich Fromm, *To Have or to Be* (London: Abacus Books, 1979 [1976]). For Fromm's thought generally see Lawrence Wilde, *Erich Fromm and the Quest for Solidarity* (New York: Palgrave, 2004).

15. Ursula K. Le Guin, *The Dispossessed: An Ambiguous Utopia*. London: Granada Books, 1983 [1974], II, 48, 50.

16. Le Guin, *The Dispossessed*, I, 14.

17. Le Guin, *The Dispossessed*, VII, 164.

18. Le Guin, *The Dispossessed*, IX, 249.

19. Le Guin, *The Dispossessed*, I, 20.

20. Le Guin, *The Dispossessed*, I, 19.

21. Le Guin, *The Dispossessed*, I, 22.

22. Le Guin, *The Dispossessed*, I, 24.

23. Le Guin, *The Dispossessed*, III, 73.

24. Ursula K. Le Guin, *The Left Hand of Darkness* (London: Virago, 1997 [1969]); Ursula K. Le Guin, *The Word for World is Forest* (London: Panther Books, 1980 [1972]).

25. Le Guin, *The Dispossessed*, I, 22.

26. Le Guin, *The Dispossessed*, VII, 180.

27. Le Guin, *The Dispossessed*, VII, 182.

28. Ursula K. Le Guin, *The Earthsea Quartet* (London: Puffin Books, 1993).

29. Le Guin, "The Child and the Shadow," *The Language of the Night*, 62.

30. See James Bittner, *Approaches to the Fiction of Ursula K. Le Guin* (Cambridge, Mass.: UMI Research Press, 1984), 16–18; Rafael Nudelman, "An Approach to the Structure of Le Guin's SF," *Science Fiction Studies: Selected Articles*, eds. Mullen and Suvin, 249; Darko Suvin, "Parables of De-Alienation: Le Guin's Widdershins Dance," in *Positions and Presuppositions in Science Fiction* (Kent: Kent State University Press, 1988), 145; Donald Theall, "The Art of Social-Science Fiction: The Ambiguous Utopian Dialectics of Ursula K. Le Guin," *Science Fiction Studies: Selected Articles*, eds. Mullen and Suvin, 293–4.

31. G. W. F. Hegel, *Hegel on Tragedy*, eds. Anne Paolucci and Henry Paolucci (New York: Doubleday, 1962).

32. G. W. F. Hegel, *Philosophy of Right*, trans. T. M. Knox (Oxford: Oxford University Press, 1979 [1817]).

33. Jurgen Habermas, "On the Pragmatic, the Ethical and the Moral Employments of Practical Reason," in *Justification and Application: Remarks on Discourse Ethics* (Cambridge: Polity Press, 1993), 1–18; see also Jurgen Habermas, *Between Facts and Norms: Contributions to a Discourse Theory of Law and Democracy* (Cambridge: Polity Press, 1996), 158–64. I discuss the views on Hegel and Habermas on this subject in Tony Burns, "Morality, Ethics and Law in Habermas and Hegel" (unpublished MS). In my view any suggestion that this distinction is characteristic of a specifically "postmodern" approach would be mistaken. Such a suggestion appears to be made by Andrew Gibson, *Postmodernity, Ethics and the Novel: From Leavis to Levinas* (Routledge, 1999), 15, who refers to Zygmund Bauman, *Life in Fragments: Essays in Postmodern Morality* (Oxford: Blackwell, 1995) in this connection.

34. Jurgen Habermas, *Between Facts and Norms: Contributions to a Discourse Theory of Law and Democracy*, 161–4.

35. Habermas, "On the Pragmatic, the Ethical and the Moral Employments of Practical Reason," 2–4.

36. Habermas, "On the Pragmatic, the Ethical and the Moral Employments of Practical Reason," 6.

37. Jurgen Habermas, "Remarks on Discourse Ethics," in *Justification and Application: Remarks on Discourse Ethics*, 23.

38. Le Guin, "Science Fiction and Mrs. Brown," 117.

39. Le Guin, "The Child and the Shadow," *The Language of the Night*, 65–66.

40. See Le Guin, "Moral and Ethical Implications of Family Planning" in *Dancing at the Edge of the World: Thoughts on Words, Women, Places* (New York: Harper and Row, 1997), 17–20.

41. Le Guin, "Moral and Ethical Implications of Family Planning," 20. See also Carol Gilligan, *In a Different Voice: Psychological Theory and Women's' Development* (Cambridge, Mass.: Harvard University Press, 1982).

42. Note that Elizabeth Cogell Cummins, "Taoist Configurations: *The Dispossessed*,"168, has associated Taoism with some kind of "virtue ethic." In her view, "the Taoists believed that the manifestation of Tao in each individual was *te*, usually translated as 'virtue.'

43. Le Guin, "The Child and the Shadow," 69.

44. Le Guin, "The Child and the Shadow," 66–67.

45. Le Guin, "The Child and the Shadow," 66–67.

46. Le Guin, "The Child and the Shadow," 66–67.

47. See Alasdair MacIntyre, *After Virtue*, 2nd ed. (London: Duckworth, 1985); Alasdair MacIntyre, *Whose Justice? Which Rationality?* (London: Duckworth, 1988); Alasdair MacIntyre, "Moral Dilemmas," in *Ethics and Politics: Selected Essays*, Volume 2 (Cambridge: Cambridge University Press, 2006), 85–100; and Tony Burns, "Whose Aristotle? Which Marx? Ethics, Law and Justice in Aristotle and Marx," *Imprints: Egalitarian Theory and Practice*, 8, 2 (2005): 125–55.

48. This was also the view of Wells. See H. G. Wells, "The Contemporary Novel," in *Henry James and H. G. Wells: A Record of Their Friendship, Their Debate on the Art of Fiction and Their Quarrel*, eds. Leon Edel and Gordon N. Ray (London: Rupert Hart Davis, 1958), 148: "All our social, political, moral problems are being approached in a new spirit, in an enquiring and experimental spirit, which has small respect for *abstract principles* and *deductive rules*" (my emhasis).

49. I have argued elsewhere that one of the limitations of MacIntyre's "virtue ethics" is its claim that it is possible to have an ethic without "rules." MacIntyre associates this way of thinking with Aristotle – in my view wrongly. See Burns, "Whose Aristotle? Which Marx? Ethics, Law and Justice in Aristotle and Marx," 131–39.

50. Le Guin, *The Dispossessed*, IX, 249.

51. Le Guin, *The Dispossessed*, I, 14: "The one law held, the one law he had ever acknowledged."

52. Ursula K. Le Guin, "The Ones Who Walked Away from Omelas," in *The Wind's Twelve Quarters*, Vol 2 (London: Granada, 1980 [1973]), 112–20. See also Lyman Tower Sargent, "The Problem of the 'Flawed Utopia': A Note on the Costs of Eutopia," in Raffaella Baccolini and Tom Moylan eds., *Dark Horizons: Science Fiction and the Dystopian Imagination* (London: Routledge, 2003), 225–32.

53. See Lyman Tower Sargent, "The Problem of the 'Flawed Utopia': A Note on the Costs of Eutopia," 226–37; and George Kateb, *Utopia and Its Enemies* (New York: Schocken Books, 1972 [1963]), 36.

54. For this see Shoshona Knapp, "'The Morality of Creation': Dostoevsky and William James in Le Guin's 'Omelas,'" *Journal of Narrative Technique*, 15, 1 (1985): 75–81; and Heinz Tschachler, "Forgetting Dostoevsky; or, The Political Unconscious of Ursula K. Le Guin," *Utopian Studies*, 2, 1–2 (1991): 63–76.

55. Le Guin, "Science Fiction and Mrs. Brown," 117.

56. Le Guin, *The Dispossessed*, IX, 250.

57. James Bittner, "Chronosophy, Aesthetics and Ethics in Le Guin's *The Dispossessed*," in *No Place Else: Explorations in Utopian and Dystopian Fiction*, eds. Rabkin, Olander, and Greenberg (Carbondale: Southern Illinois University Press, 1983), 247.

58. This observation excludes, of course, the views on ethics which Sartre developed after the publication of *Being and Nothingness*. See Jean-Paul Sartre, *Existentialism and Humanism* (Methuen, 1973 [1946]).

59. For a discussion of situation ethics see W. D. Hudson, *Modern Moral Philosophy* (London: Macmillan, 1970), 203–4, 209–23; and Alasdair MacIntyre, "What Morality is Not."

60. John Mander, *The Writer and Commitment*, (London: Greenwood Publishing Group, 1975), 11.

61. Sartre, *Existentialism and Humanism*, 38. Alasdair MacIntyre has used this idea to criticize the defense of the traditional way of thinking about "the moral point of view" outlined earlier which is to be found in the writings of the moral philosopher R. M. Hare, See again Alasdair MacIntyre, "What Morality is Not."

62. Sartre, *Existentialism and Humanism*, 36.

63. Sartre, *Existentialism and Humanism*, 28.

64. Sartre, *Existentialism and Humanism*, 52–53.

65. Sartre, *Existentialism and Humanism*, 52–53.

66. Sartre, *Existentialism and Humanism*, 52–53.

67. Sartre, *Existentialism and Humanism*, 52–53.

68. Sartre, *Existentialism and Humanism*, 52–53.

69. Simone de Beauvoir, *The Ethics of Ambiguity* (New York: Citadel Press, 1962 [1948]). See especially the section entitled "Ambiguity," 129–54.

70. For this again see, inter alia, Schrift, *Nietzsche's French Legacy: A Genealogy of Poststructuralism*.

71. See Zygmunt Bauman, *Postmodern Ethics* (Oxford: Blackwell, 1993), 47–52, 62, 69–77, 84–87, 92–93, 108, 113, 124, 219–20, 249. Also Zygmund Bauman, *Life in Fragments: Essays in Postmodern Morality* (Oxford: Blackwell, 1995); Simon Critchley, *Infinitely Demanding: Ethics of Commitment, Politics of Resistance* (London: Verso, 2007); Simon Critchley, *Ethics-Politics-Subjectivity: Essays on Derrida, Levinas and Contemporary French Thought* (London: Verso, 1999); Simon Critchley, *The Ethics of Deconstruction: Derrida and Levinas*, 2nd ed. (Oxford: Blackwell, 1999 [1992]). See also Catherine Challier, *What Ought I to Do? Morality in Kant and Levinas* (Ithaca and London: Cornell University Press, 2001).

72. For Levinas on ethics see Emmanuel Levinas, *Ethics and Infinity*, trans. Richard A. Cohen (Pittsburgh: Duquesne University Press, 1985 [1982]); Emmanuel Levinas, *Totality and Infinity* (Pittsburgh: Duquesne University Press, 1996 [1961]).

73. For Derrida's views on ethics (and his debt to Levinas) see Jacques Derrida, "Violence and Metaphysics: An Essay on the Thought of Emmanuel Levinas," in *Writing and Difference* (London: Routledge, 1993 [1967]), 79–153.

74. Plato, *Gorgias*, trans. W. R. M. Lamb (Cambridge, Mass.: 1996 [1925]), 483E, 384–7.

75. See Schrift, *Nietzsche's French Legacy: A Genealogy of Poststructuralism* and David B. Allison, ed. *The New Nietzsche: Contemporary Styles of Interpretation* (Cambridge, Mass.: MIT Press, 1985). Needless to say there is much disagreement over the issue of how Nietzsche is to be interpreted.

76. Levinas, *Totality and Infinity*, 194–95, 203.

77. Gibson, *Postmodernity, Ethics and the Novel: From Leavis to Levinas*, 57.

78. The similarities between the views of Levinas and those which are often wrongly attributed to Sartre in respect to this issue are obvious. It is not at all surprising, therefore, that Nik Farrell Fox should have written a book devoted to exploring the affinities between Sartre and postmodernism. See Nik Farrell Fox, *The New Sartre: Explorations in Postmodernism* (New York and London: Continuum Books, 2003), especially chapter 3, "Sartre: Un Homme Postmoderne?" 149–62.

79. Hilary Putnam, "Levinas and Judaism," in *The Cambridge Companion to Levinas*, eds. Simon Critchley and Robert Bernasconi (Cambridge: Cambridge University Press, 2002), 55.

80. Putnam, "Levinas and Judaism," 39.

81. Critchley, *Infinitely Demanding: Ethics of Commitment, Politics of Resistance*.

82. Robert Bernasconi, "What is the Question to Which 'Substitution' is the Answer?" in *The Cambridge Companion to Levinas*, eds. Simon Critchley and Robert Bernasconi (Cambridge: Cambridge University Press, 2002), 235: "Levinas is asking what underlies that behavior which is sometimes called superogatory, gratuitous or, as he prefers to say, ethical."

83. See Gibson, *Postmodernity, Ethics and the Novel: From Leavis to Levinas* and Gerhard Hoffman and Alfred Hornung eds., *Ethics and Aesthetics: The Moral Turn of Postmodernism* (Heidelberg: Universitätsverlag, 1996).

84. Putnam, "Levinas and Judaism," 35.

85. For postmodernism and science fiction see Andrew M. Butler, "Postmodernism and Science Fiction," in Edward James and Farah Mendelsohn eds., *The Cambridge Companion to Science Fiction* (Cambridge: Cambridge University Press, 2003), 137–48; Istvan Csicsery-Ronay Jr., "Science Fiction and Postmodernism," *Science Fiction Studies*, 18, no. 3 (1991): 305–08; Damien Broderick, *Reading by Starlight: Postmodern Science Fiction* (London: Routledge, 1995); Jenny Wolmark, *Aliens and Others: Science Fiction, Feminism and Postmodernism* (New York: Harvester, 1994); Gwyneth Jones, *Deconstructing the Starships: Science, Fiction and Reality* (Liverpool: Liverpool University Press, 1999); *Storming the Reality Studio: A Casebook of Cyberpunk and Postmodern Fiction*, ed. Larry McCaffery (Durham and London: Duke University Press, 1991).

86. Ursula K. Le Guin, "American SF and the Other," in *The Language of the Night*. For this issue generally see Carl D. Malmgren, "Self and Other in SF: Alien Encounters," *Science Fiction Studies*, 20 (1993): 15–33; *Aliens R Us: The Other in Science Fiction Cinema*, eds. Ziauddin Sardar and Sean Cubitt (London: Pluto Press, 2002); Geoffrey Whitehall, "The Problem of the 'World and Beyond': Encountering

'The Other' in Science Fiction," in *To Seek Out New Worlds: Exploring the Links Between Science*, Ed. Jutta Weldes (Palgrave,2003), 169–94. Jenny Wolmark, *Aliens and Others: Science Fiction, Feminism and Postmodernism* (Iowa City: University of Iowa Press, 1994).

87. Thomas J. Remington, "The Other Side of Suffering: Touch as Theme and Metaphor in Le Guin's Science Fiction Novels," in *Ursula K. Le Guin*, eds. Joseph D. Olander and Martin Harry Greenberg (New York: Taplinger, 1979), 157.

88. Remington, "The Other Side of Suffering: Touch as Theme and Metaphor in Le Guin's Science Fiction Novels," 157.

89. Ursula K. Le Guin, "Science Fiction and Mrs. Brown," *The Language of the Night*, 116.

90. Ursula K. Le Guin, "American SF and the Other," 99.

91. Robert A. Heinlein, *Starship Troopers* (New York: Ace, 1987 [1958]). See also Geoffrey Whitehall, "The Problem of the 'World and Beyond': Encountering 'The Other' in Science Fiction," in Weldes, ed., *To Seek Out New Worlds: Exploring the Links Between Science Fiction and World Politics*.

92. Bakunin, *Selected Writings*, ed. A. Lehning (London: Cape, 1973), 147.

93. See Samuel R. Delany, "To Read *The Dispossessed*," in *The Jewel-Hinged Jaw* (New York: Dragon Press, 1977), 239–308; Gwyneth Jones, "In the Chinks of the World Machine: Sarah Lefanu on Feminist SF," in *Deconstructing the Starships: Science, Fiction and Reality*, 127–28; Gwyneth Jones, "No Man's Land: Feminized Landscapes in the Utopian Fiction of Ursula Le Guin," in *Deconstructing the Starships: Science, Fiction and Reality*, 201–03; N. B. Hayles, "Androgyny, Ambivalence, and Assimilation, in *The Left Hand of Darkness*," in *Ursula K. Le Guin*, eds. Joseph Olander and Martin Harry Greenberg, 97–115; Naomi Jacobs, "The Frozen Landscape in Women's Utopian and Science Fiction," in *Utopian and Science Fiction by Women: Worlds of Difference*, eds. Jane L. Donawerth and Carol A. Kolmerten (New York: Syracuse University Press, 1994), 190–202; Tom Moylan, "The Dispossessed," in *Demand the Impossible: Science Fiction and the Utopian Imagination* (New York and London: Methuen, 1986), 91–120; Adam Roberts, "SF and Gender," in *Science Fiction* (London: Routledge, 2006), 71–93.

94. Carol McGuirk, "Optimism and the Limits of Subversion in *The Dispossessed* and *The Left Hand of Darkness*," in *Ursula K. Le Guin*, ed. Bloom, 243–58.

95. McGuirk, "Optimism and the Limits of Subversion in *The Dispossessed* and *The Left Hand of Darkness*," 244. See also Stanislaw Lem, "Cosmology and Science Fiction," in *Microworlds: Writings on Science Fiction and Fantasy* (New York: Harcourt Brace, 1984) 200–8.

96. McGuirk, "Optimism and the Limits of Subversion in *The Dispossessed* and *The Left Hand of Darkness*," 245.

97. McGuirk, "Optimism and the Limits of Subversion in *The Dispossessed* and *The Left Hand of Darkness*," 244.

98. McGuirk, "Optimism and the Limits of Subversion in *The Dispossessed* and *The Left Hand of Darkness*," 245.

99. McGuirk, "Optimism and the Limits of Subversion in *The Dispossessed* and *The Left Hand of Darkness*," 247.

100. McGuirk, "Optimism and the Limits of Subversion in *The Dispossessed* and *The Left Hand of Darkness*," 248.

101. McGuirk, "Optimism and the Limits of Subversion in *The Dispossessed* and *The Left Hand of Darkness*," 248–49.

102. McGuirk, "Optimism and the Limits of Subversion in *The Dispossessed* and *The Left Hand of Darkness*," 246.

103. McGuirk, "Optimism and the Limits of Subversion in *The Dispossessed* and *The Left Hand of Darkness*," 248.

104. McGuirk, "Optimism and the Limits of Subversion in *The Dispossessed* and *The Left Hand of Darkness*," 246.

105. McGuirk, "Optimism and the Limits of Subversion in *The Dispossessed* and *The Left Hand of Darkness*," 246.

106. McGuirk, "Optimism and the Limits of Subversion in *The Dispossessed* and *The Left Hand of Darkness*," 246.

107. McGuirk, "Optimism and the Limits of Subversion in *The Dispossessed* and *The Left Hand of Darkness*," 252.

108. Rottensteiner, "Le Guin's Fantasy: Review of Ursula K. Le Guin. *The Language of the Night: Essays on Fantasy and Science Fiction*," *Science Fiction Studies*, 23, no. 1 (1984), 87–90.

8

Anarchist Politics in
Zamyatin and Le Guin

In this chapter I shall consider Le Guin's "politics," and specifically the nature of her commitment to anarchism. As a preliminary it should be noted that Le Guin does not make a clear distinction between the spheres of "ethics" and "politics." She writes from within a long-standing tradition, going back at least to the ancient Greeks, according to which questions of ethics are thought of as being at the same time also questions of politics, and *vice versa*. From this standpoint, the notion of politics is understood in a very broad sense. As such it does not necessarily have anything to do with the idea of the "state." In my view this is one of the few things which Le Guin's outlook does have in common with poststructuralism. I shall also compare Le Guin's anarchism with that of Zamyatin. For, as in the case of questions relating to the philosophy of science, so also in the sphere of ethics and politics, I think such a comparison is fruitful for anyone who wishes to understand the views of Le Guin.

ENDS AND MEANS IN ANARCHIST POLITICS

Le Guin's rejection of the doctrine of ethical consequentialism implies that, in her view, the principle that "the end justifies the means" can have no place in politics, and certainly not in anarchist politics. In order to clarify Le Guin's views regarding this issue it is necessary to say something more about the different types of anarchism.[1] In what follows I shall do this by isolating four strands of anarchist thought and relating them to the problem of "ends and means" in politics. I shall make no systematic attempt to address the question of whether this account of the various types of anarchism is factually accurate when compared with the history of "actually existing anarchism."² The first of these four forms of anarchism is identical with moral nihilism. As we have seen, the philosophical source of inspiration for this kind of anarchism in modern times is the work of Stirner and Nietzsche. I have suggested that Zamyatin is an anarchist in this sense.

The second form of anarchism is different from this. For it is a political ideology, similar to other political ideologies. As such it is a certain way of looking at the world associated with a definite conceptual vocabulary. Most importantly, anarchists of this second type are not nihilists. On the contrary, they might be said to be moralists, of a kind. They have a vision of an ideal society, or at least of what they consider to be a better or morally superior society. Politically speaking, therefore, they are committed to certain moral values, and they are committed to the pursuit of definite goals or "ends." This is something which they have in common with utopian thinkers and writers.

Phillip Wegner says things which imply that he would place Zamyatin in this second category and not, as I do, in the first. For example, Wegner claims that in *We* Zamyatin's intention is not to criticize the idea of utopia generally, but specifically that of a "liberal utopia."³ Hence Zamyatin did have a utopian vision of his own, if only an implicit one. Wegner also states that Zamyatin's critique of this liberal utopia "was undertaken with the ultimate aim of opening up the possibility of an alternative path along which a different kind of reorganization of society might be accomplished."⁴ For Wegner, then, *We* is a *utopian* and not a dystopian (in the sense of being an "anti-utopian") text. As such it does contain, at least implicitly, a positive vision of an alternative society and hence, also, some kind of moral or ethical ideal. Against this reading, my own view is that it is more plausible to characterize *We* as being the anti-utopian work of an anarchist who is a nihilistic "outsider" in Colin Wilson's sense of that term. Ernst Fischer's characterization of Wilson seems to me to fit Zamyatin very well. According to Fischer, Wilson "calls upon his fellow-artist to refuse to commit himself to anything, to free himself from the 'curse' of all social obligations and try to dedicate himself solely to the redemption of his own existential 'I.'" In this manner, Wilson maintains, a "new anti-humanist epoch" is to be "ushered in."⁵ The echoes of Nietzsche's philosophy are clearly evident in Fischer's portrayal of the views of Wilson, as I think they can be discerned in the writings of Zamyatin.⁶

The views of anarchists of this second kind can be characterized by reference to the notions of ends and means. Their vision of an ideal or at least a better society does constitute a definite moral end. However, anarchists of this second type subscribe to the principle that "the end justifies the means." Consequently, although they are willing to justify the ultimate ends which they set for themselves on moral grounds, they do not feel constrained by what might be referred to as the ordinary considerations of morality when choosing the means which are to be used in order to achieve those ends. Anarchists of this type, then, can be said to be dogmatic, doctrinaire, and intolerant of the differing views of others, especially if this is a necessary means for the practical implementation of their own political program. They always think that they are "in the right." They claim to possess a privileged insight into the "Truth" in questions of ethics and politics, and are prepared to impose their views on others by the use of violence if necessary. It is arguable that Bakunin is an anarchist who falls into this second category.[7]

Anarchists of the third type reject both of these first two types of anarchism on moral grounds. They have no time at all for moral nihilism, and hence for anarchism of the first kind. But they also reject the principle of ethical consequentialism, and hence with it anarchism of the second kind. They reject outright, therefore, the principle that "the end justifies the means." According to this third view, anarchism is not so much an ideology, but more a "way of life." Anarchism and anarchists in this third sense profess to have *no* political objectives, goals, or ends at all. They are oriented not toward the future, and the question of how we might then live, but toward the present, and the question of how we ought to live now. So much so that they claim that in ethics and politics ends do not matter at all. *All* that is important are means. That is to say, they claim that life or human existence does not actually have any end or goal. It is not *where* one gets to in the end that matters. What matters is how one conducts oneself during the process of *getting* wherever one is going. The outlook associated with this form of anarchism is a *moral* one. It has a view of human nature according to which man is by nature a "moral being" or an "ethical animal"; and it also, therefore, possesses at least *some* (what might be referred to as a *formal* rather than substantive) understanding of what sort of conduct this commitment to living an "ethical life" requires.

There is at least some evidence that Le Guin should be placed in this third category. For she does occasionally appear to suggest that in political life "ends" do not matter at all. *All* that matters are "means." For example, at one point Le Guin has Shevek say that "you know that the means *are* the end to us Odonians."[8] And on another occasion she has him say that in Odonian philosophy "there was *no* end. There was process: process was all."[9] Moreover, as Peter Brigg has noted, this idea can also be found in *The Left Hand of Darkness*, where at one point the central character Genly-Ai says "it is good to have an end to journey towards, but it is the *journey* that matters, in the end [sic]."[10] Given that Le Guin does occasionally say things like this, it is not too surprising that George Slusser has claimed that an important *motif* in *The

Dispossessed (as it is in Dostoevsky's *Notes from the Underground* and in Zamyatin's *We*) is the idea that "what counts" in life "is the *living* itself, the means *without* the ends"[11] (my emphasis).

According to this third way of thinking about anarchism, and this reading of Le Guin, it is impossible for true anarchists to be dogmatic or doctrinaire, or to seek to impose their views on others. It is also impossible for them to be "ideological," in one particular (and important) sense of that much used and abused term. This is so precisely because they do not actually *have* any views regarding ultimate goals or ends. And, of course, if one does not have any views about such things one cannot seek to impose one's views about these things upon others. In short, if the ethical discourse associated with the second type of anarchism might be said to focus exclusively on ends and ignore completely the issue of means, by contrast the ethical discourse associated with this third type of anarchism focuses exclusively on the issue of means and ignores completely that of ends.

However, this account of Le Guin's views seems to me to be an exaggeration. Indeed, I am not at all convinced that the idea of a "means without an end" actually makes sense. I say this because it seems to me that these two notions are logically related to one another. A "means" is always "something which produces an end," just as an "end" is always "something which is produced by a means." There is, therefore, a logical difficulty involved in any interpretation of anarchism, or of Le Guin, which suggests that it is possible to have any kind of positive or practical political program which focuses exclusively on means and ignores completely the issue of the ends which are to be achieved by the employment of the means in question.

This brings us to the fourth type of anarchism, or the fourth way of thinking about anarchism. The ideas associated with the fourth view might be seen as a theoretical synthesis of those associated with the second and third types of anarchism just discussed. Anarchists of this type attach importance to *both* ends and means in ethics and politics. They differ from anarchists of the second type because they reject the principle that "the end justifies the means," and attach a great deal of importance to the issue of the moral constraints which ought to be placed on those seeking to create an anarchist society. At the same time, they differ from anarchists of the third type because they do not ignore altogether the issue of ends. They do have at least some idea of what a morally preferable or "better" society would be like at an interpersonal level, should it ever come into existence, even if they do not possess a detailed blue print for the social organization of that society. They insist, however, that such a society can only come into existence by the use of appropriate, that is to say, morally acceptable means. This excludes the use of physical force or violence.

In my view it is this form of anarchism which should be associated with Le Guin's more considered position. A more balanced reading of Le Guin's views would be to say that she attaches due importance to *both* "ends" and "means" for anarchist politics. Here as elsewhere Le Guin might be thought of as seeking to correct the "one sidedness" of the extreme approach to this issue which is adopted by other anarchists, especially Zamyatin. If Zamyatin attaches exclusive importance to means and none at all to ends, Le Guin does *not* counter this by doing the opposite, as anarchists of our second type do. Rather, she seeks to develop a third way of thinking which accords due importance to both—to means *as well as* ends in politics.

On the whole then, insofar as she is a political *activist* as opposed to a novelist, I think that Le Guin *is* best thought of as being an anarchist in this fourth sense. She is certainly not an anarchist in the first sense. Hence, *pace* Wegner, her outlook differs fundamentally from that of Zamyatin. She also rejects anarchism in the second sense. This is what Le Guin would refer to as "the bomb in the pocket kind" of anarchism. And although she does occasionally say things which she suggest that she might be an anarchist in the third sense, on the whole I do not think that this is her considered view.

I have suggested that Bakunin was an anarchist of the second type referred to above. It is not clear whether Dostoevsky had Bakunin specifically in mind as the prototype for the type of anarchist whose activities he evidently set out to condemn in *The Possessed*. There is some debate about this, but such a suggestion does not seem to me to be entirely implausible.[12] However, if Dostoevsky *was* thinking of Bakunin, then it is arguable that he either misunderstood or at least grossly oversimplified Bakunin's views by presenting him, and other anarchists like him, as nihilists rather than ethical consequentialists.[13] So far as Le Guin and Bakunin are concerned, Carl Freedman has rightly observed that the name of Bakunin is "conspicuous by its absence" in the commentaries on Le Guin which deal with her relationship to the anarchist tradition.[14] But this is also true of Le Guin's own writings. Like that of Zamyatin, Bakunin does not appear on any of the lists of the names of anarchist sources which Le Guin provides for her readers, although, as Freedman notes, her views are quite similar to those of Bakunin on at least some issues.

Bakunin's ethical beliefs are not entirely consistent, but it seems to me that he subscribes to some kind of moral doctrine or other. So he is certainly not a nihilist. Indeed, his endorsement of the principle that "the end justifies the means" suggests that he is some kind of ethical consequentialist. But whatever his moral beliefs were, the fact is that he is largely ignored by Le Guin, who so far as I know, nowhere discusses them explicitly. It is tempting to think that one of the reasons for this is the fact that

Le Guin accepts Dostoevsky's implicit suggestion that Bakunin was a nihilist. For example, at one point in *The Possessed* when presenting the views
of the character Kirilov to his readers, he suggests that Kirilov is "not dealing with the essence of the problem, or, as it were, its *moral* aspect. Indeed,
he rejects *morality* as such, and is in favor of the latest principle of general
destruction for the sake of the ultimate good" (my emphasis).[15] This remark demonstrates very clearly Dostoevsky's inability to conceive of the
distinction between "ethical consequentialism" and "nihilism." It is arguable that Le Guin agrees with Dostoevsky's negative evaluation of the
kind of anarchism with which Bakunin was associated. Because of
Bakunin's commitment to the principle that "the end justifies the means,"
like Dostoevsky she too associates Bakunin (and anarchists of this second
type) with "terrorism." For this reason I find it difficult to accept Phillip
Wegner's suggestion that the "Odonian anarchism" on Anarres might be
associated with the political philosophy of Bakunin.[16] At least this seems to
me to be not the case so far as the important issue of "ends and means" is
concerned. Wegner cites the work of Carl Freedman in support of his
claim. Freedman, however, takes care to emphasize that there is an important difference between Odonianism and Bakunin's anarchism with respect to this particular issue. For, as Freedman puts it, "unlike Bakunin"
the Odonians in *The Dispossessed* "are resolutely non-violent."[17]

Lyman Tower Sargent has noted that the existence of "people who are
willing to impose their utopia on others" has been a "serious problem" in
the history of utopian speculation, but that this is "not a problem with
utopianism *per se*."[18] Similarly, it might be said that for Le Guin this has
also been a serious problem in the history of anarchism, but that it is not
a problem with anarchism *per se*. When criticizing the views of anarchists
of the second type above, Le Guin suggests that the reason why they are
doctrinaire, dogmatic, and intolerant is because they are in the grip of an
"ideology." They have moral ideals which are associated with a "utopian"
vision of a better society which they consider to be objectively valid. Consequently, they claim a privileged insight into "the Truth" so far as the
"ends" which ought to be pursued in ethics and politics are concerned.
She also suggests, on occasion, that the *only* way to avoid this undesirable
outcome is to avoid "utopianism" and "ideology" and the "ends" with
which they are associated altogether. What she does not consider, on these
occasions at least, is the possibility that being dogmatic and doctrinaire is
not so much a matter of the particular beliefs which a person holds but
rather of that person's psychology or their character. In consequence she
does not explore the possibility that one might be an anarchist who does
possess a positive vision associated with a reasonably clear understanding of some morally desirable "end," without being intolerant of the
views of others who happen to disagree with you. In short, it is possible

for someone to subscribe to the belief system associated with anarchism *without* being "ideological" in the pejorative sense in which Le Guin occasionally uses that term, whilst at the same time being sensitive to the importance of the choice of "means" to be employed in pursuit of that "end." Indeed, I think that Le Guin herself is a good example of an anarchist in that sense.

LE GUIN, ANARCHISM, AND IDEOLOGY

One of the core elements of traditional conservatism from the time of Edmund Burke onward is its suspicion of the role of "theory" in the spheres of morality and politics. For Burke the European Enlightenment of the eighteenth century was, of course, The Age of Reason, and at its culmination we find the French Revolution and the Terror of Robespierre and the Jacobin Party.[19] It is arguable that the theoretical inspiration for this conservative outlook is a mistaken interpretation of the philosophy of Aristotle which emphasizes the importance of *phronesis* or "practical wisdom" in politics rather than abstract reasoning.[20] In the writings of more recent conservative thinkers this attitude is often presented as an opposition to "ideology." For it is thinking of this kind which allows ideologues to forget that their political opponents are human beings like themselves and, in consequence, to treat those opponents inhumanely. According to conservatives, it is precisely when some political ideology or other takes hold of us that we are likely to endorse the principle of "the end justifies the means," a principle which all conservatives reject. Conservative thinkers, therefore, tend to think of conservatism as being somehow nonideological, or even anti-ideological. They also tend to be hostile to utopianism in politics, for much the same reasons that they are opposed to ideology. For utopian writers also tend to be in the grip of some abstract theory or other, in the form of a vision of an alternative society which might be used to criticize existing society, and perhaps also to justify a program of radical social and political change by whatever means necessary.

It is clear, however, that a similar antipathy toward ideology, combined with a concern about the effectiveness of the use of reason for solving the problems of ethics and politics, is also to be found in the writings of Le Guin, who insists in one of her essays that her own attitude is decidedly "anti-ideological" and "pragmatic."[21] Indeed Le Guin offers a defense of J. R. R. Tolkien from accusations of conservatism along precisely these lines. As she puts it, "no ideologues, not even religious ones, are going to be happy with Tolkien, unless they manage it by misreading him. For like all great artists he *escapes* ideology by being too quick for its nets, too complex for its grand simplicities, too fantastic for its rationality, too real for its generalizations" (my emphasis).[22] Similarly, in her "Introduction" to *Planet of Exile*, Le Guin asserts that "it's one thing to sacrifice fulfillment in the service of an ideal; it's another to suppress clear thinking and honest feeling in the service of an ideology. An ideology is valuable only insofar as it is used to intensify clarity and honesty of thought and feeling."[23] And elsewhere she claims that "*ethics* flourishes in the timeless soil of Fantasy, where *ideologies* wither on the vine" (my emphasis).[24]

It is clear from a reading of Le Guin's essays that she considers "radical feminism" to be an ideology and that she considers radical feminists to be ideologues in this pejorative sense. Thomas M. Disch has argued that such a charge might be brought against Le Guin herself.[25] According to Disch far from being a "humanist" who seeks to "build bridges" by recognizing the importance, indeed the necessity, of both "Yin" and "Yang," the principles of both "feminine" and the "masculine" for any adequate view of the world, of human relationships, and of "life" more generally, in fact Le Guin attaches exclusive value to that which is "feminine" and is hostile to all things "masculine." She embraces the principle of the "Yin" entirely and rejects that of the "Yang" outright. Disch says of Le Guin that although her feminism "is less overtly phobic of the male sex than that of Andrea Dworkin," even so it "is no less absolute."[26] In Disch's opinion, Le Guin thinks that "war is wrong, and men are to blame for it," that "science is inhumane, and men are to blame for it," and that "capitalism is heartless, and men are to blame for it."[27] In my view, however, this assessment of Le Guin and her work is "one sided" and seriously misrepresents Le Guin's basic philosophical outlook.

As a counter to Disch's negative evaluation the reader is reminded that Le Guin has in the past been criticized by radical feminists precisely because of her commitment to humanism, and her refusal to privilege the members of one sex over the other. In response to criticism of this kind from radical feminists Le Guin has insisted that "I still don't care" whether people are "male or female." "One soul unjustly imprisoned, am I to ask what sex it is? A child starving, am I to ask what sex it is? The answer of some radical feminists is, Yes. Granted the premise that the root of all injustice, exploitation, and blind aggression is sexual injustice, this position is sound." However, Le Guin continues, "I cannot accept the premise; therefore I cannot act upon it." "Am I," she concludes, "to sacrifice the ideal of truth and beauty in order to make an *ideological* point?" (my emphasis).[28] Disch presents Le Guin to his readers as being an ideologist with a particular radical feminist "ax to grind." But it is obvious to anyone who is more than superficially acquainted with her work that Le Guin has consistently attempted to avoid being a writer of that kind, although she possesses both the honesty and the humility to recognize that she might not always have been as successful in this attempt as she could have been.

In Le Guin's work this lack of dogmatism is perhaps most strongly evidenced, not so much in *The Dispossessed*, but in *The Lathe of Heaven*. Consider, for example, the passage from this text which I cited earlier, which
demonstrates clearly the influence of Zamyatin upon Le Guin's thinking.[29] In this passage Le Guin is happy to associate the views of Zamyatin,
as expressed by the character Haber, not with "dystopian" thought but
rather with a particular form of "utopian" speculation. For example, she
has Orr say of Haber that "[t]hings are more complicated than he is willing to realize. He [Haber] thinks you can make things come out right, but
he won't admit it; he lies because he won't look *straight*, he's not interested in what is *true*. In what *is*; he can't see anything except his mind—
his ideas of what *ought* to be" (my emphasis).[30] In this passage, then, Dr.
Haber is presented by Le Guin as being a typical revolutionary, a "scientific" rationalist, or a Panglossian improver.[31] In matters of ethics he is a
utilitarian who wants to make things better,[32] but he will not succeed because the world just cannot be controlled in the way required. We should,
Le Guin has Orr suggest, just "let things be."[33]

In *The Lathe of Heaven* Haber represents what Le Guin refers to as the
"Judeo-Christian-Rationalist" Western tradition, which is also, of
course, the scientific tradition, committed to the idea of controlling first
nature then society.[34] At one point, for example, Orr says of Haber that
"[Y]ou're handling something outside reason. You are trying to each
progressive, humanitarian goal with a tool that isn't suited to the job."[35]
The immediate context of this statement indicates that this remark is intended as a reference to the dream technology developed by Haber—but
the wider implication is that, for whatever reason, any attempt to
change things for the better is likely not to work, or even to make things
worse, and is, therefore, undesirable. Ideas of this kind are usually associated with the conservative political tradition. In Le Guin's case, however, as the name which Le Guin gives to one of the central characters
indicates (the word "Haben" in German meaning "to have") this idea
appears to derive, at least in part, either from a familiarity with the work
of Gabriel Marcel, especially his work *Being and Having*,[36] or alternatively from an engagement with the writings of Erich Fromm, especially
Fromm's *To Have or to Be*.[37]

More than one commentator has suggested that *The Lathe of Heaven* possesses a clear "political message" and that this message is in fact a conservative one. John Huntington, for example, has noted that in this text Le
Guin makes sure that "all public activity leads to failure." The text, according to Huntington, "almost *dogmatically*, asserts the total primacy of private,
inner peace" (my emphasis) in comparison with "public" or "political" activity. For example, Dr. Haber, "the scientist who envisions creating a better
world," turns out to be "the villain." Moreover, "the novel makes it clear

that such incompetence is inevitable" and that "given man's ignorance, any public act is liable to do wrong, no matter how well intentioned."[38]

In my view, however, this interpretation of Le Guin misses something important about her work. The problem with this reading is that those who endorse it do not distinguish between Le Guin the political activist and Le Guin the novelist. Insofar as Le Guin is thought of as a novelist rather than a political activist, then it is arguable that it is inappropriate for us to think of her work as having *any* political message at all. It is, in consequence, also inappropriate for any commentator to speculate as to what that message might be. In the case of *The Lathe of Heaven*, therefore, it would be incorrect to assume that Le Guin qua novelist must "take sides"—or that she takes *any* particular "side" at all, let alone specifically that of Orr as opposed to Haber. Indeed, we have already seen that some of the views expressed by Haber are also held by Zamyatin; and they are views with which Le Guin has at least some sympathy. Indeed, in *The Dispossessed* she suggests that there is a great deal to be said for them. In her view, therefore, the point is not to reject these views outright, but rather to recognize their limitations if they are considered, in a one-sided way, to be an accurate representation of "the Truth."

It is extremely fruitful to read the passage from *The Lathe of Heaven* cited above against the background of Le Guin's discussion of the two types of "utopian" theorizing, Yang and Yin in her essay "A Non-Euclidean View of California as a Cold Place to Be." In this passage it is Haber who represents the principle of the Yang, and who evidently endorses the outlook on the world generally of Zamyatin, whereas it is Orr who provides a vocal expression for the ideas associated with Le Guin's alleged Yin "utopia." It is also clear that the views of Haber are those which in *The Dispossessed* Le Guin associates with the Sequency Theory of Time, and those of Orr are the ones which Le Guin associates with the Simultaneity Theory. Once again, however, it would be a mistake to suggest, whatever her personal views might be, that as a *novelist* Le Guin would wish to identify herself exclusively with either one or the other of these two ways of thinking. Indeed, at one point in the novel she rather playfully makes this point by having one of her characters, Lelache, refer jokingly to Orr as "Mr. Either Orr."[39] To focus exclusively on just one side of things, and ignore entirely the other dimension of Le Guin's thought, is to misunderstand the philosophical outlook which she associates with being a novelist.

ANARCHIST POLITICS IN ZAMYATIN AND LE GUIN

Elsewhere I have considered the views of Zamyatin and Le Guin with respect to questions of ethics independently of one another.[40] In this section

I will explore the relationship which exists between Le Guin's views on ethics and politics and those of Zamyatin more directly by comparing them.[41] In the past I have argued that Zamyatin is a nihilist and that Le Guin is a moralist. With respect to certain issues, then, the views of Zamyatin and Le Guin are very different from one another. It would not, however, be accurate to say that they are directly opposed to one another. For as in the case of natural science or physics, so also with respect to certain issues in ethics, Le Guin adopts a "Hegelian" strategy of "sublation" in relation to the views of Zamyatin. She gives them their due, takes them up and incorporates them within her own way of thinking, whilst at the same time being conscious of their limitations and seeking to go beyond them.

As we have seen, the idea of change or of Becoming is an important one for those who wish to understand the science or the physics which Le Guin incorporates into *The Dispossessed*, especially Shevek's "General Temporal Theory," which is a theoretical synthesis of the Simultaneity and the Sequence Theories of Time, theories which are based on the principles of Being and Becoming respectively. But this idea is also important for understanding the way in which Le Guin deals with questions of ethics and politics in her novel. For Zamyatin, as for Nietzsche, change is the law of "life." Zamyatin does not value change because he thinks that it is always for the better, or because it represents "progress," in the sense of moral improvement, or a movement toward a morally superior kind of society. For in his view it is not possible for us to achieve this. Rather, he considers change to be valuable for its own sake. This is an attitude toward change which has obvious implications for any assessment of Zamyatin's attitude toward political utopianism. In particular it is connected to Zamyatin's nihilism. Like Kirilov, one of the characters in Dostoevsky's *The Possessed*, Zamyatin considers all morality, and, therefore, by implication all society, to be a constraint on the freedom of the individual and therefore profoundly "anti-life." If a utopian society is something which is morally desirable, and if a literary utopia is considered to be a work of literature which recommends such a morally desirable state of affairs to its readers, then in Zamyatin's view these things too are profoundly anti-life. Zamyatin is not interested in moral improvement and has no ethical ideals. He therefore rejects the very idea of a "utopia" as this has traditionally been understood.

This attitude is given a striking formulation in the opening paragraphs of one of Zamyatin's early essays, entitled "Scythians." In Zamyatin's words, "a solitary, savage horseman—a Scythian—gallops across the green steppe, hair streaming in the wind. Where is he galloping? *Nowhere*. What for? For *no reason*. He gallops simply because he is a Scythian" (my emphasis).[42] Zamyatin's attitude toward change generally, and hence also change within the sphere of politics, is basically that of a Scythian. There is also a similar passage in Zamyatin's *We*. Toward the end of the novel there is a revolutionary uprising, aimed at overthrowing the Great Benefactor, organized by an underground resistance movement, the Mephi. During this uprising one of the novel's two central characters, I-330, seizes control of the Integral, a spaceship designed by the novel's other central character D-503, and exclaims "how wonderful it is to fly, not knowing where— to fly—no matter where, to fly without knowing one's destination, or even caring what that destination is."[43] This is a powerful metaphor for the expression of Zamyatin's attitude toward change, the ideas of moral and social progress, and his critique of utopianism in politics.

In his *Notes from the Underground*, Dostoevsky states that man "is interested in the process of attaining his goal rather than the goal itself." Perhaps, he goes on, "man's *sole* purpose in this world consists in this uninterrupted process of attainment, or in other words in *living*, and not specifically in the goal" (my emphasis).[44] Like Dostoevsky, Zamyatin connects the idea of change with the idea that life is a journey, and the view that what really matters in life is not the *end* of that journey, but the journey itself. For this reason Zamyatin suggests that whether we focus at the level of the individual human being or at the level of society, it does not really matter what one's ultimate objective or goal is. It does not matter *where* one is going, or indeed whether one ever actually arrives there. What really matters is the journey itself and how it is undertaken. For Zamyatin, then, the notion of "life," at both the level of the individual and that of society, has more to do with that of a *process* than it does with that of a *product*. Or, as Le Guin would put it, for Zamyatin what matters in life is only the "means" and never the "ends." Indeed, for Zamyatin's anarchism there *are* no "ends."

Le Guin is very far from rejecting Zamyatin's ideas outright. On the contrary she is positively enthusiastic about them—within limits. This is clear in both *The Lathe of Heaven* and *The Dispossessed*. For example, in an extremely interesting passage in *The Lathe of Heaven*, the character Haber says to George Orr, "when things don't change any longer, that's the end result of entropy, the heat-death of the universe. The more things go on moving, interrelating, conflicting, changing, the less balance there is—and the more life. I'm pro-life, George. Life itself is a huge gamble against all odds! You can't try to live safely, there's no such thing as safety. Stick your neck out of the shell and live fully! It's not how you get there, but where you get to that counts."[45] Up until its final sentence, the remarks which Le Guin puts into the mouth of Haber reflect very well Zamyatin's views on change and on life. It is only in the final sentence that Haber, who is, of course, a classic example of the "mad scientist" in science fiction, and, therefore, cannot be presumed to live according to the ordinary standards of scientific rationality, inverts Zamyatin's idea that life (both at the level of the individual and at the level of society) is a journey without any end point or goal by asserting that "It's not *how* you get there, but *where* you get to that counts." Anyone who is familiar with Zamyatin's ideas will find it difficult to read this passage and *not* think that when she wrote it Le Guin was in some way inspired by a reading of his works.

Zamyatin's idea that to embrace life is to embrace change for its own sake is *one* of the ideas which lies at the core of *The Dispossessed*, insofar as it contains a *critique* of the erstwhile utopian society on Anarres. This idea is most clearly formulated by the character Bedap when he says the most significant feature of life in Anarresti society is not an enthusiasm for change but, rather, its opposite—"fear of change."[46] Like I-330 in *We*, Bedap too maintains that "change is freedom, change is life."[47] He claims that nothing is "more basic to Odonian thought than that."[48] According to Bedap, a process of "dogmatization" and "ossification" has in fact set in on the planet Anarres since the founding of the anarchist settlement there. It is true that, at this particular juncture in the novel, and at this point in the biography of its central character, Shevek has little sympathy for Bedap's view. Indeed, Le Guin has him say that he found "Bedap's present opinions detestable."[49] Later, however, in consequence of his own experiences with the "authorities" on Anarres, especially his superior, the physicist Sabul, Shevek comes around to Bedap's way of thinking, when he says (regretfully) of his former friend Tirin that he was "a natural rebel," a "natural Odonian—a real one." For "he was a free man."[50]

A very good way of capturing Zamyatin's views on change is by employing the notion of "permanent revolution." This is, therefore, a notion which also has at least some importance for Le Guin. However, the vast majority of commentators on the work of Le Guin appear to have overlooked the similarities which exist between the views of Le Guin and those of Zamyatin with respect to this particular issue. Tom Moylan, for example, notes Le Guin's reference to the "ossification" or the "freezing" of the revolution in Anarresti society, and notes that the significance of Shevek is the fact that he reinvigorates or revitalizes the "process of permanent revolution" on Anarres.[51] Nowhere, however, does Moylan mention the name of Zamyatin or the obvious similarities between the views of Le Guin and Zamyatin in respect of this issue.[52]

Phillip Smith has suggested that, as in the case of the metaphor of the wall, the source for the idea of "permanent revolution" in Le Guin's *The Dispossessed* is the writings of Kropotkin. Smith maintains that "both Kropotkin and Le Guin agree that their societies must never become static."[53] As is well known, however, the idea of a "dynamic" utopia can be found much earlier in the writings of H. G. Wells,[54] and is at least partly inherited from Wells by Zamyatin.[55] It would, therefore, be surprising to say the least if Le Guin had inherited these ideas from Kropotkin rather than from Zamyatin or Wells.

In *We* Zamyatin uses the idea that the "law of life" is change, perpetual change, which must inevitably in time undermine the *status quo* in *any* society, to criticize the very idea of utopia as (rightly or wrongly) he understands it, because of its alleged commitment to the notion of static perfectionism. It might be suggested, therefore, and indeed has been suggested by some commentators, that what is interesting and original about Le Guin's emphasis on the importance of change is the fact that she does not appeal to this principle whilst developing a *critique* of the idea of utopia. Rather, as some commentators would argue, she seeks to incorporate it *within* the idea of utopia itself, in an effort to rethink the meaning of this concept. It is for this reason that Laurence Davis has suggested that although it certainly is "an offshoot of the utopian tradition," nevertheless *The Dispossessed* is at the same time "a *radical* new beginning" (my emphasis) for that tradition.[56] In my view, however, this is an exaggeration. For it ignores completely not only the fact that the same idea is to be found in Zamyatin's *We*, but also that it is can be found in the work of H. G. Wells.[57] Moreover, it also ignores the fact that there are good reasons for thinking that Le Guin herself does not consider *The Dispossessed* to be a literary utopia at all, but rather, a novel about utopianism.

Le Guin's enthusiasm for Zamyatin's views on change, and his association of the idea of change with that of life, does not mean that she is entirely uncritical, or that she simply takes Zamyatin's ideas up and employs them herself without significant alteration. Le Guin has a number of criticisms to make of Zamyatin and his ideas. Taken together, however, they all amount to just one thing, namely that Zamyatin's approach is "one sided." It does capture an aspect of life and human existence in society which Le Guin is happy to concede is valuable and important. This is something which seeks to incorporate into her own work, especially *The Dispossessed*. At the same time, however, Le Guin recognizes the limitations of Zamyatin's philosophical outlook generally, and his approach to questions of ethics in particular. In her view, Zamyatin misses something which is *also* important, and just as important. Hence, as in the case of science and physics, Le Guin seeks not to reject outright but to *supplement* Zamyatin's views in *The Dispossessed* with an alternative way of thinking which might be said to correct their deficiencies whilst at the same time incorporating what she considers to be valuable into her own work.

As an anarchist herself, Le Guin is certainly sympathetic to Zamyatin's emphasis on the value of individual freedom. However, she is unwilling to take her commitment to this idea so far as to draw a nihilistic conclusion, for in her view this would lead to "anarchy" in the bad sense, or to social "chaos," which Le Guin explicitly distinguishes from "anarchism."

Le Guin's critical engagement with Zamyatin's views on ethics can be found both in her story "Schrödinger's Cat" and in *The Dispossessed*. In "Schrödinger's Cat" she makes this very clear when she links Zamyatin's celebration of the fact that the universe is basically a "chaotic" place to the ancient Greek myth of "Pandora's Box."[58] Elsewhere Le Guin takes care to emphasize that in her view "anarchy is *not* anarchism" and, in an obvious allusion to the story of Pandora's Box (and, therefore, if only indirectly to her own story "Schrödinger's Cat") maintains that this is so because "anarchy means chaos and y'know sort of just take the lid off and let her blow," whereas "that is not what the old anarchist political movements meant at all."[59]

Le Guin presents a similar critique of Zamyatin's views in *The Dispossessed*. Perhaps taking her inspiration from Dostoevsky, Le Guin argues that one of the presuppositions for ethical life in any society is the institution of "promise keeping," and the mutual trust between individual moral agents which is associated with the making and keeping of "promises."[60] Now there is evidently a *temporal* dimension to this. A person X (say Kirilov) makes a promise at time t^1 to perform some action (murder) at a later time, t^2. For the system of promise keeping to "work," and by implication for any society to exist, it has to be the case that at time t^2 we can legitimately assume that the person who we think is obliged to keep the promise is in fact the same person as the person who actually made it. In other words promise keeping rests upon an assumption of continuous personal identity. But if Zamyatin is right about change, if like him we adopt an extreme version of the Heraclitean "flux" theory, then just as it is not possible to step into the same river twice so also it is not possible for a (putative) "person" to be the same person twice. If Zamyatin is right, then the "person" (in this case the character Kirilov) who at time t^2 is expected by others to keep a promise which he made at an earlier time t^1 could legitimately claim that *he* had not made the promise in question, that it had been made by someone else, that "he" is now a quite different person from the person who made the promise, that he cannot be morally obliged to keep a promise that someone else has made, and so on.

It is for this reason that, so far as the ethical implications of the General Temporal Theory in *The Dispossessed* are concerned, Le Guin has Shevek point out that although it is true that without a theory of time like that of Zamyatin which sees time as an "arrow" or a "running river," as the Sequency Theory does, there could be "no change, no progress, or direction, or creation," nevertheless without the necessary counter balance provided by the alternative theory of time, the Simultaneity Theory, which accounts for all of the permanence and stability that there is in the world, especially the moral or social world, there would be "*chaos*, meaningless succession of instants, a world without clocks or seasons or *promises*" (my emphasis).[61]

We may conclude that one reason why Le Guin would wish to criticize Zamyatin's "extreme" Heraclitean views on change and temporal development is precisely because of what she takes to be their undesirable ethical and political implications. She rightly appreciates that if those beliefs, as they are understood by Zamyatin, are identified with anarchism, then the anarchism in question would have to be the nihilist or immoralist kind associated with the philosophy of Nietzsche and with Sartre's early existentialism. For Le Guin, to wholeheartedly embrace Zamyatin's views on change would, if they were applied to the sphere of ethics and politics, amount, therefore, to a justification of "anarchy" in the "bad sense" referred to earlier, anarchy as it has so often been understood from at least the time of Dostoevsky's *The Possessed* onward. But this, of course, is precisely the doctrine which Le Guin rejects. It is, in Le Guin's own words, the "bomb in the pocket stuff, which is terrorism, whatever name it tries to dignify itself with."[62]

HUMAN LIFE AS AN "ODYSSEY" OF SPIRIT: *THE DISPOSSESSED* AS A *BILDUNGSROMAN*

The account of the views of Le Guin's views offered above indicates that there is at least *some* agreement between them and those of Zamyatin, especially regarding the importance of change and temporal development and the issue whether this might be said to have a definite objective or goal, both at the level of individual biography and at the level of society or social history. However, this is not complete agreement. In my view, then, Peter Brigg is mistaken when he claims that Shevek's journey in *The Dispossessed* is a "quest in which final goals cannot exist,"[63] and that "the act of *becoming* dominates Odonian philosophy. Thus the *only* goal one may have is to remain open to change" (my emphasis).[64] If these assertions were true then Odo's philosophy would be identical with that of Zamyatin. In my view, however, this is an indication that they are not true; or at least that they are only half true. For Brigg's account of Le Guin's views on change is exclusively "linear." It identifies Le Guin's outlook with that of the Sequency Theory of Time. Consequently, it ignores completely the importance which she attaches to the principle of Being, or that of "circularity," which is associated with the Simultaneity Theory of Time. It overlooks the wording of the motto "True Voyage is Return," which is carved on the tomb stone of Odo's grave on Urras, a motto which encapsulates at least one of the basic principles of Odonian anarchism in *The Dispossessed*.[65]

The difference between the views of Le Guin and Zamyatin regarding this issue is clear. For example, if we consider the issue of individual bi-

ography, according to Le Guin although in *one* important sense the journey which is undertaken in the life of any individual human being has no
endpoint or goal, nevertheless this does not mean that it is entirely "point-
less," in the sense of being meaningless or absurd. For, unlike Zamyatin,
Le Guin considers this particular process of change to be circular and not
linear. And if it is true that at the end of this particular "voyage" the individual who undertakes it has indeed come full circle, and, therefore, in
one sense remains exactly the same person as she or he was before; or has
in some important (non-geographical) sense arrived in the same "place"
from which she or he set out; nevertheless in another important sense
change and development within that individual have undeniably taken
place. A process of education or the development of *character*, which like
the Greeks Le Guin associates with the cultivation of the moral virtues,
has occurred.

Like Hegel, whose fondness for the *Odyssey* is well known,[66] Le Guin
considers the biography of an individual human being to be a personal
"odyssey of spirit," the outcome of which is always, not just the actualization of the potential as a moral being which exists in any individual
character from the moment of their birth, but also a "return home" and a
reconciliation of the individual both with him or herself and with the
world generally, especially their own society and their place within it,
whoever they are, and *whatever* that society and that place might be. In the
case of *The Odyssey* the character in question is Odysseus and the society
to which he "returns home" and with which he is "reconciled" in Hegel's
sense is that on the island of Ithaca. In the case of *The Dispossessed* the
character who undertakes the journey is the character Shevek and the society to which he returns home and with which he is reconciled is that of
the planet Anarres. It is true, of course, that the society on Anarres happens to be an anarchist society. According to this reading of *The Dispossessed*, however, this is entirely *incidental*. What really matters here is not
so much the specific character of the society on Anarres, but simply the
fact that it *is* a society which possesses a definite organizational structure
underpinned by a particular framework of moral and political values.
Shevek has a "place" in this society and the moral and political significance of the journey which he undertakes in *The Dispossessed* is the fact
that in consequence of his experiences, his adventures, and the development in his character with which these are associated (the actualization of
his potential as a moral being) he does finally "return home" in order to
reconcile himself with that society and accept his own place within it.

Tom Moylan has suggested that it would be a mistake to think of *The
Dispossessed* as an example of the literary genre known as the *Bildungsroman*.[67] It seems to me, however, that the similarities between Le Guin's
text and a *Bildungsroman* are actually quite striking. It should also be

noted that one of the classic sources for our understanding of Hegel's philosophy generally, and his views on this subject in particular, is the *Phenomenology of Spirit* which, with its root metaphor of the "odyssey of
Spirit," has itself often been referred to as an example of a (philosophical)
Bildungsroman.[68]

This way of thinking about the *Bildungsroman* as a literary genre has
been ably presented by Georg Lukács, who when discussing it refers explicitly to Hegel and the Hegelian philosophy.[69] According to Lukács,
there are basically two types of *Bildungsroman*, the "bourgeois" and the
"socialist" respectively.[70] In both cases an individual character "has to
work things out for himself and struggle for a place in the community."[71]
In both cases the process of biographical development of the character in
question is portrayed as "educational." In the case of the "bourgeois"
form, Lukács maintains that Hegel captures this process very well when
he says that "during his years of apprenticeship the hero is permitted to
sow his wild oats; he learns to subordinate his wishes and views to the interests of the society; he then enters the society's hierarchic scheme and
finds in it a comfortable niche."[72] Lukács has doubts, however, whether
this assessment by Hegel actually "fits" in the case of a number of "the
great bourgeois novels." In the case of the "socialist" *Bildungsroman*,
Lukács claims that it does not "fit" them at all, as within them "the situation is different." For in the socialist *Bildungsroman* "the end is not resignation." On the contrary, Lukács maintains, here "the process *begins* with
resignation and leads to an active participation in the life of the community." It is, therefore, no accident that "whereas the typical bourgeois *Bildungsroman* takes its hero from childhood to the critical years of early
adult life, its socialist counterpart often begins with the crisis of consciousness the adult bourgeois intellectual experiences when confronted
with socialism."[73] Although these remarks about the socialist *Bildungsroman* do not quite fit Le Guin's *The Dispossessed*, it seems to me that they do
provide us with at least a partial insight into the educational and therefore
also the political significance of Le Guin's novel.

To interpret Le Guin's *The Dispossessed* in this way is to present a reading of the text which ignores completely some things which are of fundamental importance, especially Le Guin's personal commitment to anarchism. However, it also provides an indication of why, despite that
commitment, Le Guin's approach to literature might be thought of as one
which possesses "conservative" political implications. For we have seen
that both Zamyatin and Le Guin think of "life," both at the level of individual biography and at the level of society, is a "journey," however differently this journey is conceived. They both think that there is a sense in
which it really does not matter what the ostensible end or goal of this jour-

ney actually is. They both suggest at times that what really matters is how this journey is undertaken and, in Le Guin's case at least, the effect which it has on the character or the moral development of the person who undertakes it, its producing a reconciliation between this individual and the society of which she or he happens to be a member. But it follows from this that the fact that Shevek happens to be an anarchist, or a citizen of a society organized in accordance with anarchist principles, is merely an *incidental* characteristic of Le Guin's *The Dispossessed* rather than a core feature of the novel. As in the case of a certain reading of Hegel, the conservative implications of this way of thinking about human social life, as Le Guin portrays it in *The Dispossessed,* are readily apparent.

NOTES

1. For Le Guin's relationship to anarchist political thought see John P. Brennan and Michael C. Downs, "Anarchism and Utopian Tradition in *The Dispossessed,*" in *Ursula K. Le Guin,* eds. Joseph Olander and Martin Harry Greenberg (New York: Taplinger, 1979),116–52; Winter Elliott, "Breaching Invisible Walls: Individual Anarchy in *The Dispossessed,*" in *The New Utopian Politics of Ursula K. Le Guin's* The Dispossessed, eds. Laurence Davis and Peter Stillman (Lanham, Md.: Lexington Books, 2005), 149–66; Leonard M. Fleck, "Science Fiction as a Tool of Speculative Philosophy: A Philosophical Analysis of Selected Anarchistic and Utopian Themes in Le Guin's *The Dispossessed,*" in *Selected Proceedings of the 1978 Science Fiction Research Association National Conference,* ed. Thomas J. Remington (Cedar Falls, Iowa: University of Iowa Press, 1979), 135–45; Steven A. Peterson and Douglas Saxton, "Science Fiction and Political Thought: *The Dispossessed,*" *Cornell Journal of Social Relations* 12, no. 1 (1975), 65–74; Dan Sabia, "Individual and Community in Le Guin's *The Dispossessed,*" in *The New Utopian Politics of Ursula K. Le Guin's* The Dispossessed, eds. Davis and Stillman, 111–28; Larry L. Tifft and Dennis C. Sullivan, "Possessed Sociology and Le Guin's Dispossessed: From Exile to Anarchism," in *Ursula K. Le Guin: Voyager to Inner Lands and Outer Space,* ed. Joseph de Bolt (New York: Kennikat Press, 1991 [1979]), 180–97; Lyman Tower Sargent, "Anarchism: Social and Political Ideas in Some Recent Feminist Utopias," in *Women and Utopia: Critical Interpretations,* ed. Marleen Barr (New York: University Press of America, 1983), 3–33; and Victor Urbanowicz, "Personal and Political in *The Dispossessed,*" in *Ursula K. Le Guin,* ed. Harold Bloom (New York: Chelsea House, 1985), 145–54.

2. I am grateful to Ruth Kinna for drawing this point to my attention.

3. Phillip Wegner, *Imaginary Communities: Utopia, the Nation and the Spatial Histories of Modernity* (Berkeley, Los Angeles, London: University of California Press, 2002), 196.

4. Wegner, *Imaginary Communities,* 196.

5. Ernst Fischer, *The Necessity of Art: A Marxist Approach* (Harmondsworth: Penguin Books, 1970 [1959]), 96.

6. For further discussion of this issue see Tony Burns, "Zamyatin's *We* and Postmodernism," *Utopian Studies*, 11, no. 1 (2000): 66–90.

7. If so, then any attempt to link Zamyatin too closely to Bakunin must founder. It is difficult to accept, for example, Gorman Beauchamp's and Phillip Wegner's claim that there are similarities between the views of Bakunin and Zamyatin so far as their respective visions of an ideal society are concerned, simply because Zamyatin does not have such a vision. See Gorman Beauchamp, "Zamyatin's *We*," in *No Place Else: Explorations in Utopian and Dystopian Fiction*, eds. Rabkin, Greenberg, and Olander (Carbondale: Southern Illinois University Press, 1983), 70, and Wegner, *Imaginary Communities*, 162, 172.

8. Ursula K. Le Guin, *The Dispossessed: An Ambiguous Utopia* (London: Granada Books, 1983 [1974]), V, 124. See also IX, 246: "The means *are* the end – Odo said it all her life. Only peace brings peace, only just acts bring justice!"

9. Le Guin, *The Dispossessed*, X, 276.

10. Ursula K. Le Guin, *The Left Hand of Darkness* (MacDonald, 1991 [1969]), XV, 188; Peter Brigg, "The Archetype of the Journey in Ursula K. Le Guin's Fiction," in *Ursula K. Le Guin*, eds. Olander and Greenberg, 49. See also 50: "The true reward was the journey."

11. George Edgar Slusser, *The Farthest Shores of Ursula K. Le Guin* (Chapbook: Borgo Press, 1976), 3–4.

12. For example, Isaiah Berlin, "Herzen and Bakunin on Individual Liberty," in *Russian Thinkers* (Harmondsworth: Penguin, 1979), 113, associates Dostoevsky's Stavrogin with Bakunin. On the other hand, though, E. H. Carr, "Ethics and Politics: *The Devils*," in *Dostoevsky: 1821–1881* (London: Unwin Books, 1962 [1931]), 175, maintains that any such identification would be "purely fantastic."

13. Bakunin, for example, distanced himself from Nechayev, the source of inspiration for Dostoevsky in *The Possessed*. Like Dostoevsky, Bakunin objects to Nechaev's nihilism. See Bakunin, "From a Letter to Sergei Nechaev, June 2nd 1870," in Mikhail *Selected Writings*, ed. Lehning (London: Cape, 1973), 186.

14. Carl Freedman, *Critical Theory and Science Fiction* (Hanover and London: Wesleyan University Press, 2000), fn. 15, 116. Freedman is one of the few commentators to discuss Le Guin's work in relation to Bakunin. See *Critical Theory and Science Fiction*, 115–16. See also Wegner, *Imaginary Communities*, 175.

15. Fyodor Dostoevsky, *The Devils* [*The Possessed*], trans. David Magarshack (Harmondsworth: Penguin, 1973), 106.

16. See. Wegner, *Imaginary Communities*, 175.

17. See Freedman, *Critical Theory and Science Fiction*, 115–16.

18. Lyman Tower Sargent, "The Problem of the 'Flawed Utopia': A Note on the Costs of Eutopia," in *Dark Horizons: Science Fiction and the Dystopian Imagination*, eds. Moylan and Baccolini (London: Routledge, 2003), 226.

19. I have discussed the nature of conservatism as an ideology elsewhere. See Tony Burns, *Natural Law and Political Ideology in the Philosophy of Hegel* (Aldershot: Avebury Press, 1996), chapter 3; and Tony Burns, "John Gray and the Death of Conservatism," *Contemporary Politics*, 5, 1 (1999): 7–24.

20. I discuss Aristotle and his understanding of the concept of *phronesis* in Tony Burns, "Aristotle and Natural Law," *History of Political Thought*, XIX, 3 (1998): 142–66. See also Tony Burns, "Whose Aristotle? Which Marx? Ethics, Law and Jus-

tice in Aristotle and Marx," *Imprints: Egalitarian Theory and Practice*, 8, 2 (2005): 125–55; and Tony Burns, "Aristotle," in *Political Thinkers: From Socrates to the Present*, eds. David Boucher and Paul Kelly (Oxford: Oxford University Press, 2003), 73–91. In my view Aristotle does *not* reject outright the claim that abstract reasoning has a part to play in politics. Rather, he points out that it has definite limitations as a potential source for the solution to ethical and political problems. It needs, therefore, to be *supplemented* by "practical wisdom," the function of which is to apply those abstract moral principles which are discernible by "reason" to the circumstances of particular cases.

21. Le Guin, "Dreams Must Explain Themselves," *The Language of the Night: Essays on Fantasy and Science Fiction*, ed. Susan Wood (New York: Perigee, 1979), 49.

22. Le Guin, "The Staring Eye," *The Language of the Night*, 174.

23. Le Guin, "Introduction" to *Planet of Exile*, in *The Language of the Night*, 142.

24. Ursula K. Le Guin, "European SF European SF: Rottensteiner's Anthology, the Strugatskys, and Lem," *Science Fiction Studies*, 1, no. 3 (1974), 184.

25. Thomas M. Disch, "Can Girls Play Too? Feminizing SF," in *The Dreams Our Stuff Is Made Of: How Science Fiction Conquered the World* (New York and London: Touchstone Books, 2000 [1998]), 125–32.

26. Disch, "Can Girls Play Too? Feminizing SF," 125.

27. Disch, "Can Girls Play Too? Feminizing SF," 131.

28. Ursula K. Le Guin, "Introduction" to *Planet of Exile*," in *The Language of the Night*, 141. See also Ursula K. Le Guin, "The Stone Ax and the Muskoxen," *The Language of the Night*, 230: See also 231: "No art is ladylike. Nor is any art gentlemanly. Nor is it masculine or feminine. The reading of a book and the writing of a book is not an act dependent upon one's gender (In fact, very few human acts are, other than procreation, gestation, and lactation)."

29. Ursula K. Le Guin, *The Lathe of Heaven* (London: Granada, 1984 [1971]), 119–20.

30. Le Guin, *The Lathe of Heaven*, 88.

31. Le Guin, *The Lathe of Heaven*, 65, 73.

32. Le Guin, *The Lathe of Heaven* 49, 65, 68, 73, 117.

33. Le Guin, *The Lathe of Heaven*, 74, 120.

34. Le Guin, *The Lathe of Heaven*, 73.

35. Le Guin, *The Lathe of Heaven*, 76

36. Gabriel Marcel, *Being and Having*, trans. Katherine Farrer (Boston: Beacon Press, 1951 [1935].

37. Erich Fromm, *To Have or to Be* (London: Abacus Books, 1979 [1976]).

38. John Huntington, "Public and Private Imperatives in Le Guin's Novels," in *Science Fiction Studies: Selected Articles on Science Fiction 1973–1975*, eds. R. D. Mullen and Darko Suvin (Boston: Gregg Press, 1976), 270.

39. Le Guin, *The Lathe of Heaven*, 80.

40. Tony Burns, "Zamyatin's *We* and Postmodernism"; and Tony Burns, "Science and Politics in *The Dispossessed*: Le Guin and the 'Science Wars,' in *The New Utopian Politics of Ursula K. Le Guin's* The Dispossessed, eds. Davis and Stillman, 195–215.

41. For an earlier version of the ideas presented in this section see Tony Burns, "Yevgeny Zamyatin and the Science Fiction of Ursula K. Le Guin" (paper presented

to the "Anarchism and Utopia" panel at the annual conference of the Utopian Studies Society (Europe), Tarragona, Spain, 6–8 July, 2006).

42. Yevgeny Zamyatin, "Scythians," in *A Soviet Heretic: Essays by Yevgeny Zamyatin*, ed. Mirra Ginsburg (Chicago: University of Chicago Press, 1991), 22.

43. Zamyatin, *We*, trans. Bernard Gilbert Guerney, intro. Michael Glenny (Harmondsworth: Penguin, 1972), XXXV, 200.

44. Dostoevsky, *Notes from the Underground*, trans. Jessie Coulson (Harmondsworth: Penguin, 1973), 40.

45. Ursula K. Le Guin, *The Lathe of Heaven* (London: Granada, 1984 [1971]), 119–20.

46. Le Guin, *The Dispossessed*, VI, 143.

47. Le Guin, *The Dispossessed*, VI, 143.

48. Le Guin, *The Dispossessed*, VI, 143.

49. Le Guin, *The Dispossessed*, VI, 148.

50. Le Guin, *The Dispossessed*, X, 273.

51. Tom Moylan, *Demand the Impossible: Science Fiction and the Utopian Imagination* (London: Methuen, 1986), 95, 101.

52. A similar point can be made about Angus Taylor's "The Politics of Space, Time and Entropy," *Foundation: The Review of Science Fiction*, 10 (1976): 34–44, which is a comparison of the work of Le Guin with Phillip K. Dick, but where, despite the reference to "entropy" in the title, the name of Zamyatin is nowhere mentioned.

53. Phillip E. Smith, "Unbuilding Walls: Human Nature and the Nature of Evolutionary and Political Theory in *The Dispossessed*," in *Ursula K. Le Guin*, eds. Joseph Olander and Martin H. Greenberg, 84.

54. H. G. Wells, *A Modern Utopia*, in H. G. Wells, *A Modern Utopia and Tono Bungay* (London: Odhams Press, n.d. (1905), 315. According to Frank E. Manuel, "Towards a Psychological History of Utopia," in *Utopias and Utopian Thought: A Timely Appraisal* ed. Frank E. Manuel (Boston: Beacon Press, 1966), 80, the idea of a "dynamic" utopia predates even Wells. This is also Patrick Parrinder's view, "Utopia and Meta-Utopia," in *Shadows of the Future: H. G. Wells, Science Fiction and Prophecy* (Syracuse: Syracuse University Press, 1995), 112.

55. For this issue see Burns, "Zamyatin's *We* and Postmodernism."

56. Davis, "The Dynamic and Revolutionary Utopia of Ursula K. Le Guin," in *The New Utopian Politics of Ursula K. Le Guin's* The Dispossessed, eds. Davis and Stillman, 31.

57. George Kateb, *Utopia and Its Enemies* (New York: Schocken Books, 1972 [1963]), 79. See also John S. Partington, "The Death of the Static: H. G. Wells and the Kinetic Utopia," *Utopian Studies*, 11, 2 (2000): 96–111; and John S. Partington, "*The Time Machine* and *A Modern Utopia*: The Static and Kinetic Utopias of the Early H. G. Wells," *Utopian Studies*, 13, 1 (2002): 57–68.

58. Ursula K. Le Guin, "Schrödinger's Cat," in *Universe 5*, ed. Terry Carr (New York: Random House, 1974), 33.

59. Ursula K. Le Guin and Jonathan Ward, "Interview," *Dreams Must Explain Themselves* (New York: Algol Press, 1975), 35. It should be noted that one of the central characters in Le Guin's *Always Coming Home* is also called "Pandora," and that Pandora utters sentiments strikingly similar to those of both Zamyatin and

H. G. Wells in *A Modern Utopia*. See Ursula K. Le Guin, *Always Coming Home* (London: Grafton Books, 1988), 316.

60. Dostoevsky, *The Devils* [*The Possessed*], 375–82. Although the name of Dostoevsky is not mentioned, there are also some interesting passages relating to this issue in Gabriel Marcel, *Being and Having*, 41–51.

61. Le Guin, *The Dispossessed*, VII, 188.

62. Le Guin, Introduction to "The Day Before the Revolution," in *The Wind's Twelve Quarters*, Vol. 2 (London, Granada, 1980 [1975]), 121.

63. Brigg, "The Archetype of the Journey in Ursula K. Le Guin's Fiction," 39.

64. Brigg, "The Archetype of the Journey in Ursula K. Le Guin's Fiction," 39.

65. Le Guin, *The Dispossessed*, III, 76. See also Brigg, "The Archetype of the Journey in Ursula K. Le Guin's Fiction," 39.

66. I discuss this issue in Tony Burns, "The *Iliad* and the 'Struggle for Recognition' in Hegel's *Phenomenology of Spirit*" (paper presented at the "Art, Aesthetics and Politics" panel at the *Workshops in Political Theory – Second Annual Conference*, Manchester Metropolitan University, 7th-9th September 2005).

67. Tom Moylan, "Beyond Negation: The Critical Utopias of Ursula K. Le Guin and Samuel R. Delany," *Extrapolation*, 21 (1980): 242.

68. For this see M. H. Abrams, "Hegel's "Phenomenology of the Spirit": Metaphysical Structure and Narrative Plot," in *Natural Supernaturalism: Tradition and Revolution in Romantic Literature* (New York; Norton, 1971), 225–37; Judith Butler, *Subjects of Desire: Hegelian Reflections in Twentieth Century France* (New York: Columbia University Press, 1999 [1987]), 17; George Armstrong Kelly, "Notes on Hegel's "Lordship and Bondage," in Alasdair MacIntyre ed., *Hegel: A Collection of Critical Essays* (Notre Dame: University of Notre Dame Press, 1976), 196; Leo Rauch, "Mastery and Slavery," in Leo Rauch and David Sherman, *Hegel's Phenomenology of Self-Consciousness* (New York: SUNY Press, 1999), 90; Michael S. Roth, *Knowing and History: Appropriations of Hegel in Twentieth Century France* (Ithaca: Cornell University Press, 1988), 36; Robert C Solomon, *In the Spirit of Hegel: A Study of G. W. F. Hegel's Phenomenology of Spirit* (Oxford: Oxford University Press, 1985), 22, 24, 53–54, 197–98; and Anthony Wilden, "The Belle Âme: Freud, Lacan and Hegel," in Jacques Lacan, *The Language of the Self: The Function of Language in Psychoanalysis* (Baltimore: John Hopkins University Press, 1981 [1968]), 285, 287–88.

69. Georg Lukács, "Critical Realism and Socialist Realism," in *The Meaning of Contemporary Realism* (London: Merlin Books, 1979 [1963]), 93–135, especially 111–13. See also the discussion of the *Bildungsroman* in M. H. Abrams, *Natural Supernaturalism: Tradition and Revolution in Romantic Literature*.

70. Lukács, "Critical Realism and Socialist Realism," 111.

71. Lukács, "Critical Realism and Socialist Realism," 111–12.

72. Lukács, "Critical Realism and Socialist Realism," 112.

73. Lukács, "Critical Realism and Socialist Realism," 112.

9

Conservatism in the
Writings of Le Guin

INTRODUCTION

In his Introduction to a special issue of *Science Fiction Studies* devoted to the work of Le Guin, published in 1975, Darko Suvin called for someone to attempt to integrate Le Guin's science fiction with her fantasy literature. "I'm sorry," Suvin says, "that we couldn't find anybody to integrate the *Earthsea Trilogy* [*sic*] with Le Guin's SF. This and a number of other aspects of Le Guin, a constantly evolving writer, remain to be elucidated."[1] In my view, surprising though it might seem, the solution to this particular problem is to focus on the conservative dimension which is discernible in Le Guin's work from the first volumes of the *Earthsea Quartet* through to *The Dispossessed*—a dimension which, if its existence could be established, would stand in an uneasy tension with Le Guin's personal enthusiasm for anarchism.[2]

Laurence Davis has said of *The Dispossessed* that until recently "the radical political ramifications of the *novel* remain woefully under explored."[3] We have already seen that there is evidence to support the view that *The Dispossessed* does not have any radical political ramifications at all. Indeed, one of the main arguments of this book is that, again surprising though it might seem given Le Guin's personal enthusiasm for anarchism, there is an implicit conservative dimension to much of her work. As in the case of Zamyatin's *We*, Le Guin's *The Dispossessed* might be, and indeed has been, interpreted by some commentators *not* as a utopian text, but as an implicit critique of utopianism. In the case of *We*, this critique emanates from Zamyatin's commitment to a form of nihilistic anarchism. In that of

Le Guin's *The Dispossessed* it stems, not so much from Le Guin's enthusiasm for anarchism insofar as she is a political *activist*, which she undoubtedly is, but from other sources.

So far I have discussed three reasons for thinking that there is a conservative dimension to Le Guin's work. The first of these is the fact that Le Guin, too, is skeptical about "ideological" thinking and the value of abstract rationalism as an approach to questions of morality and politics. The second is the fact that Le Guin is a *novelist*. As we have seen, Le Guin's views regarding the novel as an art form, together with her views on the social and political function of the novelist, carry with them an implicit critique of utopianism. In this case, however, the critique in question has a striking affinity, not so much with the nihilistic anarchism of Zamyatin, but rather with traditional conservatism as it is given a sophisticated theoretical justification in the philosophy of Hegel. And the third has to do with Le Guin's views concerning education, the moral development of human beings, and their integration into society.

In this chapter I shall discuss three more reasons for taking this view. The first has to do with Le Guin's commitment to Taoism. The second has to do with her implicit endorsement of the doctrine known as "scientific realism." And the third has to do with Le Guin's understanding of human nature and of the self, which underpins her philosophy of education. I should emphasize that here and throughout, my reason for drawing the attention of the reader to the existence of this conservative dimension in Le Guin's writing is neither to praise her nor to condemn her for it. The point of doing so is simply that this descriptive label seems to me to best capture the political implications of certain aspects of her work. Moreover, this observation applies only to her *persona* as a creative writer, and not to Le Guin as either a political activist or a "private" individual. There is, of course, a significant difference between claiming that someone is a conservative thinker, on the one hand, and claiming that there is a conservative dimension to their writing on the other. In the case of Le Guin the former claim seems to me to be untenable for the obvious reason that Le Guin is an anarchist. The latter (weaker) claim, however, does have something to be said for it.

LE GUIN AND THE POLITICS OF TAOISM

Some commentators have argued that Le Guin's philosophical outlook is a conservative one because it is Taoist, and because Taoism is itself a conservative doctrine. Frederic Jameson, for example, has claimed that the political "message" of Le Guin's *The Lathe of Heaven* is conservative because in this book Le Guin identifies with the views of her character

George Orr; because the views expressed by Orr are those associated with the philosophy of Taoism; and because Taoism is a conservative philosophy. According to Jameson, this is so because of its emphasis on the notions such as peace, harmony, order, rest, tranquillity, balance, and so on. On this reading, in a manner similar to the philosophy of Pythagoras, the "Way" of Taoism is associated with a belief that the universe as a whole is a system of "cosmic order."[4] The difference, however, is that in the case of Taoism this universe is thought to be, not just "paradoxical," but also in some sense "spiritual" or "mystical"; and hence beyond rational comprehension by human beings.

Le Guin's belief in the existence of such a system of "order" underpins both her fantasy literature and her science fiction. Like Jameson, Colin Manlove has argued that in the case of the former, Le Guin's outlook is, for this very reason, again in some sense conservative. As Manlove puts it, "fantasy is a profoundly conservative genre. It usually portrays the preservation of the *status quo*, looks to the past to sustain the nature and values of the present, and delights in the nature of created things." In Manlove's view, Le Guin's *The Earthsea Trilogy* "offers a striking individual instance of this." In the case of Le Guin's works of fantasy "this conservatism," Manlove goes on, "expresses itself in three modes: balance, moderation, and the celebration of things as they are."[5] It is, in short, associated with Taoism, from the standpoint of which Le Guin wrote this particular work.

But this way of looking and thinking about the world is not confined only to Le Guin's works of fantasy. Erik Rabkin, for example, has noted, speaking of *The Left Hand of Darkness*, that in that work Le Guin "seems to attempt to bring its readers around to sharing, experiencing, the Taoist point of view." According to that point of view, Rabkin continues, "The Tao is whatever is." The "Way" of the Tao is that "things happen as they must."[6] If it were true that this is what a commitment to Taoism implies; and that Le Guin did indeed identify herself with Taoism understood in this particular sense; then it would follow that her philosophical outlook might indeed, as Jameson and Rabkin suggest, legitimately be said to be a conservative one.

There are two problems with this reading of Le Guin. The first is that it ignores completely the fact that Le Guin is an anarchist. For we may take it that generally speaking anarchists think that it is desirable, somehow or other, not to conserve existing society but to radically transform it. There must, therefore, be a problem with this particular reading of Le Guin, a problem which might be resolved if a distinction is made between Le Guin the political activist and Le Guin the novelist. The second is that, as we have seen, it is not at all clear that the understanding of Taoism upon which this conservative reading of Le Guin is based is an accurate one. At least, as we saw earlier, it is arguable that this is not Le Guin's own understanding of Taoism.

THE RELATIONSHIP BETWEEN SCIENCE AND MAGIC: LE GUIN AND SCIENTIFIC REALISM

There is an analogy between Le Guin's realist views on natural science and her views on magic in the *Earthsea Quartet*.[7] In both cases she presupposes the existence of an underlying cosmic "order" which is regulated by causal laws, in the one case the laws of science, in the other the laws of magic. She thinks that it is possible to make a distinction between the empirically observable surface appearances of things and what is "really" going on beneath the surface and which is the cause of the phenomena which can be observed. She also thinks that things possess an "essential nature" which is associated with the concept which is used to designate them, that is to say, their "name." Finally, she thinks that all things possess both a "nominal essence" and a "real essence." The former is associated with the surface appearance of the thing in question; it is the name which might be used simply to identify it without really understanding it. If we wish to *properly* understand the thing in question, and therefore control it, however, it is necessary that we grasp, not its "nominal" but its "real essence." This is associated with its "real" name or its "true" name.

As Wayne Cogell has noted, Le Guin draws upon this "realist" way of thinking about the world when parodying the philosophy of Jean-Paul Sartre in one of her early short stories entitled "A Trip to the Head."[8] As Le Guin understands him, Sartre is a radical constructivist and therefore a critic of the principles of realism and essentialism. According to Sartre, things do not possess an underlying essential nature, or a "real essence," apart from their "nominal essence." Thus, for example, at one point in the story one of the characters maintains that "you can call yourself whatever you please, you know," to which the main protagonist responds "But I want to know my *real* name."[9] Similarly, elsewhere, the main protagonist maintains that "sex," far from being a social or linguistic construct, "is real, I mean *really* real."[10] It is remarks like this which have led Cogell to argue that for Le Guin there are "things hidden from view, such as internal structures of nature."[11] In Cogell's view, Le Guin's view of the natural world in this story "seems to be that each existing thing has finite structures which limit and act as its ontological ground; it has potencies which are marked by an absence of realization. Things can pass, turn away, or cease to be, but without the recognition of each living thing's finite structures, the fact of physical change and any view of nature becomes unintelligible and absurd." Le Guin, Cogell concludes, would have us "return to nature," that is to say to "the way things *really* are, nameless but *not* absurd" (my emphasis).[12]

Although Cogell does not himself pursue this issue at any length, the attitude which he (in my view rightly) attributes to Le Guin here is quite typical of the doctrine known as "scientific realism," as it is to be found, for example, in the writings of a figure like Roy Bhaskar.[13] As Bhaskar puts it, in his *A Realist Theory of Science*, "The *nominal essence* of a thing or substance consists of those properties the manifestation of which are necessary for the thing to be correctly identified as one of a certain type. The *real essences* of things and substances are those structures or constitutions in virtue of which the thing or substance tends to behave in the way it does" (my emphasis).[14] It is this way of thinking about science and the phenomena of the natural world which underpins Le Guin's view, expressed in another short story which is significantly entitled "The Rule of Names," that "to speak the name is to control the thing."[15] The same idea can also be found in *The Tombs of Atuan*, volume two of the *Earthsea Quartet*. At one point, for example, the main character Ged, who is an apprentice "magician," states that "[k]nowing names is my job. My art. To weave the magic of a thing, you see, one must find its true name out." "What a wizard spends his life at," Ged continues, "is finding out the names of things, and finding out how to find out the names of things."[16] Ged's view of the task of the "wizard" in the magical world of Earthsea, as presented here, is identical with Bhaskar's understanding of the task of the "scientist" in the "real" world.

I note in passing that this is an attitude which has also been associated by some anthropologists with the belief systems of so called "primitive" peoples. According to Ernst Fischer, in such cultures "the word" is "regarded as largely identical with the object." It is "the means of grasping, comprehending, mastering the object." Thus we find that "nearly all primitive races" believe that "by naming an object, a person, a demon, they would exercise some power over them." Thus "a means of expression—a gesture, an image, a sound or a word" is considered in such cultures to be "as much a tool as a hand axe or a knife." It is "only another way of establishing man's power over nature." This idea, Fischer maintains, is "preserved in innumerable folk tales." We need only remember the story of the "sly Rumpelstiltskin."[17]

James Bittner has observed that for Le Guin "the distinction between science and magic, or between science and myth, should not be made too rigidly, for the more rigidly it is made, the easier it is for magic to become science and science to become magic."[18] In Bittner's view the reason why Le Guin thinks that we should not distinguish too sharply between these two notions is because science is close to magic rather than because magic is close to science. Bittner refers to what he claims is the "widely held belief that science fiction is the mythology of the modern world."[19] It would, I think, be much more accurate to say, not that science *fiction* is the mythology of the modern world, but that science *itself* constitutes this mythology, at least according to contemporary postmodernism. From this standpoint *all* scientific knowledge is science *fiction*—a narrative. In my view, though, Le Guin's views are quite different from this. It is true that in Le Guin's writings the fantasy world of magic is thought of as being strikingly similar to the "real" word of science. However, this is not because, as in the case of the postmodern anarchist philosophy of science of Paul Feyerabend and Jean François Lyotard, the "real" world dealt with by science is nothing more than a conceptual or linguistic construct. It is not because, like the authors of children's fantasies, natural scientists do nothing more than "tell stories." Nor is it because the belief system associated with science is the mythology of the modern world, epistemologically no better and no worse than, say, the mythological belief system of the ancient Greeks. Rather it is because for Le Guin the magical world of fantasy, just like the world of natural science as this is conceived of by scientific realists, is governed by causal laws which are thought of as being, not social or linguistic constructs, but as part of the natural order of things, albeit in the case of the *Earthsea Quartet* an imaginary world which is based on quite different causal principles to our own.

Unlike in the case of Feyerabend, Lyotard, and postmodern anarchism, then, if for Le Guin the distinction between science and magic collapses when pressed, this is not because scientific knowledge can be thought of as being a sophisticated form of magic, but rather because in Le Guin's *Earthsea Quartet* magic is thought of in the same way as science is thought of by scientific realists like Roy Bhaskar. This, I take it, is what Le Guin is getting at in one of her early short stories, "April in Paris," when at one point the character Lenoir says, "They call me a fool, a heretic, well by God I'm worse! I'm a sorcerer, a black magician, Jehan the Black! Magic works, does it? Then science is a waste of time."[20]

As in the case of knowledge of the laws of magic in the fantasy world of *Earthsea*, so also in the "real" world of natural science, Le Guin maintains that the discovery of knowledge relating to the essential nature of things which is associated with an understanding of their "true names" gives the person who possesses that knowledge power over those things. She does not argue, as contemporary postmodern anarchists do, that it is power which enables those who possess it to have their way of thinking about the world elevated to the status of "scientific" knowledge. In this respect Le Guin's views are, once again, quite traditional. They are to be associated with the "modern" as opposed to the "postmodern" way of thinking about science. Le Guin would, I think, agree that it is Francis Bacon with his slogan that "Knowledge is Power," rather than Michel Fou-

cault with his counter-slogan that "Power is Knowledge," who has correctly understood the nature of the relationship between truth and power
in the natural sciences. This is one of the reasons why I find myself unable
to agree with Lewis Call's recent suggestion that Le Guin might be
claimed for the cause of "postmodern anarchism."[21]

It is interesting to compare Le Guin's views about this issue with those
of poststructuralist advocates of identity politics today, who follow Sartre
and maintain that personal identity is something which is entirely socially
constructed. According to this view, although the ascription or determination of identity involves the association of an individual with a definite
descriptive label or labels, that is to say, a "name" or "names," nevertheless identity is something which is *made* rather than discovered. Individuals do not have any "real" identity, or a "real essence," apart from the
identity which is socially ascribed to them, which is captured by their
name or "nominal essence." For Le Guin, however, no matter what the
merits of such an approach to issues relating to *social* identity might be,
this way of thinking could not be said to have an application to the natural world. For in the natural world there are "natural kinds" and things
just do possess a definite identity, as it were "in-themselves," quite independently of the descriptive labels which human beings attach to them.
And to get things right in this field, to attach the correct name to them,
necessarily involves a process, not of social construction, but rather of scientific discovery relating to the underlying causal structures which produce those events which natural scientists are attempting to explain.

It is not entirely clear whether Le Guin would wish to adopt the same
approach to the understanding of social and political identity as she does
to that of the identity of those things which populate the natural world.
What *is* clear, however, is that if she *were* to do so then according to her
critics this would amount, in the manner of Plato, to thinking of social
and political identity as being something which is determined in a *quasi-*
naturalistic manner. It would be to reify existing social identities by
wrongly presenting them as if they were static or fixed, a part of the fabric of the universe, or of the natural order of things. Colin Manlove has
suggested that this is exactly what Le Guin does do in *The Earthsea Quartet*, and it is for precisely this reason that Manlove believes that Le Guin's
basic philosophical outlook is a conservative one. Thus, for example, in
The Farthest Shore, Le Guin has one of the central characters, the "Archmage," express the following views: "The winds and seas, the powers of
water and earth and light, all that these do, and all that the beasts and
green things do, is well done, and *rightly done*. All these act within the
Equilibrium" (my emphasis). "But we," the Archmage continues, "'insofar as we have power over the world and over one another, we must learn
to do what the leaf and the whale and the wind do *of their own nature*. We

must learn to keep the balance. Having intelligence, we must not act in ignorance. Having choice, we must not act without responsibility" (my emphasis).[22] It is suggested here by Le Guin that, as in the case of the natural order, so also in that of the social order, generally speaking things are what they are and they do what they do. More to the point, however, in both cases things are what they *ought* to be and they do what they *ought* to do. They act in accordance with the "laws" of their own nature, or as their own essential nature dictates to them. In the case of the human beings who inhabit the social order, these laws are of course *moral* laws.

Le Guin acknowledges that there is an important difference between inanimate objects and nonhuman animate organisms on the one hand and human beings on the other, namely, that human beings possess free-will. Consequently, there is no physical or scientific (causal) necessity that they will in fact act in accordance with the requirements of their own nature or essence. This is a moral rather than a physical necessity which is placed upon them. It is their duty, and it is always possible that they will fail to do their duty. Nevertheless, despite this, Le Guin suggests that something similar to the understanding of the natural world outlined above is also appropriate for any attempt to understand the *social* world of *Earthsea*. This, too, is populated by different individuals each of which, in addition to being a human being, also possesses a determinate social identity, for example, that of a "magician" or a "wizard." Le Guin indicates that if someone in that imaginary world does possess the identity of, say, a wizard then there is a certain pattern of conduct which is appropriate for them. This identity in the society of Earthsea places moral constraints upon them. They are obliged to carry out the duties associated with their social identity or with their particular "station" in that imaginary society. Similarly, or so the argument goes, Le Guin's young readers are being encouraged by her to develop the character which they will need to carry out the duties associated with the station which, in the future, they will possess in their own society. Given this, it is again not too surprising that Colin Manlove has claimed that the political message of *The Earthsea Quartet* is a conservative one. There are times, Manlove argues, when Le Guin's writing puts one in mind of "the whole Renaissance emphasis on nature and universal order," and in particular of "Ulysses's speech on degree in Shakespeare's *Troilus and Cressida*."[23] On this reading, then, throughout the *Earthsea Quartet* Le Guin assumes that there is such a thing as a "cosmic order" and enthusiastically endorses what Arthur O. Lovejoy has referred to as the idea of "The Great Chain of Being," an idea which is central to the worldview of traditional conservatism.[24]

There are two interesting possible responses which might be made to this charge of conservatism, neither of which is successful in my view. The first is to argue that Le Guin would *not* wish to apply the same "realist" principles which she thinks are necessary for an understanding of the natural world to the social sphere. As I have attempted to show elsewhere, however, this argument does not work because there is in fact a striking homology between Le Guin's views on natural science and her views regarding questions of ethics.[25] For example, in one of her essays Le Guin argues that the world is not chaotic or random but ordered, and that the order to be discerned in the world is *not* "one imposed by man or by a personal or humane deity." She also draws a parallel between the realms of ethics and science and insists that "true laws—ethical and aesthetic, as surely as scientific—are not imposed from above by any authority, but exist in things and are to be found—discovered."[26] The second response is to argue that a distinction might be made between Le Guin's early fantasy literature and her later science fiction, especially *The Dispossessed*, because in that text at least Le Guin has a strong commitment to anarchism. In my view, however, the views on education and the development of character which underpins the *Earthsea Quartet* are *also* to be found in *The Dispossessed*. Moreover, there is an affinity between both of these texts and a *Bildungsroman*. There is, therefore, at least some truth in Manlove's claim that Le Guin's outlook is conservative, even if that is not the whole story.

LE GUIN ON HUMAN NATURE AND THE SELF

In this section I will make some remarks about Le Guin's understanding of the self and the conception of human nature upon which it is based. Throughout I will make the provisional assumption that for Le Guin all "selves" are human beings and *vice versa*. This may seem a strange assumption to make in a discussion of the views of the author of works of science fiction. In the present context, however, we are only interested in Le Guin's views regarding those selves who also happen to be human beings. Le Guin's view of the self is similar to that of Hegel, who thinks of the self as possessing a composite character. On this view, all individual "selves" possess both "universal" and "particular" characteristics. For Le Guin, just as for Hegel, an individual self is a complex, stratified entity possessing these different types of characteristic features in synthetic combination with one another.[27] The universal characteristics are those which all human beings possess in common, in virtue of which they are said to be "human." These are "essential" features which are captured in the definition of the concept of a "human being." The "particular" characteristics are what differentiate one human being from another. They include a wide range of things such as gender, race, religion, and so on. In the case of Hegel those universal features which constitute the essence of what it is to be a human being might be said to be "natural," whereas the particular features which differentiate one human being from another are "conventional," that is to say historical or cultural.

It is clear from above that Hegel and Le Guin are neither extreme "realists" nor extreme "constructivists" so far as their understanding of the self is concerned. Indeed, their view of what it is for something to be a "self" might be said to be a theoretical synthesis of the principles of realism and constructivism. For they both think that in the case of any individual self some of the characteristic features which constitute that self, the particular ones, are socially "constructed," whereas there is an important sense in which others, the universal ones, are not. These universal features are natural or "real." It may be true that human beings can only exist in society, that is to say, some society or other, and that these "human" characteristics can therefore only "emerge" in society. However, this does not alter the fact that these features are universally to be found in all human beings, and that they manifest themselves in the same way in all societies everywhere. There is a sense, therefore, in which it might be said that these characteristics are *not* socially constructed.

Whatever her views on the self might be, then, Le Guin does possess a robustly "realist" view of human nature. Like Hegel, she thinks that so far as their essential characteristics are concerned human beings are the same in all societies and all cultures, in all times and in all places. This is not to say that there are no differences at all between individual human beings or selves. Nor is it to suggest that these differences are unimportant in comparison with the similarities. It does, however, imply that Le Guin would be resistant to the thesis associated with extreme social constructivism, and with contemporary poststructuralism, that there are no similarities at all but only differences. Just as she objects to this kind of constructivism in science and in ethics, so also Le Guin rejects it in the spheres of psychology and anthropology.

Thus, for example, at one point Le Guin agrees with Carl Gustav Jung's view that as human beings "we are fundamentally *alike*; we all have the same general tendencies and configurations in our psyche, just as we all have the same general kind of lung and bones in our body. Human beings all look roughly alike; they also think and feel alike. And they are all part of the universe" (my emphasis).[28] She maintains that "if Jung is right," then "we all have the same kind of dragons in our psyche, just as we all have the same kind of heart and lungs in our body." Thus, "nobody can invent" a new psychic archetype "by taking thought, any more than he can invent a new organ in his body."[29] But this, Le Guin continues, "is no loss." Rather, it is a "gain," because it "means that we can communicate" with one another. It means that "alienation isn't the final human condition, since there is a vast common ground upon which we can meet, not only rationally, but aesthetically, intuitively, emotionally."[30]

This does not mean, of course, that Le Guin attaches no importance to the individual differences which make a particular self the particular self or the "character" that it is. Far from it. However, although she does undoubtedly emphasize the importance of "character" and that which is "individual" and "particular" in human beings, nevertheless Le Guin is *also* willing to accept that even an individual character like Virginia Woolf's "Mrs. Brown," in addition to the personal idiosyncrasies which she possesses (and she would not be the particular character she is *without* those idiosyncrasies), nevertheless *also* expresses something "eternal," and hence also universal, about what it is to be human. Mrs. Brown, Le Guin observes "*is* human nature." Consequently, she "changes only on the surface."[31] For Le Guin the subject matter of any novel if it is to be good literature must be "the human condition." In her view the theme of all novels, whether or not these are works of science fiction, "is the subject," or "that which cannot be other than subject," which for human beings is necessarily "ourselves."[32]

A consequence of this view is that for Le Guin the fundamental subject matter of all novels, whether these be the classical works associated with the literary realism of nineteenth century Europe or works of science fiction today, is always the same. Insofar as it is a novel, the focus in *The Dispossessed* on developments in science and technology is therefore of secondary importance. Le Guin tells her readers that the human beings who are its central characters just happen to "live in the universe as seen by modern science, and in the world as transformed by modern technology." According to Le Guin this, and this alone, is the reason why science fiction "remains distinct from the rest of fiction."[33] Writing in the 1970s Le Guin acknowledged that this view was even then an unfashionable one. In "Science Fiction and Mrs. Brown," referring to the constructivist critique of essentialism and of the idea of "human nature" advanced by theorists who were later to be associated with poststructuralism, Le Guin enquires "what is 'human nature' now, in 1975?" "Who dares," she laments, "to talk about it seriously?"[34]

If a more detailed picture of the view of human nature which is to be found in Le Guin's writings from the 1970s is required, then a good starting point is her assumption that by nature human beings are destined to live a moral life. Like the thinkers associated with social or ethical anarchism, as well as the young Marx, Le Guin's views on this subject are inspired ultimately by those of the ancient Greeks, especially Aristotle's idea that "man" [sic] is by nature a social and political animal destined to live a life of justice together with others in society. Like Aristotle, Le Guin associates the idea of a fully developed human being with the possession of a virtuous character, and the actualization of that potential which, in her view, all human beings share to live together in harmonious fellowship with others, in a particular moral community—although in her case, unlike that of Aristotle, without the need for any *coercive* law or system of punishment. This is not to say that such a community would have no laws at all; only that the laws in question would not need to be coercive. All that would be required to produce the spontaneous social order or harmony within such a fellowship of equals is what the character Shevek refers to in *The Dispossessed* as the principle of the "social conscience." It should hardly need pointing out that another important difference between Le Guin and Aristotle, of course, is that like all social anarchists Le Guin believes in the natural equality of all human beings.

Carol McGuirk has suggested that this view of human nature, which Le Guin associates with anarchism, with which she identifies herself as a political activist, and which she attributes to Shevek in *The Dispossessed*, is clearly "utopian," in the sense of being in some way unrealistic or overly optimistic. As such it stands in a sharp contrast with the allegedly realistic and certainly more pessimistic or even cynical view of human nature which, in the history of Western philosophy, has been associated with a long line of figures from the Callicles of Plato's Gorgias, through to Machiavelli, Hobbes, Nietzsche, and beyond. McGuirk argues that because of their shared "emphasis on the innate rationality and altruism of human character," Thomas More in his *Utopia* "sounds very much like Odo, founder of Anarres," something which makes *The Dispossessed* a much "*less* ambiguous utopia" than its subtitle "would suggest."[35] However, what McGuirk overlooks is that for Le Guin *The Dispossessed* is a novel within which the account of life on Anarres constitutes but one-half of the "story" as a whole. It would, therefore, be quite wrong to suggest that qua novelist Le Guin's should be identified with those of her character Odo, no matter how much sympathy Le Guin might have for those views insofar as she is an anarchist or a political activist.

The account offered so far has suggested that Le Guin subscribes to a view of human nature which would be considered by some commentators (namely those who, like McGuirk, are in agreement with Callicles, Machiavelli, Hobbes and Nietzsche) to be naïve, optimistic, impractical, and "utopian." But things are not quite as simple as this. For again, we must distinguish between Le Guin the anarchist and Le Guin the novelist. Insofar as Le Guin is a *novelist*, then it is arguable that she does not see things in quite the same way. Here her views are somewhat more complex. Why? We have seen that one aspect of Le Guin's commitment to Taoism is her appreciation of the necessary (dialectical) interrelation and interaction of "opposites." Thus for example, she acknowledges that there can be no "light" without there being at the same time also "darkness." In *A Wizard of Earthsea*, Le Guin has the character "Master Hand" say at one point that "[t]o light a candle is to cast a shadow."[36]

But Le Guin also applies this way of thinking to the idea of human nature. As a novelist she is well aware that human nature, too, might be said to have its "darker" side.

This way of thinking about human nature is exemplified very well in one of Le Guin's essays, which discusses the ideas of Carl Gustav Jung in connection with a short story of Hans Christian Andersen and which, tellingly, has the title "The Child and the Shadow." According to Le Guin, the shadow in question is "all that gets suppressed in the process of becoming a decent, civilized adult." It therefore represents "man's thwarted selfishness, his unadmitted desires, the swearwords he never spoke, the murders he didn't commit." The shadow is "the other side of our psyche, the dark brother of the conscious mind. It is Cain, Caliban, Frankenstein's monster, Mr. Hyde. It is Vergil who guided Dante through hell, Gilgamesh's friend Enkidu, Frodo's enemy Gollum."[37] Rollin Lasseter has perceptively observed that, in any discussion of Le Guin's view of human nature, Robert Louis Stevenson's Dr. Jekyll and Mr. Hyde immediately springs to mind, especially Stevenson's view that "man is not truly one, but truly two," and that those two are severed into "provinces of good and ill which divide and compound man's dual nature." Like Stevenson, Lasseter continues, Le Guin has also been fascinated with "the dual nature of man."[38]

For Le Guin the Jungian shadow is "the dark side of the soul" which exists in all human beings, and which is a necessary part of what it is that makes them what they are, namely, "human."[39] This "monster" must be considered to be "an integral part of the man," or any individual human being, and its existence "cannot be denied."[40] This is something which all novelists must take into account when creating their characters. If they wish the imaginary worlds which they create, and particularly the characters with which they populate them, to be remotely "realistic," then even the "heroes" of the novels in question (like Shevek) must be portrayed in a way that bears these basic principles in mind. Otherwise they will indeed become "cardboard cut out" figures—vehicles for the expression of abstract ideas of a utopian variety. For without this shadow a person or a character is nothing. As Le Guin asks, "what is a body that casts no shadow?" It is "nothing"—a "formlessness, two-dimensional, a comic-strip character,"[41] that is to say not a "character" at all in the strict sense in which she understands that term. In Le Guin's view if any individual "wants to live in the *real* world," (my emphasis) then that individual "must admit that the hateful, the evil, exists within himself."[42] Moreover for Le Guin, as for Jung, the process of psychological, emotional and moral *development* which is associated with the biography of any individual human being necessarily involves, at some point, that the individual in question should "confront" this shadow which in part makes him who

her or she is, "to accept it as himself—as part of himself."[43] For this reason the shadow might be said to be "the guide" that leads that individual
on the "journey to self-knowledge, to adulthood, to the light."[44]

Le Guin is very clear that this "journey" is "not only a psychic one, but
a moral one,"[45] having to do with personal growth and the development
of character.[46] It is, therefore, also educational. Most "great fantasies," she
says, for this reason "contain a very strong, striking moral *dialectic*" (my
emphasis). This is often expressed as "a struggle between the Darkness
and the Light," which, she says, often trivializes things by making them
"sound simple." Thus, "the tension between good and evil, light and
dark, is drawn absolutely clearly, as a battle, the good guys on the one
side and the bad guys on the other, cops and robbers, Christians and hea-
thens, heroes and villains."[47] In her view, however, this "simplistic moralism"[48] is highly misleading. For, as in the case of Greek tragic drama such
as the *Oedipus Rex* of Sophocles,[49] to which Le Guin explicitly refers, the
"ethics" involved are "not simple at all," but rather complex and contradictory, without any clear indication or certainty regarding what exactly
is "good" and what is "evil," what is "right" and what is "wrong," in the
ethical dilemmas with which a good story ought to deal.[50] Moreover, as
Hegel notes, the moral conflicts and tensions being portrayed occur not
just between the individual characters but also *within* the individual psy-
ches of those characters.[51]

Le Guin's attitude toward this issue is neatly summarized in the following passage, which is worth quoting at length. In this passage Le Guin
is discussing children's fantasy literature, specifically "fairy tales." However, what she says here also has an application to science fiction, especially to *The Dispossessed*. "Evil, then," she says, "appears in the fairy tale
not as something diametrically opposed to good, but as inextricably involved with it, as in the Yang-Yin symbol. Neither is greater than the
other, nor can human reason and virtue separate one from the other and
choose between them. The hero or the heroine is the one who sees what is
appropriate it be done, because he or she sees the *whole*, which is greater
than either evil or good."[52]

According to Le Guin, Hans Christian Andersen must be considered to
be "one of the great *realists* of literature" (my emphasis). precisely because
he was able to confront his own shadow. Like Shevek in *The Dispossessed*,
this shadow is "part of him, but not all of him, nor is he ruled by it." Moreover, Andersen's "creative genius" came "precisely from his acceptance
and cooperation with the dark side of his own soul."[53] Speaking more
generally Le Guin states that if an "artist," specifically a novelist, tries to
ignore "evil" in this sense of the term then he or she "will never" achieve
success in their chosen task—"will never enter into the House of Light."[54]
There is, therefore, something to be said for David Porter's claim that for

Le Guin "the unity and equilibrium of good and evil in human nature reflects on the individual scale the larger universal balance and interdependence of opposites in the broader natural world."[55] Porter notes that Le Guin's works "abound with vivid examples of those who fail to comprehend themselves as the unification of opposites" (e.g., Haber in *The Lathe of Heaven*).[56] By contrast, he says, "those who see the unity behind their own internal conflicts" become Le Guin's "leading protagonists" (e.g., Shevek in *The Dispossessed*).[57]

From the standpoint of this view of human nature, Shevek should not be and is not portrayed as a model of virtue whose conduct is in no way influenced by such base motivations as vanity, pride, selfishness, and so on, which are so often associated with the concept of vice. On the contrary, if the portrayal of his character is to be realistic Le Guin appreciates that, in any given situation where he must decide what it is that he ought to do, Shevek must be presented (like all of us) as having to confront these baser impulses associated with his own shadow. According to Le Guin, the notions of virtue and of vice are dialectically related. "Neither of them without the other, can approach the truth" about the human condition.[58] And the task of the novelist just is to portray this moral "truth."

For this reason I am unable to agree with Gregory Benford's claim that in *The Dispossessed* "the principal *ignored* problem of Anarres is the problem of evil and thus violence" (my emphasis).[59] At least, in my view this judgment requires a strong qualification. For although it may perhaps be true that, strictly speaking, Le Guin *does* suggest that on the planet Anarres this is less of a problem than it is on Urras, nevertheless it could hardly be said that in the novel which is *The Dispossessed* as a whole, or indeed as we have seen elsewhere in her writings, she ignores this particular problem. Nor, therefore, is Benford correct to claim that for Le Guin "fundamentally, the *real* world does not matter" (my emphasis).[60] Indeed, this second judgment seems to me to be the very opposite of the truth.

One could think of the planet Urras in *The Dispossessed* as being the "shadow" of the planet Anarres, in the technical sense in which Jung uses the term. As such it represents that side or aspect of human nature which Le Guin associates with "vice," just as the planet Anarres might be thought of as representing that side or aspect which she associates with "virtue," or that which is "good" in human beings. If one thinks, not in spatial or geographical terms, about the notions of utopia and dystopia, but rather in terms which are psychic and/or ethical, then one might say that Anarres and Urras between them represent that articulated totality or whole which is an individual human being. From this point of view, each of the two planets in *The Dispossessed*, Anarres and Urras, is associated with a *necessary* component element or part of what it is to be a human being, but neither on its own will provide us with a *sufficient* characterization, if the intention is to write a novel which realistically portrays the complex reality of human existence. Thought of in this way, although Shevek is certainly a citizen of Anarres, and as Le Guin occasionally suggests therefore of "utopia," nevertheless if he is to be successfully portrayed as being potentially a real person, a "character" in Le Guin's sense of that term, then Le Guin the novelist must make sure that he also carries within himself something of the principle of Urras. For without that he would not be a convincing character. Nor could he be plausibly presented as possessing the qualities which are usually associated with "real" human beings.

Just like H. G. Wells, insofar as she is a novelist rather than a utopian theorist, or writer of literary utopias, Le Guin appreciates that because of what she considers to be the "imperfections" in human nature, no real live human being could actually *live* in a sociological "utopia,"[61] if by that term one has in mind anything like an ideal or perfect society. A utopian society would be a society of "angels," not of human beings. This, I take it, is what Brennan and Downs have in mind when they say that Shevek could not "be completely at home in either society. To be true to himself, he must, in Camus' phrase, be 'in revolt' against both." Consequently, he "is not a typical Anarresti any more than he is a typical Urrasti."[62] As Judah Bierman has written, "in moving between two worlds, but always keeping them both in his mind," Shevek "demonstrates to the reader the complementing strengths and weaknesses" of both Anarres and Urras.[63] Brennan and Downs rightly associate this feature of *The Dispossessed* with the fact that it is *"novelistic* rather than visionary" (my emphasis).[64] In my view, however, they go wrong when they claim that it is the "Odonian planet" which is "ambiguous" because "it is not perfect, because it is a utopia that comes to terms with man as he *is*—mortal, weak, and potentially spiteful—rather than with man as he *would* be were he angelic" (my emphasis).[65] There is, of course, nothing wrong with the account which Brennan and Downs offer of Le Guin's views on human nature here, at least insofar as she is a novelist. What does, however, seem to me to be wrong is their claim that the planet Anarres is a "utopia" which "comes to terms with man as he is." In my view, it would be more accurate to say that it is not the *planet* Anarres in *The Dispossessed*, but rather the *novel* itself (and, of course, its author) which attempts to come to terms with man as he is. Indeed, it is arguable that for Le Guin Anarres *is* a utopian *society* precisely because it does *not* come to terms with man as he is, whereas *The Dispossessed* is *not* a utopian *text* precisely because it *does* do this. In short, *The Dispossessed* is neither a literary "utopia" nor a "dystopia," but a *novel* which recognizes the contradictory utopian and dystopian impulses in human nature and within each individual human psyche.

Margaret Esmonde has said that Jung describes the shadow as "the dark half of the human *totality*," (my emphasis) warning that one cannot omit the shadow that belongs to the light figure; for without it, this figure lacks body and humanity."[66] Esmonde also maintains that for Jung "in the empirical self, light and shadow form a *paradoxical unity*" (my emphasis).[67] These remarks suggest an affinity between the views of Jung and those of Hegel on the issue of the nature of the self. Indeed, as Esmonde points out, Jung is the author of an essay entitled "The Phenomenology of the Spirit in Fairy Tales."[68] Given her undoubted enthusiasm for the work of Jung, this also brings Le Guin close to Hegel. According to Le Guin, "Jung saw the ego, what we usually call the self, as only a part of the Self, the part of it which we are consciously aware of." This other "self," or the "Self" with a capital letter "S" is, she says, "transcendent, much larger than the ego; it is not a private possession, but collective—that is, we share it with all other human beings, and perhaps with all beings. It may indeed be our link with what is called God."[69] Whether Le Guin is aware of it or not, this Jungian way of thinking about the individual self in relation to some wider or universal Self is strikingly similar to that of Hegel.

In his *Phenomenology of Spirit,* published in 1807, Hegel refers at one point to "the 'I' that is 'We' and the 'We' that is 'I.'"[70] Somewhat later, Bakunin is recorded as having said "I don't want to be 'I,' I want to be 'We.'"[71] On reading these words of Bakunin it is difficult not to think of Hegel. It is also difficult not to think of the title of Zamyatin's *We.* So far as Hegel is concerned, I have suggested elsewhere that his remarks about the notion of the "I" and that of the "We" in the *Phenomenology* can be linked to his account of the dialectic of "mastery" and "slavery."[72] To be more specific, the principle of the "I" is that of the "master," which is the principle of free self-consciousness and unrestrained individual liberty. The principle of the "We," on the other hand is that of the "slave," which here at least Hegel associates with the possession of a determinate social identity, as a member of a particular society or ethical community at a particular time, and with carrying out the moral duties associated with one's "station" in that society, in virtue of which one possesses the identity which one has. It might therefore be argued that for Hegel these two principles of the "I" and the "We" are component elements in the psyche of all individual human beings in all societies at all times and everywhere.

Carl Freedman has suggested that the Marxist (more accurately Hegelian) aesthetics of Georg Lukács, especially his analysis of "the historical novel," is especially significant for those who are interested in science fiction.[73] According to Lukács's reading of Hegel's *Lectures on Aesthetics*, there is a "classical heritage" in the history of aesthetics which "consists in the great arts which depict man as a whole in the whole of society."[74] Lukács maintains that this classical heritage, as it is understood by Hegel, was inherited by Marx and Marxism, the aesthetics of which he characterizes by the expression "proletarian humanism." For this Marxist aesthetics the "object" of art is "to reconstruct the complete human personality and free it from the distortion and dismemberment to which it has been subjected in class society."[75] It is by reference to this principle that Marxism establishes a "bridge" back to the classics whilst at the same time discovering "new classics in the thick of the literary struggles of our own time." In Lukács's view, in the history of human civilization over the last two millennia, from the ancient Greeks, through to Dante, Shakespeare, Goethe, Balzac, and Tolstoy, all great writers have given "adequate pictures of great periods of human development," pictures which are "signposts in the ideological battle fought for the restoration of the unbroken human personality."[76] Lukács argues that those active in the spheres of literature and politics address the same fundamental issues. In literature "the central problem of realism" in the modern era is again that of "the adequate presentation" of "the complete human personality," just as in politics the problem of the restoration of "the complete human personality" is the most important (indeed, the one and only) "social and historical task" which "humanity has to solve."[77]

According to Lukács's understanding of Hegel's aesthetics, the diremption in the human personality to be found in contemporary society, which is associated with the phenomenon of "alienation," exists because of the "class divided" nature of that society. It is not a "natural" phenomenon. Hence it is not a consequence of "the human condition," observable in all societies everywhere. On the contrary, it is a sociological phenomenon which occurs only in a particular *type* of society. Thought of in this way, the problem of alienation, or of "the divided self," is a purely historical problem. As such, it is a problem that could in principle be solved by a radical transformation of existing society. This argument of Lukács's is based on a particular reading of Hegel's philosophy in general, and of Hegel's *Lectures on Aesthetics* in particular, a reading which differs fundamentally from my own.

In my view the problem of alienation dealt with by both Hegel and Lukács is relevant for a proper appreciation of Le Guin's *The Dispossessed*. It might be suggested, however, that it is not *Lukács's* reading of Hegel (a reading which is in certain respects strikingly similar to that developed in France by Alexandre Kojève) but rather the alternative reading put forward by Jean Wahl, and later inherited by Jean-Paul Sartre, which best helps us to understand the way in which Le Guin thinks about this particular issue.[78] For there are times when, just like Wahl and Sartre, but unlike Lukács and Kojève, Le Guin suggests that the split in the human personality referred to earlier is an inevitable consequence of the human condition. It is a natural rather than a purely sociological or historical phenomenon and, as such, is something which could never be overcome. On this reading of Hegel, the separation or internal division within the individual human personality which Lukács associates with the condition of alienation is to be found in all human beings in all societies everywhere. It is in the very nature of human beings that they possess such a divided self. The human condition is inevitably one of alienation, understood in just this sense. The phenomenon of alienation, therefore, should be associated not with what Hegel refers to in his *Phenomenology of Spirit* as "the *unhappy* consciousness" (the unhappiness of *some* consciousness) but rather with the similar sounding though in fact fundamentally *different* notion of "the *unhappiness* of consciousness" (the unhappiness of *all* consciousness). It occurs not, as Lukács, Kojève, and Freedman suggest, because of the character of a particular type of human society, specifically (in recent times) capitalist society,[79] but rather because it is inherent in all societies and in the very nature of human existence. On this view the separation of the particular part of the "self," from that other part of the self which is "universal" to which Hegel refers in his *Phenomenology of Spirit*, is something which could never be historically transcended. There could be no self which is not a divided self. In short, for Hegel there can be no "I" without there also being a "We," just as there can be no "We" without there also being an "I."

It seems to me that it is this reading of Hegel's philosophy, rather than that of Lukács, Kojève, and Freedman, which is most relevant for anyone seeking to understand Le Guin's view of the self and their relevance for *The Dispossessed*.[80] For what is the psychic and ethical principle which Le Guin associates with the planet Urras if it is not that of the "I"? And what is the psychic and ethical principle which she associates with the planet Anarres if it is not that of the "We"? And is this not why Le Guin attaches so much importance to Zamyatin and his novel *We*, whilst at the same time being critical of it because, with its exclusive focus on the principle of the "I," or of individual liberty and the absence of *all* restraint, including that voluntary self-restraint which Le Guin associates with "morality" and with moral "virtue," it tells only one-half (the dystopian, nihilistic half) of the "story" which is the human condition?

This suggests that just as for Hegel the notions of the "I" and the "We" are abstractions which cannot even be thought of separately from one another, let alone subsist independently of one another, so also for Le Guin the same can be said for two planets, Anarres and Urras, and the utopian and dystopian principles associated with them. Neither of these psychic or ethical principles, considered in what could only ever be a relative isolation from the other, is capable of an actual existence. Once again, therefore, Le Guin must be thought of as a quintessentially dialectical thinker. But the important point, here, is that if we look at *The Dispossessed* in this way then Anarres and Urras, or the complex of motivational principles associated with them, are indeed abstractions in Hegel's technical sense of that term. Neither of them can even be thought of, let alone actually exist, independently of the other. Each is necessary and neither is on its own sufficient for a properly human existence. That is why it is impossible for us to choose between them, and why we should approach the situation with a "both-and" rather than an "either-or" mentality.

If we think of the concepts of utopia and dystopia in this way, then we may say that according to Le Guin these two concepts and the motivational principles associated with them are both a part of the human condition precisely because they are both component elements of the self. Moreover, the conceptual duality of utopia/dystopia can be correlated to other similar dualities such as those of altruism/egotism, optimism/pessimism, being/having, wisdom/immaturity, age/youth, reason/passion, and so on, thereby generating two sets of binary oppositions. Insofar as she is a novelist, Le Guin is of the opinion that there is no reason to identify the human condition with either one or the other of these. Bearing this in mind we may also say that, so far as Le Guin the novelist is concerned, the planets Anarres and Urras in *The Dispossessed* might be seen as representing a unified ethical system structured around a cluster of such dualities, within which the planet Anarres is associated with the "positive" poles of utopia/altruism/optimism/being, and so on, whereas the planet Urras is associated with the "negative" poles of dystopia/egotism/pessimism and having, and so on. From this standpoint, Phillip E. Smith is right to say that in *The Dispossessed* Le Guin "tempers her optimism by clearly showing that in human nature the will to dominance" is "a force co-equal" with the "will to mutual aid." According to Smith, the "political systems of each planet," correspond to "the cultural acceptance" of one or other of "these two aspects of human nature."[81]

As in the case of our knowledge of the natural world, and the example of "Schrödinger's Box" discussed earlier, Le Guin suggests that her task as a novelist, so far as *The Dispossessed* is concerned, is to rise above this situation, this "either-or" choice, and refuse to make it. It is to avoid both horns of the dilemma by looking at the situation in a new way. Once we recognize the complex and contradictory nature of the world generally, including both the natural world (as demonstrated by quantum physics) and that of the social world, more specifically the ethical life of human beings, then we can appreciate that we do not *have* to make such an "either-or" choice. We can confine ourselves simply to recognizing and indeed embracing the "contradiction," whilst in some way also seeking to reconcile ourselves to it. That way, Le Guin suggests, is where true wisdom lies.

In my view, then, Phillip E. Smith is wrong to suggest that Le Guin's "thesis" or her "political message" in *The Dispossessed* "is that the anarchism on Anarres, despite its imperfections, represents the best hope for human political, moral, and evolutionary progress."[82] Insofar as she is an anarchist this may indeed be what Le Guin thinks. However, insofar as *The Dispossessed* is not an anarchist tract but a novel about anarchism, or about the life of an individual anarchist, Shevek, then Smith's claim is at best inaccurate. This is so because if the account offered above has anything to be said for it then *The Dispossessed* could have no political message at all—no "thesis" in the sense in which Smith uses this term. As a *novelist* Le Guin does not have, or at least tries very hard not to have, a preference for life on Annares in comparison with that on Urras. Moreover, Smith is also wrong to suggest that in the novel the Anarresti "have forgotten" or do not know "the dichotomy in human nature."[83] For it seems clear that for Le Guin the Anarresti (insofar as their conduct is influenced by the ethical ideals associated with Odonian anarchism) are intended to represent just one dimension of what it is to be a human being, and not both. And it is also clear that Le Guin herself, insofar as she is a novelist, does not ignore or "forget" about the other aspect. Again that is why *The Dispossessed* is best thought of as a novel rather than a literary utopia.[84]

For Le Guin, then, the principle of social organization on Anarres corresponds to just one side or part of the self, the "better" side, the social, cooperative, altruistic side, which undeniably exists. But it is still just one side and not the whole story—even on Anarres. A human life in the sense outlined here is not a cooperative life of the sort depicted on Anarres. Rather, it is a complex and self-contradictory life which embraces the two principles of social organization represented by Anarres and Urras (A-Io), and which, therefore, is practically embodied on neither planet, or nowhere. Perhaps, more accurately, one should say that it is practically embodied on *both* planets in their conjunction with one another, or within the "ethical system" of which the social systems of the two planets are the component parts. Alternatively it might be said to be embodied on *each* planet, although the tension between its component elements is mediated differently on Anarres from the way in which it is mediated on Urras. So just as on Anarres we find the principles of selfishness and greed operating (Sabul), so also on Urras not everyone is motivated by these same principles. Again this is why according to Le Guin *The Dispossessed* should be thought of as a novel and not a work of political theory or a political pamphlet. As such it steadfastly refuses to "take sides." At least it makes a heroic effort not to do so. Although of course, as Le Guin herself occasionally suggests, it is not clear that this effort entirely succeeds. Indeed, one might say that the supreme practical embodiment of this contradiction is in the central character of the novel, Shevek, who has a foot on both planets, and who indeed traverses the ethical as well as the geographical distance between them. It is precisely this which makes Shevek an individual "character," in Le Guin's sense of that term, that is to say, someone who, despite being a fictitious person, is nevertheless intended by his creator to be a realistically portrayed human being.[85]

NOTES

1. Darko Suvin, "Introduction," special issue on "The Science Fiction of Ursula K. Le Guin," *Science Fiction Studies*, 2, no. 3 (1975), 234. For some illuminating remarks which might be considered as a response to Suvin's call by attempting to connect Le Guin's "children's literature" with her science fiction see Margaret Esmonde, "The Master Pattern: The Psychological Journey in the *Earthsea Trilogy*," in *Ursula K. Le Guin*, eds. Joseph D. Olander and Martin Harry Greenberg (New York: Taplinger, 1979), 15–16.

2. For the claim that Le Guin's fantasy literature is associate with an outlook which is politically conservative see especially Gregory Benford, "Reactionary Utopias," in *Storm Warnings: Science Fiction Faces the Future,* eds. George E. Slusser, Colin Greenland, and Erik Rabkin (Carbondale: Southern Illinois University Press, 1987), 75–77; and Colin R. Manlove, "Conservatism in the Fantasy of Le Guin," *Extrapolation,* 21 (1980): 287–97.

3. Laurence Davis, "Introduction" to *The New Utopian Politics of Ursula K. Le Guin's* The Dispossessed, eds. Laurence Davis and Peter Stillman (Lanham, Md.: Lexington Books, 2005), ix.

4. According to Elizabeth Cogell Cummins, for example, "Taoist Configurations: *The Dispossessed*," in *Ursula K. Le Guin: Voyager to Inner Lands and to Outer Space,* ed. Joe de Bolt (New York: Kennikat Press, 1979), 156, Joseph Needham (one of Le Guin's sources) describes it as "the way in which the Universe worked; in other words, the Order of Nature."

5. Colin R. Manlove, "Conservatism in the Fantasy of Le Guin," 287; see also 295: "The Earthsea trilogy is in large part panegyric, a celebration of things as they are."

6. Erik S. Rabkin, "Determinism, Free Will and Point of View in *The Left Hand of Darkness*," in *Ursula K. Le Guin,* ed. Harold Bloom (New York: Chelsea House, 1985), 168.

7. The discussion of Le Guin's views on natural science which follows is complementary to some earlier comments of mine regarding the same issue. See Tony Burns, "Science and Politics in *The Dispossessed*: Le Guin and the 'Science Wars,'" in *The New Utopian Politics of Ursula K. Le Guin's* The Dispossessed, eds. Laurence Davis and Peter Stillman, 195–215.

8. Ursula K. Le Guin, "A Trip to the Head," in *The Wind's Twelve Quarters*, Vol. I (London: Granada, 1978 [1969]).

9. Le Guin, "A Trip to the Head," 20.

10. Le Guin, "A Trip to the Head," 22. See also Le Guin, *The Left Hand of Darkness* (London: MacDonald, 1991 [1969]), XIII, 144: "It is what it looks like and is called. It is a jail. It is not a front for something else, not a façade, not a pseudonym. It is *real*, the real thing, the thing behind the words" (my emphasis). I am unable to accept Rabkin's claim that Le Guin subscribes to the "Sapir-Whorf Thesis," and therefore

endorses the principle of the "linguistic construction of reality." See Rabkin, "Determinism, Free Will and Point of View in *The Left Hand of Darkness*," 159.

11. Wayne Cogell, "The Absurdity of Sartre's Ontology: A Response by Ursula K. Le Guin," in *Philosophers Look at Science Fiction*, ed. David Nichols (Chicago: Nelson Hall, 1982), 151.

12. Cogell, "The Absurdity of Sartre's Ontology: A Response by Ursula K. Le Guin," 151.

13. Roy Bhaskar, *A Realist Theory of Science* (Sussex: Harvester Press, 1978 [1975]).

14. Bhaskar, *A Realist Theory of Science*, 209–11. Bhaskar continues, "In general to classify a group of things together in science, to call them by the same *name*, presupposes that they possess a real essence or nature in common, though it does not suppose that the real essence or nature is known" (my emphasis).

15. Ursula K. Le Guin, "The Rule of Names," in *The Wind's Twelve Quarters*, Vol. I, 85.

16. Ursula K. Le Guin, *The Tombs of Atuan*, in *The Earthsea Quartet* (Harmondsworth: Penguin Books, 1993 [1972]), 266–67.

17. Ernst Fischer, *The Necessity of Art: A Marxist Approach* (Harmondsworth: Penguin Books, 1970 [1959]), 31. It is also worth noting Hegel's observation that "the fundamental desideratum" of all language is "the name." See G. W. F. Hegel, *Hegel's Philosophy of Mind: Being Part Three of the Encyclopaedia of the Philosophical Sciences*, trans. William Wallace and A. V. Miller (Oxford: Oxford University Press, 1971), 218.

18. James W. Bittner, *Approaches to the Science Fiction of Ursula K. Le Guin* (Ann Arbor: UMI Press, 1984), 21.

19. Bittner, *Approaches to the Science Fiction of Ursula K. Le Guin*, 67.

20. Ursula K. Le Guin, "April in Paris," *The Wind's Twelve Quarters*, Vol. I, 35.

21. See Lewis Call, "Postmodern Anarchism in the Novels of Ursula K. Le Guin," *SubStance* 36, no. 2 (2007): 87–105.

22. Ursula K. Le Guin, *The Farthest Shore*, in *The Earthsea Quartet*, 361.

23. Manlove, "Conservatism in the Fantasy of Le Guin," 293–94.

24. Arthur O. Lovejoy, *The Great Chain of Being: A Study of the History of an Idea* (New York: Harper and Row, 2005 [1936]). See also E. M. W. Tillyard, *The Elizabethan World Picture: A Study of the Idea of Order in the Age of Shakespeare* (Harmondsworth: Penguin, 1970 [1942]).

25. Tony Burns, "Science and Politics in *The Dispossessed*: Le Guin and the 'Science Wars.'"

26. Ursula K. Le Guin, "Dreams Must Explain Themselves," in *The Language of the Night: Essays on Fantasy and Science Fiction* (New York: Perigee Books, 1979), 49.

27. For an account of Hegel's views on the self along these lines see Tony Burns, "Hegel, Identity Politics and the Problem of Slavery." *Culture, Theory and Critique*, 47, 1 (2006): 87–104.

28. "Le Guin, "The Child and the Shadow," *The Language of the Night*, 62–3.

29. Le Guin, "Myth and Archetype in Science Fiction," in *The Language of the Night*, 78–9.

30. Le Guin, "Myth and Archetype in Science Fiction," 78–9.

31. Le Guin, "Science Fiction and Mrs. Brown," *The Language of the Night*, 103.

32. Le Guin, "Science Fiction and Mrs. Brown," 103.

33. Le Guin, "Science Fiction and Mrs. Brown," 109.

34. Le Guin, "Science Fiction and Mrs. Brown," 113.

35. Carol McGuirk, "Optimism and the Limits of Subversion in *The Dispossessed* and *The Left Hand of Darkness*," in *Ursula K. Le Guin*, ed. Bloom, 252.

36. Ursula K. Le Guin, *A Wizard of Earthsea*, in *The Earthsea Quartet*, 288.

37. "The Child and the Shadow," *The Language of the Night*, 63–64.

38. Rollin A. Lasseter, "Four Letters About Le Guin," in *Ursula K. Le Guin*, ed. De Bolt, 90.

39. Le Guin, "The Child and the Shadow," 60.

40. Le Guin, "The Child and the Shadow," 61.

41. Le Guin, "The Child and the Shadow," 64–65.

42. Le Guin, "The Child and the Shadow," 64.

43. Le Guin, "The Child and the Shadow," 65.

44. Le Guin, "The Child and the Shadow", 65.

45. Le Guin, "The Child and the Shadow," 65.

46. For an interesting attempt to apply these ideas to the interpretation of Le Guin's *A Wizard of Earthsea* see Esmonde, "The Master Pattern: The Psychological Journey in the *Earthsea Trilogy*," 16–20.

47. Le Guin, "The Child and the Shadow," 67.

48. Le Guin, "The Child and the Shadow," 69.

49. Le Guin, "The Child and the Shadow," 68.

50. Le Guin, "The Child and the Shadow," 65–66.

51. G. W. F. Hegel, *Hegel on Tragedy*, eds. Anne Paolucci and Henry Paolucci (New York: Doubleday, 1962), 281. In the case of Greek tragedy, Hegel notes that the "opposition of ethical powers" which exists in all tragedy, as represented for example by the conflict between Antigone and her uncle Creon in Sophocles' *Antigone*, "contradicts" the principle of "the unity of the self." For in the case of both Antigone and Creon "the one character like the other is divided into a conscious element and an unconscious" one. Moreover, because of the irresolvability of the contradiction which exists between these opposed moral forces within the individual psyche, "each falls into the guilt which consumes it."

52. Le Guin, "The Child and the Shadow," 66.

53. David Porter, "The Politics of Le Guin's *Opus*," in *Science Fiction Studies: Selected Articles on Science Fiction 1973–1975*, eds. R. D. Mullen and Darko Suvin (Boston: Gregg press, 1976), 273.

54. Le Guin, "The Child and the Shadow," 62.

55. Porter, "The Politics of Le Guin's *Opus*," 273.

56. Porter, "The Politics of Le Guin's *Opus*," 273.

57. Porter, "The Politics of Le Guin's *Opus*," 273. Porter also places the character George Orr from *The Lathe of Heaven* in this category, together with Shevek, but I am not so sure about this. It is arguable that the Orr character is just as "one sided" as that of Haber – and hence, paradoxical though it may seem, that he is not really a "character" at all, in the sense in which Le Guin uses this term in "Science Fiction and Mrs. Brown." This is perhaps a weakness in *The Lathe of Heaven*, insofar as it has aspirations to possess the qualities of a novel.

58. Le Guin, "The Child and the Shadow," 64.

59. Benford, "Reactionary Utopias," 77.

60. Benford, "Reactionary Utopias," 79.

61. The impossibility of "real" people actually living in a utopian society is the central theme of H. G. Wells, *Men Like Gods* (London: Sphere Books, 1976 [1923]). I am unable to accept the view of Davenport and Kumar that this is a *utopian* work. See Basil Davenport "Introduction," to Basil Davenport ed., *The Science Fiction Novel: Imagination and Social Criticism* (Chicago: Advent, 1969 [1959]), 12; and Kumar, *Utopia and Anti-Utopia in Modern Times* (Oxford: Blackwell, 1991 [1987]), 129. Interestingly, this view is shared by Zamyatin who in his essay "H. G. Wells," in *A Soviet Heretic: Essays by Yevgeny Zamyatin*, ed. Mirra Ginsburg (Chicago: University of Chicago Press, 1991), maintains, 286–87, that Wells's "*only* utopia is his latest novel, *Men Like Gods*"(my emphasis) and, 288, that "The elements of classic utopia," generally speaking, "are absent from Wells's works (with the sole exception of his novel *Men Like Gods*)." This implies that, unlike other commentators, Zamyatin did not consider Wells's *A Modern Utopia* to be a "utopian" text.

62. John P. Brennan and Michael C. Downs, "Anarchism and Utopian Tradition in *The Dispossessed*," in *Ursula K. Le Guin*, eds. Olander and Greenberg, 146.

63. Judah Bierman, "Ambiguity in Utopia, *The Dispossessed*," in *Science Fiction Studies: Selected Articles on Science Fiction 1973–1975*, eds. Mullen and Suvin.

64. Brennan and Downs, "Anarchism and Utopian Tradition in *The Dispossessed*," 151.

65. Brennan and Downs, "Anarchism and Utopian Tradition in *The Dispossessed*," 151.

66. Esmonde, "The Master Pattern: The Psychological Journey in the *Earthsea Trilogy*," 17.

67. Esmonde, "The Master Pattern: The Psychological Journey in the *Earthsea Trilogy*," 17.

68. Esmonde, "The Master Pattern: The Psychological Journey in the *Earthsea Trilogy*," 19. The essay to which Esmonde is referring here can be found in C. G. Jung, "The Phenomenology of the Spirit in Fairy Tales," in *Four Archetypes: Mother, Rebirth, Spirit, Trickster* (London: Ark Paperbacks, 1989). For discussion of the link between Jung and Hegel see Sean M. Kelly, *Individuation and the Absolute: Hegel, Jung, and the Path Toward Wholeness* (New York: Paulist Press, 1993); and John Dourley, *The Illness That We Are: A Jungian Critique of Christianity* (London: Inner City Books, 1984), 45–47.

69. Le Guin, "The Child and His Shadow," 62–3.

70. Hegel, *Phenomenology of Spirit*, trans A. V. Miller (Oxford: Oxford University Press, 1977), §177, 110.

71. Bakunin, cited Irving Howe, *Politics and the Novel* (London: New Left Books, 1961), 64.

72. Tony Burns, "Hegel, Identity Politics and the Problem of Slavery," 101–02.

73. Freedman, "The Critical Dynamic: Science Fiction and the Historical Novel," in Carl Freedman *Critical Theory and Science Fiction* (Hanover and London: Wesleyan University Press, 2000), 44–62.

74. Georg Lukács, *Studies in European Realism: A Sociological Survey of the Writings of Balzac, Stendhal, Zola, Tolstoy, Gorki and Others* (London: Merlin Press, 1972), Preface, 5.

75. Lukács, *Studies in European Realism,* 7.

76. Lukács, *Studies in European Realism,* 7.

77. Lukács, *Studies in European Realism,* 7.

78. See Jean Wahl, *Le Malheur de la conscience dans la philosophie de Hegel* (Paris: Rieder, 1929). For Sartre and Hegel see Christopher Fry, *Sartre and Hegel: The Variations of an Enigma in "L' Étre et le néant"* (Bonn: Bouvier, 1988); George L. Kline, "The Existentialist Rediscovery of Hegel and Marx," in *Sartre: A Collection of Critical Essays,* ed. Mary Warnock (New York: Doubleday, 1971), 284–314.

79. Lukács, *Studies in European Realism,* "Preface," 5.

80. For a discussion of the "I-We" issue in the context, not of *The Dispossessed,* but Le Guin's *The Lathe of Heaven,* see Carol S. Franko, "The I-We Dilemma and a 'Utopian Unconscious' in Wells's *When the Sleeper Awakes* and Le Guin's *The Lathe of Heaven,*" in *Political Science Fiction,* eds. Donald M. Hassler and Clyde Wilcox (Columbia, Sth. Carolina: University of South Carolina Press, 1997), 76–98. Franko overlooks the link with Hegel, Bakunin, Zamyatin, Lukács, and Sartre.

81. Phillip E. Smith, "Unbuilding Walls: Human Nature and the Nature of Evolutionary and Political Theory in *The Dispossessed,*" in *Ursula K. Le Guin,* eds. Olander and Greenberg, 79. See also Susan Wood, "Discovering Worlds: The Fiction of Ursula K. Le Guin," in *Ursula K. Le Guin,* ed. Bloom, 202: "[T]he walls are not built by any failure of Odonian theory, but by flaws in human nature," especially "[t]he will to dominance" which is "as central in human beings as the impulse to mutual aid is."

82. Smith, "Unbuilding Walls," 79.

83. Smith, "Unbuilding Walls," 86.

84. Frederick Pohl, "The Politics of Prophecy, in *Political Science Fiction,* eds. Hassler and Wilcox, 14, has stated that "we don't need to get out our decoder rings to find the political message in some of the best science fiction. The messages are quite explicit." As an example he cites *The Dispossessed,* which he maintains is "an anarchist utopia (though a downbeat one)." In my view, this oversimplifies what Le Guin is trying to do in this particular text.

85. The reader is reminded of Franz Rottensteiner's criticisms of Le Guin in respect to this issue in "Le Guin's Fantasy: Review of Ursula K. Le Guin. *The Language of the Night: Essays on Fantasy and Science Fiction.*" *Science Fiction Studies,* 8, no. 1 (1981): 87–90. For a similar view see also Gwyneth Jones, "*In the Chinks of the World Machine*: Sarah Lefanu on Feminist SF," in *Deconstructing the Starships: Science Fiction and Reality* (Liverpool: Liverpool University Press, 1999), 128, who agrees with Sarah Lefanu that so far as its attempt at individual characterization is concerned *The Dispossessed* is a failure: "Le Guin insists that she writes novels of character, and has been firm in her dismissal of fashionable critical theory. However Sarah Lefanu easily discovers that the central characters—Genly Ai in *The Left Hand of Darkness,* Shevek in *The Dispossessed*—of her two best known novels are as thin as paper. 'Who is Genly Ai? Who is Shevek? Who remembers what they look like, what they say or feel?' The answer, I would suggest, is very simple . . . Shevek is Le Guin."

10

Conclusion: Le Guin's Relevance for Political Theory Today

Although, as we have seen, there is a conservative dimension to her work as a creative writer, in other areas of her life Le Guin is undoubtedly on the "left" of the traditional political spectrum. It is not too surprising, then, that in recent years she has been "claimed" both by adherents of "postmodern anarchism," such as Lewis Call,[1] and by those who associate themselves with the critical theory of the Frankfurt School, like Carl Freedman.[2] Since the "collapse of communism" in 1989 there has been a welcome revival of interest in anarchism, both in theory and in practice. And generally speaking I am sympathetic toward this recent historical development. I consider myself to be on the "left, specifically an extremely unorthodox type of Marxist, and have always been sympathetic to the kind of "libertarian" approach to politics which is usually associated with anarchism, and consequently toward the idea of some kind of *rapprochement* between Marxism and anarchism. In particular, without being uncritical, I am broadly sympathetic toward anarchism as it is understood by Ursula Le Guin. Otherwise I would not have written this book.

On the other hand, though, for reasons I have already given, it seems to me that the ideas which underpin Le Guin's commitment to anarchism cannot be associated with poststructuralism or postmodernism. Whether one is talking about Le Guin's attitude toward questions of philosophy, science, ethics, politics or aesthetics, it makes no difference. In my view, in each case, Le Guin's outlook is typically "modern" rather than "postmodern," although as I have also said I am not sure that the best way to capture her outlook is by employing temporal categories of that kind. I find myself unable to accept, therefore, Lewis Call's claim that Le Guin can be located within the tradition of "postmodern anarchism." Indeed, this book might be considered to be a more or less systematic refutation of that interpretation. In fact Le Guin's views have much more in common with the "classical anarchism" of the nineteenth century, the anarchism of Bakunin, Proudhon, and Kropotkin, than they do with thinkers such as Friedrich Nietzsche, Michel Foucault, Emmanuel Levinas, and Jacques Derrida.

What about Freedman's attempt to demonstrate an affinity between the outlook of Le Guin and the critical theory of the Frankfurt School? I shall discuss Freedman's reading of Le Guin in some detail shortly. However, let me say here that although I am critical of it, I think that Freedman's attempt as a Marxist to engage positively with the views of Le Guin is most welcome. For Le Guin's Marxist critics have not always been so constructive, even those who read her from the standpoint of critical theory. And this, I think, is a great pity. For Marxists and anarchists are involved in a common project. Despite their differences they do also have at least some things in common. And despite its weaknesses elsewhere there are some areas at least where anarchism in general, and Le Guin's version of it in particular, have a great deal to offer to Marxism. Before turning to discuss Freedman's interpretation of Le Guin, therefore, I would like to say something about how Marxist commentators in the past have approached her work.

MARXISM, LITERATURE, AND LE GUIN

The relationship between Le Guin and Marxism has not always been an easy one. For as in the case of Zamyatin, some of Le Guin's most forceful critics in the past have been Marxists with an interest in science fiction.[3] There are three criticisms in particular which have been made of Le Guin by Marxist commentators. The first of these is that there is no strong sense of the importance of political economy in her work for our understanding of the things which she considers to be morally wrong, for example, the American involvement in Vietnam which provides the background for her *The Word for World is Forest*, which she published in 1972. The second is because, as a result, Le Guin does not have much to offer when it comes to the question of what those who are opposed to such things on ethical grounds could actually do about them in practical terms, for example by creating a political organization committed to opposing them.[4] The third, which I shall discuss at greater length, is that works like *The Dispossessed* are not sufficiently "engaged" politically. The broad thrust of this last criticism is twofold. First it is assumed that it is appropriate to evaluate a work of fiction from the point of view of its contribution to the cause of producing a radical transformation of existing society. Does it make a positive contribution to the "class struggle" by raising the level of political consciousness of its readers? Second it is claimed that when assessed in this way, as in the case of Zamyatin's *We*, Le Guin's *The Dispossessed* can be found wanting.

According to George Steiner, in the early years of the twentieth century, before the Russian Revolution, Lenin took the view that all literature should be *partisan*. In Lenin's own words, "literature must become a part of the general cause of the proletariat" or "a part of the organized, methodical and unified labors" of the Russian Social Democratic Party. Literature, Lenin insisted, "must become party literature." Lenin's motto at that time was "down with unpartisan *littérateurs!*"[5] This is the attitude which is usually associated with the movement known as "socialist realism" in post-revolutionary Russia. It is also, of course, the attitude which led to the persecution of the "heretic" Zamyatin and to his decision to leave the Soviet Union and go into exile in Paris in the 1920s. Surprisingly, this was also the attitude which somewhat later, and despite his philosophical differences with "orthodox Marxism" over other issues, was adopted by Jean-Paul Sartre.

As Istvan Csicsery-Ronay Jr. has noted, most of Le Guin's Marxist critics in the period immediately after the publication of *The Dispossessed* were associated with the journal *Science Fiction Studies*. In the 1970s and 1980s this journal was, according to Csicsery-Ronay Jr., the "primary venue for neo-Marxist criticism" of science fiction, especially whenever and wherever it was guilty of "ideological complicity with established capitalist interests."[6] Key figures associated with the journal at the time were the editors Darko Suvin and R. D. Mullen (who was not a Marxist), as well as Marc Angenot, Peter Fitting, Carl Freedman, Frederic Jameson, and Tom Moylan. All of these figures had an interest in Marxism and science fiction. However, they wrote about science fiction, not from the standpoint of "orthodox Marxism," but rather from that of the Critical Theory of the Frankfurt School.[7] Broadly speaking, the difference between these two strands of thought within the history of Marxism is that those theorists who are associated with the Frankfurt School claim to be less "scientistic" (or as they would say "positivistic") than orthodox Marxists. They have a particular interest in science and society, or the ethical and political issues raised by developments in science and technology. They are less hostile to the employment of moral categories as a weapon of social criticism and subscribe to a form of "ethical Marxism." And they have a more positive attitude toward political utopianism. Indeed, they maintain that even Marx himself might be said to have had, if not a blue print for an ideal society, then at least some idea of what a better world, morally speaking, would be like.[8] From this point of view then, as Csicsery-Ronay Jr. notes, science fiction and "the closely related genre of utopian fiction" have "deep affinities with Marxist thought."

This is so because in *both* cases what we find is authors who have "been concerned with imagining progressive alternatives to the *status quo*" which often imply "critiques of contemporary conditions or possible future outcomes of current social trends."[9]

Similar views have also been expressed by Mark Rose and Hoda Zaki. Rose contrasts science fiction with the writing of "fantasy." In his view, "one might call fantasy a conservative form, whereas *in principle* science fiction might be called subversive" (my emphasis).[10] Given that Le Guin has written both works of fantasy and what most people consider to be works of science fiction, this is an interesting judgment. However, it overlooks the fact that a number of works of science fiction, perhaps even most, are not at all radical or subversive of existing society. For example, this might be said of the later works of Robert Heinlein.[11] Indeed, if we consider the claim made earlier that Le Guin's *The Dispossessed* is a novel written in the tradition of European realism, in the light of the views of Csicsery-Ronay Jr. and Rose, then the appropriate conclusion would have to be that Le Guin does not write what *they* consider to be science fiction at all. Nor, as a number of commentators have pointed out, do many other writers who are usually thought of as working within the genre of science fiction. From this point of view, then, if science fiction is supposed to present its readers with a vision of an alternative future which can be used to critically evaluate existing society or societies, then the vast majority of works which are conventionally thought of as falling into the category of science fiction must be said to be a failure. Indeed, C. M. Kornbluth has argued, against the position adopted by Csicsery-Ronay Jr. and Rose, that "the science fiction novel is *not* an important medium of social criticism" (my emphasis).[12] This is a view which is shared by both Basil Davenport and Keith Booker. For example Davenport has argued that "by and large science fiction has been at its *least* imaginative in inventing alternative societies, especially alternative *good* societies" (my emphasis).[13] He also claims, in my view rightly, that "science fiction has produced very few Utopias, and those not very imaginative, or even tempting; it has done better with Utopias in reverse."[14] Similarly, as we have seen, Booker has claimed that "in general dystopian fiction *differs* from science fiction" (my emphasis) precisely because of "the specificity of its attention to social and political critique."[15] There is, therefore, at least some evidence to support Tom Moylan's contention that "science fiction is not essentially progressive or conservative," and that "it does not automatically come down on the side of angels or devils."[16]

According to Csicsery-Ronay Jr., all of the Marxist theoreticians associated with *Science Fiction Studies* in the 1970s and 80s were interested in contemporary culture, especially so called "popular culture" because of its ideological implications as a vehicle for either sustaining or transforming the class domination associated with contemporary (capitalist) social relations. Csicsery-Ronay Jr. maintains that central to the work of this group was the idea, first systematically developed in the work of Tom Moylan, of the "critical utopia." The members of the group were interested in analyzing specific examples of such "critical utopias" because they saw in them, not just a critique of the present, combined with some discussion of a possible alternative future, but *also* a potential for the construction of an alternative "resisting consciousness." They therefore cast about them in an attempt to identify "recent works" of science fiction" that would fit into this category; worlds which would "criticize the *status quo*" and offer hopeful alternatives," thereby alerting their readers to "potentially subversive works" whilst at the same time "cultivating radical inspiration."[17] It was for this reason that members of the group took such an interest Le Guin's *The Dispossessed*, which rightly or wrongly they considered to be (or perhaps more accurately *hoped* would be) an example of such a "critical utopia."

It is not clear to me that these remarks of Csicsery-Ronay Jr. adequately capture what Moylan has in mind by the notion of a "critical utopia." After all, even the earlier or more traditional literary utopias could be thought of as possessing such a "critical" function. Why then should it be thought to be necessary to conjoin the word "critical" with that of "utopia" in order to characterize what is often claimed to be a new genre of "utopian" writing originating in the 1970s? The point of describing these later works as "critical utopias" has, in fact, more to do with their literary *form* than it does their sociopolitical *content*. They are "critical" utopias, not because they can be used to criticize existing society, but rather because their authors are considered to be *self*-critical. They are aware of the dangers of overenthusiastic utopian speculation. It must be conceded, however, that Moylan himself has a tendency, occasionally, to suggest that the works he refers to as "critical utopias" are indeed "critical" for the very reason suggested by Csicsery-Ronay Jr. So it could not be said that Csicsery-Ronay Jr. has missed the point entirely. On one occasion, for example, Moylan follows Herbert Marcuse and Ernst Bloch and identifies "the utopian imagination as being part of that human activity which consists of imagining (and then desiring) a way of life different from the one offered by the contemporary social system."[18] Utopia therefore "represents a challenge to the dominant ideology of a particular social system." In Moylan's view it is for this reason that "[u]topian texts are counter-hegemonic." As such they "tend to undermine the degrading and totalitarian mechanisms of modern capitalism and centralized bureaucracy." Moylan argues that "utopian writing" like that of "Delany, Russ, Piercy, *Le Guin,* and others" (my emphasis) can thus "be read as expressions of unfulfilled desire resisting the limitations of the present system and breaking beyond with 'figures of hope' not yet realized in our everyday lives."[19]

In response to this it might be suggested that if this were the only thing which made the "utopias" written in the 1970s "critical" then it would be difficult to understand why these utopias were at the time considered to represent a new development in the history of utopian literature. It is only if we focus our attention on questions relating to aesthetic form, specifically the fact that these texts are *novels* in the strict sense of the term, that it is possible for us to properly understand their significance. It is precisely this which makes them *self* "critical"—or "critical" in a quite different sense from that indicated by Csicsery-Ronay Jr. and also, occasionally, by Moylan himself.

Although Le Guin's Marxist critics in the 1970s and 1980s were not orthodox Marxists, the underlying attitude which informed their criticism at the time was much the same as that of Sartre referred to earlier. As examples of this we may take the views of Frederic Jameson, Nadia Khouri, and again Tom Moylan. Writing in the early 1970s, Jameson identified the views of George Orr, one of the two central characters in Le Guin's *The Lathe of Heaven*, with Taoism whilst at the same time also attributing those views to Le Guin. According to Jameson, Le Guin has a "predilection for quietistic heroes."[20] Her "work as a whole is strongly pacifistic" and this leads to a "valorization of an anti-political, anti-activistic stance."[21] Jameson also referred to the "temperamental opposition between the Tao-like passivity of Orr and the obsession of Haber with apparently reforming and ameliorating projects of all kinds,"[22] suggesting that Le Guin herself strongly identifies with the views expressed by Orr in the novel rather than with those of Haber.[23] In short, according to Jameson, *The Lathe of Heaven* supports the view that, despite her evident fondness for "dialectics," something which as we have seen Le Guin has in common with Taoism as she understands it, the political implications of Le Guin's basic philosophical outlook are obviously in some sense conservative. Precisely because of their eschewal of didacticism and their refusal to condemn the existing social and political order outright Le Guin's writings, especially *The Dispossessed*, tend, therefore, to preserve the *status quo* rather than contribute toward the effort to radically transform it.

Similarly, writing in 1980, Nadia Khouri suggested that Le Guin remains "stuck in her own aesthetic project."[24] Khouri's critique of Le Guin and her work, undertaken from the standpoint of orthodox Marxism, is a particularly severe one. *The Dispossessed*, she maintains, has three "ideological stumbling blocks." First there is its preoccupation with questions of "moral philosophy" and its consequent belief that moral beliefs could actually change the world (a belief which is evidently incompatible with the basic assumptions of the materialist conception of history). Second there is what Khouri, with some justification, characterizes as its "regressive" understanding of "dialectics," which is imbued with a "dynamism" which is more "apparent" than real. And third there is its "reduction of the dialectic to binary oppositions with points of gravity congealed in static equilibrium." According to Khouri, Le Guin "seems incapable of transcending these oppositions" and her way of thinking about "dialectics" actually harks back "to closed and entropic models," including that of "the unhappy consciousness" of Hegel.[25] In other words, by implication, Khouri argued that to be a novelist, in Le Guin's sense of that term, is in effect a *petit-bourgeois* self-indulgence, of very little political value so far as Marxism's emancipatory project is concerned.

Finally, as we saw earlier, Tom Moylan (writing in 1986) observed that Le Guin's writing style appears to have more in common with "the realist novel or the tragedy rather than the utopia."[26] Not surprisingly, in Moylan's then view, this was a serious weakness in Le Guin and her work.[27] *The Dispossessed* is, Moylan maintained, "an *apparently* critical text which *asserts* utopia and radical activism" (my emphasis), but is nevertheless "flawed" so far as its aspirations to be a utopia are concerned precisely because of its "compromise with the *status quo*."[28]

All of these criticisms of Le Guin seem to me to rely on the principle that those authors who do not unequivocally condemn existing society in their writings must inevitably condone it. Such authors are, therefore, clearly on the wrong side in the political struggle to radically transform that society or to replace it with a new and better one. How could Le Guin respond to such criticism? If, for example, we focus on Moylan's critique, it should, I think, be clear that in Le Guin's opinion criticism of this kind misses the point, and it does so because those who make it assume that, when she wrote *The Dispossessed*, her intention *was* to write a literary utopia, which could be used to critically valuate existing society, rather than a novel about utopianism. What Moylan considers to be a flaw in Le Guin could hardly be a flaw in her insofar as she is a novelist writing in the realist tradition. On the contrary, it is a strength rather than a weakness. So, if it is a flaw at all, then it could only be so insofar as she is a political activist, whose task is considered to be a didactic one, namely that of raising the level of political consciousness of her readers by instructing them what to think, rather than to overcomplicate matters, or weaken their political resolve, by presenting "both sides of the story" in relation to the ethical dilemmas with which the novel deals. In the end, then, Moylan's then criticism amounted to the claim that when she wrote *The Dispossessed* Le Guin was writing as a *novelist* rather than as a political activist, specifically an anarchist. She was in effect wasting her time writing novels, which "muddy the waters" because they do not clearly take sides, rather than doing what she *should* have been doing, namely, engaging in political activism and/or writing literary utopias which (even if they are not detailed blueprints) are at least schematic outlines for ideal societies which might be used to critically evaluate existing ones. In short, in the view of her Marxist critics Le Guin was then, like Zamyatin, an "unpartisan *littérateur*" in Lenin's sense of the term. It is, therefore, not at all surprising that, as we saw earlier, Le Guin should have identified herself so strongly with that other "internal *émigré*," her literary predecessor Zamyatin, when subjected to criticism of this kind by some Marxists in the 1970s and 1980s.

We have seen that Le Guin distinguishes between the didactic texts which are produced by political activists, on the one hand, and the novels which are produced by artists or creative writers on the other. As an author she thinks that didacticism "gets in the way." It prevents one from producing a good work of literature. Moreover the aesthetic criteria to be adopted when evaluating texts as works of literature are quite different from the political criteria which might be used to evaluate them as contributions to the emancipatory project of transforming existing society. It is for this reason that, in her opinion, Zamyatin's *We* deserves praise as a work of art, rather than condemnation for its suspect moral and political views.

From Le Guin's point of view, Jean-Paul Sartre's understanding of the nature and function of literature generally, and of the novel in particular, would fall into the "preaching" or "moralizing" category. Le Guin would, in my view, side with Zamyatin against Sartre and other Marxists over this issue. The irony is that, as George Steiner notes, this brings Le Guin into agreement with Frederick Engels, whose views on art and literature are much more nuanced and not at all what one would expect from someone who is usually presented as a classic example of an orthodox Marxist. Le Guin would, I think, accept Engels's somewhat surprising assertion that so far as a novel is concerned "there is no compulsion for the writer to put into the reader's hands the future historical resolution of the social conflicts which he is depicting."[29] She would also accept Engels's observation that "the more the opinions of the author remain hidden, the better for the work of art."[30] Indeed, these remarks of Engels seem to me to capture very well the understanding of art and literature which underpins Le Guin's work generally. At least this was Le Guin's aspiration when she wrote *The Dispossessed* even if, as she herself occasionally admits, her efforts to achieve it were not entirely successful.

LE GUIN, SCIENCE FICTION, AND THE CRITICAL THEORY OF THE FRANKFURT SCHOOL

One recent commentator who has not been as critical of Le Guin as Marxists have in the past is Carl Freedman. Writing from the standpoint of the

Frankfurt School, rather than that of orthodox Marxism, Freedman has praised Le Guin both for her moral vision and for what he takes to be her commitment to political "utopianism"—neither of which, in his opinion, are incompatible with the outlook of a "critical theory" of society. Indeed, Freedman's interpretation of Le Guin might be read as an attempt to "claim" her as an author who writes from a standpoint which is strikingly similar not, as Lewis Call maintains, to contemporary postmodernism, but to that of critical theory. Thus, for example, Freedman notes the "dialectical" or the "Hegelian" character of Shevek's (and by implication Le Guin's) approach to science and scientific knowledge, as this is evidenced by the General Temporal Theory referred to in *The Dispossessed*. According to Freedman's interpretation of Le Guin "there ought," so far as Shevek's General Temporal Theory is concerned, "to be no question of choosing between simultaneity and sequency," because each "becomes a reified dogmatism to the degree that it is abstracted from the other." What is required, therefore, is a "unified approach" which "critically engages both viewpoints, sublating them in the classically Hegelian sense of cancelling them on one level while, on another, preserving them in a higher and more complex synthesis." For Le Guin, therefore, as Freedman understands her, the "dialectical approach" which is necessary for an adequate understanding of the world generally has a clear application to "the epistemology even of the physical sciences."[31]

As I have noted, Freedman considers *The Dispossessed* to be a consequence of Le Guin's attempted "reinvention of the positive utopia" in the 1970s.[32] In his view, *The Dispossessed* is "not only the central text in the postwar American *revival* of the *positive utopia*, but, arguably, the most vital and politically acute instance of the positive utopia yet produced, at least in the English speaking tradition" (my emphasis).[33] As such, it contains a definite vision which might be used to criticize existing social conditions and suggest a possible alternative future. At the same time, though, Freedman is well aware that *The Dispossessed* is a novel. Indeed, he praises Le Guin's employment of this stylistic device because, in his view, it constitutes an improvement on the form adopted by the authors of traditional utopias. It enables Le Guin to more effectively realize her didactic intentions. Like a number of other commentators, therefore, Freedman is of the opinion that, even if it did not itself *initiate* a new development in the history of utopian literature, namely, the birth of the utopian novel, Le Guin's *The Dispossessed* can at the very least be associated with that development. Although it is indeed a novel, it is nonetheless legitimate to think of it as being *also* a literary utopia, or a work of utopian literature.

According to Freedman, the fact that a work like *The Dispossessed* is a novel rather than a more traditional literary utopia actually strengthens rather than weakens its force as a critical instrument for the evaluation of

existing society.³⁴ In his view, the novel's "insistence upon the unavoid-
able complexities and ambivalences of social organization" nevertheless
"coexists with a definite radical commitment" on the part of its author.³⁵
This radical critique of existing society is something which, Freedman
maintains, brings Le Guin much closer to "critical, dialectical Marxist
thought" than to "the anarchist thought of the author's own political lin-
eage."³⁶ Moreover, this critique is made possible for two reasons: firstly
because, unlike traditional literary utopias, works of science fiction like
The Dispossessed depict imagined alternative societies which can be clearly
"connected" historically to the present by a process of extrapolation; and
secondly because, again unlike a traditional literary utopia, being a novel,
Le Guin's text possesses a *dialogic* rather than a *monologic* form.³⁷

So far as the first of these points is concerned, Freedman acknowledges
his debt to Lukács's discussion of "the historical novel," which he ingen-
iously adapts to the analysis of the genre of science fiction.³⁸ As Freedman
himself states, both works of science fiction and the historical novel, as
Lukács understands it, "manifest a radically *critical* impulse" (my emphasis). This is so because "both are radically dialectical and historicizing
literary tendencies." Both genres, Freedman maintains, "operate by
means of a post-Hegelian dialectic of historical identity and historical difference." That is to say, in both, "the empirical present of the reader and
of the text's own production is put into contrast with an alternative significantly different from the former, yet different in a way that remains rationally accountable." In the historical novel, this "alternative to actuality" is located in a knowable *past*, whereas in science fiction "the mundane
status quo shared by the author and reader is *contrasted*, while also *connected*, to a potential *future*" (my emphasis).³⁹

In my view, however, this particular explanation of what it is about the
genre of science fiction which makes it "critical" only works if it is assumed that, so far as its intellectual content is concerned, science fiction
can be identified with *dystopian* political thought and writing. Freedman
suggests that it is the method of *extrapolation*, a method which is central to
dystopian science fiction, which allows us to evaluate a society in the
present by comparing it with some imagined and morally *undesirable* society of the future, a *possible* future society which might come into existence if those tendencies observable in present society which the author
considers to be malign continue to operate unchecked. If there is any
utopian vision to be associated with writing of this kind, and some commentators think that in principle there could be,⁴⁰ then this is contained in
such texts only *implicitly* and not explicitly. Writing of this kind could not
be said to be overtly utopian. The type of critique associated with it is an
"immanent" or "negative" critique, rather than the "positive" type of critique associated with traditional works of utopian literature.

It is clear from what Freedman says about Le Guin, however, that in his opinion *The Dispossessed* is a "critical" text for a quite different reason from this. It is critical not because, like dystopian works of science fiction, it extrapolates undesirable trends existing in present society, but simply because it contains a positive vision of a possible, ethically superior, alternative society in the future. In other words, it is critical because it is a *utopian* rather than a dystopian work. The reason which Freedman gives for thinking that science fiction in general is critical of existing society is, therefore, quite different from the reason he gives for thinking that Le Guin's *The Dispossessed* is critical of existing society. In short, his analysis of the significance of *The Dispossessed* for a "critical theory of society" does not actually follow from his account of the critical character of science fiction more generally. It suggests that in Freedman's view what makes *The Dispossessed* critical is the fact that it is a literary utopia rather than the fact that it is a work of science fiction. Indeed, Freedman's account actually casts doubt on the status of *The Dispossessed* as a work of science fiction.

So far as the second point is concerned, namely, the issue of the dialogic form of the novel in contrast to the monologic form of the traditional literary utopia, Freedman does not satisfactorily explain why we should think of this dialogic form as being radical in terms of its potential for criticizing existing social condition, or indeed why we should think of it as being critical at all. It is true that a well-crafted novel is likely to touch the sympathies of its readers and encourage them to engage with the moral dilemmas with which it deals, in a way that the traditional literary utopia does not. It is likely to "move" its readers in some sense of that term. Freedman appears to think, however, that this will amount in practice to readers being moved to "take sides," or to act in a certain way, because they will come to identify with just *one* of the two points of view which are in collision with one another in the moral conflict being depicted in the novel in question. This is certainly possible, of course; but it is by no means inevitable. It is also possible that readers might be moved to take the *other* side. Another possibility is that readers of a novel, whether this be a historical novel or a work of science fiction, will be moved in the *tragic* sense of identifying or empathizing with *both* sides at the same time. In such circumstances it may well be the case that like Shakespeare's *Hamlet*, although they are certainly in some sense moved by what they have read, they will nevertheless feel unable to take either one side or the other and will, in consequence, be reduced to passivity so far as their involvement in any similar moral conflicts in the present are concerned.

In his discussion of Le Guin, Freedman does not distinguish between what I have referred to as Le Guin the anarchist political *activist* and Le Guin the *novelist*. In his view there is just one Le Guin, who is consistently both an activist and a novelist at the same time. Here, Freedman does *not* follow the lead of Georg Lukács. Referring to Sir Walter Scott, Lukács states at one point that "undoubtedly there is a certain contradiction here between Scott's directly *political* views and his *artistic* world picture" (my emphasis). For, Lukács continues, Scott too, like so many great realists, such as Balzac or Tolstoy, "became a great realist *despite* his own political and social views" (my emphasis).[41] Here Lukács makes a clear distinction between, on the one hand, Scott the *novelist* and Scott the "private" individual. The former was a writer whose work was in practice, if not in theory, informed by a profoundly "dialectical" approach to the problems of human existence and who steadfastly refused, as an artist, to "take sides" when portraying them in his writings. Consequently, Scott was compelled by his artistic calling to have a certain degree of sympathy for the "victims" of historical and social "progress" whose lives he depicts in his novels. The latter, on the other hand, certainly did take sides, and possessed a political outlook which, according to Lukács, was quite typical of a late eighteenth century English "conservative" or "honest Tory" gentleman.[42]

It is worth noting in this connection that H. G. Wells was of the opinion that Sir Walter Scott "was a man of intensely *conservative* quality" (my emphasis). According to Wells, he "accepted willfully the established social values about him" and "hardly had a doubt in him of what was right or wrong."[43] Against this Lukács would have argued that Wells's assessment of Scott is true only of that "Scott" who was a nineteenth century Tory gentleman, and not of the Scott who was a writer of historical novels.

If we take this distinction of Lukács and apply it to Le Guin, as the author of a science fiction novel, then as we have seen it becomes possible for us to distinguish between Le Guin the private individual, who as a political activist is, of course, not a conservative but an anarchist, and Le Guin the *novelist*, who in a manner strikingly similar to Sir Walter Scott also adopts a profoundly "dialectical" approach to the moral dilemmas with which her work deals, and who, therefore, again like Scott, as an *artist* refuses on principle to "take sides" when dramatizing them in her writings.

Freedman makes some extremely interesting remarks about the issue of didacticism in Le Guin's work.[44] In his view, because Le Guin is indeed a writer working in the utopian tradition it inevitably follows that she *must* be "in some measure a didactic writer." According to Freedman, "the dialectical complexity of *The Dispossessed* should not be confused with a refusal to take sides. Indeed, far from resolving into any sort of Olympian apoliticism which is 'above' politics, Le Guin's text is able to *enforce* its anarcho-communist political vision with special power precisely because of its theoretical self-critique, and it is perhaps here that the novel's greatest achievement is located."[45] Unlike Le Guin, then, Freedman maintains that a tendency toward didacticism should not be considered to be a weakness in her writing. Far from it. The "didactic impulse," he argues, is a "per-

fectly legitimate component of artistic production." As such it is "deval-
ued" only by the "precritical prejudices of a naively contemplative middle class aesthetic."[46]

Freedman distinguishes between two quite different forms of didacticism. Someone who is didactic in the first of these two senses is so in a
"narrow" and "an insufficiently critical way," precisely because they
"fail" to be "dialectical." This is the didacticism of the traditional literary
utopia, of which as we have seen Le Guin is critical. Someone who is didactic in Freedman's second sense certainly does "take sides," but not in
such a crude way. In Le Guin's case, for example, Freedman claims that
she does not "make things too easy" when presenting the anarchist vision
that she recommends to her readers in *The Dispossessed*. On the contrary
she is willing to "make things difficult for herself" by incorporating into
her text "as many rigorous objections to her own viewpoint as possible."
She "prefers," Freedman maintains, "on intellectual and aesthetic principle to make her case as strong as possible by not flinching from the most
cogent counter-arguments that might be mounted." In this way Le Guin
has produced a text which "achieves a genuine critical victory," and not
just "a formal win by default."[47] According to Freedman, then, there is no
logical inconsistency involved in maintaining both that *The Dispossessed* is
a "positive utopia" and that its author adopts a "dialectical" outlook on
the world; just as there is no contradiction involved in claiming that it is
a literary utopia as well as being a novel. Indeed, Freedman thinks that
The Dispossessed is much more successful in realizing its author's didactic
intentions than earlier, more traditional literary utopias, precisely because
it is a novel rather than a political pamphlet or tract.

It cannot be denied that this is a plausible, as well as an interesting,
reading of Le Guin; a reading which transforms her adoption of a "dialectical" style of writing (that is to say, the fact that she chose to write a
novel rather than a traditional literary utopia) into an instrument, not just
for criticizing existing society, but also for recommending to her readers a
definite alternative to that society. On Freedman's reading *The Dispossessed* could indeed be considered to be both a novel and a literary utopia
at one and the same time. However, I am not so sure that when she wrote
The Dispossessed in the 1970s Le Guin herself would have agreed with
Freedman's account of her position. Indeed, when making these remarks
Freedman seems to me to be defending Le Guin against herself. For although her views on this subject are not always consistent, nevertheless a
case could be made for the view that Le Guin did not herself make a distinction between these two different forms of didacticism; that she considered *all* didacticism to be a bad thing; that she tried as hard as she
could to avoid it in her own work; that she recognized that there is at least
some substance to the criticism that her efforts to do this were not entirely

successful; that she was, therefore, to some extent guilty of the charge of didacticism; and, finally, that in her view this did indeed diminish the quality of *The Dispossessed*, her novel, if it is evaluated by purely aesthetic criteria, as a work of art.

Like Freedman's interpretation, my own reading of Le Guin's work generally, and of *The Dispossessed* in particular, attaches decisive importance to the notion of "dialectics" and to the affinity which Le Guin's work has with Hegelianism. I agree with Freedman that Le Guin's philosophical outlook is indeed a "dialectical" one. In my view, however, her adoption of the stylistic device of the novel is associated, not with an effort to be more successful in achieving her own didactic intentions but rather, on the contrary, with an attempt to avoid didacticism altogether in her own writing. From this point of view, then, *The Dispossessed* should not be thought of as a "critical utopia," or as a "positive utopia" as Freedman understands that expression. Indeed, it should not be thought of as being a literary utopia at all.

It is interesting to compare Freedman's "Hegelian" reading of Le Guin with the spectrum of different possible interpretations of Hegel's own philosophy referred to earlier. That spectrum identified three different interpretations of Hegel's philosophy, namely, Left, Right, and Centrist Hegelianism. But where does Freedman's understanding of Hegel, and of Le Guin, fit into this schema? The answer to this question is not entirely clear. Given Freedman's association of Le Guin with the critical theory of the Frankfurt School it would seem that the kind of Hegelianism which he considers to be present in her work is neither Right Hegelianism nor Centrist Hegelianism. For in Freedman's view *The Dispossessed* presents a radical critique of existing society and it does so because it contains a vision of an alternative society in the future which is fundamentally different from our own. On the other hand, however, it does not seem appropriate to associate Le Guin with Left Hegelianism either, as the hallmark of Left Hegelianism is its rejection of political utopianism on the grounds that utopian writers assume that there is such a thing as a perfect or ideal society which would, if it were ever achieved, necessarily remain static as it would have no need to change.

Freedman's Hegelian interpretation of Le Guin does not, therefore, fit neatly into the categorical schema presented above. The type of critique of existing society which Freedman associates with Le Guin and her work appears to be associated with an abstract moral ideal, or a positive vision of an alternative society which is morally superior to our own, and with which our own society can be compared and found wanting. Such a critique might be said to be a transcendent rather than an immanent critique. It is arguable, however, that the kind of critique which is (or ought to be) associated with the outlook of the Frankfurt School is quite different from

this. For the critique that is associated with "critical theory" is an immanent rather than a transcendent critique—a negative rather than a positive
critique. From the standpoint of critical theory, therefore, any transcendent critique of existing society of the kind which Freedman appears to attribute to Le Guin would be "undialectical."[48] It is, therefore, arguable
that, as Freedman understands it, Le Guin's approach to questions of
ethics and politics is not properly speaking a dialectical one at all.

My own interpretation of Le Guin, insofar as she is a novelist, associates her philosophical outlook with what I have referred to as Centrist
Hegelianism. In my view, if we are talking about Le Guin the novelist as
opposed to Le Guin the political activist then the interpretation of Hegel
which lies closest to her philosophical outlook is not one which is associated with a commitment to the radical transformation of existing society,
but rather (as in the case of Taoism) with a conservative attitude of resignation or of reconciliation with that society and with the world generally.
It is for this reason that *The Dispossessed* is best thought of as a novel rather
than a literary utopia. For that is the genre of writing which is most appropriate for an author with such an outlook.

Earlier I cited Freedman's claim that for Le Guin "there ought," as far
as Shevek's General Temporal Theory is concerned, "to be no question of
choosing between simultaneity and sequency," because each "becomes a
reified dogmatism to the degree that it is abstracted from the other." What
is required, therefore, is a "unified approach" which "critically engages
both viewpoints, sublating them in the classically Hegelian sense of cancelling them on one level while, on another, preserving them in a higher
and more complex synthesis." For Le Guin, therefore, as Freedman understands her, the "dialectical approach" to the world generally applies to
"the epistemology even of the physical sciences."[49] Thus far, Freedman's
reading of Le Guin seems to me to be absolutely correct. However, considered from the standpoint of a Centrist Hegelian interpretation of *The
Dispossessed*, it is noteworthy that what Freedman does *not* do in his discussion of Le Guin is appreciate that a similar line of reasoning might also
be applied to Le Guin's understanding of the social systems on Anarres
and Urras and their respective moral values. Thus, for example, it is possible to take the remarks cited above and substitute the words "Anarres"
and "Urras" for the words "simultaneity" and "sequency" within them. If
we do this then we get the following result, which seems to me to accurately capture Le Guin's views with respect to this issue. The revised version runs as follows: "there ought to be no question of choosing between
Anarres and Urras," because each "becomes a reified dogmatism to the
degree that it is abstracted from the other." What is required therefore, in
their case also, is a "unified approach" which "critically engages both
viewpoints, sublating them in the classically Hegelian sense of cancelling

them on one level while, on another, preserving them in a higher and more complex synthesis." This, I think, is precisely what Le Guin does in *The Dispossessed*, and that is why the text should be thought of as a *novel* (in Le Guin's sense of that term) about utopianism in politics rather than, as Freedman suggests, some kind of literary utopia. Although Freedman would not agree with me, in my view his insistence that Le Guin is indeed a "utopian artist" and in consequence someone who *does* commit herself to "choosing" the society of Anarres in preference to that of Urras, is an indication that he has not consistently applied his own (basically correct) understanding of the dialectical approach to questions of science (and the world generally) which underpins *The Dispossessed* to his analysis of Le Guin's views on ethics and politics. Nor does he appreciate that for Le Guin it is the novel and *not* the literary utopia which is the most appropriate aesthetic form for someone with such a "dialectical" outlook. If Le Guin the political activist does indeed make the choice which Freedman attributes to her, and opts for anarchism, Le Guin the *novelist* feels unable to do so.

LE GUIN, CLASSICAL ANARCHISM, AND ETHICAL MARXISM

The above remarks are intended to apply only to Le Guin insofar as she is a novelist and not to her insofar as she is an anarchist. They amount to saying that although there are some similarities between Le Guin's philosophical outlook and that of critical theory, nevertheless there are also some fundamentally important differences. Despite the fact that Le Guin's views do have an affinity with those of Hegel, then, this is not enough to justify Freedman's claim that her outlook is basically the same as that of the critical theory of the Frankfurt School.

It seems to me, however, that the case for claiming that, insofar as she is an anarchist, Le Guin's ethical vision is similar to that of the Frankfurt School, or of "ethical Marxism" is a much stronger one.[50] We saw earlier that central to this anarchist ethical vision is the assumption, which Le Guin considers to be "essential," that "we" human beings "are not objects" but "subjects." Hence, "whoever among us treats us as objects is acting inhumanly, wrongly, against nature."[51] Le Guin insists that "if you deny any affinity with another person or kind of person, if you declare it to be wholly different from yourself" then you inevitably deny its "spiritual equality" and hence also its "human reality." In her view, "the only possible relationship" we could have with an "other" which is thought of in this way is "a power relationship" and not an ethical one.[52] Le Guin's criticism of those who seek to "objectify" others, to reduce them to the status of a "thing," a "tool," or an "instrument," in short to "enslave" them, has an obvious affinity with the Frankfurt School's rejection of the principle of "instrumental rationality." It also has an affinity with the notion of "alienation," as this is developed in the writings of the young Marx, especially the *Economic and Philosophical Manuscripts of 1844*. Like Marx she thinks that if you have alienated another person in this way then you have also "alienated yourself," and have in consequence "fatally impoverished your own reality" as a human being, as a moral being.[53]

This is not to say, however, that Le Guin's views on this subject must have been derived as a consequence of her critical engagement with Marxism. That is certainly possible, of course. However it is also possible that they were derived independently. For these ideas can also be found in the classical anarchist tradition, especially in the writings of Mikhail Bakunin. And in the case of both Marxism and anarchism they can be traced back to a joint source, namely, German philosophy at the end of the eighteenth and beginning of the nineteenth centuries, especially the moral philosophies of Kant and Hegel. This is one of the reasons why Le Guin should be thought of as a "modern" rather than a "postmodern" anarchist so far as questions of ethics and politics are concerned.

If someone is a creative writer and an artist, whilst at the same time also being committed to a particular ideological position in politics, whether this is Marxism or anarchism, it is inevitable that this will create tensions. To the extent that one overtly preaches a particular political message in one's work, to that extent the value of the work in question as a work of art will be diminished. To the extent that one is keen to preserve the integrity of a novel as a work of art, to that extent it is inevitable that one's own political commitments will become diluted in the process. Le Guin has been criticized in the past from both sides, both by those who think that she is overly didactic in her work and by those who think that her work is not sufficiently committed when it comes to raising the level of political consciousness of her readers. In the case of *The Dispossessed*, in my view it is arguable that she gets the balance about right. The political significance of *The Dispossessed* is not so much that Le Guin tells her readers what to think and offers them the "right answers" to the moral and political problems with which it deals. How could she do that, given that her intention was to write a novel and not a political pamphlet? It is, rather, that Le Guin engages her readers with these problems, and encourages them to think for themselves about them.

Perhaps the most important thing about Le Guin's work is the fact that it stimulates and encourages her readers to think in ethical terms, something which in the young especially Le Guin considers to be an important contribution to the development of character or virtue. In particular, in both her "children's" literature and in her science fiction Le Guin seeks to stimulate and encourage the development of the creative imagination, the

ability that in her view all human beings natively possess to imagine entire "worlds" which are radically different from and ethically superior to
our own. To encourage this is, of course, is at the same time to suggest that
there might also be a possible alternative future for our own world. Although Le Guin the novelist would disagree, this is where the political
significance of Le Guin's work as a creative artist truly lies.

This is an attitude which puts one in mind of the work of Herbert Marcuse in the area of aesthetics and politics.[54] In a marvellous essay entitled
"Why are Americans Afraid of Dragons?" which might have been inspired
by the humanist Marxism of Erich Fromm,[55] a one-time member of the
Frankfurt School, Le Guin neatly summarizes what she considers to be the
political significance of her own work. "[A]n adult," she says, "is not a dead
child but a child who survived. I believe all the best faculties of a mature
human being exist in the child and that if these faculties are encouraged in
youth they will act well and wisely in the adult, but if they are repressed
and denied in the child they will stunt and cripple the adult personality.
And finally, I believe that one of the most deeply human, and humane, of
these faculties is the power of imagination: so it is our pleasant duty, as li-
brarians, or teachers, or parents, or writers, or simply as grownups, to encourage the development of that faculty of the imagination in our children,
to encourage it to grow freely, to flourish like the green bay tree, by giving
it the best, absolutely the best and purest, nourishment that it can absorb.
And never, under any circumstances, to squelch it, or sneer at it, or imply
that it is childish, or unmanly, or untrue. For fantasy is true, of course. It
isn't factual, but it is true. Children know that. Adults know it too, and that
is precisely why many of them are afraid of fantasy. They know that its
truth challenges, even threatens, all that is false, all that is phony, unneces-
sary and trivial in the life they have let themselves be forced into living.
They are afraid of dragons because they are afraid of freedom."[56] These remarks, first published in 1974, the same year as *The Dispossessed*, remain as
valid today as they were then. In my view, no matter what legitimate criticisms might be brought against Ursula K. Le Guin or against anarchism in
other areas, a Marxism that does not feel able to respond positively to such
sentiments, a Marxism which is not both a libertarian and an ethical Marxism, has definitely lost its way.

The criticisms made of Le Guin by Marxists when she first published
The Dispossessed may have appeared to possess greater force thirty years
ago than they do now. At that time, with the exception of the Frankfurt
School, Marxists had a tendency to think that they should be opposed on
principle to any kind of ethical critique of capitalism, or to any kind of
utopian speculation, both of which were considered to be irredeemably
"bourgeois." The fact that Le Guin was and is a self-professed anarchist
cut no ice with her then critics, who considered anarchism to be nothing

more than a form of pseudo-radical liberalism. Today however, post 1989, such criticisms seem much less persuasive. Happily, those who still consider themselves to be Marxists are on the whole much less sectarian and much more sympathetic to Le Guin than Marxists have been in the past.

NOTES

1. See Lewis Call, "Postmodern Anarchism in the Novels of Ursula K. Le Guin," *SubStance* 36, no. 2 (2007): 87–105, and Lewis Call, *Postmodern Anarchism* (Lanham, Md.: Lexington Books, 2002).

2. Carl Freedman, *Critical Theory and Science Fiction* (Hanover and London: Wesleyan University Press, 2000).

3. Istvan Csicsery-Ronay Jr., "Marxist Theory and Science Fiction," in *The Cambridge Companion to Science Fiction*, eds. Edward James and Farah Mendelsohn (Cambridge: Cambridge University Press, 2003), 113–24.

4. See, for example, Frederic Jameson, "World Reduction in Le Guin: The Emergence of Utopian Narrative," in *Archaeologies of the Future: The Desire Called Utopia and Other Science Fictions* (London: Verso, 2005), 251–60, and Nadia Khouri, "The Dialectics of Power: Utopia in the Science Fiction of Le Guin, Jeury and Piercy," *Science Fiction Studies*, 7, (1980), 49–61.

5. George Steiner, "Marxism and the Literary Critic," in *Sociology of Literature and Drama*, eds. Elizabeth Burns and Tom Burns (Harmondsworth: Penguin, 1973), 59–60. But see also Terry Eagleton, *Marxism and Literary Criticism* (London: Methuen, 1976), 40–41: "Lenin's remarks, interpreted by unsympathetic critics as applying to imaginative literature, were in fact intended to apply to party literature . . . Lenin had in mind not novels but party theoretical writing." See also Alan Swingewood, *The Sociology of Literature* (London: Paladin Books, 1972), 48, and Alan Swingewood, *The Novel and Revolution* (London: Macmillan, 1975), 74–75.

6. Istvan Csicsery-Ronay Jr., "Marxist Theory and Science Fiction," 117.

7. Istvan Csicsery-Ronay Jr., "Marxist Theory and Science Fiction," 117.

8. The literature on the Frankfurt School is vast. Standard reference works include David Held, *Introduction to Critical Theory: Horkheimer to Habermas* (Cambridge: Polity Press, 1990); Martin Jay, *The Dialectical Imagination: A History of the Frankfurt School and the Institute of Social Research, 1923–1950* (Berkeley: University of California Press, 1996); and Rolf Wiggerhaus, *The Frankfurt School: Its History, Theories, and Political Significance* (Cambridge: Polity Press, 1994).

9. Csicsery-Ronay Jr., "Marxist Theory and Science Fiction," 113.

10. Mark Rose, "Genre," in *Alien Encounters: Anatomy of Science Fiction* (Cambridge, Mass.: Harvard University Press, 1981), 21.

11. Adam Roberts, *The History of Science Fiction* (London: Palgrave, 2005), 202–03, characterizes Heinlein's attitude in *Starship Troopers* as being at worst "quasi-fascistic," and at best "right wing," "hawkish," and "militaristic."

12. C. M. Kornbluth, "The Failure of Science Fiction as Social Criticism," in *The Science Fiction Novel: Imagination and Social Criticism*, ed. Basil Davenport (Chicago: Advent, 1969 [1959]), 50.

13. Basil Davenport, "Introduction" to *The Science Fiction Novel: Imagination and Social Criticism*, 11–12. See also Robert Bloch, "Imagination and Modern Social Criticism," in *The Science Fiction Novel: Imagination and Social Criticism*, ed. Davenport, 97–121.

14. Davenport, "Introduction" to *The Science Fiction Novel: Imagination and Social Criticism*, 11–12. Interestingly, Davenport claims that H. G. Wells was a writer of science fiction "utopias," citing Wells's *Men Like Gods* as an example. Against this it might be argued that *Men Like Gods* is neither a utopian text nor a work of science fiction. However, whatever the status of this particular text, generally speaking (as Zamyatin suggests in his essay on Wells) the science fiction tales which Wells wrote in the 1890s are best thought of as being "dystopian" rather than "utopian." For this see the appropriately titled work by Mark Hillegas, *The Future as Nightmare: H. G. Wells and the Anti-Utopians* (New York: Oxford University Press, 1967), 4–5, 17–20, 30–31, 34, 36–37, 47–48, 57.

15. Booker, "Introduction," in *The Dystopian Impulse in Modern Literature: Fiction as Social Criticism* (Westport, Conn.: Greenwood Press, 1994), 19.

16. Tom Moylan, *Scraps of the Untainted Sky: Science Fiction, Utopia, Dystopia* (Boulder, Colo.: Westview Press, 2000), 29. See also Frederick Pohl, "The Politics of Prophecy," in *Political Science Fiction*, eds. Donald M. Hassler and Clyde Wilcox (Columbia: University of South Carolina Press, 1997), 12–13: "The political affiliations of science fiction writers are as diverse as those of any random selection of Americans."

17. Csicsery-Ronay Jr., "Marxist Theory and Science Fiction," 119–20.

18. Tom Moylan, "The Locus of Hope: Utopia Versus Ideology," in *Utopia and Anti-Utopia*, Special Issue of *Science Fiction Studies* 9, no. 2 (1982), 163–65.

19. Moylan, "The Locus of Hope: Utopia Versus Ideology," 163–65.

20. Frederic Jameson, "World Reduction in Le Guin: The Emergence of Utopian Narrative," in *Science Fiction Studies: Selected Articles on Science Fiction 1973–1975*, eds. Mullen and Suvin, 275. This is reprinted in Frederic Jameson, *Archaeologies of the Future* without revisions. We may assume, therefore, that Jameson's assessment of Le Guin today (2008) is the same as it was thirty years ago.

21. Jameson, "World Reduction in Le Guin: The Emergence of Utopian Narrative," 275.

22. Jameson, "World Reduction in Le Guin: The Emergence of Utopian Narrative," 275.

23. Jameson, "World Reduction in Le Guin: The Emergence of Utopian Narrative," 275.

24. Nadia Khouri, "The Dialectics of Power: Utopia in the Science Fiction of Le Guin, Jeury and Piercy," *Science Fiction Studies*, 3, no. 1 (1980), 53.

25. Khouri, "The Dialectics of Power: Utopia in the Science Fiction of Le Guin, Jeury and Piercy," 53.

26. Tom Moylan, *Demand the Impossible: Science Fiction and the Utopian Imagination* (London: Methuen, 1986), 103.

27. Moylan, *Demand the Impossible*, 114, 120.

28. Moylan, *Demand the Impossible*, 114, 120.

29. Engels, Letter to Minna Kautsky, November, 1885, cited Steiner, "Marxism and the Literary Critic," 159. Terry Eagleton has noted, *Marxism and Literary Criticism* (London: Methuen, 1976), 44–45, that "Marx and Engels by no means

crudely equated the aesthetically fine with the politically correct," and that "the idea that art is in some sense an end in itself crops up even in Marx's mature work." According to Eagleton, the remarks made by Marx and Engels about art and aesthetics generally, and about literature in particular, are "rarely if ever accompanied by an insistence that literary works should be politically prescriptive." See also Alan Swingewood, *The Novel and Revolution,* 12; and Alan Swingewood, *The Sociology of Literature,* 47–48.

30. Engels, Letter to Margaret Harkness, April 1888, cited George Steiner, "Marxism and the Literary Critic," 159.

31. Freedman, *Critical Theory and Science Fiction,* 112.

32. Freedman, *Critical Theory and Science Fiction,* xvii.

33. Freedman, *Critical Theory and Science Fiction,* 114.

34. Freedman, *Critical Theory and Science Fiction,* 79–81.

35. Freedman, *Critical Theory and Science Fiction,* xviii.

36 Freedman, *Critical Theory and Science Fiction,* xviii. This claim overlooks the importance (even the very existence) of the influence of Hegel's "dialectical" philosophy on the history of anarchism. Freedman's suggestion (xviii, 122) that Le Guin's alleged radical vision and the "dialectical" outlook associated with it are to be associated with the works of Trotsky, especially the notion of "permanent revolution," seems to me to be misguided. For this idea is also to be found in the anarchist tradition which runs back through Zamyatin, to Nietzsche, to the Left Hegelianism of the 1840s. For a discussion of some of the similarities which exist between Le Guin's understanding of anarchism and Marxism see Tony Burns, "Marxism and Science Fiction: A Celebration of the Work of Ursula K. Le Guin." *Capital and Class,* 84 (2004): 141–51.

37. Freedman, *Critical Theory and Science Fiction,* 79–80, 86. For Lukács emphasis on the importance of "dialogue" for the historical novel in relation to its potential for presenting a critique of existing society, see Georg Lukács *The Historical Novel* (Harmondsworth: Penguin, 1976 [1936]), 30, 42.

38. For Freedman's appropriation of the ideas of Lukács see "The Critical Dynamic: Science Fiction and the Historical Novel," in *Critical Theory and Science Fiction,* 44–62.

39. Freedman, *Critical Theory and Science Fiction,* 54. For relevant passages from Lukács see *The Historical Novel,* 40, 57–58, 67–68. It should be noted that in these passages Lukács has a tendency to refer directly to Hegel's philosophy rather than Marx's social theory when discussing the extent to which the historical novel is relevant for a critique of existing society.

40. For the important suggestion that it is necessary to distinguish between two types of dystopian literature, namely, between dystopian texts which are "anti-utopian," and which, therefore, contain no utopian vision at all, and dystopian texts which *do* contain some kind of utopian vision if only implicitly, see Lyman Tower Sargent, "Utopia – The Problem of Definition," *Extrapolation,* 16 (1975), 138; Lyman Tower Sargent, "The Three Faces of Utopianism Revisited," *Utopian Studies,* 5, no. 1 (1994), 9; and Moylan, *Scraps of the Untainted Sky,* 72, 74, 122, 127, 133–35, 137–39, 155, 309, 312–13.

41. Lukács, *The Historical Novel,* 59.

42. Lukács, *The Historical Novel,* 32.

43. H. G. Wells, "Digression About the Novel," in *Henry James and H. G. Wells: A Record of Their Friendship, Their Debate on the Art of Fiction and Their Quarrel*, eds. Leon Edel and Gordon N. Ray (London: Rupert Hart Davis, 1958), 222.

44. Freedman, *Critical Theory and Science Fiction*, 127.

45. Freedman, *Critical Theory and Science Fiction*, 127.

46. Freedman, *Critical Theory and Science Fiction*, 127. Needless to say, the aesthetic in question is one endorsed by Hegel.

47. Freedman, *Critical Theory and Science Fiction*, 127.

48. See, for example, *Herbert Marcuse, One Dimensional Man: Studies in the Ideology of Advanced Industrial Society*, intro. Douglas Kellner (London: Routledge,1991 [1964]), 141–42; Robert J. Antonio, "Immanent Critique as the Core of Critical Theory: Its Origins and Developments in Hegel, Marx and Contemporary Thought," *The British Journal of Sociology*, 32, no. 3 (1981), 330–45; Andrew Buchwalter, "Hegel, Marx, and the Concept of Immanent Critique," *Journal of the History of Philosophy*, XXX, no. 2 (April 1991): 253–79; Steven Helmling, "Immanent Critique" and "Dialectical Mimesis" in Adorno and Horkheimer's *Dialectic of Enlightenment*," *Boundary 2*, 32, no. 3 (2005), 97–117.

49. Freedman, *Critical Theory and Science Fiction*, 112.

50. For "ethical Marxism" see Lawrence Wilde ed., *Marxism's Ethical Thinkers* (London: Palgrave, 2002), and Lawrence Wilde, *Ethical Marxism and Its Radical Critics* (London: Palgrave, 1998).

51. Ursula K. Le Guin, "Science Fiction and Mrs. Brown," *The Language of the Night: Essays on Fantasy and Science Fiction* (New York: Perigee, 1979), 116.

52. Ursula K. Le Guin, "American SF and the Other," *The Language of the Night*, 99.

53. Ursula K. Le Guin, "American SF and the Other," 99.

54. See Herbert Marcuse, *The Aesthetic Dimension: Toward a Critique of Marxist Aesthetics* (London: Macmillan, 1979).

55. Erich Fromm, *The Fear of Freedom* (London: Routledge, 2001 [1942]).

56. Ursula K. Le Guin, "Why are Americans Afraid of Dragons?" *The Language of the Night*, 46.

Bibliography

Abrams, M. H. "Hegel's 'Phenomenology of the Spirit': Metaphysical Structure and Narrative Plot." in Pp. 225–37 in *Natural Supernaturalism: Tradition and Revolution in Romantic Literature*. New York: Norton, 1971.

Adereth, Max. *Commitment in Modern French Literature: A Brief Study of "Littérature Engagée" in the Works of Péguy, Aragon and Sartre*. London: Victor Gollancz, 1967.

———. "What is *Littérature Engagée*"? Pp. 15–54 in *Commitment in Modern French Literature: A Brief Study of "Littérature Engagée" in the Works of Péguy, Aragon and Sartre*.

Aldridge, Alexandra. *The Scientific World View in Dystopia*. Ann Arbor, MI: UMI Research Press, 1984 [1978].

———. "Ambiguities in the Scientific World View: The Wellsian Legacy." Pp. 19–32 in *The Scientific World View in Dystopia*.

Antonio, Robert J. "Immanent Critique as the Core of Critical Theory: Its Origins and Developments in Hegel, Marx and Contemporary Thought." *The British Journal of Sociology*, 32, no. 3 (1981): 330–45.

Arblaster, Antony. "Literature and Moral Choice." Pp. 29–44 in Horton and Baumeister, eds., *Literature and the Political Imagination*.

Avineri, Shlomo. *Hegel's Theory of the Modern State*. Cambridge: Cambridge University Press, 1970.

Baccolini, Rafaella and Tom Moylan eds., *Dark Horizons: Science Fiction and the Dystopian Imagination*. London: Routledge, 2003.

Baier, Kurt. *The Moral Point of View: A Rational Basis of Ethics*. New York: Random House, 1966 [1958].

Bailey, J. O. *Pilgrims Through Space and Time: Trends and Patterns in Scientific and Utopian Fiction*. Westport, CT: Greenwood Press, 1972 [1947].

Bakunin, Mikhail. *Selected Writings*, ed. A. Lehning. London: Cape, 1973.

———. "The Reaction in Germany." Pp. 37–58 in *Selected Writings*, ed. A. Lehning.

Bakunin, Mikail. "From a Letter to Sergej Nechaev, June 2nd 1870." Pp. 182–94 in *Selected Writings*, ed. Lehning.

Ball, Terence. *Transforming Political Discourse*. Oxford: Blackwell, 1988.

Barbour, Douglas. "Wholeness and Balance: An Addendum." Pp. 146–55 in *Science Fiction Studies: Selected Articles on Science Fiction 1973–1975*, eds. R. D. Mullen and Darko Suvin.

Baring, Maurice. *Landmarks of Russian Literature*. London: Methuen, 1960 [1910].

Barr, Marleen, ed. *Women and Utopia: Critical Interpretations*. New York: University Press of America.

Baugh, Bruce. *French Hegel: From Surrealism to Poststructuralism*. London: Routledge, 2003.

Bauman, Zygmunt. *Postmodern Ethics*. Oxford: Blackwell, 1993.

———. *Life in Fragments: Essays in Postmodern Morality* (Oxford: Blackwell, 1995).

Beauchamp, Gordon. "Zamyatin's *We*." Pp. 56–77 in *No Place Else: Explorations in Utopian and Dystopian Fiction*, eds. Rabkin, Greenberg and Olander.

Benford, Gregory. "Reactionary Utopias." Pp. 73–83 in *Storm Warnings: Science Fiction Faces the Future*, eds. George E. Slusser, Colin Greenland, and Erik Rabkin.

Berlin, Isaiah. "Herzen and Bakunin on Individual Liberty. Pp. 82–113. in *Russian Thinkers* Harmondsworth: Penguin, 1979.

Berlin, Isaiah. *Karl Marx*. London: Home University Library, 1965.

Bernasconi, Robert. "What is the Question to Which 'Substitution' is the Answer?" Pp. 234–51 in *The Cambridge Companion to Levinas*, eds. Simon Critchley and Robert Bernasconi.

Berneri, Marie Louise. *A Journey Through Utopia*. London: Freedom Press, 1982 [1950].

Berthold-Bond, Daniel. *Hegel's Grand Synthesis*. New York: SUNY, 1989.

Bhaskar, Roy. *A Realist Theory of Science*. Sussex: Harvester Press, 1978 [1975].

Bierman, Judah. "Ambiguity in Utopia, *The Dispossessed*." Pp. 279–85 in *Science Fiction Studies: Selected Articles on Science Fiction 1973–1975*, eds. Mullen and Suvin.

Bittner, James W. *Approaches to the Fiction of Ursula K. Le Guin*. Ann Arbor, MI: UMI Press, 1984.

———. "Chronosophy, Aesthetics and Ethics, in Le Guin's *The Dispossessed: An Ambiguous Utopia*." Pp. 243–70 in *No Place Else: Explorations in Utopian and Dystopian Fiction*, eds. Rabkin, Greenberg, and Olander. *Ursula K. Le Guin: Voyager to Inner Lands and to Outer Space*, ed. De Bolt.

———. "A Survey of Le Guin Criticism." Pp. 31–49.

Bloch, Robert. "Imagination and Modern Social Criticism." Pp. 97–121 in *The Science Fiction Novel: Imagination and Social Criticism*, ed. Davenport.

Bloom, Harold, ed., *Ursula K. Le Guin*. New York: Chelsea House, 1985.

Blotner, Joseph L. *The Political Novel*. New York: Doubleday, 1955.

Booker, Keith. *The Dystopian Impulse in Modern Literature: Fiction as Social Criticism*.

———. "Introduction." Pp. 1–23 in *The Dystopian Impulse in Modern Literature: Fiction as Social Criticism*.

———. "Zamyatin's *We*: Anticipating Stalin." Pp. 25–46 in *The Dystopian Impulse in Modern Literature: Fiction as Social Criticism*.

——. "Introduction." Pp. 1–23 in *The Dystopian Impulse in Modern Literature: Fiction as Social Criticism.*

Bradley, A. C. "Hegel's Theory of Tragedy". Pp. 367–88 in *Hegel on Tragedy*, eds. Paolucci and Paolucci.

Brennan, John P., and Michael C. Downs. "Anarchism and Utopian Tradition in *The Dispossessed*." Pp. 116–52 in *Ursula K. Le Guin*, eds. Joseph Olander and Martin Harry Greenberg.

Brigg, Peter. "The Archetype of the Journey in Ursula K. Le Guin's Fiction." Pp. 36–63 in *Ursula K. Le Guin*, eds. Joseph Olander and Martin Harry Greenberg.

Broderick, Damien. *Reading by Starlight: Postmodern Science Fiction*. London: Routledge, 1995.

Brown, E. J. "The Legacy of H. G. Wells." Pp. 46–53 in *Brave New World, 1984 and We: An Essay on Anti–Utopia*. Ann Arbor, MI: Ardis, 1976.

Browning, Gary, ed. *Hegel's Phenomenology of Spirit: A Reappraisal*. Dordrecht: Kluwer, 1997.

Buchwalter, Andrew. "Hegel, Marx, and the Concept of Immanent Critique." *Journal of the History of Philosophy*, XXIX, no. 2 (April 1991), 253–79.

Bucknall, Barbara. J. *Ursula K. Le Guin*. New York: Ungar, 1981.

Burns, Elizabeth, and Tom Burns, eds. *Sociology of Literature and Drama*. Harmondsworth, UK: Penguin, 1973.

Burns, Tony. "Hegel and Anarchism." Paper presented at the annual meeting of the Political Studies Association of Great Britain, University of Bath, UK, 11–13 April 2007.

——. "Yevgeny Zamyatin and the Science Fiction of Ursula K. Le Guin." Paper presented to the "Anarchism and Utopia" panel at the annual conference of the Utopian Studies Society (Europe), University of Tarragona, Spain, 6–8 July, 2006.

——. "Hegel, Identity Politics and the Problem of Slavery." *Culture, Theory and Critique*, 47, 1 (2006): 87–104.

——. "Science and Politics in *The Dispossessed*: Le Guin and the 'Science Wars.'" Pp. 195–215 in *The New Utopian Politics of Ursula K. Le Guin's* The Dispossessed, eds. Laurence Davis and Peter Stillman, 2005.

——. "Hegel." Pp. 45–58 in *Palgrave Advances in Continental Political Thought*, eds. Terrell Carver and James Martin. London: Palgrave, 2005.

——. "Whose Aristotle? Which Marx? Ethics, Law and Justice in Aristotle and Marx." *Imprints: Egalitarian Theory and Practice*, 8, no. 2 (2005): 125–55.

——. "The *Iliad* and the 'Struggle for Recognition' in Hegel's *Phenomenology of Spirit*." Paper presented to the "Art, Aesthetics and Politics" panel at the Workshops in Political Theory – Second Annual Conference, Manchester Metropolitan University, 7–9 September 2005.

——. "Aristotle and the *Nomos* Versus *Physis* Debate in Ancient Greek Political Thought." Paper presented to a panel on Ancient Greek Political Thought at the Annual Conference of the American Northeastern Political Science Association, Philadelphia, PA, United States, 17–19 November, 2005.

——. "Marxism and Science Fiction: A Celebration of the Work of Ursula K. Le Guin." *Capital and Class*, 84 (2004): 141–51.

——. "Aristotle." Pp. 73–91 in *Political Thinkers: From Socrates to the Present*, eds. David Boucher and Paul Kelly. Oxford: Oxford University Press, 2003.

——. "Sophocles' *Antigone* and the History of the Concept of Natural Law." *Political Studies*, 50, 3 (2002): 545–57.

——. "Hegel (1770–1831)." Pp. 162–79 in *Interpreting Modern Political Philosophy from Machiavelli to Marx*, eds. Alastair Edwards and Jules Townshend. London: Palgrave, 2002.

——. "Karl Kautsky: Ethics and Marxism." Pp. 15–50 in *Marxism's Ethical Thinkers*, ed. Lawrence Wilde. London: Macmillan, 2001.

——. "Zamyatin's *We* and Postmodernism." *Utopian Studies*, 11, no. 1 (2000): 66–90.

——. "The Purloined Hegel: Semiology in the Thought of Saussure and Derrida." *The History of the Human Sciences*, 13, 4 (2000): 1–24.

——. "John Gray and the Death of Conservatism." *Contemporary Politics*, 5, no. 1 (1999): 7–24.

——. "Aristotle and Natural Law." *History of Political Thought*, XIX, no. 3 (1998): 142–66.

——. "Metaphysics and Politics in Aristotle and Hegel." Pp. 387–99 in *Contemporary Political Studies: 1998*, Vol. 1, eds. A. Dobson and G. Stanyer. The Political Studies Association of Great Britain, 1998.

——. "Hegel's Interpretation of the Philosophy of Heraclitus: Some Observations." Pp. 228–39 in *Contemporary Political Studies: 1997*, Vol. I, eds. G. Stoker and J. Stanyer. The Political Studies Association of Great Britain, 1997.

——. *Natural Law and Political Ideology in the Philosophy of Hegel*. Aldershot: Ashgate, 1996.

——. "The Ideological Location of Hegel's Political Thought." Pp. 1301–08 in *Contemporary Political Studies: 1995*, Vol. 3, eds. J. Lovenduski and J. Stanyer. The Political Studies Association of Great Britain, 1995.

Burns, Tony, and Ian Fraser, eds. *The Hegel–Marx Connection*. London: Palgrave–Macmillan, 2000.

——. "Introduction: An Historical Survey of the Hegel–Marx Connection." Pp. 1–33 in *The Hegel–Marx Connection*, eds. Tony Burns and Ian Fraser.

Burton, Deirdre. "Linguistic Innovation in Feminist Utopian Fiction." *Journal of English Language and Literature*, 29, no. 1 (1983): 31–54.

Butler, Andrew M. "Postmodernism and Science Fiction." Pp. 137–48 in *The Cambridge Companion to Science Fiction*, eds. James and Mendelsohn.

Butler, Judith. *Subjects of Desire: Hegelian Reflections in Twentieth Century France*. New York: Columbia University Press, 1999 [1987].

Call, Lewis. "Postmodern Anarchism in the Novels of Ursula K. Le Guin," *SubStance* 36, no. 2 (2007): 87–105.

Call, Lewis. *Postmodern Anarchism*. Lanham, MD: Lexington Books, 2002.

Carr, E. H. "Ethics and Politics: *The Devils*." Pp. 169–82 in *Dostoevsky: 1821–1881*. London: Unwin Books, 1962 [1931].

Carver, Terrell. *The Postmodern Marx*. Penn State University Press, 1999.

Challier, Catherine. *What Ought I to Do? Morality in Kant and Levinas*. Ithaca, NY, and London: Cornell University Press, 2001.

Clute, John. "Science Fiction from 1980 to the Present." Pp. 64–78 in *The Cambridge Companion to Science Fiction*, eds. Edward James and Farah Mendelsohn. Cambridge: Cambridge University Press, 2003.

Cogell, Wayne. "The Absurdity of Sartre's Ontology." Pp. 143–51 in *Philosophers Look at Science Fiction*, ed. Nicholas Smith. Chicago: Nelson Hall, 1982.

Cogell Cummins, Elizabeth. "Taoist Configurations: *The Dispossessed.*" Pp. 153–79 in *Ursula K. Le Guin: Voyager to Inner Lands and to Outer Space*, ed. Joe de Bolt.

Colletti, Lucio. *Marxism and Hegel*. London: Verso Books, 1973.

———. "Hegel and the 'Theory of Reflection.'" Pp. 52–67 in *Marxism and Hegel*.

Collins, Christopher. "Zamyatin, Wells and the Utopian Literary Tradition." *Slavonic and East European Review*, 44 (1966): 351–60.

Critchley, Simon. *Infinitely Demanding: Ethics of Commitment, Politics of Resistance*. London: Verso, 2007.

———. *Ethics–Politics–Subjectivity: Essays on Derrida, Levinas and Contemporary French Thought*. London: Verso, 1999.

———. *The Ethics of Deconstruction: Derrida and Levinas*, 2nd ed. Oxford: Blackwell, 1999 [1992].

Critchley, Simon, and Robert Bernasconi, eds. *The Cambridge Companion to Levinas*. Cambridge: Cambridge University Press, 2002.

Csicsery-Ronay Jr., Istvan. "Marxist Theory and Science Fiction." Pp. 113–24 in *The Cambridge Companion to Science Fiction*, eds. James and Mendelsohn.

———. "Science Fiction and Postmodernism." *Science Fiction Studies*, 18, no. 3 (1991): 305–08.

Crow, John H., and Richard D. Erlich. "Words of Binding: Patterns of Integration in the Earthsea Trilogy." Pp. 200–24 in Olander and Greenberg eds., *Ursula K. Le Guin*.

Curtis, Claire. "Ambiguous Choices: Skepticism as a Grounding for Utopia." Pp. 265–82 in *The New Utopian Politics of Ursula K. Le Guin's* The Dispossessed, eds. Davis and Stillman.

Davenport, Basil, ed. *The Science Fiction Novel: Imagination and Social Criticism*. Chicago: Advent, 1969 [1959].

———. "Introduction." Pp. 7–13 in *The Science Fiction Novel: Imagination and Social Criticism*.

Davis, Laurence, and Peter Stillman, eds. *The New Utopian Politics of Ursula K. Le Guin's* The Dispossessed. Lanham, MD: Lexington Books, 2005.

Davis, Laurence. "The Dynamic and Revolutionary Utopia of Ursula K. Le Guin." Pp. 3–36 in *The New Utopian Politics of Ursula K. Le Guin's* The Dispossessed, eds. Davis and Stillman.

de Beauvoir, Simone. *The Ethics of Ambiguity*. New York: Citadel Press, 1962 [1948].

de Bolt, Joseph. ed. *Ursula K. Le Guin: Voyager to Inner Lands and to Outer Space*. New York: Kennikat Press, 1979.

Deery, June. "H. G. Wells's *A Modern Utopia* as a Work in Progress." Pp. 26–42 in *Political Science Fiction*, eds. Donald M. Hassler and Clyde Wilcox. Columbia, SC: University of South Carolina Press, 1997.

Delany, Samuel R. *The Jewel-Hinged Jaw*. New York: Dragon Press, 1977.

———. "To Read *The Dispossessed*." Pp. 239–308 in *The Jewel-Hinged Jaw*.

Derrida, Jacques. *Positions*, trans. Alan Bass (Chicago: University of Chicago Press, 1981), 77–78.

———. *Writing and Difference*. London: Routledge, 1993 [1967].

———. "Violence and Metaphysics: An Essay on the Thought of Emmanuel Levinas." Pp. 79–153 in *Writing and Difference*.

Dickson, Lovat. *H. G. Wells: His Turbulent Life and Times*. London: Macmillan, 1971.

Disch, Thomas M. "Can Girls Play Too? Feminizing SF." Pp. 115–36 in *The Dreams Our Stuff Is Made Of: How Science Fiction Conquered the World*. New York and London: Touchstone Books, 2000 [1998].

Dolman, Everett Carl. "Military, Democracy and the State in R. A. Heinlein's *Starship Troopers*." Pp. 196–213 in Donald M. Hassler and Clyde Wilcox, eds. *Political Science Fiction*.

Donawerth, Jane, and Carol A. Kolmerten, eds. *Utopian and Science Fiction by Women: Worlds of Difference*. New York: Syracuse University Press, 1994.

Dostoevsky, Fyodor. *Notes from the Underground*, trans. Jessie Coulson. Harmondsworth: Penguin, 1973.

———. *The Devils* [*The Possessed*], trans. David Magarshack. Harmondsworth: Penguin, 1973.

Dourley, John. *The Illness That We Are: A Jungian Critique of Christianity*. London: Inner City Books, 1984.

Dudley, Will. *Hegel, Nietzsche and Philosophy: Thinking Freedom*. New York: Cambridge University Press, 2002.

Eagleton, Terry. *Marxism and Literary Criticism*. London: Methuen, 1976.

Easterbrook, Neil. "State, Heterotopia: The Political Imagination in Heinlein, Le Guin and Delany." Pp. 43–75 in *Political Science Fiction*, eds. Donald Hassler and Clyde Wilcox.

Edel, Leon, and Gordon N. Ray, eds. *Henry James and H. G. Wells: A Record of Their Friendship, Their Debate on the Art of Fiction and Their Quarrel*. London: Rupert Hart Davis, 1958.

Elliott, Robert C. *The Shape of Utopia: Studies in a Literary Genre*. Chicago: University of Chicago Press, 1970.

———. "The Aesthetics of Utopia." Pp. 102–28 in *The Shape of Utopia*.

Elliott, Winter. "Breaching Invisible Walls: Individual Anarchy in *The Dispossessed*." Pp. 149–66 in Davis and Stillman, eds. *The New Utopian Politics of Ursula K. Le Guin's* The Dispossessed.

Ellis-Fermor, Una. *The Frontiers of Drama*. London: Methuen, 1945.

Engels, Frederick. *Ludwig Feuerbach and the End of Classical German Philosophy*. Pp. 358–402 in Marx and Engels, *Selected Writings*, Vol. II.

Esmonde, Margaret "The Master Pattern: The Psychological Journey in the *Earthsea Trilogy*." Pp. 15–35 in *Ursula K. Le Guin*, eds. Olander and Greenberg.

Euben, Peter J. *The Tragedy of Political Theory: The Road not Taken*. Princeton: Princeton University Press, 1990.

Euben, Peter J., ed. *Greek Tragedy and Political Theory*. Berkeley and Los Angeles, CA: University of California Press, 1988.

Farrell Fox, Nik. *The New Sartre: Explorations in Postmodernism*. New York and London: Continuum Books, 2003.

———. "Sartre: Un Homme Postmoderne?" Pp. 149–62 in *The New Sartre: Explorations in Postmodernism*.

Feenberg, Andrew. *Transforming Technology: A Critical Theory Revisited*. Oxford: Oxford University Press, 2002.

———. *Critical Theory of Technology*. Oxford: Oxford University Press, 1991.

Fekete, John. "Circumnavigating Ursula Le Guin: Literary Criticism and Approaches to Landing: A Review of Joseph de Bolt, *Ursula K. Le Guin: Voyager to Inner Lands and to Outer Space*," *Science Fiction Studies*, 8, no. 1 (1981): 91–98.

Ferns. Chris. "Future Conditional or Future Perfect? *The Dispossessed* and Permanent Revolution." Pp. 249–62 in *The New Utopian Politics of Ursula K. Le Guin's* The Dispossessed, eds. Davis and Stillman.

Fischer, Ernst. *The Necessity of Art: A Marxist Approach*. Harmondsworth: Penguin Books, 1970 [1959].

Fitting, Peter. "Positioning and Closure: On the 'Reading Effect' of Contemporary Utopian Fiction, *Utopian Studies*, I (1987): 23–36.

Fleck, Leonard M. "Science Fiction as a Tool of Speculative Philosophy: A Philosophical Analysis of Selected Anarchistic and Utopian Themes in Le Guin's *The Dispossessed*." Pp.135–45 in *Selected Proceedings of the 1978 Science Fiction Research Association National Conference*, ed. Thomas J. Remington. Cedar Falls, IA: University of Iowa Press, 1979.

Forster, E. M. *Aspects of the Novel*. Harmondsworth, UK: Penguin, 1963 [1927].

Franko, Carol S. "The I–We Dilemma and a 'Utopian Unconscious' in Wells' *When the Sleeper Awakes* and Le Guin's *The Lathe of Heaven*." Pp. 76–08 in *Political Science Fiction*, eds. Hassler and Wilcox.

Freedman, Carl. *Critical Theory and Science Fiction*. Hanover and London: Wesleyan University Press, 2000.

———. "The Critical Dynamic: Science Fiction and the Historical Novel." Pp. 44–62 in *Critical Theory and Science Fiction*.

———. "Science Fiction and Utopia: A Historico-Philosophical Overview." Pp. 72–97 in *Learning from Other Worlds: Estrangement, Cognition and the Politics of Science Fiction and Utopia*, ed. Patrick Parrinder.

———. "*The Dispossessed*: Ursula Le Guin and the Ambiguities of Utopia." Pp. 111–28 in *Critical Theory and Science Fiction*.

Frege, Gottlöb. "On Sense and Reference." Pp. 56–78 in *Translations from the Philosophical Writings of Gottlöb Frege*, trans. Peter Geach and Max Black. Oxford: Basil Blackwell, 1977.

Fromm, Erich. *The Fear of Freedom*. London: Routledge. 2001 [1942].

———. *To Have or to Be*. London: Abacus Books, 1979 [1976].

Fry, Christopher. *Sartre and Hegel: The Variations of an Enigma in "L'Être et le néant."* Bonn: Bouvier, 1988.

Geoghegan, Vincent. *Utopianism and Marxism*. London: Methuen, 1987.

Gerber, Richard. *Utopian Fantasy: A Study of English Utopian Fiction Since the End of the Nineteenth Century*. London: Routledge, 1973 [1955].

Gibson, Andrew. *Postmodernity, Ethics and the Novel: From Leavis to Levinas*. Routledge, 1999.

Gilligan, Carol. *In a Different Voice: Psychological Theory and Women's Development*. Cambridge, MA: Harvard University Press, 1982.

Greenberg, Martin Harry, and Joseph D. Olander, eds. *International Relations Through Science Fiction*. New York and London: Franklin Watts, 1978.

Gregg, Richard A. "Two Adams and Eve in the Crystal Palace: Dostoevsky, the *Bible* and *We*." Pp. 202–08 in *Major Soviet Writers: Essays in Criticism*, ed. Edward J. Brown. New York: Oxford University Press, 1973.

Gribbin, John. *In Search of Schrödinger's Cat: Quantum Physics and Reality*. New York: Bantam Books, 1988.

Gribbin, John. *Schrödinger's Kittens and the Search for Reality*. London: Phoenix Books, 1995.

Habermas, Jurgen. *Between Facts and Norms: Contributions to a Discourse Theory of Law and Democracy*. Cambridge: Polity Press, 1996.

———. *Justification and Application: Remarks on Discourse Ethics*. Cambridge: Polity Press, 1993.

———. "On the Pragmatic, the Ethical and the Moral Employments of Practical Reason." Pp. 1–18 in *Justification and Application: Remarks on Discourse Ethics*.

———. "Remarks on Discourse Ethics." Pp. 19–111 in *Justification and Application: Remarks on Discourse Ethics*.

———. "Technical Progress and the Social Life-World." Pp. 50–61 in *Toward a Rational Society*. Boston: Beacon Press, 1970 [1968].

———. "The Scientization of Politics and Public Opinion." Pp. 62–80 in *Toward a Rational Society*. Boston: Beacon Press, 1970 [1968].

———. "Technology and Science as 'Ideology.'" Pp. 81–122 in *Toward a Rational Society*. Boston: Beacon Press, 1970 [1968].

Hamner, Everett L. "The Gap in the Wall: Partnership, Physics and Politics in *The Dispossessed*." Pp. 219–32 in *The New Utopian Politics of Ursula K. Le Guin's* The Dispossessed, eds. Davis and Stillman.

Hansot, Elizabeth. "H. G. Wells' *A Modern Utopia*." Pp. 147–58 in *Perfection and Progress: Two Modes of Utopian Thought*. Cambridge, MA: MIT Press, 1974.

Hare, R. M. *The Language of Morals*. Oxford: Oxford University Press, 1991 [1952].

———. *Freedom and Reason*. Oxford: Oxford University Press, 1990 [1963].

Harris, H. S. "Hegel's Correspondence Theory of Truth." Pp. 11–22 in *Hegel's Phenomenology of Spirit: A Reappraisal*, ed. Browning.

Hassler, Donald M., and Clyde Wilcox, eds., *Political Science Fiction*. Columbia, SC: University of South Carolina Press, 1997.

Hayles, N. B. "Androgyny, Ambivalence, and Assimilation, in *The Left Hand of Darkness*." Pp. 97–115 in *Ursula K. Le Guin*, eds. Joseph Olander and Martin Harry Greenberg.

Hegel, G. W. F. *Philosophy of Right*, trans. T. M. Knox. Oxford: Oxford University Press, 1979.

———. *Phenomenology of Spirit*, trans. A. V. Miller. Oxford: Oxford University Press, 1977.

———. *Hegel's Philosophy of Mind: Being Part Three of the Encyclopaedia of the Philosophical Sciences*, trans. William Wallace and A. V. Miller. Oxford: Oxford University Press, 1971.

———. *Hegel on Tragedy*, eds. Anne Paolucci and Henry Paolucci. New York: Doubleday, 1962.

Heinlein, Robert A. *Starship Troopers*. New York: Ace, 1987 [1958].

Held, David. *Introduction to Critical Theory: Horkheimer to Habermas*. Cambridge: Polity Press, 1990.

Helmling, Steven. "'Immanent Critique' and 'Dialectical Mimesis' in Adorno and Horkheimer's *Dialectic of Enlightenment.*" *Boundary 2*, 32, no. 3 (2005): 97–117.

Hexter, J. H. "Intention, Words and Meaning: The Case of More's *Utopia*," *New Literary History*, 6, 3, (1975): 529–41.

Hillegas, Mark. R. *The Future as Nightmare: H. G. Wells and the Anti-Utopians.* New York: Oxford University Press, 1967.

Hoffman, Gerhard, and Alfred Hornung, eds. *Ethics and Aesthetics: The Moral Turn of Postmodernism.* Heidelberg, Germany: Universitätsverlag, 1996.

Hollinger, Veronica. "Feminist Theory and Science Fiction." Pp. 125–36 in *The Cambridge Companion to Science Fiction*, eds. Edward James and Farah Mendelsohn. Cambridge: Cambridge University Press, 2003.

Hook, Sidney. *From Hegel to Marx: Studies in the Intellectual Development of Karl Marx.* New York: Humanities Press, 1958.

Houlgate, Stephen. *Hegel, Nietzsche and the Criticism of Metaphysics.* Cambridge: Cambridge University Press, 1986.

Horton, John, and Andrea Baumeister, eds., *Literature and the Political Imagination* London: Routledge, 1996.

Howe, Irving. *Politics and the Novel.* London: New Left Books, 1961.

———. "The Idea of the Political Novel." Pp. 15–24 in *Politics and the Novel.*

Hughes, David Y. "The Mood of *A Modern Utopia.*" *Extrapolation* 19 (1977): 59–67.

Huntington, John. *The Logic of Fantasy: H. G. Wells and Science Fiction.* New York: Columbia University Press, 1982.

———. "Thinking by Opposition." Pp. 21–40 in *The Logic of Fantasy: H. G. Wells and Science Fiction.*

———. "The Logical Web." Pp. 57–84 in *The Logic of Fantasy: H. G. Wells and Science Fiction.*

———. "The Dreams of Reason." Pp. 109–38 in *The Logic of Fantasy: H. G. Wells and Science Fiction.*

———. "Utopian and Anti-Utopian Logic." Pp. 139–70 in *The Logic of Fantasy: H. G. Wells and Science Fiction.*

———. "Anti-Utopia in Wells' *A Modern Utopia.*" Pp. 167–70 in *The Logic of Fantasy: H. G. Wells and Science Fiction.*

———. "Utopian and Anti-Utopian Logic: H. G. Wells and his Successors." *Science Fiction Studies*, 21 (1982): 122–46.

———. "Public and Private Imperatives in Le Guin's Novels." Pp. 267–72 in *Science Fiction Studies: Selected Articles on Science Fiction 1973–1975*, eds. Mullen and Suvin.

Inwood, Michael. *A Hegel Dictionary.* Oxford: Blackwell, 1992.

Jacobs, Naomi. "The Frozen Landscape in Women's Utopian and Science Fiction." Pp. 190–204 in *Utopian and Science Fiction by Women: Worlds of Difference*, eds. Jane L. Donawerth and Carol A. Kolmerten.

———. "Beyond Stasis and Symmetry: Lessing, Le Guin, and the Remodeling of Utopia." *Extrapolation*, 29, no. 1 (Spring 1988): 34–45.

Jackson, R. L., *Dostoevsky's Underground Man in Russian Literature.* Mouton: The Hague, 1958.

James, Edward. "Utopias and Anti-Utopias." Pp. 219–29 in *The Cambridge Companion to Science Fiction*, eds. James and Mendelsohn.

James, Edward, and Farah Mendelsohn, eds. *The Cambridge Companion to Science Fiction*. Cambridge: Cambridge University Press, 2003.

Jameson, Frederic. *Archaeologies of the Future: The Desire Called Utopia and Other Science Fictions* (London: Verso, 2005).

———. "The Utopian Enclave." Pp. 10–21 in *Archaeologies of the Future*.

———. "How to Fulfill a Wish." Pp. 72–84 in *Archaeologies of the Future: The Desire Called Utopia and Other Science Fictions*.

———. "Synthesis, Irony, Neutralization and the Moment of Truth." Pp. 170–81 in *Archaeologies of the Future*.

———. "Journey into Fear. Pp. 182–210 in *Archaeologies of the Future*.

———. "World Reduction in Le Guin." Pp. 251–60 in *Archaeologies of the Future: The Desire Called Utopia and Other Science Fictions*.

———. *Marxism and Form: Twentieth Century Dialectical Theories of Literature* (Princeton: Princeton University Press, 1974 [1971]).

———. "The Case for Georg Lukács." Pp. 160–205 in *Marxism and Form: Twentieth Century Dialectical Theories of Literature*.

Jay, Martin. *The Dialectical Imagination: A History of the Frankfurt School and the Institute of Social Research, 1923–1950*. Berkeley: University of California Press, 1996.

Jones, Gwyneth. *Deconstructing the Starships: Science, Fiction and Reality*. Liverpool, UK: Liverpool University Press, 1999.

———. "In the Chinks of the World Machine: Sarah Lefanu on Feminist SF." Pp. 123–30 in *Deconstructing the Starships: Science, Fiction and Reality*.

———. "No Man's Land: Feminized Landscapes in the Utopian Fiction of Ursula Le Guin." Pp. 199–208 in *Deconstructing the Starships: Science, Fiction and Reality*.

Jung, C. G. "The Phenomenology of the Spirit in Fairy Tales." Pp. 83–132 in *Four Archetypes: Mother, Rebirth, Spirit, Trickster*. London: Ark Paperbacks, 1989.

Jurist, Elliott. *Beyond Hegel and Nietzsche: Philosophy, Culture and Agency*. Cambridge, MA: MIT Press, 2000.

Kateb, George. *Utopia and Its Enemies*. New York: Schocken Books, 1972 [1963].

———, ed. *Utopia*. New York: Atherton Press, 1971.

———. "Introduction." Pp. 1–20 in *Utopia*, ed. George Kateb.

Kaufmann, Walter. *Nietzsche: Philosopher, Psychologist, Antichrist*. Princeton: Princeton University Press, 1974 [1950].

———. "Hegel's Ideas About Tragedy." Pp. 201–29 in *New Studies in Hegel's Philosophy*, ed. Warren E. Steinkraus.

Kellner, Douglas. *Critical Theory, Marxism and Modernity*. Cambridge: Polity, 1989.

———. *Herbert Marcuse and the Crisis of Marxism*. London: Macmillan, 1984.

Kelly, George Armstrong. "Notes on Hegel's 'Lordship and Bondage.'" Pp. 196–203 in *Hegel: A Collection of Critical Essays*, ed. Alasdair MacIntyre.

Kelly, Michael. *Hegel in France*. Birmingham: Birmingham Modern Languages Publications, 1992.

Kelly, Sean M. *Individuation and the Absolute: Hegel, Jung, and the Path Toward Wholeness*. New York: Paulist Press, 1993.

Khouri, Nadia. "The Dialectics of Power: Utopia in the Science Fiction of Le Guin, Jeury and Piercy," *Science Fiction Studies*, 7 (1980): 49–61.

Klein, George. "'Nietzschean Marxism' in Russia." Pp. 166–83 in *Demythologizing Marxism*, ed. Frederick J. Adelman. The Hague: Martinus Nijhof, 1969.

———. "Nietzschean Marxism in Russia." *Boston College Studies in Philosophy*, 2, (1969): 166–83.

———. "The Nietzschean Marxism of Stanisklav Volsky." Pp. 177–95 in *Western Philosophical Systems in Russian Literature: A Collection of Critical Studies*, ed. Anthony M. Mlikotin. Los Angeles: University of Southern California Press, 1979.

———."Foreword." Pp. ix–xvi in Bernice Glatzer Rosenthal, *Nietzsche in Russia*.

Klein, Gerard. "Le Guin's 'Aberrant' Opus: Escaping the Trap of Discontent." Pp. 85–97 in *Ursula K. Le Guin*, ed. Bloom.

Kline, George. "The Existentialist Rediscovery of Hegel and Marx." Pp. 284–314 in *Sartre: A Collection of Critical Essays*, ed. Mary Warnock.

Knapp, Shoshona. "'The Morality of Creation.' Dostoevsky and William James in Le Guin's 'Omelas.'" *Journal of Narrative Technique*, 15, 1 (1985): 75–81.

Koper, Peter T. "Science and Rhetoric in the Fiction of Ursula Le Guin." Pp. 66–88 in *Ursula K. Le Guin: Voyager to Inner Lands and Outer Space*, ed. Joseph de Bolt.

Kornbluth, C. M. "The Failure of Science Fiction as Social Criticism." Pp. 49–76 in *The Science Fiction Novel: Imagination and Social Criticism*, ed. Basil Davenport.

Kuhn, T. S. *The Structure of Scientific Revolutions*, 2nd ed. Chicago: University of Chicago Press, 1970 [1962].

Kumar, Krishan. *Utopianism*. Milton Keynes: Open University Press, 1991.

———. *Utopia and Anti-Utopia in Modern Times*. Oxford: Blackwell, 1991 [1987].

———. "Science and Utopia: H. G. Wells and *A Modern Utopia*." Pp. 168–223 in *Utopia and Anti-Utopia in Modern Times*.

———. "A Book Remembered: A Modern Utopia." *New Universities Quarterly*, 36 (1982): 3–12.

Lacan, Jacques. *The Language of the Self: The Function of Language in Psychoanalysis*, ed. Anthony Wilden. Baltimore: John Hopkins University Press, 1981 [1968].

Lao Tzu, *Tao Te Ching: A Book About the Way and the Power of the Way*, a new English version, ed. Ursula K. Le Guin. Boston and London: Shambhala Books, 1998.

Lasseter, Rollin A. "Four Letters About Le Guin. Pp. 89–114 in *Ursula K. Le Guin*, ed. De Bolt.

Le Guin, Ursula K. "Head Cases: A Review of Jeanette Winterson's *The Stone Gods*." *The Guardian*, Saturday, 22nd September, 2007.

———. "A Response, by Ansible, from Tau Ceti." Pp. 305–08 in *The New Utopian Politics of Ursula K. Le Guin's The Dispossessed*, eds. Davis and Stillman. Lanham, MD: Lexington Books, 2005.

———. *The Earthsea Quartet*. Harmondsworth, UK: Penguin Books, 1993.

———. *A Wizard of Earthsea*. Pp. 9–168 in *The Earthsea Quartet*. Harmondsworth, UK: Penguin Books, 1993 [1968].

———. *The Tombs of Atuan*. Pp. 169–300 in *The Earthsea Quartet*. Harmondsworth, UK: Penguin Books, 1993 [1972].

———. *The Farthest Shore*. Pp. 301–478 in *The Earthsea Quartet*. Harmondsworth, UK: Penguin Books, 1993 [1973].

———. *The Left Hand of Darkness*. London: MacDonald, 1991 [1969].

———. *Dancing at the Edge of the World: Thoughts on Words, Women, Places*. New York: Harper and Row, 1989.

——. "Moral and Ethical Implications of Family Planning." Pp. 17–20 in *Dancing at the Edge of the World*.

——. "A Non-Euclidean View of California as a Cold Place to Be." Pp. 80–100 in *Dancing at the Edge of the World: Thoughts on Words, Women, Places*.

——. *Always Coming Home*. London: Grafton Books, 1988.

——. *The Lathe of Heaven*. London: Granada Books, 1984 [1971].

——. *The Dispossessed: An Ambiguous Utopia*. London: Granada Books, 1983 [1974].

——. *The Language of the Night: Essays on Fantasy and Science Fiction*, ed. Susan Wood. New York: Perigee Books, 1979.

——. "Why are Americans Afraid of Dragons?" Pp. 39–46 in *The Language of the Night*.

——. "Dreams Must Explain Themselves." Pp. 47–56 in *The Language of the Night*.

——. "The Child and the Shadow." Pp. 59–72 in *The Language of the Night*.

——. "Myth and Archetype in Science Fiction." Pp. 73–82 in *The Language of the Night*.

——. "American SF and the Other." Pp. 97–100 in *The Language of the Night*.

——. "Science Fiction and Mrs. Brown." Pp. 104–26 in *The Language of the Night*.

——. "Introduction to Planet of Exile." Pp. 139–44 in *The Language of the Night*.

——. "Introduction" to *The Word for World is Forest*." Pp. 149–54 in *The Language of the Night*.

——. "Introduction to *The Left Hand of Darkness*." Pp. 155–59 in *The Language of the Night*.

——. "Is Gender Necessary?" Pp. 161–69 in *The Language of the Night*.

——. "The Staring Eye." Pp. 171–74 in *The Language of the Night*.

——. "Escape Routes." Pp. 201–06 in *The Language of the Night*.

——. "The Stalin in the Soul" Pp. 211–21 in *The Language of the Night*.

——. "The Stone Ax and the Muskoxen." Pp. 223–36 in *The Language of the Night*.

——. *The Wind's Twelve Quarters*, Vol. 2. London, Granada, 1980 [1975].

——. "The Stars Below." Pp. 60–81 in *The Wind's Twelve Quarters*, Vol. 2.

——. "The Ones Who Walk Away from Omelas." Pp. 112–20 in *The Wind's Twelve Quarters*, Vol 2.

——. "The Day Before the Revolution." Pp. 121–38 in *The Wind's Twelve Quarters*, Vol 2.

——. *The Wind's Twelve Quarters*, Vol 1. London: Granada, 1978 [1969].

——. "A Trip to the Head." Pp. 18–24 *The Wind's Twelve Quarters*, Vol. I.

——. "April in Paris." Pp. 31–45 in *The Wind's Twelve Quarters*, Vol. I.

——. "The Masters." Pp. 46–63 in *The Wind's Twelve Quarters*, Vol. 1.

——. "The Rule of Names." Pp. 82–93 in *The Wind's Twelve Quarters*, Vol. I.

——. "Nine Lives." Pp. 128–57 in *The Wind's Twelve Quarters*, Vol. 1.

——. "A Response to the Le Guin Issue." *Science Fiction Studies*, 3 no. 8 (1976): 43–46.

——. *Dreams Must Explain Themselves*. New York: Algol Press, 1975.

——. "European SF: Rottensteiner's Anthology, the Strugatskys, and Lem." *Science Fiction Studies*, 1 no. 3 (1974): 181–85.

——. "Schrödinger's Cat." Pp. 26–34 in *Universe 5*, ed. Terry Carr. New York: Random House, 1974.

——. "Surveying the Battlefield." *Science Fiction Studies*, 1, no. 2 (1973): 88–90.

——. "On Norman Spinrad's *The Iron Dream*." *Science Fiction Studies*, 1, no. 1 (1973): 41–44.

Lem, Stanislaw. *Solaris*. Trans. Joanna Kilmartin and Steve Cox. London: Faber and Faber, 2003 [1961].

——. *Microworlds: Writings on Science Fiction and Fantasy*. New York: Harcourt Brace, 1984.

——. "Cosmology and Science Fiction." Pp. 200–08 in *Microworlds: Writings on Science Fiction and Fantasy*.

Levinas, Emmanuel. *Totality and Infinity*. Pittsburgh: Duquesne University Press, 1996 [1961].

——. *Ethics and Infinity*, trans. Richard A. Cohen. Pittsburgh: Duquesne University Press, 1996 [1982]).

Levitas, Ruth. *The Concept of Utopia* (Syracuse, NY: Syracuse University Press, 1990).

Löwith, Karl. *From Hegel to Nietzsche: The Revolution in Nineteenth Century Thought* London: Constable, 1965.

Lovejoy, Arthur O. *The Great Chain of Being: A Study of the History of an Idea*. New York: Harper and Row, 2005 [1936].

Lucas, F. L. *Tragedy: Serious Drama in Relation to Aristotle's Poetics*, 2nd ed. London: Chatto and Windus, 1972 [1927].

Lukács, Georg. *The Meaning of Contemporary Realism*. London: Merlin Books, 1979 [1963].

——. "Critical Realism and Socialist Realism." Pp. 93–115 in *The Meaning of Contemporary Realism*.

——. *The Theory of the Novel: A Historico-Philosophical Essay on the Forms of Great Epic Literature*. London: Merlin Press, 1978.

——. *The Historical Novel*. Harmondsworth, UK: Penguin, 1976 [1936].

——. *Studies in European Realism: A Sociological Survey of the Writings of Balzac, Stendhal, Zola, Tolstoy, Gorki and Others*. London: Merlin Press, 1972.

MacIntyre, Alasdair. *Ethics and Politics: Selected Essays*, Volume 2. Cambridge: Cambridge University Press, 2006.

——. "Moral Dilemmas." Pp. 85–100 in *Ethics and Politics: Selected Essays*, Volume 2.

——. *A Short History of Ethics*, 2nd ed. London: Routledge, 1998 [1967].

——. *Whose Justice? Which Rationality?* London: Duckworth, 1988.

——. *After Virtue*, 2nd ed. London: Duckworth, 1985.

——. *Against the Self Images of the Age: Essays on Ideology and Philosophy*. Notre Dame: University of Notre Dame Press, 1978.

——. What Morality is Not," Pp. 136–56 in Alasdair MacIntyre, *Against the Self Images of the Age: Essays on Ideology and Philosophy*.

——, ed. *Hegel: A Collection of Critical Essays*. Notre Dame, IN: University of Notre Dame Press, 1976.

MacLeod, Ken. "Politics and Science Fiction." Pp. 230–40 in *The Cambridge Companion to Science Fiction*, eds. Edward James and Farah Mendelsohn.

Malmgren, Carl D. "Self and Other in SF: Alien Encounters." *Science Fiction Studies*, 20 (1993): 15–33.

Mander, John. *The Writer and Commitment*. London: Secker and Warburg, 1961.

Manlove, Colin R. "Conservatism in the Fantasy of Le Guin.' *Extrapolation*, 21 (1980): 287–97.

Manuel, Frank E. and Fritzie Manuel. *Utopian Thought in the Western World*. Oxford: Blackwell, 1975.

Manuel, Frank E. "Towards a Psychological History of Utopia." Pp. 69–100 in *Utopias and Utopian Thought: A Timely Appraisal*, ed. Frank E. Manuel. Boston: Beacon Press, 1966.

Marcel, Gabriel. *Being and Having*, trans. Katherine Farrer. Boston: Beacon Press, 1951 [1935].

——. *The Mystery of Being*, Vol. I, *Reflection and Mystery*, trans. G. S. Fraser. Chicago: Regnery, 1950.

Marcuse, Herbert. *One Dimensional Man: Studies in the Ideology of Advanced Industrial Society*, intro. Douglas Kellner. London: Routledge, 1991 [1964].

——. "From Negative to Positive Thinking: Technological Rationality and the Logic of Domination," Pp. 144–69 in *One Dimensional Man: Studies in the Ideology of Advanced Industrial Society*.

——. *The Aesthetic Dimension: Toward a Critique of Marxist Aesthetics*. London: Macmillan, 1979.

——. *Reason and Revolution: Hegel and the Rise of Social Theory*. London: Routledge, 1948.

Marks, Jon. *Gilles Deleuze: Vitalism and Multiplicity*. London: Pluto Press, 1998.

Marx, Karl. *Capital: A Critical Analysis of Capitalist Production*, Vol. 1, ed. F. Engels, trans. Samuel Moore and Edward Aveling. London: Lawrence and Wishart, 1974 [1873].

——. "Afterword." Pp. 22–29 in *Capital: A Critical Analysis of Capitalist Production*, Vol. 1.

——. *The Poverty of Philosophy: Answer to 'The Philosophy of Poverty' by M. Proudhon*. Moscow: Progress Publishers, 1973 [1846].

——. *Economic and Philosophical Manuscripts of 1844*, trans. Martin Milligan. Moscow: Progress Publishers, 1967.

Marx, Karl, and Frederic Engels, *Selected Writings* in 2 volumes. Moscow: Foreign Languages Publishing House, 1958.

May, Todd. *The Political Philosophy of Poststructuralist Anarchism*. University Park, PA: Pennsylvania State University Press, 1994.

——. "Is Poststructuralist Political Theory Anarchist?" *Philosophy and Social Criticism*, 15, 2 (1989): 275–84.

McCaffery, Larry, ed. *Storming the Reality Studio: A Casebook of Cyberpunk and Postmodern Fiction*, ed. Durham, NC, and London: Duke University Press, 1991.

——. "An Interview with Ursula K. Le Guin." Pp. 151–75 in *Across the Wounded Galaxies: Interviews with Contemporary American Science Fiction Writers*. Urbana, IL: University of Illinois Press, 1991.

McConnell, Frank. *The Science Fiction of H. G. Wells*. Oxford: Oxford University Press, 1981.

McCormack, Win, and Ann Mendel. "An Interview with Ursula K. Le Guin: Creating Realistic Utopias." P. 128 in Le Guin, *The Language of the Night*.

McDermott, K. A. "Ideology and Narrative: The Cold War and Robert Heinlein," *Extrapolation*, 23, no. 3 (1982): 254–69.

McGuirk, Carol. "Optimism and the Limits of Subversion in *The Dispossessed* and *The Left Hand of Darkness*." Pp. 243–58 in *Ursula K. Le Guin*, ed. Bloom.

McLellan, David. *Marx Before Marxism*. Harmondsworth, UK: Penguin Books, 1972.

———. *Karl Marx: His Life and Thought*. London: Macmillan, 1973.

———. *The Young Hegelians and Karl Marx*. Harmondsworth, UK: Penguin, 1969.

McLennan, Greg. "Sociology, Eurocentrism and Postcolonial Theory," *European Journal of Social Theory*, 6, no. 1 (2003): 69–86.

Milner, Andrew, Matthew Ryan and Robert Savage, eds. *Imagining the Future: Utopia and Dystopia*. Arena Journal New Series, 25/26 (2006).

———. "Framing Catastrophe: the Problem of Ending in Dystopian Fiction." Pp. 333–54 in *Imagining the Future: Utopia and Dystopia*, eds. Andrew Milner, Matthew Ryan and Robert Savage.

Morson, Gary Saul. *The Boundaries of Genre: Dostoevsky's Diary of a Writer and the Traditions of Literary Utopia*. Evanston, IL: Northwestern University Press, 1981.

———. "Utopia as a Literary Genre." Pp. 69–106 in *The Boundaries of Genre: Dostoevsky's Diary of a Writer and the Traditions of Literary Utopia*.

Morton, A. L. *The English Utopia*. London: Lawrence and Wishart, 1978 [1952].

Moylan. Tom. *Scraps of the Untainted Sky: Science Fiction, Utopia, Dystopia*. Boulder, CO: Westview Press, 2000.

———. "Beyond Negation: The Critical Utopias of Ursula K. Le Guin and Samuel R. Delany," *Extrapolation*, 21 (1980): 236–53.

———. *Demand the Impossible: Science Fiction and the Utopian Imagination*. London: Methuen, 1986.

———. "The Dispossessed." Pp. 91–120 in *Demand the Impossible: Science Fiction and the Utopian Imagination*.

———. "The Locus of Hope: Utopia Versus Ideology." *Science Fiction Studies*, 9, 2 (1982): 163–65.

———. "Introduction: Dystopia and Histories." *Dark Horizons: Science Fiction and the Dystopian Imagination*, eds. Moylan and Baccolini.

Mueller, Gustav E. "The Hegel Legend of 'Thesis-Antithesis-Synthesis.'" *Journal of the History of Ideas*, 19, 3 1958, 411–14.

Mullen, R. D., and Darko Suvin, eds. *Science Fiction Studies: Selected Articles on Science Fiction 1973–1975*. Boston: Gregg Press, 1976.

Murdoch, Iris. *Sartre: Romantic Rationalist*. London: Collins, 1967 [1953].

Newman, Saul. *Power and Politics in Poststructuralist Thought: New Theories of the Political*. London: Routledge, 2005.

———. *From Bakunin to Lacan: Anti-Authoritarianism and the Dislocation of Power* Lanham, MD: Lexington Books, 2001.

Nicholls, Peter, ed. *The Science in Science Fiction*. New York: Alfred Knopf, 1983.

Nicol, Charles. "The Good Witch of the West Processed: A Review of Warren G. Rochelle. *Communities of the Heart: The Rhetoric of Myth in the Fiction of Ursula K. Le Guin*," *Science Fiction Studies*, 29, no. 1 (2002): 127–28.

Nussbaum, Martha. *Frontiers of Justice: Disability, Nationality, Species Membership*. Cambridge, MA, and London: Belknap Press, 2006.

——. "Human Functioning and Social Justice: In Defense of Aristotelian Essentialism," *Political Theory*, 20, non. 2 (1992): 202–46.

——. *The Fragility of Goodness: Luck and Ethics in Greek Tragedy and Philosophy.* Cambridge: Cambridge University Press, 1986.

Olander, Joseph D., and Martin Harry Greenberg, eds. *Ursula K. Le Guin.* New York: Taplinger, 1979.

——. "Introduction." Pp. 11–14 in *Ursula K. Le Guin*, eds. Joseph Olander and Martin Harry Greenberg, 1979.

Orwell, George. "Writers and Leviathan." Pp. 463–70 in *The Collected Essays, Journalism and Letters of George Orwell*, in 4 volumes, Volume 4, *In Front of Your Nose: 1945–50*, eds. Sonia Orwell and Ian Angus. Harmondsworth, UK: Penguin, 1970 [1948].

——. "Inside the Whale." Pp. 540–78 in *The Collected Essays, Journalism and Letters of George Orwell*, Volume 1, *An Age Like This: 1920–1940*, eds. Harmondsworth, UK: Penguin, 1971 [1968].

——. "Review of *The Novel Today*, by Phillip Henderson." Pp. 288–92 in *The Collected Essays, Journalism and Letters of George Orwell*, Volume 1.

——. "The Frontiers of Art and Propaganda." Pp. 149–53 in *The Collected Essays, Journalism and Letters of George Orwell*, in 4 volumes, Volume 2, *My Country Right or Left: 1940–1943*, eds. Harmondsworth, UK: Penguin, 1970 [1968].

——. "Tolstoy and Shakespeare." Pp. 153–57 in *The Collected Essays, Journalism and Letters of George Orwell*, Volume 2.

——. "Literature and Totalitarianism." Pp. 161–64 in *The Collected Essays, Journalism and Letters of George Orwell*, Volume 2.

——. "Literature and the Left." Pp. 334–37 in *The Collected Essays, Journalism and Letters of George Orwell*, Volume 2.

——. "Why I Write." Pp. 183–86 in *The Decline of the English Murder and Other Essays.* Harmondsworth, UK: Penguin, 1980 [1965].

Parrinder, Patrick, ed. *Learning from Other Worlds: Estrangement, Cognition and the Politics of Science Fiction and Utopia.* Durham, NC: Duke University Press, 2001.

——. *Shadows of the Future: H. G. Wells, Science Fiction and Prophecy.* Syracuse University Press, 1995.

——. "The Future as Anti-Utopia: Wells, Zamyatin and Orwell." Pp. 115–26 in *Shadows of the Future: H. G. Wells, Science Fiction and Prophecy.*

——. "Utopia and Meta-Utopia." Pp. 96–114 in *Shadows of the Future: H. G. Wells, Science Fiction and Prophecy.*

——, ed. *Science Fiction: A Critical Guide.* London: Longman, 1979.

——. "Science Fiction and the Scientific World View." Pp. 67–89 in *Science Fiction: A Critical Guide.*

——. "The Alien Encounter: Or, Ms. Brown and Mrs. Le Guin." Pp. 148–61 in Parrinder, ed. *Science Fiction: A Critical Guide.*

Partington, John. "*The Time Machine* and *A Modern Utopia*: The Static and Kinetic Utopias of the Early H. G. Wells." *Utopian Studies*, 13, no. 1 (2002): 57–68.

——. "The Death of the Static: H. G. Wells and the Kinetic Utopia." *Utopian Studies*, 11, no. 2. (2000), 96–111.

Pegg, Barry. "Down to Earth: Terrain, Territory and the Language of Realism in Ursula K. Le Guin's *The Left Hand of Darkness* and *The Dispossessed*." *Michigan Academician*, 27, no. 4 (1995): 481–92.

Peterson, Steven A., and Douglas Saxton. "Science Fiction and Political Thought: *The Dispossessed*." *Cornell Journal of Social Relations* 12, 1 (1975): 65–74.

Plato, *Gorgias*, trans. W. R. M. Lamb. Cambridge, MA, 1996 [1925], 483E, 384–7.

Plaw, Avery. "Empty Hands: Communication, Pluralism and Community in Ursula K. Le Guin's *The Dispossessed*." Pp. 283–304 in *The New Utopian Politics of Ursula K. Le Guin's* The Dispossessed, eds. Davis and Stillman.

Pohl, Frederick. "The Politics of Prophecy." Pp. 7–17 in *Political Science Fiction*, eds. Hassler and Wilcox.

Pomerants, G. "Euclidian and Non-Euclidian Reasoning in the Works of Dostoevsky." *Kontinent*, 3 (1978): 141–82.

Popper, Karl. *The Open Society and Its Enemies*, Vol. 2, *The High Tide of Prophecy: Hegel, Marx and the Aftermath*. London: Routledge, 1966.

———. *Conjectures and Refutations: The Growth of Scientific Knowledge* (London: Routledge and Kegan Paul, 1972 [1963].

———. "Truth, Rationality and the Growth of Knowledge." Pp. 215–52 in *Conjectures and Refutations: The Growth of Scientific Knowledge*.

———. "Back to the Presocratics." Pp. 136–65 in *Conjectures and Refutations: The Growth of Scientific Knowledge*.

———. "Normal Science and Its Dangers." Pp. 51–58 in *Criticism and the Growth of Knowledge*, eds. Imre Lakatos and Alan Musgrave. Cambridge: Cambridge University Press, 1974 [1970].

———. "The Problem of Induction." Pp. 101–17 in *A Pocket Popper*, ed. D. A. Miller. London: Fontana Books, 1983.

Porter, David. "The Politics of Le Guin's *Opus*." Pp. 273–78 in *Science Fiction Studies: Selected Articles on Science Fiction 1973–1975*, eds. Mullen and Suvin.

Putnam, Hilary. "Levinas and Judaism." Pp. 33–62 in *The Cambridge Companion to Levinas*, eds. Simon Critchley and Robert Bernasconi.

Rabkin, Erik S. "Determinism, Free Will and Point of View in *The Left Hand of Darkness*." Pp. 155–69 in *Ursula K. Le Guin*, ed. Harold Bloom. New York: Chelsea House, 1985.

Rabkin, Eric, Martin H. Greenberg, and Joseph D. Olander, eds. *No Place Else: Explorations in Utopian and Dystopian Fiction*. Carbondale, IL: South Illinois University Press, 1983.

Raphael, D. D. *The Paradox of Tragedy*. London: Allen and Unwin, 1960.

Rauch, Leo, and David Sherman. *Hegel's Phenomenology of Self-Consciousness*. New York: SUNY Press, 1999.

Rauch, Leo. "Mastery and Slavery." Pp. 87–102 in Rauch and Sherman, *Hegel's Phenomenology of Self-Consciousness*.

Remington, Thomas Joseph. "The Other Side of Suffering: Touch as Theme and Metaphor in Le Guin's Science Fiction Novels." Pp. 153–74 in *Ursula K. Le Guin*, eds. Olander and Greenberg.

Roberts, Adam. *Science Fiction*. London: Routledge, 2006.

———. "SF and Gender." Pp. 71–93 in *Science Fiction*.

————. *The History of Science Fiction*. London: Palgrave, 2005.

Rocco, Christopher. *Tragedy and Enlightenment: Athenian Political Thought and the Dilemmas of Modernity*. Berkeley and Los Angeles: University of California Press, 1997.

Rochelle, Warren. *Communities of the Heart: The Rhetoric of Myth in the Fiction of Ursula K. Le Guin*. Liverpool, UK: Liverpool University Press, 2001.

Rodgers, Jennifer. "Fulfillment as a Function of Time: Or The Ambiguous Process of Utopia." Pp. 181–94 in *The New Utopian Politics of Ursula K. Le Guin's* The Dispossessed, eds. Davis and Stillman.

Roemer, Kenneth M. "H. G. Wells and the Momentary Voices of *A Modern Utopia*." *Extrapolation*, 23 (1982): 117–37.

Rorty, Richard. *Philosophy and the Mirror of Nature*. Oxford: Blackwell, 1980.

Rose, Mark. *Alien Encounters: Anatomy of Science Fiction*. Cambridge, MA: Harvard University Press, 1981.

Rose, Mark. "Genre." Pp. 1–23 in *Alien Encounters: Anatomy of Science Fiction*.

Rosenthal, Bernice Glatzer. *New Myth, New World: From Nietzsche to Stalinism*. University Park, PA: Pennsylvania State University Press, 2002.

————. *Nietzsche in Russia*. Princeton: Princeton University Press, 1986.

Roth, Michael S. *Knowing and History: Appropriations of Hegel in Twentieth Century France*. Ithaca, NY: Cornell University Press, 1988.

Rottensteiner, Franz. "European Science Fiction." Pp. 203–26 in *Positions and Presuppositions in Science Fiction*. Kent, OH: Kent State University Press, 1988.

————. "Le Guin's Fantasy: Review of Ursula K. Le Guin. *The Language of the Night: Essays on Fantasy and Science Fiction*." *Science Fiction Studies*, 8, no. 1 (1981): 87–90.

Ruppert, Peter. *Reader in a Strange Land: The Activity of Reading Literary Utopias*. Athens, GA: University of Georgia Press, 1986.

————. "The Ambiguous Utopia: A Third Alternative." Pp. 121–49 in *Reader in a Strange Land: The Activity of Reading Literary Utopias*.

Sabia, Dan. "Individual and Community in Le Guin's *The Dispossessed*." Pp. 111–28 in *The New Utopian Politics of Ursula K. Le Guin's* The Dispossessed, eds. Davis and Stillman.

Sanders, Scott. "Invisible Men and Women: The Disappearance of Character in Science Fiction." Pp. 137–147 in Parrinder ed., *Science Fiction: A Critical Guide*.

Sardar, Ziauddin. *Thomas Kuhn and the Science Wars*. London: Icon Books, 2000.

————. *Postmodernism and the Other: New Imperialism of Western Culture*. London: Pluto Press, 1997.

Sardar, Ziauddin, and Sean Cubitt, eds. *Aliens R Us: The Other in Science Fiction Cinema*. London: Pluto Press, 2002.

Sartre, Jean-Paul. *Existentialism and Humanism*. London: Methuen, 1973 [1946]).

————. *What is Literature?* London: Methuen, 1967 [1948].

Scholes, Robert. "The Good Witch of the West." Pp. 35–45 in *Ursula K. Le Guin*, ed. Harold Bloom.

Schrift, Alan D. *Nietzsche's French Legacy: A Genealogy of Poststructuralism*. London and New York: Routledge, 1995.

Science Fiction Studies. Special issue on "The Science Fiction of Ursula K. Le Guin." 2, no. 3 (1975).

Sherman, David. "The Denial of the Self: The Repudiation of Hegelian Self-Consciousness in Recent European Thought." Pp. 163–222 in Rauch and Sherman, *Hegel's Phenomenology of Self-Consciousness*.

Shklar, Judith. "The Political Theory of Utopia: From Melancholy to Nostalgia." Pp. 101–15 in *Utopias and Utopian Thought*, ed. Frank Manuel. Boston: Beacon Press, 1966.

Slusser, George Edgar. *The Farthest Shores of Ursula K. Le Guin*. Chapbook: Borgo Press, 1976.

Slusser, George E., Colin Greenland, and Erik Rabkin eds. *Storm Warnings: Science Fiction Faces the Future*. Carbondale, IL: Southern Illinois University Press, 1987.

Smith, Phillip E. "Unbuilding Walls: Human Nature and the Nature of Evolutionary and Political Theory in *The Dispossessed*." Pp. 77–96 in *Ursula K. Le Guin*, eds. Joseph Olander and Martin H. Greenberg.

Solomon, Robert C. *In the Spirit of Hegel: A Study of G. W. F. Hegel's Phenomenology of Spirit*. Oxford: Oxford University Press, 1985.

Somay, Bulent. "From Ambiguity to Self-Reflexivity: Revolutionizing Fantasy Space." Pp. 233–48 in *The New Utopian Politics of Ursula K. Le Guin's The Dispossessed*, eds. Davis and Stillman.

———. "Towards an Open Ended Utopia." *Science Fiction Studies* 11 (1984): 25–38.

Spivack, Charlotte. *Ursula K. Le Guin*. Boston: Twayne, 1984.

Steiner, George. "Marxism and the Literary Critic." Pp. 159–78 in *Sociology of Literature and Drama*, eds. Burns and Burns.

Stepelevich, Steven, ed. *The Young Hegelians: An Anthology*. Cambridge: Cambridge University Press, 1983.

Stow, Simon. "Worlds Apart: Ursula K. Le Guin and the Possibility of Method." Pp. 37–54 in *The New Utopian Politics of Ursula K. Le Guin's The Dispossessed*, eds. Laurence Davis and Peter Stillman.

Suvin, Darko. *Positions and Presuppositions in Science Fiction*. London: Macmillan, 1988.

———. "Parables of De-Alienation: Le Guin's Widdershin's Dance." Pp. 134–50 in *Positions and Presuppositions in Science Fiction*.

———. *Metamorphoses of Science Fiction*. New Haven, CT, and London: Yale University Press, 1979.

———. "Introductory Note." *Science Fiction Studies*, 2, no. 3 (1975): 231. Special issue on "The Science Fiction of Ursula K. Le Guin."

Swingewood, Alan. *The Novel and Revolution* London: Macmillan, 1975.

———. *The Sociology of Literature*. London: Paladin Books, 1972.

———. "George Orwell, Socialism and the Novel." Pp. 249–75 in *The Sociology of Literature*.

"Symposium on Marxism and Fantasy." *Historical Materialism: Research in Critical Marxist Theory*, 10, no. 4 (2002).

"Symposium on Change, Science Fiction and Marxism: Open or Closed Universes?" *Science Fiction Studies*, 1 (1973): 84–98; reprinted in *Science Fiction Studies: Selected Articles on Science Fiction 1973–1975*, eds. Mullen and Suvin, 48–58.

Taylor, Angus. "The Politics of Space, Time and Entropy." *Foundation: The Review of Science Fiction*, 10 (1976): 34–44.

Theall, Donald. "The Art of Social-Science Fiction: The Ambiguous Utopian Dialectics of Ursula K. Le Guin." Pp. 286–94 in *Science Fiction Studies: Selected Articles on Science Fiction 1973–1975*, eds. Mullen and Suvin.

Tifft, Larry L., and Dennis C. Sullivan. "Possessed Sociology and Le Guin's Dispossessed: From Exile to Anarchism." Pp. 189–97 in *Ursula K. Le Guin: Voyager to Inner Lands and Outer Space*, ed. Joseph de Bolt.

Tillyard, E. M. W. *The Elizabethan World Picture: A Study of the Idea of Order in the Age of Shakespeare*. Harmondsworth, UK: Penguin, 1970 [1942].

Todorov, Tzvetan. "The Origin of Genres." *New Literary History*, 8 (1976): 159–70.

Tower Sargent, Lyman. "The Problem of the 'Flawed Utopia': A Note on the Costs of Eutopia." Pp. 225–32 in *Dark Horizons: Science Fiction and the Dystopian Imagination*, eds. Moylan and Baccolini.

———. "The Three Faces of Utopianism Revisited." *Utopian Studies*, 5, 1 (1994): 1–38.

———. "Utopia: The Problem of Definition." *Extrapolation*, 16 (1975): 137–48.

———. "Anarchism: Social and Political Ideas in Some Recent Feminist Utopias." Pp. 3–33 in *Women and Utopia: Critical Interpretations*, ed. Marleen Barr. New York: University Press of America, 1983.

———. "Eutopias and Dystopias in Science Fiction: 1950–75." Pp. 347–66 in *America as Utopia*, ed. Kenneth M. Roemer. New York: Burtt Franklin, 1981.

Tschachler, Heinz. "Forgetting Dostoevsky; or, The Political Unconscious of Ursula K. Le Guin." *Utopian Studies*, 2, nos. 1–2 (1991): 63–76.

Tunick, Mark. "The Need for Walls: Privacy, Community and Freedom in *The Dispossessed*." Pp. 129–48 in *The New Utopian Politics of Ursula K. Le Guin's The Dispossessed*, eds. Davis and Stillman.

Turner, George. "Paradigm and Pattern: Form and Meaning in *The Dispossessed*." *Science Fiction Commentary* 41/42 (February 1975): 65–74.

Urbanowicz, Victor. "Personal and Political in *The Dispossessed*." Pp. 145–54 in *Ursula K. Le Guin*, ed. Harold Bloom.

Utopian Studies. Special Issue on "Ursula K. Le Guin's 'The Ones Who Walked Away From Omelas.'" 2, nos. 1–2 (1991).

Wagar, W. Warren. *H. G. Wells and the World State*. New Haven, CT: Yale University Press, 1963.

Wahl, Jean. *Le Malheur de la conscience dans la philosophie de Hegel*. Paris: Rieder, 1929.

Walsh, Chad. *From Utopia to Nightmare*. Westport, CT.: Greenwood Press, 1975 [1962].

Ward, Jonathan. "Interview With Ursula K. Le Guin." Pp. 34–5 in Le Guin, *Dreams Must Explain Themselves*.

Warnock, G. J. *The Object of Morality*. London: Methuen, 1971.

Warnock, Mary, ed. *Sartre: A Collection of Critical Essays*. New York: Doubleday, 1971.

Warrick, Patricia. "The Sources of Zamyatin's *We* in Dostoevsky's *Notes from the Underground*." *Extrapolation*, 17, no. 1 (1975): 63–77.

Wegner, Phillip E. *Imaginary Communities: Utopia, the Nation and the Spatial Histories of Modernity*. London: University of California Press, 2002.

———. "A Map of Utopia's 'Possible Worlds': Zamyatin's *We* and Le Guin's *The Dispossessed*." Pp. 147–82 in *Imaginary Communities: Utopia, the Nation and the Spatial Histories of Modernity*.

Weldes, Jutta, ed. *To Seek Out New Worlds: Exploring the Links Between Science Fiction and World Politics.* Palgrave Macmillan, 2003.

Wells, H. G. *The War of the Worlds,* ed. Patrick Parrinder, intro. Brian Aldiss, notes Andy Sawyer. Harmondsworth, UK: Penguin, 2005 [1898].

——. *A Modern Utopia and Tono Bungay* London: Odhams Press. n.d. [1905].

——. *Men Like Gods.* London: Sphere Books, 1976 [1923].

——. "Skepticism of the Instrument." Appendix to *A Modern Utopia.* Pp. 494–504 in *A Modern Utopia and Tono Bungay.*

——. "Of Art, of Literature, of Mr. Henry James." Pp. 244–45 in *Henry James and H. G. Wells: A Record of Their Friendship, Their Debate on the Art of Fiction and Their Quarrel,* eds. Edel and Ray.

——. "Letter to Henry James, 8 July 1915." Pp. 263–64 in *Henry James and H. G. Wells,* eds. Edel and Ray.

——. "The Contemporary Novel." Pp. 131–55 in *Henry James and H. G. Wells,* eds. Edel and Ray.

——. "Digression About the Novel." Pp. 215–33 in *Henry James and H. G. Wells,* eds. Edel and Ray.

——. "Utopias." *Science Fiction Studies,* 27 (1982): 117–21.

——. *First and Last Things: A Confession of Faith and Rule of Life.* London: Watts, 1930 [1929].

——. "Metaphysics." Pp. 1–42 in *First and Last Things: A Confession of Faith and Rule of Life.*

West, Anthony. "The Dark World of H. G. Wells." *Harper's,* 214 (1957): 68–73.

White, Donna K. *Dancing with Dragons: Ursula K. Le Guin and the Critics.* New York: Camden House, 1999.

——. "The Great Good Place." Pp. 82–106 in *Dancing with Dragons: Ursula K. Le Guin and the Critics.*

Whitebrook, Maureen, ed. *Reading Political Stories: Representations of Politics in Novels and Pictures.* Lanham, MD: Rowman and Littlefield, 1991.

Whitehall, Geoffrey. "The Problem of the 'World and Beyond': Encountering 'The Other' in Science Fiction." Pp. 169–94 in *To Seek Out New Worlds: Exploring the Links Between Science Fiction and World Politics,* ed. Jutta Weldes.

Widmer, Kingsley. "Utopian, Dystopian, Diatopian Libertarianism: Le Guin's *The Dispossessed.*" *The Sphinx,* 4, 1 (1981): 55–66.

Wiggershaus, Rolf, *The Frankfurt School: Its History, Theories, and Political Significance.* Cambridge: Polity Press, 1994.

Wilde, Lawrence. *Erich Fromm and the Quest for Solidarity.* New York: Palgrave, 2004.

——, ed. *Marxism's Ethical Thinkers.* London: Palgrave, 2001.

——. *Ethical Marxism and Its Radical Critics.* London: Palgrave, 1998.

Wilden, Anthony. "The Belle Âme: Freud, Lacan and Hegel." Pp. 284–90 in Lacan, *The Language of the Self: The Function of Language in Psychoanalysis.*

Williams, D. G. "The Moons of Le Guin and Heinlein." *Science Fiction Studies,* 21, no. 2 (1994): 164–72.

Williams, Howard. *Hegel, Heraclitus and Marx's Dialectic.* London: Harvester, 1989.

Williams, Raymond. "Science Fiction and Utopia." Pp. 52–66 in *Science Fiction: A Critical Guide,* ed. Patrick Parrinder.

Williams, Robert R. "Recent Views of Recognition and the Question of Ethics." Pp. 364–412 in *Hegel's Ethics of Recognition*. Berkeley, CA: University of California Press, 1998.

Williamson, Jack. *H. G. Wells: Critic of Progress*. Baltimore: Mirage Press, 1973.

Wolmark, Jenny. *Aliens and Others: Science Fiction, Feminism and Postmodernism*. New York: Harvester, 1994.

Wood, Susan. "Introduction." Pp. 11–18 in Le Guin, *The Language of the Night*.

———. "Discovering Worlds: The Fiction of Ursula K. Le Guin." Pp. 183–210 in Bloom, ed., *Ursula K. Le Guin*.

Woodcock, George. *Anarchism*. Harmondsworth, UK: Penguin Books, 1975.

Woolf, Virginia. *The Captain's Bed and Other Essays*. New York: Harcourt Brace Jovanovich, 1978 [1924].

———. "Mr. Bennett and Mrs. Brown." Pp. 94–119 in *The Captain's Bed and Other Essays*.

Zaki, Hoda M. *Phoenix Renewed: The Survival and Mutation of Utopian Thought in North American Science Fiction: 1965–1982*. San Bernadino, CA: Borgo Press, 1988.

———. "Utopian Thought and Political Theory." Pp. 1–25 in *Phoenix Renewed: The Survival and Mutation of Utopian Thought in North American Science Fiction: 1965–1982*.

Zamyatin, Yevgeny. *We*, trans. Bernard Gilbert Guerney, intro. Michael Glenny. Harmondsworth, UK: Penguin, 1972.

———. *A Soviet Heretic: Essays by Yevgeny Zamyatin*, ed. Mirra Ginsburg. Chicago: University of Chicago Press, 1991.

———. "Scythians." Pp. 21–33 in Zamyatin, *A Soviet Heretic*, ed. Mirra Ginsburg.

———. "Contemporary Russian Literature." Pp. 34–50 in Zamyatin, *A Soviet Heretic*, ed. Mirra Ginsburg.

———. "Tomorrow." Pp. 51–52 in Zamyatin, *A Soviet Heretic*, ed. Mirra Ginsburg.

———. "On Synthetism." Pp. 81–91 in Zamyatin, *A Soviet Heretic*, ed. Mirra Ginsburg.

———. "The New Russian Prose." Pp. 92–106 in Zamyatin *A Soviet Heretic*, ed. Mirra Ginsburg.

———. "On Literature, Revolution, Entropy and Other Matters." Pp. 107–12 in Zamyatin, *A Soviet Heretic*, ed. Mirra Ginsburg.

———. "H. G. Wells." Pp. 259–90 in Zamyatin, *A Soviet Heretic*, ed. Mirra Ginsburg.

Index

aesthetics, 7, 14, 17, 19, 32, 34–36, 40–41, 46, 101, 119, 132, 138–40, 149n78, 159, 174, 188–89, 195, 206, 249, 267, 279–80, 282, 287–88; the form of the novel, 8, 12, 14, 31–32, 35–36, 40–41, 46–47, 50n61, 119, 132–33, 135–36, 138, 153, 156, 272, 277; Hegel and, 9, 153–54, 175n3, 257–59; Lukács and, 9, 153–54, 156, 257–59; Marxism and, 9, 13, 153–54, 156, 257–58, 272–74, 278–79, 284, 286n29. *See also* conservatism, didacticism, utopia

alienation, 76n28, 115, 187, 250, 258–59, 283. *See also* anarchism, ethics, Hegel, Marx

ambiguity, 60, 105, 118, 120, 142, 158, 163, 256; and dialectics, 26, 56, 74nn5–6; in ethics, 212n69; in literature, 26, 52n98, 100, 109n34, 126, 144n16, 146n32, 207, 252; in science, 48n4, 51n67, 103–7; in writings of H. G. Wells, 26–27. *See also* dialectics, Hegelianism, situation ethics, utopia

anarchism: classical, 6, 10, 60, 62–63, 71, 187, 204, 268, 282–85;

Dostoevsky's critique of in *The Possessed*, 5, 170–73, 185, 220–22, 232, 236n13; ends and means in, 73, 217–23, 227–28; ethical, social anarchism, 6, 13, 76n28, 115–17, 185–87, 194, 199, 219–23, 230–32, 251, 261; different types of, 5–6, 12–13, 69–70, 217–23; and Hegel's philosophy, 10, 14–15, 60, 63–68, 71–72, 76n39, 90, 203, 287n36; and Marxism, 67–68, 76n28, 268, 276, 282–85; and Nietzsche, 6, 66–67, 72–73, 90, 185, 218; and nihilism, 5–6, 13, 185, 194, 199, 218, 221–22, 227, 230–32, 242; and postmodernism, 6, 63, 68–73, 90, 186, 203–4, 246–47, 267–68; and Zamyatin, 66–68, 185, 218, 221, 228, 242. *See also* Bakunin, Kropotkin, postmodernism, poststructuralism, Proudhon

Andersen, Hans Christian, 253–54

Aristotle, 75n16, 75n27, 175n5, 200, 208n3, 209n9, 223, 237; and conservatism, 164, 223; and *eudaimonia*, 190; and heliocentrism, 87–88, 92–94, 99; and human

About the Author

Tony Burns is associate professor in the School of Politics and International Relations, University of Nottingham, UK. He is author of *Natural Law and Political Ideology in the Philosophy of Hegel* (Avebury Press, 1996). He is co-editor (with Ian Fraser, Nottingham Trent University, UK) of *The Hegel-Marx Connection* (Palgrave, 2000) and (with Simon Thompson, University of West of England, UK) of *Global Justice and the Politics of Recognition* (Palgrave, forthcoming 2009). He is currently writing a book entitled *The Politics of Recognition in the History of Political Thought Before and After Hegel*. His main areas of research interest are the Aristotelian natural law tradition in the history of political thought; the philosophy and politics of Hegel and Marx, especially the influence of Hegel on French thought in the nineteenth and twentieth centuries; and the philosophy and politics of science, especially as this is dealt with in works of science fiction. His earlier contributions on Le Guin include 'Science and Politics in *The Dispossessed*: Le Guin and the "Science Wars",' in Laurence Davies and Peter Stillman eds., *The New Utopian Politics of Ursula K. Le Guin's The Dispossessed* (Lanham, MD: Lexington Books 2005); 'Marxism and Science Fiction: A Celebration of the Work of Ursula K. Le Guin.' *Capital and Class*, 84 (2004); and 'Zamyatin's *We* and Postmodernism,' *Utopian Studies*, 11, 1 (2000).